D0051968

SKINHEAT

AVA GRAY

BERKLEY SENSATION, NEW YORK

THE BERKLEY PUBLISHING GROUP
Published by the Penguin Group
Penguin Group (USA) Inc.
375 Hudson Street, New York, New York 10014, USA
Penguin Group (Canada), 90 Eglinton Avenue East, Suite 700, Toronto, Ontario M4P 2Y3, Canada
(a division of Pearson Penguin Canada Inc.)
Penguin Books Ltd., 80 Strand, London WC2R 0RL, England
Penguin Group Ireland, 25 St. Stephen's Green, Dublin 2, Ireland (a division of Penguin Books Ltd.)
Penguin Group (Australia), 250 Camberwell Road, Camberwell, Victoria 3124, Australia
(a division of Pearson Australia Group Pty. Ltd.)
Penguin Books India Pvt. Ltd., 11 Community Centre, Panchsheel Park, New Delhi—110 017, India
Penguin Group (NZ), 67 Apollo Drive, Rosedale, North Shore 0632, New Zealand
(a division of Pearson New Zealand Ltd.)
Penguin Books (South Africa) (Pty.) Ltd., 24 Sturdee Avenue, Rosebank, Johannesburg 2196,
South Africa

Penguin Books Ltd., Registered Offices: 80 Strand, London WC2R 0RL, England

This is a work of fiction. Names, characters, places, and incidents either are the product of the author's imagination or are used fictitiously, and any resemblance to actual persons, living or dead, business establishments, events, or locales is entirely coincidental. The publisher does not have any control over and does not assume any responsibility for author or third-party websites or their content.

SKIN HEAT

A Berkley Sensation Book / published by arrangement with the author

PRINTING HISTORY
Berkley Sensation mass-market edition / January 2011

Copyright © 2011 by Ann Aguirre.
Excerpt from *Skin Dive* copyright © 2011 by Ann Aguirre.
Cover design by Lesley Worrell.
Cover art by Danny O'Leary.
Interior text design by Kristin del Rosario.

ISBN: 978-0-425-23920-9

BERKLEY® SENSATION
Berkley Sensation Books are published by The Berkley Publishing Group,
a division of Penguin Group (USA) Inc.,
375 Hudson Street, New York, New York 10014.
BERKLEY® SENSATION and the "B" design are trademarks of Penguin Group (USA) Inc.

PRINTED IN THE UNITED STATES OF AMERICA

10 9 8 7 6 5 4 3 2 1

For Bree and Donna.
Thanks for your support, knowledge,
and your friendship; it means more to me than you know.
Well . . . I guess you know *now*, don't you?
I'm bad at keeping secrets.

ACKNOWLEDGMENTS

As always, I thank my agent first. Without Laura Bradford, none of this would be possible. She is one of the bravest people I know; she doesn't hesitate to take chances and I benefit directly from that courage.

I also offer infinite gratitude to Cindy Hwang. These are the romances I dreamed of writing, years ago, when I first started reading the genre, and I will never be able to repay her for believing in me.

Next, I must mention Bree Bridges and Donna Herren. Without these two amazing ladies (and dear friends), this book wouldn't be finished, let alone half so good. Bree listened to me with endless patience and helped me work through the snarly bits. Donna offered her invaluable expertise regarding forensic information and legal procedures. Halpern County is fictitious, but I did my best to make it feel real. As always, any mistakes or liberties are my own. Both Bree and Donna supported me when I had doubts, cheered me when I was tired, and were my biggest fans while I wrote, making me want to finish so they could read it. Thanks, guys. This book is for both of you since you loved Zeke from the moment I dreamed him up.

Thanks also to my husband, Andres. I broke my foot while on vacation in Acapulco, and though he had to be weary with working, running all errands for the kids, helping out at home, as well as doing all the shopping, he never once complained. He always made me feel like it was something he wanted to do, so I could focus on working and healing. Likewise, both kids pitched in and helped out, even more than I realized they could. I have seldom felt more cherished, despite the pain and inconvenience. So thanks to them all. They are the best family I could ever want. And thanks especially to Alek, who helped me figure out what sadness smelled like.

Here's a shout to my friend, Ivette. It was wonderful seeing you in Mexico City. I appreciate everything you do; it makes my life much easier. I have made wonderful friends these past few years and you are among the best. Your achievements make me smile: I look at everything you've accomplished, and I'm so proud of you! I'm so fortunate to know you.

Thanks to Ashley Whitney, who came up with the name for Neva's pet clinic. Thanks to all for being there to give me an encouraging word when I had a minute of downtime. Additionally, I'm sending a special thank-you to the Skin Posse, made up of fiction vixens and book chicks who first loved Reyes and couldn't wait to read about Foster. Here's hoping you love Zeke as much; he's a different kind of hero. Many thanks to Stefanie Gostautas, the best proofreader ever. And thanks to the rest of my readers, who make it possible for me to keep writing. You guys are the best, and I love hearing from you.

CHAPTER 1

All the animals were gone.

Stolen, Zeke guessed. Or he hoped so, at least. He didn't like to think they might've wandered off and died. At one point, he had some chickens and a cow. He'd planted what he could tend and harvest by himself; he'd never been able to afford laborers, not even the migrant kind. He grew most of what he ate. So he'd never had much money, just enough to pay taxes and keep the lights on. It was a simple life, but it had suited him well enough.

But he'd been gone a long time... and not by choice, so the farm carried a desolate air, the land bleak with winter. Standing in the drive, he had a clear view of the dead fields and the pine and oak forest that framed them. The earth still showed the last furrows he'd dug and the rotten harvest he hadn't been here to bring in.

He couldn't see the road, but he heard vehicles passing now and then. The detail unsettled him. Zeke knew when a car had a loose muffler, what engines needed the timing adjusted, and which ones could use a change of spark plugs.

The surety made him sick because it wasn't right. With a faint sigh, he started toward the steps.

The house, in all its Depression-era glory, had seen better days. Posts supported a sagging porch, and it had been charcoal gray, but the months of neglect and a hot, dry summer had left it looking worse than ever. It was lucky nobody had broken in—not that there was anything worth stealing. Maybe they'd even scouted the place through the windows and come to that conclusion themselves. A few panes were cracked—vandals, most likely, or just bored kids. Those repairs would keep.

His shoes crunched on loose gravel as he went up the drive. He'd walked the last two miles, after being dropped off by a friendly truck driver. The man hadn't done anything to set off the prickly way Zeke felt about sharing the cab with him, but he hadn't been able to stop watching him out of the corner of his eye, every muscle tensed. Every time the guy moved, Zeke felt like defending his territory. Stupid, considering he'd occupied the passenger seat in an eighteen-wheeler that didn't belong to him.

With a tired glance, he took in the filthy gutters and the patchy roof. He didn't like to think about how long it had taken him to get home. Hitchhiking wasn't a safe way to travel, and these days sometimes people didn't stop. It had been a long walk, complicated by the fact that sometimes he had to stop and take odd cash jobs in order to eat. If he'd been willing to steal to buy a bus ticket, he could've gotten here faster. But he hadn't been willing. Robbing other people only compounded the crime done to him, so he'd taken it slow, worked his way home as best he could.

But no wonder things were in such a mess. The place required regular upkeep, and six months ago, before he was taken, he'd put things off because he needed to finish the planting. If he didn't, then he didn't eat come winter. It was just that simple.

Too clearly, he remembered going to a bar over in Aker-ville with a friend. A local band he liked had been playing and he'd had a beer or two while they ran through their sets.

When he came out for some fresh air during the intermission, two men had grabbed him. Everything went dark, and when he woke up, it felt like a nightmare—only it had no end. Just pain.

But he was here now. They'd escaped, and he had to forget or he'd go nuts. Some men might want answers or vengeance, but at this point, he only wanted to survive. With some effort, Zeke pushed the past from his mind.

The spare key was still buried in a plastic bag to the side of the steps. He knocked it against the post, and chips of graying paint flaked away along with the loose dirt. Zeke dug out the key and let himself into the house. It smelled musty, felt damp, and it was cold. If he'd taken any longer, the pipes might have frozen.

There was no power, of course, and he needed money before he could get it turned back on. Same with the phone. At least he'd never had cable, so one less thing to miss while he tried to put the pieces back together.

In the kitchen, it smelled worse than musty. In the twilight, he located a box of matches and lit some candles. Everything in the refrigerator had to be tossed. Though he was exhausted—and starving—he found a garbage bag in the cupboard and pulled all the rotten stuff out. He fought the urge to hurl it out the window in a burst of rage.

Control, he told himself. If he started yielding to those impulses, it would lead down a slippery slope. This, he knew. If he wanted to live in the human world, his instincts couldn't rule him. He hadn't eaten in the last twelve hours, and it was a miracle he'd made it back to the farm with no money in his pocket. Though he'd stolen the shoes and clothing, he'd refused to take any cash. He'd just needed to get out of the institutional garb or he would never have found anyone willing to give him a ride. In addition to his feet, three kind souls had gotten him where he needed to go, and he didn't even know their names.

He made himself carry the bulging bag out to the rusty silver can behind the house before looking for food. Rituals mattered. They would keep him sane and drive away the voices in his head. Like a mental patient, he had to focus on one thing at a time. *Baby steps.*

That wasn't such a bad analogy. He'd been confined like a loon while they jabbed needles in him, shone lights in his eyes, and then seemed disgusted by his lack of response. Based on their mutterings, they hadn't been pleased with his results, not that he had any clue what those people wanted with him. Most days, he felt less than human. He'd never had a lot of self-esteem, thanks to his family history, but nobody had succeeded in eroding his sense of self . . . until now. It took men and women in white coats with charts and wires and electrodes to make him feel like nothing at all.

Zeke studied the contents of the cupboard. Sparse. He hadn't bought a lot of food at the grocery. He usually canned his own vegetables, but he hadn't been around to do it this year. Black despair weighed on him, and he forced that away, too. A can of ravioli should still be good. But he couldn't make himself wait for it to heat. Instead he popped the top and ate it from the can. It wasn't until he'd finished that he realized he should've used a fork. People did.

Because the farm had its own well, he had water at least, even if he had to use the old-fashioned hand pump. After he cleaned up, Zeke realized he hadn't noticed the cold. Not like he used to. He wasn't shivering when he finished. That was a blessing since without power, there would be no hot water, but it was hard to wrap his head around.

He pushed the confusion down as he dried off and found "clean" clothes in his closet. They'd been hanging for a while and the smell bothered him more than he thought it should. Dust all but choked him. The whole way home from Virginia, he'd been troubled by the sense the world didn't fit: smells were too sharp, colors too bright, noises too loud. And he was hanging on by a thread.

Grimly, Zeke dressed. The jeans hung loose on his hips. If he could ever afford new ones, the waist needed to be three inches smaller. T-shirts mattered less, but he had lost some bulk in his arms and shoulders as well. Where he'd once been strong, his shadow self in the dark mirror looked thin and desperate.

Zeke turned away and headed downstairs, seeking the candles he'd left burning in the kitchen. Most of them needed to be put out. It was then he heard the sputtering cough of a car on the road. But he shouldn't have.

It was too far away. He'd never heard engines inside before. Not through the windows and across the fields, through muffling trees. In silence, he listened to the vehicle choke and die. He could hear what was wrong with it. Zeke fought the urge to shove his fingers in his ears.

Not crazy.

Then he heard a woman's soft curse.

With every fiber of his being, he wanted to crawl in bed, regardless of how the sheets smelled, and sleep. Without worrying about what would happen to him. He'd escaped that awful place, and he'd prefer to pretend it never happened.

Only he couldn't leave the lady out there alone on a country road. That was how most horror movies started. With a low growl, he slammed out of the house.

The last step bowed a little under his weight, but he leapt clear before it snapped. *Fast. Too fast. Should've taken some damage there.* But he balled that up and refused to think about it. Instead he'd focus on doing something good. He realized he should've gotten a jacket, but he didn't need one and there was no point pretending.

Zeke covered the distance at a run, even with weariness weighing on him. When he ran around the bend where his driveway met the county road, he saw a car pulled off on the dirt shoulder. This time of night, with the headlights on, he couldn't tell what color it was. The woman he'd heard cussing must have gotten back inside.

He jogged toward the vehicle and then slowed, so he didn't frighten her. Scents of gas and oil, burnt rubber and hot metal nearly overwhelmed him. Zeke took a few seconds before he approached. God only knew how he looked to her, probably like a crazy mouth-breather appearing on a lonely road.

"You okay?" Clearly she wasn't. But he didn't have the command of words he wanted or needed.

She was smart, cracking the window only enough to reply. "Car trouble."

"Call somebody?"

"The battery in my phone died. Do you have a cell I could borrow?"

He shook his head. "Wish I did."

Not that he had anyone to call, or the money to pay for one. But it'd be nice to help her right now.

"Service station three miles that way," he said, jerking his head. "I'll go."

"Do you have a car?"

Damn. He did. The truck might not run, after sitting for so long, but he'd left it parked at the farm. It hadn't even occurred to him to drive. He'd *wanted* to run. The realization sent tension coiling through him again.

"Kinda. Be back soon."

He turned then and headed back the way he'd come. The farm was closer. It made no sense that he hadn't thought of checking things out in the truck. Maybe they'd broken his brain.

It took him a little while to find the keys, and then a bit longer to coax the old Ford into motion. Eventually the motor caught, but he didn't find driving natural anymore. He felt tense and scared, wrestling the wheel as he sent it down the drive. Sickness rose in his belly, and by the time he got to the service station, thankfully still open, he was covered in cold sweat.

Tim Sweeney, the owner, recognized him, leathery face creasing in a smile. "Haven't seen you in a coon's age, Zeke. Where you been?"

"Traveling," he muttered. "Lady down the road a piece needs a tow."

"Scooter!" Tim called. "Mind the front. I'm taking the truck out."

A kid made some noise of affirmation and Tim headed for the parking lot. Zeke followed, hands shaking. He tried to hide it, though the jingling of his keys gave it away.

"I'll show you." He got back in the cab and pulled out onto the empty road.

The fear scaled up. He had no place behind the wheel. It was all kinds of wrong. He wished he'd just *run* for help. By the time they reached the site, he barely had a grip on his emotions.

He flashed his lights, and the woman had the presence of mind to signal back, showing Tim where she was. Zeke turned off into his driveway then and brought the truck to a ragged stop before the farmhouse. For long moments he leaned his sweaty forehead on the wheel and listened to the knocking of the engine.

Distant car doors slammed. Voices whispered in the wind. *Too far away. I can't . . . This ain't possible.*

"Who was that?" the woman asked. "I didn't get to thank him."

"Zeke Noble. He ain't been back long."

Their voices bled away, swamped by nearer noises. He caught squirrels in the dark trees, and the rustling of bird wings as they settled in for the night. *Crazy.* How he wished it weren't true, but normal people didn't hear this stuff. Maybe he hadn't been kidnapped. Maybe there had been no secret underground facility, just a mental institution he'd managed to slip away from. Maybe he'd simply been locked up for his own good because he *was* nuts. Just like his mother.

Blood stained Geneva Harper's gloved hands. That wasn't unusual. She'd just finished operating and her patient looked like he'd be fine. Since he was a big fellow, he was already shaking off the anesthetic. Julie, her assistant, rubbed his head, and his tail gave a weak, corresponding thump. Duffy, a black Labrador, was still groggy, but soon he'd need a cone to keep him from worrying his incision site.

"Dogs eat the strangest things," she said, not for the first time.

Julie nodded her agreement. "But at least you saved him."

That was her job, after all, and she was good at it. Leaving

Julie to clean up, she went to wash her hands and then she checked her schedule; the day looked pretty full. In ten minutes, she had a poodle coming in for routine vaccinations, but Kady didn't like needles. She'd need the muzzle.

Most places had a couple of vet techs, a receptionist and office manager, maybe even a couple more doctors in the rotation, but Paws & Claws ran on a skeleton crew, which meant it was pretty much herself and Julie, five days a week. And she stayed on call for weekend emergencies, too. It was exhausting, but this was what she'd always wanted, and she didn't regret any of her choices. There had been problems, of course, but she didn't want to think about her string of bad luck today.

She *did* regret that she couldn't seem to keep an attendant on staff: someone to clean the cages and kennels, wash the pets, take the dogs out for walks, and handle general maintenance, like replacing lightbulbs and painting lines in the parking lot. But two men had quit in the last three months alone. It wasn't glamorous work, admittedly—it was tough and menial, but if you liked animals, it could be rewarding.

And it wasn't like Harper Creek was overflowing with jobs. Her dad had been steadily laying people off at the mill for the last year. As a result, Neva expected an influx of applications from men who used to work maintenance there, but so far it hadn't happened. Puzzling and upsetting, but she didn't have time to reflect on why things weren't working out like she'd thought.

Mrs. Jones was here; she could tell by the yapping in the foyer. She came out of her office, tucked just around the corner from the waiting room. Julie's desk sat in the waiting area, so she handled the hellos, if she wasn't working on a pet; her friend expressed anal glands, cleaned ears, and clipped nails on her own. But before she started any such services, Julie pulled all the medical histories and put them in order in the file holder outside the exam room. Neva snagged the first one.

File in hand, she smiled as she waved Mrs. Jones back. "How are you and Kady doing today?"

The other woman smiled. "Well, I'm old. Kady's lively as ever."

"You'll outlive us all." She led the way back to the exam room.

If only dealing with a cantankerous, spoiled pet comprised the worst of her worries. She made small talk while she fastened the muzzle and then prepared the shots. If Julie wasn't cleaning up from surgery, she'd have already done this. But there was no point in wishing for more help. Some nights she cleaned the place before going home, too—and her mother never tired of telling her it was beneath her.

Harpers don't work like you do, Lillian would say, clad in one of her endless pastel suits. Neva had never been clear if she meant with animals or just the whole idea of employment. It didn't matter; she had long ago resigned herself to the fact she'd never be the daughter her mother wanted. Nor could she make up for the son they'd lost.

It hadn't always been that way, of course. She remembered when Lillian was less concerned about appearances, when she laughed more freely. But Neva had been a lot younger then, and Luke's loss had only frozen her mother more. Putting those thoughts aside, she went to work with the vaccines.

Naturally, the little dog yipped more than the shots warranted; in response, Mrs. Jones hovered and cooed. Tiredly, Neva feigned cheer as she finished.

"Same time next year?" she said with a smile.

"I will if you will."

Neva let the old woman deal with the muzzle while she disposed of the empty vials. Mrs. Jones was a good client; she always bought all the boosters, not just rabies. People like her kept the clinic in the black. Barely. It was a matter of pride for Neva that she made ends meet without touching her trust fund. Not that she could anymore, in any case. Her parents had it frozen after their last argument.

The rest of the day went quickly. More appointments. More pets. Neva gave shots and examined sickly animals. Most just needed minor treatments or medicine, except a dog she took as a walk-in near closing time. He was clearly in bad shape.

"He's not eating or drinking," the man told Julie. "I'm at my wit's end."

She didn't recognize him, and in the two years since she'd been open, she'd thought she had treated all the animals in the area at one time or another. Of course, some people didn't believe in spaying or neutering or regular vaccines. They only brought the pet in if it was sick—and sometimes not even then. So while he filled out the new-patient intake card, she assessed the dog from across the room and winced. Neva braced herself to deliver bad news—she'd learned to recognize the look of a dying animal. He wasn't a big breed, maybe thirty pounds, and he showed mixed heritage in his fuzzy dun coat.

After asking the usual questions, she performed a routine prelim exam, but as she'd suspected, it would take a CT to know for sure what was wrong. She hated this part of the job because she was almost sure she wouldn't be able to offer a cure. If Amos had brought Duke in sooner, maybe. But not now. The dog was just too weak.

Still, she had to try. Her instincts, while good, were not infallible. Neva scooped the dog into her arms and took him in back. He didn't fight as she laid him on the table. Julie came back to assist, but she paused in the doorway when she saw how much Neva had done on her own.

"Are you okay?"

She heard the question in the tech's voice. Julie had a boyfriend and a life outside work and she was ready to be done for the day. "Yeah, I can handle this. Go on home to Travis."

It didn't take long to find the problem—tumor on the spleen. Fatal. This one was such a good size, it was no wonder the dog didn't want to eat. There wasn't room inside him.

Neva closed her eyes and took a deep breath, bracing herself for the encounter to come. Then she squared her shoulders and picked Duke up, cradling him with the same tenderness most people would show a small child. His yellow fur contrasted with her white coat as she carried him back to the exam room.

Amos came to his feet with an anxious look. "You find out what's ailing him?"

"Yes. I'm sorry." Using her doctor's voice, she explained the medical condition and his options. He could take some pain meds home and let the dog live as long as possible, or she could euthanize tonight. "I understand it's a tough decision. I can give you some medicine for him if you want to think about it."

His face fell. "So there's nothin' you can do?"

"I'm sorry," she said again, wishing she could fix it.

No matter how many animals she saved, this never got any easier. The losses always overshadowed the wins. Sometimes she thought it would break her heart, but quitting would just prove her parents right. She'd refused the life they'd chosen for her; they must learn to accept her on her own terms . . . or not at all, though that wasn't what she wanted, either.

But he surprised her. "Let's get it done then. I don't want Duke in pain."

"If you're sure, I have some forms for you to fill out."

An hour later, she finished up. Amos was in tears when he left, and she felt heavy as a carton of bricks. Neva hated days that ended like this.

She jumped a little when a man stepped into view through the frosted glass of her front window. If he held a sick animal, she just might cry. Her lunch had consisted of a soggy sandwich; she was starving and she needed some rest.

Halfheartedly she pointed at the "Closed" sign. In answer, he indicated the "Help Wanted" sign on the other side of the door. As she peered at him, she realized she knew him. He'd helped her the other day when she was stranded. Zeke Noble, the tow truck driver had said. *A good Samaritan, and more importantly, not a stranger, thief, or vandal.* If he'd wanted to hurt her, he'd had a better shot at it on that lonely road. He'd struck her as strange and wary, but not dangerous. So there was no need to call the sheriff to shoo him off.

Counting herself lucky that was all he wanted, Neva pulled an application off the pad on the front desk—covered with pictures of Julie's family, her boyfriend, and her dog—and then went out into the dark.

CHAPTER 2

The woman looked tired, Zeke thought. Her scrubs were stained, and she wore a long tan jacket over the top of them, carelessly unbelted. It was chilly but not freezing today. The extremes ranged wildly; one day it could be below thirty with frost on the ground, and the next it might be sixty-six with threat of tornadoes. Tonight it was about forty-five, and she really should have her coat buttoned up.

Zeke stepped back so as not to crowd her. He didn't often care what people made of him, hadn't for years, but he didn't want to scare a woman after dark, especially not one he hoped would give him a job. She locked the door behind her and then turned, offering him the form. Nodding his thanks, he took it and headed toward his truck. Her voice stopped him halfway there.

"You're not much for talking."

He recognized her voice, though he hadn't gotten a good look at her the other night. She spoke with a honey-sweet drawl that almost made him retrace his steps. The power of those soft, almost teasing words flowed over him in a soothing wave; he'd like to listen to her a little longer, and maybe the knots in him would unwind. Right now he felt ten kinds of exposed —twitchy—as if unfriendly eyes watched him from all dark corners.

Zeke imagined how angry dogs must listen to her whispering reassurances until their hackles smoothed and they stopped showing teeth. Pretty soon they'd be belly up, whining for a rub. He knew that because he fought the same urge.

"Reckon not," he answered at length.

"You never let me thank you."

So she knew him, too. Tim Sweeney had told her his name, but they'd met before, a long time ago. Not that she'd remember. There was no reason for Geneva Harper to recall the boy who'd mowed their lawn while she was away at college. Their paths had only crossed the summer she came home instead of taking extra classes. He'd watched her a lot, those months, with quiet, hopeless longing.

The one time they'd spoken, she had come into the kitchen while he was eating his lunch to ask the cook to make some lemon squares. She'd said hello to him and given him a sweet smile. He'd mumbled something, hoping she'd linger, hoping she wouldn't. She didn't.

Zeke turned then, watching her cross the pavement toward him. She'd put on some weight since he'd seen her last, but she carried it well. Back then, he'd thought she looked like a fawn, all legs and eyes. Now she had curves, the kind that made a man want to see how deep the softness ran. But she still had the big brown eyes and pretty skin. Her hair was brown, too, caught at her neck in a clip. And she was smiling at him.

Annoyance surged through him. It was full dark; she should be more wary. Even though it was a small town, bad things happened here. *He* ought to know.

"Thank me with a job." He emphasized the words with a rattle of the paper.

"I just might. Bring it back during business hours."

"Yes, ma'am."

Her smile flickered. "Don't. Ma'am makes me feel old."

You're not old. The words stuck in his throat, too personal to be spoken. He just inclined his head. *Best not rile her.* At this point any job would do, and he'd visited every other business in town before stopping here. Nobody else had looked thrilled when he asked for an application. They remembered him from his mother, he supposed, and later, his father had done the family name no service, either. If things got worse, he'd heed the voices in his head telling him to slide deeper into the woods and never come out again. But Zeke wasn't quite ready to give up. Not yet.

She smelled of blood and death. He'd fight hard to get past that, if he went to work here. Beneath the disturbing scents, she had others: honey, almonds, and warm cotton. Maybe it was just because he hadn't been with a woman in over a year, but disturbing urges coiled up inside him. He wanted to pull her hair out of the clip, knot his hands in her hair, and *growl* as he—

No more. You're not *an animal.*

"Sorry, Ms. Harper."

"Neva," she corrected gently.

Zeke hadn't known people called her that. But then why would he? They didn't travel in the same circles; he felt like he'd been granted an undeserved intimacy. It was vaguely shaming that he wanted her to remember his name—and that they'd met before—but she never would.

"Won't keep you," he muttered. "Thanks."

Before she could stop him again, he wheeled and headed for his truck. He climbed inside, and by the overhead light, he looked at the job application. He had a stack of them on the seat beside him. And *none* of them made sense. The letters kept changing shape on him, translating into symbols that made no sense. He'd once understood what they meant. At least, he was pretty sure he had.

Now he could only figure signs out based on past experience. He knew what an exit sign looked like, and he'd seen enough "Help Wanted" signs to recognize one in red and white because it was two words and the correct number of letters; he just couldn't make them out separately as words. And it helped a lot that public bathrooms had pictures on them. His hands trembled as he put the form atop the others. There was no way he could fill these out without help and it enraged him.

"What the hell did y'all do to me?" he asked aloud.

With a little snarl, Zeke started the truck, and then he realized he'd waited until Neva made it to her car. In town, with lights all around, he could see it was an old Honda Civic—same one that'd stalled on his road, so she must've gotten it fixed; it was a little surprising Geneva Harper didn't drive a more expensive car. Only after she drove away did he feel free to do the same. Weird, but his inner hound relaxed its guard once he knew she was safe.

To fill out these applications, he needed help. And there was only one person he could turn to.

Half an hour later, he sat in his aunt's kitchen, listening with half an ear to her complaints. His excuses didn't matter—nobody would believe the real story anyway. More importantly, with his mother's history, he couldn't *trust* anyone with the true story. Not even Auntie Sid, much as it grieved him.

"I was worried," she concluded with a scowl. "I can't believe you just run off like that. What would your daddy say?"

Nothing, Zeke thought. *Being dead and all.* But nobody mouthed off to her. Not if they knew what was good for them. Sid was short for Sidonie; it was a French name, as she never tired of reminding people, because their people had moved to Alabama from New Orleans. She was a small woman, barely came up to his chin, and her hair had more silver in it than it used to. He hoped the crow's feet around her eyes weren't because of him. It was lucky she didn't look anything like his father, or he might have a hard time looking at her. People said he favored her around the eyes.

He mumbled something apologetic and ate the last of his pie—Granny Smith apple, and one of the pleasures he'd forgotten during his captivity. Luckily he remembered to use a fork. His cheeks burned with remembered embarrassment,

With any grace, he would avoid humiliating himself like that in front of folks.

Once she wound down and joined him at the kitchen table, he said, "Need your help with these," and scooted the stack of forms toward her.

With reading glasses perched on her nose, she looked a lot like his mamaw, too, but there were no dark memories attached to his grandmother. She'd passed on before everything turned at the farm.

Sid had always been his favorite auntie; the others didn't have much time for him. They were a big family, lots of cousins and such, but Zeke had never felt connected to any of them. As a kid, he'd spent his time in the woods, looking for frogs and trying to save squirrels that his kin wanted to shoot.

"Something wrong with your writin' hand?"

Now he'd have to lie to her. Trying not to squirm, he answered, "Need glasses but I gotta work 'fore I can pay the eye doctor."

She nodded like that made good sense. "Well, I'm just glad you're back. Don't take off on me like that again, hear?"

No. I'll die first.

It took everything he had to answer her questions like nothing was wrong. Like he couldn't hear the mice scurrying in the walls. Once she'd gotten all the facts for the first form, it was simple for her to fill in the blanks on all the applications. Most had pictures on them so he could tell which ones needed to go back to what businesses. By the time she finished, Sid was complaining her hand hurt.

"Sorry for that. But anything I can do . . ." He glanced around her kitchen, looking for work. A few of the cabinets looked loose. Tomorrow he'd come back and fix them.

"Psht," she scoffed. "You're the first one I'll call, something needs doing. The rest of these Nobles are a shiftless lot, I tell you what."

Zeke stood. "Need to get on home."

"Guff. You'll stay until you're back on your feet. I know dang well you don't have power at the farm."

His aunt had a cozy little bungalow in town, so it would be

nice to stay with her. But he was afraid of what he might say or do. Sometimes dreams came, and when he woke, he wasn't where he'd been when he went to sleep. Best not to expose her to that. Reluctantly he shook his head. "Can't. You done enough."

He read the love and concern in her face as she hugged him. "Then I want you for dinner, once you get one of these jobs. Hear?"

"Yes, ma'am."

"Be careful in that truck. It'll be the death of you."

She might not be wrong about that.

"You smell like dog," Lillian Harper said.

Neva felt her smile slip. "I do not. I showered."

"Stay away from James Marchand. He's allergic." Her mother lifted her chin in greeting at a newly arrived guest and swept away in a slim Chanel cloud.

Harper Court teemed with people invited to the country for a long weekend. It could be long, despite the lack of any corresponding holiday, because most of the guests had money and were not engaged in the business of making it. The next holiday would be Thanksgiving, and if her mother had any say in it, the house would be full then, too; anything to drive off the silence.

I put on my good black dress for this? These days, she had only the one. Her wardrobe consisted of scrubs, jeans, and T-shirts. When she got her own place, she'd given her old clothes to charity. And she still heard about it. *Why you live in that terrible firetrap when you have a lovely suite at Harper Court, I will never understand.*

Bennett Reed slipped up to stand at her elbow. Though she didn't look around, she recognized his cologne. It was an expensive blend of cedar, pine, and musk, mixed with lower notes, and she didn't like it any better this time around. Like him, it was slick and polished, bought for the brand more than the scent.

"You look tense."

Tension pinched at her temples, but she forced herself to offer a perfunctory smile as she swung around to face him. "Hi, Ben. How've you been?"

"Missing you," he said softly.

Dating him had been the biggest single mistake of her life. Her parents had been so distraught after . . . well, she didn't want to think about Luke. She had wanted to comfort them, and Ben had a reassuring way about him. In those early, awful days, he consoled her parents in a way she never could, always calm and capable, always wearing that gentle half smile. They'd coasted along while they were all numb with grief, and then one day, she'd woken up to realize he quietly ran all their lives.

Neva didn't like being managed. He'd laughed at her complaints and that was the last straw. The resulting argument ended in her moving to her own place and out of Harper Court for good. It hadn't been that long ago, either, so she came to functions like these grudgingly, and for appearance's sake. Not that she cared.

Her mother did. And if Lillian got too upset, she made life miserable for Neva's dad. He'd then visit it on her. So most times it was worth it to put in a few polite hours in the interest of keeping the peace. And honestly, she didn't want to upset either of them. Despite their disagreements, she loved them.

"I doubt that, somehow." Her smile became fixed as a politician stopped to shake her hand. "Nice to see you again, Congressman. Will y'all be doing some hunting while you're here?"

"You know it. Your daddy has some of the best woods around."

"So I hear." And it was an old argument, one she wouldn't go into again.

They made small talk while servers circulated with trays of canapés and flutes of wine. Music tinkled from the baby grand piano and the lights sparkled through the polished teardrop chandelier overhead. Neva found no charm in any of it. Only Luke had made this place feel like a home, and with him gone, she couldn't bear being here. Hard to say how her parents stood it. But then, they had each other, and whatever their faults, she had never doubted their devotion. Unlike most of her friends, her parents had a solid marriage, which meant they always offered a unified front in any argument with her. She found that frustrating.

Eventually, the congressman excused himself and went off to greet his constituents and drink a little more wine. From his rosy flush, Neva guessed he'd already had plenty, but he was a good old boy with a hollow leg. He probably went around half sloshed as a matter of course.

Unfortunately that left her with Ben. She'd thought him handsome enough once. He had the look of a Ken doll come to life, but Ben was anatomically correct, at least so far as she knew. They'd never gotten that far. He'd said he didn't want to press her, which sounded like he was doing the right thing and being a gentleman, but at the bottom of it, she hadn't trusted his control. It made her feel like he was just going through the motions, using her to further his connection with her father.

"Can we talk?"

"We *are* talking."

From across the room, Lillian noted Ben at her side and gave an approving smile. She'd never stopped hinting that it wasn't too late—Neva could still atone for her misdeeds and marry that fine young man. She could sell her vet practice and come back to the fold, no harm done. That was the last thing she wanted. Her life might not be glamorous, but she'd built it on her own sweat, and it wasn't hollowed out with loss of Luke. Work filled her hours, not grief. That was how it had to be.

"That's not what I meant, and you know it." He took her elbow. Ostensibly it seemed a courtly gesture, but his fingers gripped like steel bands. "One turn on the terrace."

"It's cold." She couldn't object without causing a scene at her mother's party. Since she'd come to avoid drama, it was best to accede. "I'll get my coat first and meet you outside." While she was at it, she'd also get her car keys.

Ben gazed down at her as if weighing her words. "Promise?"

Stifling a sigh, she nodded and wove through the crowd. A

few people stopped her on the way out. Neva made conversation politely for a moment or two, answering questions about people's pets. Unlike her mother, most of the guests appeared to find her work charming. They probably wouldn't if they saw the reality of it.

Ten minutes later, she slipped around the front of the house, heels tapping on the flagstone. She found Ben waiting as promised. No surprises there. He needed her family connections to further his own career and would take her to get them, however little he wanted her.

"Here I am." She stopped a few yards away from him and gazed up at the stars. It was a chill, clear night.

"I want you to know I mean it when I say I miss you," he began. "I know you don't believe that, and I know I can be overbearing. I took control because it's the way I know how to help. I'm not very good at knowing what to say, so I do instead."

That was not *true,* Neva thought. He always knew *exactly* what to say, which was why he wanted her father's help to get into politics. It was also why he wanted to marry old money, if only she'd stop cutting up sick animals and get her hair done and buy some pretty shoes. And it was why they'd never fit together in a million years.

"I'm glad you make life easier for my parents," she answered. "But I prefer to captain my own ship."

He offered a wry smile. "You made that very clear."

Her cheeks heated. During their last fight, she'd screamed something to that effect at him, but with less grace and more profanity. But Ben never lost his temper. That wasn't natural, or at least, it didn't work for her. She didn't want everything to be explained and rationalized away. Sometimes you just knew what you knew in your gut and there was no reason why. That was why she couldn't accept Luke was dead, though he'd been missing for almost two months.

I'd know. Though people said twins could sometimes sense each other's thoughts and feelings, they'd never had that. But they had been close. Surely she would feel his loss . . . or maybe she just wanted to believe that because it was easier than the alternative. From his expression, Ben knew what she was thinking, but he had the sense this time not to lecture her about the stages of grief and how she was stuck in denial. Before, she'd almost punched him.

The heels hurt her feet. Neva shifted and rested an arm on the balustrade. Ornate carvings etched the stone, creating a frame for the terrace. She gazed out over the dead garden. In summer, there would be roses, camellias, wisteria, daisies, asters, foxglove, and bleeding hearts. Her mother took special pride in the grounds, kept the gardeners tending the plants until all hours. When Neva was a kid, Lillian had worked out there herself, at least until Grandmother Harper told her it was unseemly.

"Let's cut to the chase, Ben. I'm never coming to my senses. I like my life the way it is, and I don't ever want to be a politician's wife."

"We could go all the way to the state capital," he said softly. "We'd make a good team if you could just be a little less hands-on with your causes. Maybe you could take up fund-raising instead?"

She laughed, tickled at his persistence. If he channeled that into his work, he would certainly go far. "Ben, I don't want to be a 'good team' with the man I marry. It calls to mind towel slaps on the ass and sweaty shorts."

"I didn't mean like that," he said, obviously stung.

"We're done. Tell my mama I had a headache and I went on home, will you?"

Neva felt him watching as she walked away. Ben was *always* watching. The problem was, she had no idea what he was thinking; it was like staring down into a well and seeing your own face gazing back.

CHAPTER 3

The next day, Zeke dropped off the applications. He stopped first at Felton's Pharmacy. He recognized the manager as someone he'd gone to school with, and it rankled to ask the man for a job because he'd never liked Skip Felton. The guy acted like he thought he was something special because his old man owned the drugstore.

Skip had put on forty pounds and was losing his hair. But when Zeke stepped up to the prescription counter, the jackass puffed his chest like he thought the red vest made him look manly. "Something I can do for you?"

"Just turning in an application."

"I know you, don't I?" Felton pretended to think, but he knew it for a lie from the sour-smug smell. "Zeke Noble. Haven't seen you around in a while."

He made himself smile when he really wanted to punch him in the face. Might prove troublesome if he couldn't stand a man in a position of authority over him, especially since Felton was the type to give him shit for no reason at all. Still, he needed a job.

"Been traveling."

"Well, I'll put this with the other apps and I'll give you a buzz when we start interviews." Another lie. He had no intention of calling, let alone hiring him.

For all the good it was doing, Aunt Sid had let him put her phone number down for interview calls, since it would take a paycheck to get his phone turned back on. And he might not bother. Who would he call? Zeke spun grimly and stalked toward the door.

"That you, boy?" The voice came booming from the shampoo aisle.

This day just gets better and better. He turned to greet his uncle, who had his cousins in tow. "Uncle Lew. Wil. Jeff."

"I saw Sid today. She said you come out to the house for supper. When you planning on seeing us?"

"Not sure. Need to find work and get the farm fixed up first."

"I know Carleen would love to make a big mess of fried chicken and hear about your adventures."

"My—"

"Aunt Sid said you was seeing the world," his cousin put in.

"And I was glad to hear it," Lew went on. "Thought you done ended up like your ma."

And that was why he didn't like his uncle. The man had all the tact of a bull elephant, and no awareness of it, so it wasn't like yelling at him would do any good. Lew would just claim he was doing the person a favor with his straight talk. Zeke had been down that road before—and when he was more capable of debate.

"Can see I didn't."

Lew laughed, like that was a joke. "Me and the boys'd love to take you out with us. We're gonna shoot some squirrel this weekend."

"Need to get settled."

"I'll let you get on then. We got shopping to do anyhow. I'm just glad your aunt ain't making me buy her woman junk anymore. Change of life and all."

He could've survived without hearing that. Funny how little some things changed when everything felt different in his own head. Zeke lifted a hand in passing and pushed past his cousins. Jeff and Wil had never liked him. From their dark expressions, that didn't look to be changing anytime soon.

None of his other stops gave him hope. They brushed him off at the grocery store and the rest of the jobs needed him to do some reading. By the time he got to his last application in the stack, he felt pretty low. He'd saved the vet clinic for last because he prickled at the idea of seeing Neva again. It wasn't entirely a bad feeling, some gladness mixed in with the boyish nerves.

The strip mall was pretty new; he remembered when it had been built. Cement first, and then the brick facing. A tall, backlit sign at the edge of the lot read Five Oaks Shopping Plaza. That sounded a lot fancier than it was. When he was here before, he'd checked at Tammy's Nail Hut, Shoe Connection, and GameZone, but they had no jobs for him. Neva's clinic occupied the end position on the far right. On the far left sat a sub shop called Armando's. Other than the Walmart near the highway, and the cluster of stores downtown, this was it for shopping in Harper Creek. Not that he'd ever spent money like some.

He parked the truck far enough away that it wouldn't be visible from the front and for good measure stashed it on the far side of an SUV. Then it took him a minute longer to master his nerves. As he walked up, he saw that the clinic sign had both paws and claws swiping at letters he couldn't read. Someone had taped merry-looking turkeys along the front of the window, and the door had a horn of plenty overflowing with paper fruit. A bell jingled as he went inside.

This time, a petite red-haired girl sat at the front desk. She glanced up with a smile. Like Neva, she wore blue scrub pants, but puppies and kittens covered her shirt. "Can I help you?"

"Here." He handed her the form.

Her expression brightened. "Oh, you're here about the job. If you want to wait ten minutes or so, Neva can probably squeeze in an interview."

Shit. If he had to wow her with smooth talk, he'd never get hired. But Zeke nodded and sat down. To make it look good, he picked up a magazine. The words still refused to make sense but he could admire the pictures. Anger simmered inside him. He'd never be . . . right again.

It took longer than the redhead said, but eventually Neva escorted a kitten-carrying girl to the front door. They were both smiling, so it must be good news. Today she didn't smell of blood and death, just the warm musk of healthy animals and the honey-almond scent he'd noticed before. She wore her hair in a braid today, different than the tail, all twisted up. It made his fingers itch to unwind the strands.

"I have a fifteen-minute break between appointments," she said in greeting. "Come on back and we'll talk a bit."

Wordlessly, he followed her. He studied the swell of her butt even through baggy scrubs. She carried her extra weight in her hips and thighs, and he liked it fine. Her waist was small by comparison, and she had fragile-looking shoulders. She couldn't be weak, though, if she treated big animals. He'd heard she made farm visits since she was the only vet in the county. She ran what he'd heard the assistant call a *mixed practice* on the phone.

Inside, her office felt too small, just enough space for her desk and a plastic chair across from it. He tried not to think about the size of the room or the lack of light. It reminded him of the cell, and he refused to go there again, even in his mind.

"First, I'll tell you what I'm looking for." Neva described the duties and none of them sounded too tough. He could handle manual labor. "I can afford to give the successful applicant twenty hours a week at minimum wage. That's four hours, five days a week. No benefits." She paused. "Before we go on, so as not to waste our time, does this still sound like something you'd be interested in?"

Zeke nodded. *About all I'm fit for, too.* He tried not to show his despair.

"Then we'll move on to my usual questions. Why do you want to work here?"

"Need a job."

She gave a soft, surprised laugh. "People aren't usually so

forthright about it. Most wrap it up in pretty talk about loving animals."

"Could try that if you want me to."

"No, that's fine. But you *do* like them?" She hesitated, as if she wasn't sure what he'd think about the next thing. "The job requires some handling help and they sense fear or dislike. It can complicate matters."

Oh. People probably made fun of her for giving animals that much credit. But she was right. "Yeah. Won't hamper me."

"Excellent. I see on your application you worked at the mill for a while. Can I ask why you left?"

"Can."

"But you won't answer?" she asked, raising a brow.

"Past is past. Need work and need somebody to take a chance on me." He read subtle astonishment in her face, and he heard the faintest intake of breath. Nobody else would've caught it.

"I like your honesty. To put my cards on the table likewise, I'm not exactly overwhelmed with applicants. I'll call your references, and if they recommend you, I'll offer you a two-week trial. We'll see how it goes."

"Sounds good," he said.

Zeke pushed to his feet and offered his hand. It was a privilege he'd offered nobody since his escape. After being poked and prodded and having no say about anything, now he wanted complete control over who touched him. She curled her warm fingers around his and it felt like a fist around his heart. Letting go of her hurt.

With a nod of farewell, he turned. But she stopped him again with that sweet molasses voice. Her careless interest would cut him wide open, if he didn't watch out.

"Have you always been so quiet?"

He'd lost some of his old life while they had him locked up. Things were blurred or felt like they'd happened to someone else. It helped with the sad things, but he didn't like losing the precious thoughts as well. The bell jingled up front.

"Yeah." It was the easy answer, and he'd sure never talked as much as some.

That time, she let him go because the red-haired girl called, "Your next appointment is here!"

"Coming! I'll be in touch, Zeke. It was nice talking to you." Her smile said she meant it, and her scent agreed, deepening to caramel and smoky apple wood. Before the change, emotions had barely registered for him at all, and now he could smell them. Was this how animals read humans?

Neva walked him out of her office and then took over with the clients; her assistant had started the visit by putting the pet owners in the exam room. He admired the way they worked together. Maybe one day he'd fit that smoothly. Dim hope. He never fit anywhere.

The assistant came back to the lobby. Her face was covered in freckles and she had a faint gap between her two front teeth. She didn't seem to care it showed when she smiled, because she did it a lot.

"I'm Julie Fish." She waited, as if expecting a response.

"Pleasure. Zeke Noble."

Puzzlement flickered. "It's okay, you can laugh."

"Why?"

"Because my last name is Fish and I work at a place called Paws and Claws."

Then he *did* laugh. The sound surprised him. It felt like something had torn loose inside; some weight had lifted. "Funny."

"I'm used to it. So you really want a job here, huh?"

"Yeah." And he meant it.

"She works harder than anybody I've ever met."

Though he felt guilty at the impulse, he got the feeling Julie would chatter if he didn't walk away. He didn't. "Oh?"

"Yeah." Julie glanced at the closed exam room door and lowered her voice. "Since Luke disappeared anyway."

Zeke drew a blank. He didn't know much about the Harpers, other than what the rest of the town did—that they had money, owned the mill, and threw fancy parties out at Harper Court. And it took a full day to trim their lawns.

"Who?"

"Been gone awhile, I take it?" He didn't answer, and she

went on, "Lucius Harper was Neva's twin. He went missing and the family hasn't been the same since."

Lucius. That name, he remembered. Geneva and Lucius. Luke and Neva. They'd both chosen simpler names than the ones they'd been given. That spoke to their characters.

"Sorry to hear," he said, belatedly seeing she wanted a response.

"Anyway, I tell you that so you understand why she's always here."

"So she won't have time to grieve."

"You got it. But don't worry. She doesn't expect us to match her schedule. She's a great boss."

"Seems you like her a lot."

Julie nodded. "We've been friends since fifth grade."

His best friend was in the military. The last time he'd seen the guy was the night he'd been taken. Danny had been in town briefly, just before shipping out again, and he probably thought Zeke was a bastard who had gone home with some chick without bothering to say good-bye or good luck. They wouldn't be bridging that gap. Just as well—Zeke wouldn't want Danny to see him now.

The phone rang, saving him from making up his mind whether to ask for more. It seemed wrong, so that was best. He went out to the truck and headed to his aunt's house. She'd insisted on cooking him a casserole to take out to the farm. Hungry as he was these days, it wouldn't last long enough to spoil. Zeke ate and ate without gaining back any of the weight he'd lost. It appeared they had fucked up his metabolism, too.

Sid had left the key in the usual place, though she was at work at the insurance office, so he let himself in. He found everything packaged up in the fridge with a little note. Regret panged through him because he couldn't read it.

Zeke took out his frustration on her cabinets, repairing them with angry slams of the hammer. He went home heavy-hearted, and after eating, he started on the house overhaul. Before he could put full faith in a fresh start, he had a lot of cleaning to do.

* * *

His references were impeccable. Neva studied the notes she'd taken. HR departments often just confirmed dates of employment, but these were personal references, and the people had nice things to say about Zeke Noble. Most were post-scripted with comments like, *poor boy*, and *such a shame*, though. Such tantalizing hints made her hungry for gossip; Julie would surely know. She heard about *everything* in Harper Creek.

Neva debated silently before deciding to indulge her curiosity. Julie had just hung up the phone and was penciling in an appointment when she stepped out of her office. "Do you know anything about the Nobles?"

"I was wondering if you'd ask." She set down her pencil, her freckled face sober. It was an odd expression on her, like catching a pixie in a pensive moment. "In a nutshell, his mom was quiet-crazy. These days, they'd call it postpartum depression, but she went untreated for years. Eventually she killed herself."

"Shit. How old was he?" This didn't speak to whether he could do the job, of course. It just filled the gaps in her local knowledge.

"Not very." Julie shrugged. "Still a kid, anyway. I'm not sure. I could find out, if you want. My cousin—"

"No," she said hastily. "Don't call Emmylou."

Emmylou Fish waited tables at Tom's Diner—they had been tickled with the Suzanne Vega song—and if Julie called, she would repeat the question and the story to everyone in the place. The last thing Neva wanted to do was stir up ancient history. Zeke didn't need that. But it was typical of the town where something that happened years ago would still be the first thing that came to mind when his name came up. It wasn't fair, but people had long memories.

"You thinking about hiring him?"

"Mm-hm. How did he seem to you?"

"Polite. Watchful. He paid more attention to the animals than their owners while he waited."

Neva nodded. "Good sign in somebody angling to work here."

"That's what I thought. Okay for me to head out now? I've got to run some errands and then stop at Pie in the Sky."

"Sure."

Once Julie had gone, she returned to her office and studied the application. So he was twenty-seven, nearly twenty-eight. Almost four years younger than she was. They might've attended school together, if she hadn't been sent to a private academy an hour away. After elementary school, drivers had ferried her back and forth. Without slumber parties at Julie's house, she would've had no idea what normal life should be like.

At six, she dialed the number from Zeke's application, and a woman answered. She didn't sound young, but it couldn't be his mother. "Hello?"

"I'm calling for Zeke. Is he there?"

"No, he's out at the farm doing some work. I'll get a message to him."

Interesting. Maybe he had a bad harvest and needed some cash flow to get him through the winter. It wouldn't be the first time she'd heard that story. But it boded ill for her if he turned out to be a good worker and next year's yield brought more.

"Then tell him I'm offering him the job at Paws and Claws, if he still wants it."

"Oh, that's wonderful news! I'll let him know."

"Thank you. He can start as soon as tomorrow, if he wants."

That finished, after she did all the paperwork, put away files, and saw to the final care on her two inpatients, she knocked off "early." By that point, it was nearly eight. Neva turned off all the lights, and then set the alarm. Armando's would be closing soon. She tried never to stay past their business hours. Otherwise, she would be alone on the property, and that wasn't a good idea.

Zeke surprised her again as she was locking up; her heart gave a little jolt as he slid out of the dark, a lean shadow moving around his ancient truck. The lamps in the parking lot glazed his skin with ashen light and made deep hollows of his eyes.

"What time tomorrow? Tried to call but the machine picked up."

"Most attendants did nine to one, but if you have other obligations, you can work in the afternoon, say two to six?"

"That'd be better." He didn't say why.

Before she knew she meant to, she found herself inviting, "I'm heading to Julie's for pizza night. Want to come along?"

He froze, still with shock and something else, something she couldn't identify. Longing, maybe, but that seemed like too strong a word for such a simple thing. "Sure I'm welcome?"

"Of course. I hang out with Julie and her boyfriend once a month. I bet Travis'll be happy to have you even the numbers. We order pizza from Pie in the Sky and chill with some action movies. We're doing a Mad Max-a-thon tonight."

He hesitated so long that she wondered if she'd oversold the invitation. Finally he answered, "Sounds good."

"Their place is out on Ringer Road. Follow me?"

Zeke nodded and she went to her Civic, conscious of his gaze on her the whole way. He was a strange man. Her step faltered. *Oh, crap.* Did he think this was a *date*? She'd invited him because she and Julie were so close; she thought it might make him feel included. It might help him stay on the job longer, too. The other guys might've quit because of one too many inside jokes. That, plus the work was hard, dirty, and paid very little.

Well, no help for it now. At some point she'd have to make it clear she wasn't hitting on him. How awful. But overall, she didn't regret asking him.

Julie and Travis lived on the far side of town, toward the highway. Their place was bigger than Neva's, which was why they always got together there. Not bigger than Harper Court, of course, but she never would've felt comfortable inviting them over for pizza and beer there anyway.

She stopped at the liquor store, amused to see Zeke pull up behind her. His Ford really was ancient, made in the fifties, she guessed, by the curved front end. It had been red at some point, but it was mostly rust now. The engine ran loud, banging in a way that couldn't be healthy.

As she went past, she called, "I'm running in to pick up a cold six-pack. That's my contribution to the meal. Next time I'll get the pizza."

That was more than he needed to know, but she didn't want him feeling like he had to pay for anything when she'd invited him. He obviously needed work and being short of cash could prick a man's ego. Zeke seemed the prickly type; his jaw was certainly set tight enough right now to make her think he was worried. He waited outside while she ran her errand and then they headed off in tandem.

The house on Ringer Road sat back from the highway, not quite in the town limits. There was supposed to be a proper development out here, but the project had run out of money and only a few houses were built. The investor took a loss, and sold them off cheap, which was why her friends already owned a home. Though they weren't married yet, they planned to tie the knot soon, and they'd bought as a couple. They were good together, giving Neva hope she might find somebody who worked for her on that level.

When she pulled up, Travis opened the front door before she got out of the car, likely because of the way Zeke's truck was knocking. She snagged the beer and stepped out. Gravel crunched under the soles of her sensible shoes.

Travis gave her a quizzical look. "You brought a date? Who's this?"

Oh, God. Awkward. She didn't want to hurt Zeke's feelings by denying it too quickly but a nondenial might worry him in a different way. *No, you're not obligated to perform routine vaginal maintenance on the boss to keep your job.*

"He's a new hire," she said, skirting the question.

"Ah, fresh blood at the clinic." Travis waved them up.

The three-bedroom ranch house had a small covered porch attached to the front of the house, just big enough for a swing. Neva secretly wanted one just like it. She *loved* their house. It was warm and homey; it felt lived in. The shiny wood floor showed some scratches from their dog, Doof, who was a mix of shepherd and Dane. He was a big brindle fellow with clumsy paws, but he overflowed with slobbery love. Julie always said he'd lick an intruder to death.

Handing the beer to Travis, she made Doof sit down before she'd pet him. He'd knocked visitors off their feet a time or two before they taught him it was rude. Then she knelt down and gave his ears a rub. The dog thumped his tail on the floor and gave a rapturous sigh as he flipped over and offered his belly for rubs. From her lower vantage point, she studied Zeke while he checked out the place. The way he cocked his head, almost as if he were listening and smelling, struck her as strange. She'd seen dogs and cats do that. Never a man. But he seemed to be taking the place in as much with his ears and nose as with his eyes.

Travis went into the kitchen, talking the whole way. "Julie's not home yet." Once he came back, the other man offered his hand. "I'm Travis Delaney."

Zeke shook but she saw his discomfort. "Pleasure. Kind of you to let me barge in like this."

"You'll need some support if you're gonna be working with Jules and Neva. They're an evil duo for sure."

Neva grinned as she straightened. "Enough of that. Let me get a beer or two in him before you start telling embarrassing stories."

"You mean like the time you two—"

"I *mean* it," she said, though she didn't know for sure why it mattered.

Only that it did—and that was one of her gut certainties that Ben had never understood. He'd probe for why, because there had to be a reason or she couldn't feel what she felt. Maddening.

Watching them, a smile broke the solemnity of Zeke's face like clouds clearing away from the sun. Until that moment, she hadn't realized how dark he looked. Now it was like seeing a different man. He had eyes like twilight, she thought, shot with gray and blue and green, all the colors of a sky before a powerful storm. And he smiled with such tentative fear, like he didn't think he was allowed to share in their amusement.

"You got the DVDs, right?"

"Netflix delivers," Travis said. "The front room is all set up if you two want to head on in. I have a little more work to do yet."

He had a CS degree and he worked as a contractor coding for a company in California. When projects hit, he often worked insanely long hours, leading Julie to compare him to Neva. In many ways they were opposites. Travis was tall where Jules was tiny. He was also seventy-five percent geek. In a good way.

Because it meant he loved gadgets, which included the huge plasma TV and surround sound, great for movies. Besides Travis's work computers, it was the single most expensive item in the house. Zeke seemed suitably impressed. Like any guy, he stopped and gazed at the big screen.

"It's as good as it looks," she said.

"Few things are." His words held a weight she didn't understand.

She *wanted* to. And that was bad, bad news.

CHAPTER 4

Zeke felt out of place.

It wasn't that his hosts had done anything to make him feel unwelcome; they hadn't asked Neva why she'd invited him. His new job at the clinic seemed to be enough. His trouble came from somewhere else. The room had a brown couch and love seat, framing the TV. Travis and Julie cuddled together on the latter while he perched on the edge of the sofa. He couldn't relax.

This house was Travis's territory, and it smelled like him. The man had lived here long enough with Julie that Zeke's nerves prickled. He expected a challenge. He wasn't sure he'd ever be able to allow another male to spend so much time at the farm. His jaw clenched. He knew normal behavior when he saw it in other people. *He* was the broken one, not Travis.

The pizza was delicious, though—light, crisp crust, plenty of cheese, spicy tomato sauce, extra sausage, light peppers. When Julie carried it in, she'd joked that the peppers served as a nod to the four food groups. He tried to follow the conversation afterward, but they laughed too much and switched topics too fast. Three voices talking over one another, and the words turned into noise.

Once they finished eating, everyone settled down to watch the movie. That was easier. They dimmed the lights and then he only needed to understand one person talking at once. His muscles eased a bit. But he wasn't sure he could stay for two more movies. He needed to be moving. Doing something. Sitting still like this didn't work unless he was sleeping.

During the first intermission, Julie and Travis went to the kitchen for more beer. They couldn't know he heard them whispering about him and then the soft little sounds that came from kissing. He didn't *want* to be able to hear this. Her soft sighs should be for her man alone. The need to run rose up.

"You okay?" Neva asked.

Surprise washed over him. He'd thought he was doing a decent job of hiding his unease. "Why?"

"You look . . ."

You wouldn't believe it if I told you. Hell, sometimes he didn't. Sometimes he thought weak minds ran in his family, and that his mother's sickness had finally taken him. Maybe he *was* crazy.

"Sad," she finished.

That wasn't it but it helped that she'd paid enough attention to notice. He calmed some. Listening to her voice let him block out what was happening in the kitchen. For the first time, he found he could turn it off. He shifted and found her gazing at him with concerned eyes.

"Hasn't been easy," he said.

"I guess not." She hesitated, as if she wanted to ask him something more, maybe *what* hadn't been easy, but Julie and Travis came back with the beer, putting a stop to further talk. *Just as well.* Still, he relaxed as he'd been unable to before. Even the faint scent of sexual arousal that clung to Neva's friend didn't alarm him.

After the second movie, Travis went to the bathroom and Julie called Neva into the kitchen. To talk about him, he guessed. Shortly, he was proven right.

"So is this a date?" she whispered, right away.

He gazed at the big, blank screen, trying to pretend he couldn't hear. But he wanted to know the answer to that himself, so he didn't block. His hands curled into fists on his knees.

Neva sounded shocked. "Of course not. I just hired the guy. I wanted him to feel more at ease working at the clinic and I hoped this might help."

"Just checking. But you'll never meet anyone if you don't get out there and start looking."

"You sound like my mother. Not everyone's as lucky as you, Jules."

The other woman sighed. "I know. I'm sorry."

Zeke's heart lifted. It could've been a lot worse. She could've said she felt sorry for him or that she'd never want someone like him. He almost smiled.

Travis came back down the hall, drying his hands on the thighs of his jeans. "You want that last slice?"

"If nobody else does."

"Go for it. Are you sticking around for the third one?" It was a friendly inquiry, but the question told Zeke he'd stayed long enough.

Maybe it wasn't personal. Maybe the guy just wanted to be alone with Julie. Given how they'd been messing around in the kitchen, he'd want private time with his woman; that was for sure. He stood up, still chewing the last of the pizza.

"Should get home. Thanks."

"Not a prob. Next month we're watching the *Weekend at Bernie's* movies." He grinned. "My turn to pick. Maybe you can make it?"

Huh. So Travis hadn't been asking him to leave? God, he'd lost so much in his ability to read other human beings. He could figure out more from their breathing and their smell than from their words and expressions. But since he'd already said he needed to go, he just nodded.

"Sounds good."

Travis called, "Zeke's heading out. Want to say bye?"

The women came out of the kitchen together. Julie offered a warm smile. "It was great having you. See you at work tomorrow."

Pleasure washed over him. As of tomorrow, he'd have somewhere to go and work to be doing. At the end of the week, there would be money to get the power back on and put food in his cupboards. Neva couldn't know how much she'd done for him by giving him a job.

"Good night," he said.

Lifting a hand, he headed for the door. Neva surprised him by saying to the others, "I'll walk him out."

Outside, the air was crisp and cool. No clouds in the sky. Stars glittered overhead, and the night sang with sounds other people wouldn't even notice. He could hear a raccoon prowling in the bushes. There were squirrels in the trees, too, and nesting birds as well. He saw the shadow of open wings and the sensation of swooping rushed through him. Owl. For a dizzying moment, he saw through its eyes just as it dove after a mouse.

He stumbled, barely catching himself on the hood of the truck. Tremors ran through him. Christ. Just when he thought it couldn't get worse, it did. *Can there be any doubt I'm nuts?*

"What happened? Did you step in the hole?"

Still dizzy, he couldn't speak. Zeke let her go on about some defect in Travis's driveway maintenance program. He lost the thread of her words. Instead he just breathed, trying to regain control of his own head. When he finally did, he realized she had her hand on his arm.

Warm.

The heat shocked him. He couldn't remember how long it had been since a woman other than Aunt Sid had touched him. Here it was, skin to skin. He would've pulled away from anyone else, but for her, he stood quiet, drinking in the feeling.

"How many beers did you have?"

"One."

"So you should be fine to drive."

Sid would call Neva a caretaker, someone who made sure everyone else was okay. But who looked after *her*? He never could've imagined a world where Geneva Harper would be asking about him like this.

"Just tripped," he said. "Tired. Been a long day."

He wanted to say more but the words wouldn't come. He wanted to tell her that it mattered she cared—that she was kind and decent—and that he'd known little enough of either in recent months. But his tongue seemed to swell in his mouth, and he couldn't.

"Would you like me to follow you home? I owe you. Anything could've happened to me the other night."

He shook his head. "You done plenty."

By the time he got in the truck, the dizziness had passed. The owl had flown away, mouse in talons, though Zeke didn't like to think about his surety. Blood scented the night air, surely not just from one small mouse. Just more of his crazy. Best not to speak it or think of it.

"'Night, Zeke." Neva stood in the shine of his headlights, watching him drive away.

He had a strange feeling about leaving her, like it was the last thing he should ever do. The urge to slam the truck into park and run back to her nearly overwhelmed him. Gritting his teeth against his quiet horror about being behind the wheel, he held on tight, ignored the impulse, and went on home. He just had to hang on a little longer.

Day by day, he told himself that. One day he'd wake up and the world would be right again. A quiet little voice said, *No, that's not happening. Not ever.*

Zeke ignored that whisper. If he didn't, they won.

That night, the dream came. It was always the same. He lay strapped on a hospital-style bed, his arms buckled at the wrists, straps on his ankles as well. He was completely naked, bright lights shining down while people stood all around him talking about him like he wasn't a person. The low murmurs were indistinguishable, but he heard displeasure in their tones. Then the pain began.

Needles at first, jabbing into his skin, over and over. He had no way of knowing how much time passed while they worked on him. After the needles, they used electricity: electrodes on his head, his chest, and his sex. The current made him howl; the shocks went on and on, until he screamed and it all went dark. Awakening found him back in the cell, still naked, blood trickling from his arms and legs. Unlike the others, he couldn't scream or weep. He had no voice. No words. So he curled into himself and waited for the torture to start again.

Zeke woke in a pool of sweat, ready to kill someone for what had been done to him. They'd stolen almost a year of his life, all told, between the time he was held hostage, and the long months it took him to work his way home. But he didn't kid himself that he had the resources to find answers, so he'd do the next best thing.

You bastards thought you broke me, but you didn't. I will rise. Then he began the long hike back to the house because when he woke from one of those nightmares, he was never in his own bed.

Neva worked at a mad pace, and the following week went in a rush. Hunting season always brought its share of calamities. Having an extra body around helped greatly, and Zeke proved amenable to pitching in as needed. Sometimes there was no substitute for a strong man willing to hold a frightened animal. She and Julie occasionally had trouble with the larger dogs.

Over time, she noticed he had a real rapport; injured creatures calmed around him. He was as patient and capable around animals as he was strange and awkward in the presence of people. And unlike the others who had come and gone, he was dead reliable. With him on board, she found herself working shorter hours because she didn't have to stay late and clean up.

The downside? Most nights, she had too much time to think.

Fortunately, this wasn't one of those times. She had a Great Dane in the exam room and a worried owner to deal with. She donned her professional smile and went in. To her surprise, she found Zeke in with them. The dog had been whimpering pitifully when they arrived, but she was fine now. Maybe that was just because she was lying down. That suggested a wide variety of possible causes.

"Got a sec?" he asked.

Nonplussed, she stepped into the hall with him with a parting smile for the client. "What's up?"

"Her hips hurt."

"The owner told you that?"

He shrugged.

"Great Danes are prone to hip dysplasia and Yancy's getting on in years. Thanks for letting me know."

She didn't understand why they'd needed to have that conversation in private, but Neva had given up trying to make sense of Zeke's quirks. It was enough that he helped so much; the practice ran smoother than it ever had. He'd picked up their routine quickly and cleaned the exam room between patients without being asked. He never complained, no matter how dirty the job, and sometimes . . . it got pretty bad.

The rest of the day sped by in a blur of appointments. At seven that night, she stood resting her head against her office door. She had finished the last chart and it was time to go home, if she could muster the energy, because in the morning, she had another full day scheduled.

"Tired?" Zeke asked.

She had gotten used to the idea he wouldn't leave until she did, though she only paid him for four hours a day. Which was why she'd started trying to get out of the building earlier. He seemed worried about her safety. But then she'd noticed the way he was always scanning the darkness, like he thought something scary lurked out there. He never seemed to relax fully; she just didn't know why.

"Just hungry most likely."

"No lunch?"

Thinking back brought none to mind. An emergency surgery had screwed up her afternoon, requiring a couple of routine checks to be bumped until tomorrow. "Nope. But I'm ready to head out, if you are."

They checked the place once more and then she led the way to the front door, where she set the alarm and then locked up. He went out first, his expression wary as he checked the shadows. It was almost like he expected somebody laying in wait.

"Dinner?"

Neva paused, keys in hand. "Are you asking if I plan to eat?"

"Wanna get some? Tom's Diner?"

Now she had date confusion. Maybe he just meant for them to share a meal since they were leaving at the same time. Nobody liked eating alone. If it had been Julie issuing the invitation, she wouldn't hesitate, so maybe she was making it more complicated than it needed to be. The other attendants had been . . . different than Zeke. The first man had been in his late fifties, and the second had the drawn features of the habitual drinker, though he had been careful not to come to work drunk. If either of them had asked her to dinner, she wouldn't have hesitated over the no.

"Sure. I'll follow you."

"No need. Can ride with you and then run back."

"It's two and a half miles."

He shrugged in answer and walked to her Honda. She got in and leaned over to unlock the door for him and then scrambled to clear the junk off the passenger seat. It was easy to tell she hadn't had anyone in her car in a while. Once he joined her, she felt conscious of his height, though he didn't try to take up more space.

Nerves made her ramble about the pets she'd seen today, and she was relieved when the diner lights appeared on the left. The place was pretty packed, since apart from Armando's and Pie in the Sky, there were no other options for dining out. And Tom's had the most varied menu by far. The diner had a retro air: black and white trimmed in red neon. A chalkboard announced the daily specials.

She chose a booth near the bathrooms, mostly because it was the last one left. Emmylou Fish hustled over with the laminated page that comprised the menu. Zeke took his with an air of abstraction.

"Today's special is chicken fried steak with mashed potatoes, gravy, and corn. Served with your choice of roll or biscuit. Y'all know what you want?"

"Sounds good," Zeke said. "Biscuit, please."

"I'll have the bacon cheeseburger. Salad instead of fries."

"Sure thing." Emmylou scrawled the order and took it to the window behind the counter.

People watched them, whispering, and soon it would be all over town where she'd gone and who she'd been with. When she was a kid, it made having fun in this town damn near impossible. This time, Neva didn't let it bother her. She ignored the stares, but they appeared to trouble Zeke. Trying to make small talk proved fruitless while he fiddled with the salt and pepper and flipped his thumb back and forth across the sugar and sweetener packets. Eventually he went to the bathroom to wash up, but his mood hadn't improved when he came back.

He sat back down, his jaw tight. "Maybe this was a bad idea."

"You get used to it."

"Yeah?"

"Okay, no. But you learn to deal. When I was a kid, I made faces at people." She glanced over at Mrs. Gillespie—still watching their every move—and stuck out her tongue. "As you can see, sometimes I still do. It helps."

He laughed, and then exhibited the most charming astonishment, as if he didn't immediately recognize the sound. The smile eased his face of its sharp tension, and she couldn't stop looking at him. *The color of those eyes ought to be called nightfall in heaven. Oh no.* She really couldn't think this way about him.

"Thanks," he said softly.

Emmylou returned with their food, interrupting the moment. Probably just as well—she had been staring in a decidedly unbosslike way. Over the course of the meal, Neva noticed he ate with excessive care, paying attention to his knife and fork at all times. He acted almost as if he had trouble with minor motor functions but she didn't think that was the case, based on his graceful, almost predatory walk.

By the time the waitress brought the checks, the atmosphere had eased between them. Emmylou had split them into two, but she raised a brow and grinned, obviously in search of gossip. "Should I have put it on one?"

"No," Neva said. "This is fine."

"Let me." He plucked her green ticket from her hand and strode toward the cash register.

It's not a date, she told herself. *Even if he buys. Nothing wrong with that.*

But from Emmylou's avid expression, she scented a juicy story and leaned in, effectively blocking Neva's retreat. "So you're seeing Zeke Noble? What's *that* like?" Her green gaze lingered on his butt.

Dammit, she had to try and head this off. Maybe a big tip would work; she fished a ten out of her wallet. "It's not like that. We work together."

The other woman just grinned. "Well, aren't you the dirty girl?"

With a huff of breath, she gave up and edged her way out of the booth and went to join Zeke, who was finishing up at the register. Mrs. Gillespie still nursed her coffee, eyeing them with undisguised speculation. Damn, sometimes she hated being a Harper. Neva made her face impassive, like she didn't know or care what everyone thought. It was none of their business.

"Ready?" she asked.

"No need to wait on me."

"I know that. But there's no way I'm letting you walk back to your truck at this hour. It's not that far."

A small smile plucked at the corners of his mouth, tugging simultaneously on her heartstrings. "Worried 'bout me?"

"Yeah."

"Can't have that." His hand brushed her waist, as he guided her toward the door with inborn courtesy, and she felt the touch all the way to her toes.

November sped toward Thanksgiving. It was a Wednesday like any other, Neva thought. Might even have been quieter than usual—until the end of the day. The last patient was a pregnant female cat, and she wasn't on the books.

A woman brought her in, nearly in tears. "I don't know what happened to her. She's not mine. I found her . . . I think maybe she was hit."

Or she could've been tossed from a moving car—Neva had seen it before. People could be unspeakably cruel.

"It's all right. You can go. I'll take it from here."

"Don't I have to pay you?"

She smiled. "Not for this."

Though her heart clenched, she went to work. The mother cat was beyond saving; she could tell at a glance, but her kittens might not be. If she had been near term . . . yes, she had been. Three of them were dead. It hurt. It never stopped hurting. On days like today, she could almost see her mother's point. Why *do* this?

Well, for the three of them she saved. That was why. Miraculously, they seemed to be as healthy as three orphaned kittens could be.

"Julie!" she shouted. "I need the heating pad, a box, a towel, and the kitten formula."

She'd be sleeping here tonight, of course. That was why she kept a cot in the storeroom. Sometimes patients required overnight care and she couldn't afford to pay a night attendant. The practice wasn't hemorrhaging money but neither was she rolling in it. Corners had to be cut.

"Saving kitties, are we?"

"I'm sure going to try."

"Do you need me to stay over?"

Smiling, she shook her head. Julie always asked and she always said no. Such rituals were comforting. "Just flip the 'Closed' sign. I can handle this."

Neva used a warm, damp cloth to clean them up because it would feel to them like the comfort of their mother's tongue. Once she'd done that, Neva set up the box with heating pad, covered that with the towel, and then started the feeding rotation. The next three weeks were going to be grueling since newborn kittens couldn't eliminate without help. Ordinarily the mother cat would take care of it.

Now it was all up to her.

At some point, Zeke appeared beside her, and he seemed to know what to do, so she let him feed one of the kittens. It was late by the time they finished, and in two or three hours, it would be time to do it all again.

She arched her back, so tired she ached all over. It was a good feeling. Despite the four losses, she had three tiny wins snuggled up together in their box. The heating pad beneath them would keep them nice and warm; it was specially designed for newborns and post-op animals.

"This happen a lot?"

"Twice in two years. I don't know if that qualifies as a lot."

"Will they make it?"

She glanced up and found him closer than she'd realized. "I'll do my damnedest to make sure they do."

"Pleasure watching you with them."

Maybe it was just because she was exhausted but the comment felt like it had a personal connotation. A happy flush suffused her. "I love animals, always have. My mother said I'd drive her wild, always dragging something home."

"To fix it up," he guessed.

"Yeah." But she'd always had trouble letting go. Once she healed something, she never wanted to send it back into the wild. She wanted to keep it and love it, no matter how ill-advised that seemed.

To her surprise, Zeke sat down on a crate nearby, seeming in no hurry to leave. "My cousins hunted. Used to run around after them in the woods, making a racket so they'd get no game."

"Did they hunt for sport or food?"

Though she loved animals, she wasn't a vegetarian, and she understood the latter. Just . . . not the former. It seemed like the height of cruelty to kill something for the pleasure of it. Even worse to put its carcass on the wall as proof of the deed.

"Both."

And he still hadn't wanted to see the deer shot? *Interesting.* He was a puzzling man, one she had a hard time reading. She had the sense he was hiding something, but then, wasn't everyone? With her family and Luke and Ben Reed, she didn't exactly go around broadcasting her personal issues, either. As long as she could depend on him to do his job, things would be fine.

Now, the part she hated . . . dealing with the dead. A pet cremation service would pick up if she called, but it meant out-of-pocket expense on this one. Ordinarily she passed the cost along to the owner—and felt guilty doing so—but she couldn't charge the woman for kindness. That discouraged people from doing the right thing.

"Could you—"

"Already did," he said. "Bagged them. And cleaned the exam room."

She gazed at him in stupefied weariness. "I'm not paying you enough. It's well past six, and I can't afford more hours."

Her parents could. *She* couldn't. She'd spent the money she'd gotten from Grandmother Devereaux on an education. The rest remained in trust, administered by her father, and he'd never give her a dime until she became the daughter he wanted instead of the one he had. It didn't matter; she'd never be Luke, even if she broke her back trying. Better not to go down that road.

"Don't need money to do the right thing."

It seemed to Neva she had never heard anyone say that. *Ever.* In her parents' world, it was all about appearances and fund-raisers and knowing the right people, going to the right parties. She'd walked away from that life at eighteen, and she felt as though she'd lost her place in the world at the same time. Apart from Julie and Travis, she belonged nowhere. She'd always been too emotional, unable to make the decisions that would've earned her favor.

"You're a rare person," she said softly.

Sadness rushed in. She didn't know if it was the weight of the day or remembered grief, but she found herself drowning. To keep from losing it, she focused on the kittens. Tiny, curled up together. She watched them breathe and tried to fight back the tears. She hadn't cried when Luke went missing. She never cried. Instead she worked and pretended and worked some more. As Julie had told her more than once, that wasn't living, but it was the best she could do.

His hand lit on her shoulder, so light that if she flinched, he'd pull away. Tenuous heat filled her. Oh, to get inside his silence. Neva gazed up into his face. For the first time, she noticed he had a strong jaw and a well-shaped mouth. His wariness detracted from his appeal, made one see only his suspicion. She'd noticed his eyes before, but now she realized he was beautiful.

His light brown hair had been cropped close. She wanted to run her palms over it and see if the new growth prickled. And his deep blue eyes—*God, he has such haunted eyes*. She'd only seen eyes like that before in animals that had been tied and whipped, starved of all human affection.

"Don't," he said, and she didn't even know what he was asking her not to do.

The moment ended when one of the kittens needed to burp, a good thing, too. Zeke hated how she'd been looking at him, like she saw more than she was supposed to, more than he could let anyone see. Thankfully she went back to caring for them. She truly loved her work, but there was loneliness about her as well. Yet he understood why she preferred the company of animals.

She was busy, so he took the spare key from the hook in her office—one day maybe he'd have one of his own—and slipped out back. It was dark; the lights didn't go all around the building, but he could see just fine. Another side effect of whatever they'd done to him.

Halfway to Armando's, he froze. Footfalls sounded behind him, as if the person was trying to be quiet. But he wasn't very good at it. *Shit. Someone's creeping toward the back door of the clinic.*

He wheeled and loped along the edge of the pavement, alert for more movement. A man rounded the corner, heading for the back door. It locked automatically, but a determined thief could get in. Unlike the other man, Zeke could move silently. He was on him before the guy sensed a presence and turned.

"Need something?"

"I wanted to speak to Neva." He had a polished, newscaster accent. "I know she's working late. Would you get her for me?"

Close up, Zeke could see he was wearing expensive clothes and he had a hundred-dollar haircut. He didn't like the look of him any better.

"Don't think so. Go home and call her."

The other man's mouth curled. "Which are you, her social secretary or her bodyguard?"

"She pays me, not you."

"Are you asking for a bribe?" He reached for his wallet.

"No. Go on now. Clinic's closed."

Zeke folded his arms and waited. Silence would drive the guy away; he knew the type. With a muttered curse, he left. Zeke waited until he was sure it was safe and then he retraced his steps toward the sub shop.

Armando's was deserted when he stepped inside. No surprise, since it was nearly eight. Julie was right: Neva did work hard. With the money he had from cashing his first paycheck, he bought her a turkey sandwich, a drink, and a cookie. He didn't have a lot of money, but it pleased him to provide for her in a small way, even if she didn't notice or care. She'd given him back his pride, and that was a priceless gift. Now he could afford to get the power back on and stop living in the dark. Tomorrow he'd buy some groceries and try to remember how to be a man instead of the monster they'd made him.

Bag in hand, he scouted the place, front to back, and to his surprise, he found the asshole in a car out front. The headlights were off and he was there, *sitting*, hands on the wheel. His face was tight with anger, and something else. He didn't know what to call that look; it was almost greed, but it went deeper, too. Ownership? Zeke fought back an instinctive territorial growl. Though he hadn't been here that long, he thought of this place as his. That meant the two women who came with it were his to protect, Neva more than Julie.

But by now she would be hungry. She often worked through lunch and he didn't know if she had breakfast before coming to the clinic. Before anything else, he'd give her the food and tell her about the guy watching the place. Maybe she knew him and would like to talk to him. He pushed back a surge of anger at the idea, knowing he had no right to it.

Zeke used the key to let himself in the back door. She was where he'd left her, sitting with the kittens, but her eyes shone, wet, as if she wanted to cry but couldn't.

"Brought you dinner," he said.

She shifted, obviously startled. "I thought you left. You didn't have to, Zeke. I didn't even give you any money."

"Wanted to. Need anything else tonight?"

"I should probably take a bathroom break and get the cot set up in here."

"Go on then." He took her place beside the kitten box.

They slept now, all their physical needs tended for a little while. She moved off and he felt them in a way he couldn't explain: tiny, questing things, scared and uncertain. They got inside his head. Loss. It was a blurry feeling, but these kittens knew they had lost something. They just didn't know what. They huddled together and took comfort in each other while looking for something that wasn't there.

When Neva came back, he asked, "Got a stuffed toy to put in with them?"

He expected her to ask why he'd suggest such a thing. Instead her face brightened. Her smile reminded him of the time he'd skipped school to go fishing with his best friend, Danny, so long ago now. It was a hazy, springtime memory. They hadn't caught anything, but instead lay on the grassy banks of the river, listening to the birds and feeling the sun on their skin. She warmed him like that, only backward, from the inside out.

"Good idea. I have a few plushies for sale out front. Sometimes parents bring their kids and I convince them to take home a toy as a gauge of whether they're ready for the responsibility of a real one."

Zeke stayed while she got the surrogate mama cat and

tucked her in the box. He wondered what it would be like if she touched him with such gentleness. But he couldn't let himself want her. In all ways, she stood above him. Dinner at the diner proved that much—everyone had been so shocked to see her in his company. They were probably still talking about it.

"Guy tried to get in the back," he said then.

"Let me guess . . ." And then she described him to a tee.

"Know him?" Zeke could go get the guy, easy enough. He just didn't want to. He'd rather be whipped. The angry beast stirred in him again.

"Yes. But I'm not interested in talking. He's my ex," she added, as if she owed him any explanations. Still, he appreciated it. "He just won't accept we're done."

"Get that," he said, before he could stop himself.

She straightened, eyes on his, and they shared another of those long moments where he feared he might do something wrong. Because that look of hers tore straight through him like a gunshot wound. He had to close his hands so he didn't brush away the dark strands that had slipped out of her ponytail.

"You mean you understand why somebody wouldn't want to let me go?"

Zeke flinched. But he couldn't disown the truth. "Yeah."

"That's sweet. But it isn't me he wants. It's just because I'm a Harper. He wants to go into politics." Her expression reflected surprise, as if she couldn't believe she'd said that aloud. "You're almost *too* easy to talk to."

"Won't repeat it," he promised.

"No, I know you wouldn't. And thanks for making him go away."

"Part of the job." He found himself smiling, a little lighter in some way he couldn't name. "Sure you'll be all right?"

"I'll turn on the alarm after you leave. Don't worry, this isn't the first time I've pulled an all-nighter."

"'Night, then."

He'd planned to pay the electric bill today, but the office had long since closed. That would have to wait until tomorrow morning. But he could hit the grocery store. He'd been eating from cans and whatever Aunt Sid brought by.

In the morning he'd run his errand at the power company and then get home to do some repairs on the farm. He could make it livable again. He could do this.

CHAPTER 5

"It's time," the shrink said.

Emil Hebert had been in counseling for almost four months. The knife in his gut had almost killed him, and the loss of his partner did worse than that; it shook his faith in himself. He'd worked with Rina for almost ten years.

In that time, she'd started as his colleague and became his best friend. He didn't make them easily. Life had taught him too much about how to shut people out. Not enough about letting them in. But Rina hadn't minded his brusqueness or that he focused on the job too much. When they were paired up, she was the experienced one, four years on the job already, and a lot wiser. He'd learned so much from her.

Belatedly he noticed the doc waiting for a reply. "I'm ready."

"Then go see Birch."

Nodding, he pushed to his feet and offered the other man a firm handshake. It was funny how they thought certain things had a shelf life or an expiration date. *Make him talk about her once a week for X number of months and he'll be fine. Ready to get back out there.*

And he was, but not because they'd worked some magical cure. He just couldn't stand the silence of his apartment anymore. He left and made his way to Birch's office on the third floor. Hebert tapped lightly on the closed door. Waited.

"Come on in." His immediate boss was a man in his early fifties with salt-and-pepper hair. He'd softened up some from his years on the desk. Birch was a career man; he'd retire from the ABI one day. Pictures dotted the wall behind his desk; he'd shaken hands with some important people in his time.

"Got my clearance papers here. My brain's fixed."

The other man grinned, but Hebert could see he was uneasy. Everyone was, these days. They didn't know whether to console him, bake him cookies, or treat him like they always had. "You feeling all right?"

He'd spent some time on leave, after the surgery that put his guts back together. *Eight times. The knife went in eight times. And while I was bleeding—*

"Nothing I can't handle."

"Good. I wanted to talk to you because there are two things we can do, here."

"What do you mean?" He just wanted to get back to work, however difficult that might be at first.

"Given your track record, they want me to offer you a promotion." Birch held up a hand, forestalling protest. "There's a vacancy in region six. So it would mean a move. We'd miss you, but maybe a change of scenery would do you good."

Hebert considered the offer for all of thirty seconds. "And the other option?"

"You come back to work." Birch hesitated. "But we won't be replacing Rina. Hiring freeze, budgetary considerations."

A promotion, or work alone? A smart man would take the first offer. Get out of the field and start a new chapter in life. But right now, he felt like that'd be turning his back on everything he'd accomplished with his partner, and maybe just a hint of running scared. He'd never know if he had the stones to do the job if he didn't try.

"I don't want to work the desk," he said. "Ask me again in ten years."

Birch grinned. "In ten years, I'll be fishing off a boat in Cabo. But maybe I'll make you take *my* job when I'm ready to go."

"I may be fine with it by then."

"And Emil . . ." That told him something serious was coming. Birch never used his first name. "I'm really sorry."

Me, too.

He'd missed her funeral, hadn't been there to say goodbye. *I wasn't there when she died. The one time we split up to chase down separate leads . . .*

Well, there was no point going down that road. In the early days after his discharge from the hospital, he'd spent some time fondling his gun and chasing pain meds with cheap whiskey. But in the end, it was unworthy of her. He could almost hear Rina saying, *Man the fuck up, Hebert. You gonna cry in your beer forever?*

And remembering her made him smile. That smile gave him the strength to pour the liquor down the drain, ease off on the medications, and start climbing out of that dark hole. People had lost their best friends before. They went on. So could he.

"It was just a bad break," he said then, and was surprised at how rough his own voice sounded.

"I'm glad you know it wasn't your fault. Sometimes there just isn't anything you can do, and it doesn't matter that you did everything right." By the man's tone, he'd suffered a loss, too, but one just didn't ask Hal Birch to talk about his feelings.

"Well, they played us. Divide and conquer. I should've known better."

"You had no reason to think they were working together. They hate each other. I catch you talking guilt again, and I'm sending you back to Marlow."

He winced. Spending another month of appointments talking about how he was dealing with Rina's loss sounded like a special circle of hell. "Got it."

"I expect you back at work on Monday. You'll spend the first week on the desk, getting back into the groove. Once you're sure you're good, I'll have the others shuffle some cases your way. I know they're buried."

With Rina . . . gone and him out on sick leave, it wasn't surprising. The workload must be staggering. "I'm ready to get back to it."

"Not today. Go home, Hebert. Take one more weekend. This is probably the last peaceful Friday you'll see for a while."

He couldn't argue, though he wanted to. Quiet wasn't the same as peaceful. In his silent apartment, he had no choice but to turn things over in his mind. Weigh what he could've done differently and wonder whether it would've mattered. If there was any confluence of events in which he could save her.

Because she hadn't *just* been his best friend. Though he'd never told her—and Rina had been happily married for fifteen years—he'd loved her. Desperate, unspoken, and hopeless, it had always been. He'd known that, and would never have acted on it. She'd adored her husband and their two children.

Hebert didn't like thinking of Preston, who had the real right to fall into a dark hole over her. Instead, he seemed to be coping better than Emil, maybe because of the kids. He didn't have the luxury of falling apart; he had to keep it together for them. When he'd first gotten out of the hospital, he'd paid his respects to their family.

He wouldn't be doing it again. Envy ate him up inside because Preston had had fifteen years with her, partner in every way. He'd been the one she was eager to get home to, and it hurt him to see mementoes of their life—the life *he'd* wanted with her—all over that house.

Once he left the ABI, he didn't go home. Only emptiness and a hidden bottle of booze waited for him. Instead he stopped by a flower shop and bought a mixed bouquet of roses. *Yellow for friendship. Red for love.* He knew such things because he'd once been a romantic, before the army ground it out of him.

They'd told him where she rested so he found Rina's grave without trouble. It had a vase built in, and he removed the dead flowers, adding his roses instead. She was buried in a new plot with a twin plot reserved for Preston, and it was lovely, laid beneath a beautiful oak tree. The man had bought a double headstone carved with angels, his side still blank. Hers read:

KATRINA SLATER
Beloved Wife and Mother
1967–2009

Preston had also included a copper plaque, imprinted with her favorite loss-related poem. *Do not stand at my grave and weep* . . . Damn the man, he did everything right. He had been a good husband, and he was still a good father. And even now he wasn't alone.

Hebert hated him.

He had been watching her for weeks, learning her patterns. She wasn't the one; he wasn't crazy. He *knew* that. She was merely a stand-in, and he harbored no particular animosity toward her. But she fit, and he needed the practice.

One did not start at the top, after all. It took time to work up to such goals. He must ensure that when the time came, he was ready, and everything would be perfect. He had spent years picturing how he would make everything right.

She was pretty with her long chestnut hair and her big dark eyes. And she was young. So his work would prove no hardship. Since his needs were specific and precise, it had taken him a while to find her. He'd watched countless women before choosing her as the first of his girls.

Now that he had, he would never let her go.

Every morning, she went to work at the hair salon. She wore impractical shoes for standing all day, but from the way the other stylists dressed, high heels must be part of the uniform, as much as the pink smock, white shirt, and black slacks. Her hair looked different, practically every day, and if business was slow, they fixed each other's hair. It was almost like watching a slumber party.

That night, she locked up alone. He knew she would be

leaving at half-past eight, after she had balanced the accounts and finished closing the salon. Everything was falling into place. He had been so deliciously careful.

There were no other cars in the lot. Just hers. And his, nearby. But not where she could see it. He waited outside the range of the security cameras. Days before, he had calculated where he could stand without being seen, at least nothing more than a hint of his shadow. That idea pleased him. When people started asking questions, they would find nothing of him here. Just the echo of her absence.

When she came outside, she had her keys already in hand. As he knew, she had taken self-defense courses at the Y. She had pepper spray on her key ring. She wasn't a stupid woman, nor would she prove easy prey. That was why he had chosen her, for what was the point of a simple test? She comprised part of his dark gauntlet, and facing this would make him ready for what was to come.

She noticed right away, but then, he *had* slashed her front right tire so it was obvious. A low curse escaped her as she dug in her bag for her phone. Ah, that mistake would cost her. She should've gotten in her car immediately in case the flat was meant as a distraction.

It was.

He slipped up behind her, handkerchief in hand. She didn't even scream. The cloth muffled her struggles, but she went limp in his arms with a satisfying speed. Keeping the cloth over her mouth, he lifted her, checked the area, and then strode toward his car.

He didn't put her in the trunk. On such small details hung the difference between success and failure. Instead he tenderly eased her into the passenger side of the car and buckled her in. To a policeman or passing car, she would seem to be asleep. Not so unusual at this hour. To keep her unconscious, he slipped a surgical mask over her face to secure the handkerchief across her nose and mouth.

As with everything else, he drove with care, leaving the lights of the city behind. The country road was desolate, and he kept driving until he reached their destination. There were no lights inside. He did not need them.

When he carried her inside, she still had not stirred. He took her downstairs to the room where he had spent so many nights in his youth. Each crack in the stained cement he knew by heart, each shadow thrown by the bare bulb swinging on its loose wire. He lay her down on the table and fastened her in place.

Any new endeavor required a certain amount of experimentation. Otherwise how could he ever learn what worked or what he liked best? Anticipation radiated through him in a low-grade hum. He had her laid out for his pleasure, anything he wanted . . . anything at all.

Something like love surged. She would help make him ready for the one. He was going to make them pay, soon now. The years of waiting and watching would soon be over, and then Daddy could sleep. Only one thing could stop the screaming.

He removed the mask, but she still did not move. Worried now, he leaned closer and took her pulse. Nothing. When he peeled back her eyelids, they showed no signs of life. *God-dammit, you killed her too fast*, the old man snarled. *She didn't feel a thing. You used too much chloroform, you moron. Or maybe you just left the rag on too long, because you were so fucking scared of being caught. Pussy. They'll ride you like a horse in prison.*

Furious, now, he took the knife to her, trying to drown his father's voice. He'd planned to use her for practice; now it was all ruined. *Slash, slash*. He imagined it was the bastard who'd sired him instead. It was his one regret—that the devil had died in a car accident instead of by his hand.

He hadn't wanted to come back. But he couldn't live with the noise in his head. If he could've shut the old man up any other way, he would've stayed in Florida. But over the years, the screaming grew louder and pretending got harder. At the age of nine, he *had* promised. He'd sworn to make all them pay in exchange for light and food and warmth. At last, he'd yielded and come back to Harper Creek, the heart of darkness.

He had been planning ever since. But now, there was only one way to proceed—only one course that would satisfy the old man. First, however, he had to dispose of his mistake. In this business, there was no margin for error. The next time, he'd get it right. Next time, it would be perfect.

CHAPTER 6

Thursday night was rough, and life got worse thereafter.

Neva ran home early Friday morning to shower and pack a bag full of clean uniforms. She hated leaving the kittens alone at their age, even for that long, but she couldn't bring them to her apartment. *I'll be quick*, she thought, until she stepped through the front door.

A mildew odor greeted her, and she found a puddle of water nearly an inch deep on her living room floor. Overhead, the dark stains on the ceiling had finally given way to a ragged hole, where pipes and supports were visible. Restraining a whimper, she splashed through to the bedroom and saw there was damage in here as well. Her clean uniforms were no longer so pristine; they needed to be laundered before she could wear them.

She went downstairs to confront her landlady. Mrs. Popović took nearly five minutes to open the door, probably because she knew the conversation wouldn't be pleasant. The woman answered in her housecoat, hair up in curlers, a cigarette dangling from her orange mouth.

"Good morning," the woman greeted her.

"Not so much. Are you aware part of the upstairs has fallen down into my apartment along with a significant amount of water?"

"Yes." Mrs. Popović bobbed her head. "I have my grandson coming out to fix the problem."

"And how long do you expect that to take?"

A lift of bony shoulders, shifting pale blue flowered fabric. "Not long."

Considering it took two weeks to replace a broken window pane, Neva didn't have much confidence in that assessment. "I can't live like that."

"So go visit relatives. Stay with good friend. Don't worry, I knock it off your rent."

Neva clutched her bag full of uniforms and fought the urge to scream, but she didn't have time to argue. The clinic had to be open and there were kittens who would die without her care.

"Fine. Let me know as soon as the repairs are finished."

By that afternoon, Neva wasn't sure she could last the month. Though the kittens were fine, she was flagging. Sleeping on the cot at night, working all day, and almost never leaving Paws & Claws left her sputtering like an engine running out of gas. It was costing her—not that the babies weren't worth it—but she didn't want to make some stupid diagnostic error on one of her patients, either. People needed her to make the best choices for their pets' health. She was no longer in top form and she knew it.

But at least she *could* sleep in the clinic while Mrs. Popović had the ceiling fixed. *Other people are much worse off*, she told herself. It was just a string of bad luck; that was all. Everybody went through rough patches, and then the universe evened it out with good fortune down the line. *It has to turn around . . . and soon.*

When Zeke came in at two, she didn't know how she was going to make it until six. And then another endless night lay before her. She hid the worst of it from Julie, who was distracted anyway with talk about Thanksgiving. Her friend

was worried about meeting her in-laws-to-be, which she suspected was part of the reason the two still hadn't tied the knot.
According to Julie, Travis had a mother who could best be
termed possessive—and she didn't approve of young people
living in sin.

She didn't see Zeke until an hour after his shift started.
Patients kept her tied up, so she didn't have to think about his
mystery, his silence, or his unexpected kindness. But they ran
into each other in her office, both checking on the kittens. It
was almost time for the next feeding, and they were mewing,
clambering over each other looking for teats on the surrogate
mother he'd suggested.

"You take one, I'll take one," she said by way of greeting.
"And first done gets a bonus baby."

His eyes lightened a little, though he didn't smile. Sitting
down opposite her on a crate of dog food, he got right to work.
She noted his gentle competence in making sure the little fur-
face got what he needed. The quiet between them felt comfortable, surprisingly, though they hadn't known one another
that long. She felt at ease with him as she had with few folks
since returning to Harper Creek after college.

Luke had been one of them. But she wasn't going to think
about him today.

Experience led her to finish first, so she took the other
one, and he went to work on burping detail. Next, they'd have
bathroom duty. It was an endless, exhausting cycle, but it'd be
worth it when she found homes for these darlings.

"Look tired," he commented at length.

She'd gotten used to his laconic, truncated sentences,
though she supposed he might sound strange to someone else.
"It's going to be a long few weeks."

"Why not take them home?"

Oh, how she wished. But she couldn't even live there, let
alone the kittens, but she wouldn't complain to Zeke. Her
problems weren't his. "I can't. My landlady is picky about
pets, and I can't afford to piss her off. There aren't a lot of
places to rent around here."

At least, that my parents don't own. But she didn't say that aloud.

From his expression, he extrapolated the unspoken subtext. Zeke didn't comment. Neva decided she liked that about him. He knew when to keep quiet.

"Julie?"

"Travis is allergic." To cats, not dogs. Otherwise, it would never work with Julie, who loved Doof almost as much as her boyfriend.

And besides, this was her pet project. She'd decided to save these three newborns, and it didn't seem right to stick Julie with the task just because it was tiring. Life didn't work that way, unless you were selfish, and Neva had never been one to bail on trying times.

"Something else, too." It wasn't a question, and surprise rippled through her. Already, he read her so well.

Since he'd asked, she wouldn't lie. "My apartment's got some plumbing problems, too. So even if Mrs. Popović liked cats, it wouldn't be an option."

"Ah." He finished with the black-and-white fuzzball he was holding, gently put him back beside his "mother," and lifted his sibling for his turn. His face went distant, as if he were weighing a grave matter.

She couldn't resist asking, "What's on your mind?"

After a long silence, he said without looking at her, "Could come to the farm."

"The kittens, you mean?" Neva began framing a polite refusal. There was no way she could relinquish this burden to him. It wasn't her way.

You're determined to be a martyr, she heard her mother saying. *You and your causes. Why can't you understand we need you* here?

But their need came braided together with commitment, obligation, and a hundred thousand rules that would suck the joy out of her life. Okay, so maybe there wasn't much joy at present, but there had been, once, and there were always little flickers, reminding her of why she loved the work.

His answer astonished her. "All of you. Just 'til they're eating right and your place is fixed up. Can help with the night care." `

Could he really be offering that? "You understand I'd be there for a month or longer." She didn't care to mention how long it might take to get her apartment livable again, the way the younger Popović worked. "They'll get stronger as they're older, of course, but—"

"Get that."

"And you still want us to come?"

"Yeah."

Some expression crossed his face that kindled warmth she couldn't let herself feel. The situation was already fraught and she was pretty close to the breaking point. His sweetness might drive her to do something stupid, something irrevocable, and he might not feel free to decline, because she was his boss, and she was a Harper. The two factors combined gave her too much power.

Sleeping at the clinic and taking showers at Julie's could offer a stopgap; she shouldn't accept. It was a bad idea. But she could see his wariness, like she might feel she was too good to set foot in his home. Just the fact that he'd offered touched her, and that made up her mind.

"Then we accept gratefully." Neva tilted her head at the squirming kittens. "I'll try to keep a lid on all the office gossip at the water cooler."

She invited him to share the joke with a little grin, and it was obvious when he registered that they only had Julie to worry about, benefit of a small work force. And honestly, Julie would probably encourage her to seduce him and to hell with sexual harassment suits. She was convinced great sex would cheer Neva up. As her friend had said, *If it doesn't fix your mood, hey, at least you had the great sex.*

He nodded. "Can ride together after work."

"I have my car. I'll just follow you, if that's all right."

"Was hoping you'd drive us."

That gave her pause. "Where's your truck?"

"Home."

Despite herself, Neva laughed softly. It was like trying to get blood from a stone. "But why?"

"Wanted to run."

Good God. Was he some kind of fitness buff? She'd known a few people who ran everywhere as part of their fitness regimen, but Zeke hadn't seemed the type. Not because he wasn't superbly fit; he was. He was lean and hard in the best possible ways, a whipcord and tensile strength that brought to mind a bow drawn taut. And she really shouldn't be looking at his chest or his arms, or the way his raw-knuckled hands cradled a kitten. She shouldn't think about how it would feel if he touched her.

"That's about eight miles," she said in disbelief. "Were you going to run that home, too?"

"Sure. But don't need to now."

Sixteen miles, plus his normal workday—Neva did *not* know what to make of him. "True enough. Well, I think these three are settled. With any luck, they'll keep until we get them to your place."

God, she was going to love sleeping in an actual bed again. Assuming he had a spare room. Even the old farmhouses had at least two bedrooms, one for husband and wife, the other for young'uns. But even a couch would be better than the cot in her office. She was tired of spending all her time at the clinic . . . and she'd be lying if she said she wasn't inappropriately interested in getting to know him outside work. With an eye toward becoming friends, of course. As his boss, she couldn't see him any other way.

"Not fancy."

For a hideous, guilt-inducing moment, she thought he was warning her off, telling her he wasn't a fancy man, and wouldn't put out. Heat suffused her cheeks. She was already framing a mortified apology when he added, "The farm. Needs work. But it's cozy."

Oh. Thank God.

"If you could see my apartment, I'm sure you'd think yourself lucky by comparison. I bet you don't have a foot of water on your floor and a hole in your ceiling. And I remember where you live, the area anyway, and that means your neighbors are squirrels, raccoons, and woodchucks. Mine are drunken Albanians who scream at each other all day and then bang the walls making up all night."

Okay, so she was exaggerating. Somewhat. But it was so worth it when some of the worry faded from his face, replaced by soft amusement. Could it be . . . yes. Zeke was actually smiling.

"Maybe get some earplugs?"

"I use my earbuds." At his blank look, she explained, "Headphones for my iPod. They go in your ears, not over them."

"Uh-huh."

It seemed weird he hadn't heard of earbuds, but who was she to judge? Maybe he didn't follow tech trends. She'd find out more about him when she saw the inside of his house. A forbidden, secret thrill surged through her, as if she'd been invited to some exclusive party. This was better, actually, because she liked Zeke, and she *didn't* like the ones who would attend such a gala.

She tucked a kitten into her shirt and Zeke did likewise. They'd deliver the other one to Julie to provide the daily required dosage of snuggle time.

"Well, I have patients." Neva thought she might live through the day after all. "See you at six."

CHAPTER 7

Zeke watched her—and tried to seem as if he wasn't. If he hadn't managed to get the power back on and clean the place, he never would've invited her out here. He felt strange and anxious, but he didn't regret it. Having Neva here pushed back the loneliness and the feeling of hovering an inch away from some new disaster.

He couldn't tell what she thought. The walls needed a fresh coat of paint. In the kitchen, the floor was cracked and worn. No new furniture had been bought in years, so it was all faded, stuff his mother had chosen more than twenty years before. The house was pretty small for the plot of land—one bedroom downstairs and two upstairs, along with kitchen, parlor, and a mudroom out back for the laundry.

First thing, they took care of the kittens, who were mewing plaintively again. Afterward, she asked, "Where's my room?"

"Upstairs." He led the way, ignoring the empty room downstairs.

Nobody had slept in there since his dad died. Nobody would. That space needed more than a simple cleaning; it might take a young priest and an old priest to get rid of the badness. Kitten box in hand, he nodded at the second door.

"Here, I take it?"

He watched her step inside. It was a plain room with a mattress and box springs on a steel frame, no headboard. The only other piece of furniture was a battered dresser with four drawers. There was a closet, too, but it was empty.

"Gonna start supper," he muttered, uneasy with how much he liked seeing her in his home.

"I'll bring the kids to the kitchen. It should be warmer anyway." She hesitated before asking, "Would it be all right if I left them with you? I need to go home and pack some things . . . I only have work clothes with me. Do you have a washer and dryer?"

"Yeah." It was the answer to both her questions.

Warmth dawned. She trusted him. Not just with the kittens, but with herself, too. They were going to be alone out here, and it was pretty isolated. He'd make sure he deserved that faith. Somehow he'd keep a lid on his crazy night-prowling, and do whatever it took not to scare her.

Zeke tucked the box in the corner near the fridge. Warm there, but not too much so. He'd planned to make his own favorite dinner to honor the feat of getting things back to normal. Lights on at night, a working radio. It might seem like a small thing to anyone else, but having music to drown out the noises he shouldn't be able to hear helped a lot. The radio was old, a clunky black thing his dad had bought at Sears in the seventies. But it still worked.

He found a country station and then he went to work on the meal—meatloaf, mashed potatoes, and green beans. Over the years, he'd become a good cook. If he didn't want to go hungry, he fixed his own food; it was just that simple. Sid was the only person who'd ever done for him, but she had her own kids. Two of them had moved out of state, just as soon as they could, which meant she now had more time to fuss over him. Only his cousin Amber still lived in Harper Creek, and she showed no signs of wanting to settle down.

The potatoes were cut up and boiling, and he had just slid

the meatloaf into the oven when Neva got back. Tension he
hadn't even been aware of eased out of him. Deep down he'd
thought maybe she'd taken a look at the place and decided
to dump the kittens off on him. His heart had been pretty
sure she wouldn't do that, but the rest of him had been kicked
enough not to trust so easily.

"Something smells good." She had changed out of her
scrubs into a pair of faded jeans and an Auburn sweatshirt;
Zeke recognized the colors and the school logo, and he
remembered she'd gone to school there.

"Thanks. Will be done in about an hour."

He wasn't surprised when Neva checked on the kittens.
She scooped them out of the box and tucked all three of them
into her sweatshirt. Then she started squirming while they
tried to get comfortable. Her grin lightened her whole face,
and he found it hard not to watch her. Zeke admired everything about her. She'd committed to looking after them, and
she didn't take it lightly. He didn't know what to make of her.
She came from money; she didn't have to live like she did or
drive that old car. Julie had said she was sad, and he could see
hints of it in her eyes. It made him wonder what he'd have to
do to make her laugh.

"Anything I can do to help?"

In answer, he gave her the spatula and nodded at the beans.
"Don't let 'em scorch."

He made them with onion and bacon, just like his aunt.
This meal wasn't healthy, but he'd wanted it—to feel like he
was home—for longer than he cared to recall. The food in the
cell . . . *no*, he wasn't thinking about that. Horror rose up in
him. The longer he was free, the more he worried he might be
crazy—that he'd invented the whole thing. How else could he
explain the changes, though? And he had some scars they'd
left behind as proof, nothing he'd gotten on his own working
at the mill and on the farm.

No, it *had* been real. He'd never made up stories or seen
things that weren't there. Even his mother's crazy hadn't
gone that route. Over the years she just got quieter and sadder
until there was nothing left.

"Julie's mom has a kitchen like this." Neva gazed around at the scarred cabinets as if what she saw appealed to her. "It has character. Lots of living."

He guessed that was true. And somehow, having her here balanced out the bad history. Instead of neglect and darkness, the room lit with welcoming light. It didn't all come from the fixture overhead, either.

Silently he set the grey and white Formica table for two. It had banded metal around the edges, stylish in the forties. For Zeke, it had always been enough that it was sturdy. Things didn't need to be pretty; they just needed to work. So it was rare for him to find such fascination in a woman who offered both.

"Got Coke, milk, or juice," he said.

"Juice, please. I left my bag in the hall so you didn't end up making dinner by yourself, after everything else. If it's all right, I'll take it up now."

Why was she asking him? He stared at her in confusion until he realized she was being polite. He owned the house. She was unsure of her place. He fought down the urge to tell her she could do whatever she wanted—to his house and him. For an awful moment, he turned into that untried sixteen-year-old boy again, watching her glide across the emerald lawn he'd just trimmed while his heart went wild in his chest and his hands clenched on the silent mower.

She had been wearing a yellow sundress, he remembered, in some fancy fabric with little holes that showed glimpses of her tan skin. The breeze blew the skirt against her thighs, and he'd had to look away. That summer, he'd thought she was the closest thing to heaven on earth. He'd gone home that night and lay in bed daydreaming about a day where she noticed him working and led him off into the flower garden. He'd spent himself more than once, imagining what she felt and tasted like, imagining the clasp of her legs and the hot welcome of her body.

Neva wasn't the same girl anymore, and he wasn't that boy. But he still wanted her with the same awful, hopeless ache. And now she was standing in his kitchen, a little lost and forlorn. That look stirred all kinds of needs, tangled up so he couldn't separate them.

"No problem," he got out.

He reduced the heat on the beans. They'd come from a can so they wouldn't take as long to cook down. It was about time to mash the potatoes; he did it by hand, adding milk and butter and garlic powder. By the time she got back, they were only waiting on the meatloaf, and it should be done soon. His stomach rumbled. It felt like forever since he'd eaten.

"The quilt in my room looks like an antique," Neva said from the doorway.

Once again, her voice soothed him. Even if she'd created knots of unwelcome desire in him, she also made them go. Some of the raw edges smoothed away.

"My grandma made it."

"It's beautiful."

She meant it. Since coming home, he'd discovered sincerity had a scent. He could smell when people were lying to him. Like Skip Felton at the drugstore. Zeke had known he was going to crumple his application as soon as he walked out the door. *We don't want any crazy Nobles working here,* his eyes said.

But Neva didn't do that. She was often sad or angry or exhausted, or some combination of the three. But she wore those feelings openly. It made her an honest island in a sea of liars.

They ate in silence, listening to the radio. She looked absolutely worn out, so once they finished, he said, "Get some sleep."

"You'll wake me when it's my turn to look after them?"

Zeke made some noncommittal noise, but when the time came, he didn't. She needed somebody to take care of her for a little while. Maybe he'd never have what he wanted of her, but he could have this much. He'd make do.

When Neva got up in the morning, she felt amazingly good. And then she realized she hadn't lifted a finger all night. He'd said he would get her up but clearly that hadn't happened. Oh, crap. If they'd both slept through the night, the kittens could be in bad shape. Without getting dressed, she bolted from her room. She'd left them in the kitchen—

"Don't worry," he said. "They're fine."

"You did it all."

"Yeah."

"Oh, Zeke, you *shouldn't* have. I committed to these babies, not you."

"Reckon they're as much mine as yours, now."

Well, that was true. Some of the fear dialed back. She had the irrational surety that if she could save these three kittens, then Luke would be all right, too, somehow. It was illogical, sympathetic magic, the kind people practiced as kids. *Step on a crack, break your mother's back*. Most days, Neva was very careful not to step on any cracks because she loved her mom. Other days, if Lillian had been hard on her, she would stomp them. It never made any difference but it gave the illusion of having some power to change circumstances. She couldn't overlook the value of that.

Everyone else believed Luke was dead.

The sheriff was still investigating, of course. But the trail had gone cold, and they all thought the best possible resolution would be to discover his body, so their family received closure. There were no leads. Just an empty car on the highway.

"When did they eat last?"

"An hour ago. Breakfast's on the table."

"Good Lord," she said. "I didn't agree to this so you could wait on me. You're doing too much."

"Can't cook pancakes for one," he said.

It was impossible to argue with him. He just didn't offer enough words in a single go to give her complaints traction. Further, after his kindness, it just seemed churlish to protest. Plus, she was hungry.

"I can't tell you how much I appreciate this."

"Woulda been a long weekend," he agreed.

Holy crap, he was right. Today was Saturday. He'd saved her from spending a whole weekend alone in the clinic with the kittens. She really *had* to thank him properly.

All men appreciate sex, Julie's voice suggested. It was a

testament to Neva's inner workings that her mischievous side always sounded like her best friend. When they were kids, it had always been Julie suggesting stuff that got them in trouble. Neva would follow along more reluctantly, conscious of what people would think because she was a Harper, and she ought to be better than this. The only thing she'd ever done, against her family's wishes, was go to vet school. She didn't regret the decision, despite all the complications.

Breakfast was oddly comfortable. She thanked him for the meal and then showered. It was rare that she found herself not besieged with work calls, even on a Saturday. Her cell phone served as her emergency number; people rang up if their pets suffered any life-threatening injuries or illnesses. Neva hoped they didn't today, though this time of year was notorious for trouble. If it wasn't a hunting accident, then somebody's dog ate something he shouldn't at a holiday party, and then wound up in her office. To say nothing of cats chewing on Christmas lights.

But a good night's sleep had gone a long way toward restoring her energies. She appreciated Zeke's kindness more than she could say, but he wasn't in the kitchen when she came downstairs. Banging drew her toward the porch; Neva grabbed her jacket from the hall closet before going outside. She'd noticed one of the steps was broken coming in last night; he'd guided her over it. Now, she watched as he repaired it. His hands were quick and deft. Maybe it wasn't enlightened but she'd seen men doing such things so rarely that she liked it. There was just something about a guy who knew how to swing a hammer.

She admired the bunch and pull of his muscles with each movement. Despite the chill, he wore only a thin white T-shirt, which seemed strange. But he didn't appear to notice the cold. No goose bumps. When he bent to place the last nail, his jeans slid down, revealing the taut slope of his lower back; they were loose in a way that spoke of recent weight loss. His skin was smooth and beautiful. He hitched them up in an absent movement, but not before she saw the gorgeous curve of his hipbone.

Oh, God, he didn't have anything on beneath his jeans. How she wished she didn't know that . . . because it invited all manner of unsuitable thoughts. *I'm his boss,* she told herself. *This is inappropriate. He's helping you out, and you respond by ogling him? Nice, Neva. Really nice.*

Plus, he could look to younger women for his hook ups. She was thirty-one, and men always seemed to want the nubile coed, no matter how old they were. Four years wasn't a huge age difference, but that, coupled with her role as his boss, rendered her interest ten kinds of wrong. A lawsuit would destroy her practice, so she had to keep things respectable, even under these odd circumstances.

"Anything I can do to help?"

He shook his head. While she looked on, he finished securing the new step in place and checked how secure it was by putting his weight on it. "Don't mind me. Just have work I need to be doing."

It rankled that he wanted her to sit around like a hothouse flower. If she was going to accept room and board from him, he ought to let her help. What was she supposed to do all day, between kitten feedings? She suspected he wouldn't budge on this particular argument, however.

Remodeling an old house would be fun for her, not that she expected him to believe it, especially with her background. She had quiet dreams for when the practice was stable and she'd fought clear of the bad luck. One day, she'd buy a place like this and restore it by hand. She had a bunch of DIY books at the apartment; Neva never called her landlady when something minor needed fixing. That self-sufficiency didn't extend to holes in the ceiling or broken glass, unfortunately, but she'd unplugged the drains more than once.

"Me, too," she said firmly. "I just need you to tell me what it is." He glanced up then, wearing a doubtful look. She didn't let that deter her. "It looks to me like you should replace that support column or the porch is coming down, sooner rather than later. Do you have the wood?"

"Yeah. But that's a two-person job."

"Well, I'm here."

To her surprise, he nodded without further protest and went toward the garage. When he returned, he carried the raw column, already cut in proper shape. How he'd expected to do it on his own, though, she had no idea. But maybe he'd intended to call a friend over today. She didn't know that much about him, after all.

"Need you to hold this while I get the other one."

She knew what he needed her to do. But she hadn't been expecting for him to flip a bucket, step up on it, and pull the weak column loose with his bare hands. He caught the sagging roof with one hand and motioned for the replacement. Thanks to her secret interest in repair work, Neva handed him the proper tools without being asked, and pretty soon, he had the new one affixed in place.

"You are insanely strong," she said, wide-eyed.

It was a mistake. His face closed, as if she'd accused him of spying on teenage girls. He muttered a response and headed for the barn. The taut line of his shoulders warned her not to follow.

Shit. She had the feeling she owed him an apology, but didn't men always like hearing two things? *You're so strong* and *wow, you're so big.* Her experience said this was true.

She sighed. "Apparently not."

Neva went back inside. Even if he didn't feel the cold, she did. The kittens were crying, so she collected the three of them and snuggled them into her shirt. Then she dug a book out of her backpack and read until they needed their next feeding. Since he'd done it all night by himself, she didn't expect him to come back to the house to help—and he didn't. It wasn't the lack of aid that bothered her, just the feeling she'd stepped wrong and didn't know how.

Later, banging on the roof told her he was replacing the worn shingles. He seemed dead serious about making this place nice again. Neva looked around the kitchen, mentally imagining it with a fresh coat of paint and some new curtains. She liked the retro table; it would be fun to get some antique canisters to go with it. But this wasn't her home.

It was almost dark by the time he came back inside and

she'd tended the kittens again. This time, she'd kept them in her lap, on top of the heating pad, while she stroked their tiny bodies with her fingertips. In a few days, their eyes would start to open. Right now they were so tiny and helpless; all they could do was eat, squirm, poop, and sleep.

His shadow fell across the doorway to the parlor. In the kitchen, she'd left the radio on, trying to dispel some of the silence. Neva didn't look at him because she didn't know what to say. Her hair fell into her face and she didn't brush it away. It offered camouflage from his intent regard.

"Sorry," he said roughly.

"About what?" Petty, but she'd make him talk by feigning ignorance.

"How I bailed on you before. Wasn't right."

"It's okay." And it was. She could breathe a little easier, just because he'd come in with an apology. Neva didn't like how much emotional weight he'd acquired, but there was no changing the truth.

"Meatloaf sandwiches okay for dinner?"

"Sure. I think there are still some beans, too."

How domestic they sounded, as if they were lovers tentatively making up after an unexpected quarrel. The fact that he lived in a proper home added to the illusion, and God, it was dangerous. She couldn't allow herself to get comfortable here.

Tomorrow, they both had another day off, and she didn't know how they'd spend the time. An odd, unacceptable flutter started in her stomach.

An idea struck her. It was a way to distract herself from this unwanted attraction, and to repay him for his kindness, and she would not take no for an answer. "I'm going to the hardware store after dinner."

"If you need something, might have it here."

Oh, how she wished he hadn't put it quite like that. Despite her good intentions, her gaze roved his chest and shoulders. Thankfully he didn't seem to notice. He had no awareness of her as a woman, as far as she could tell. Which was good. It would be disastrous if he found her as attractive as she did him.

He used a pan to heat the green beans while she sliced up the meatloaf cold. He put extra ketchup on his sandwich and she enjoyed watching him. He had a small scar on his chin, and the scruff on his cheeks was almost golden, lighter than his hair. Neva tried not to study his mouth—the lower lip was a longer and fuller than the top one, which had a tender little divot—but when he licked them, a shiver went through her. She'd never wanted to kiss anyone quite so much.

No, she scolded herself. *You can't. No matter how sweet he is. No matter how strong or how much you wonder what it would take to bring a smile to those eyes.*

After dinner, they tidied up together, and it was so normal, so companionable, that it left her aching. Until now, she hadn't realized how much she missed having another person around. But her nights were silent unless she spent them with Julie and Travis—and she didn't want to cramp his style all the time.

He laid down the cloth he'd used to wipe the table. "Want me to ride along?"

"Please," she said.

"Kittens?"

His concern made her feel like the chocolate and marshmallow center of a hot s'more. "Don't worry about them. They're warm and full and they've been held plenty already today. We'll be back before they need us again."

He nodded and followed her out to the car. She didn't explain until they reached the hardware store. Mandy Wilson, the cashier, noted their arrival, and within ten minutes, she'd be telling everyone she knew that she'd seen Neva and Zeke together again, this time on a Saturday night. She found she didn't care. Let them talk.

She chose three different cards from a wall display. "Which do you like?"

His look said he didn't understand why she wanted his opinion on home décor. "I'm going to help you paint," she explained. "You said the farm needs sprucing up. Since I'm imposing on you, I need to pay for my room and board."

She knew very well he wouldn't accept rent, though he

could use the money. But maybe this, he would allow. Neva held her breath, belatedly worried he might take it the wrong way. She was braced to explain herself, why she'd thought it was a good idea, something she could offer.

"This," he said, pointing to a lemon yellow.

Her breath went out in a relieved sigh. "For which room?"

"Kitchen."

"That'll be pretty with the cupboards."

They obviously needed plain white for trim and to redo the cabinets. Now that she had his approval, she was already planning to redo the whole downstairs. A soft cream would suit the parlor; it wasn't a big room, so it needed the pale walls to open it up. She'd never been in the downstairs bedroom.

"Just the kitchen and front room," Zeke said. "Not the bedroom."

He didn't want to change it? Odd. But she didn't press. It was his house.

"Do you have any ideas for the bathroom?"

It was too small for a three-bedroom home and it seemed to be the only one. But from what she remembered, the tiles were sound, and he'd obviously given them a good scrubbing because the grout was clean.

He shrugged. "What goes with green and white?"

She hesitated a little. Should she really be redecorating his house for him? It seemed presumptuous. And yet if he minded, surely he'd say something?

"I'd paint the room white and then put up an ivy border to bring it together."

He also needed a new shower curtain and some new bath accessories, but she wouldn't find them here. Plus, she suspected she shouldn't buy such things. Paint was one thing, less personal somehow.

His eyes gave away his uncertainty. "Let's do it."

Moving on, Neva showed him some options and he liked Bavarian cream for the parlor. They went with a low-maintenance, low-odor paint that promised to resist stains and clean up easily. She guessed at how much paint would be needed for each room, but based on a quick conversation with the salesman about the dimensions, which Zeke confirmed, they worked it out.

The total came to several hundred dollars, once they added plastic and rollers to the cost of the paint, but it was going to be so worth it. She gave the clerk her credit card without so much as a flinch. She couldn't get enough of shows like *Trading Spaces*, *Extreme Makeover: Home Edition*, and *While You Were Out*. Living first at Harper Court, then in dorms, and now in an apartment she didn't own, she'd never been given a chance to do anything like this. God, she wanted to please him. She didn't know why it mattered so much—only that it did.

Once they'd finished, they headed out to the car. She started it, fairly bubbling with anticipation. "This is going to be so much fun."

"It is?" He sounded dubious.

"Absolutely. You've given us a great start with all the cleaning you did. The walls are ready. Since they're all white"— which was a kind word for the dingy hue—"we should have no problems getting the color to cover in one coat."

"Seems like you know a lot about this."

Heat rose in her cheeks as she drove toward the farm. "Mostly from TV. But I promise I know what I'm doing. I helped Julie and Travis paint their place."

He seemed to register her dismay. "Not worried about that. Was just wondering why you wanna do this on your day off. It's work."

"I like work. It keeps me from thinking."

"Ah," he said, and she had the unmistakable impression he understood.

CHAPTER 8

Worthless. His father's voice rang in his head.

He could almost feel the dark closing in on him. A tremor rocked him as if he'd been struck. He listened to the old man's tirade patiently and then he went to get the plastic. But first, he stripped her naked. Not for lascivious reasons, but in case trace evidence lingered on her clothing.

The slashes he'd made sent a shock down his spine. They weren't clean and pretty; he could see where his hand shook and they marred her pale skin in crooked gashes. Finished at last, he wrapped the woman's body so she wouldn't leave any signs in his vehicle, and then wrapped her in another layer of plastic to be safe. The woods would provide a safe dumping ground. Out here, he had no neighbors to see what he was doing.

He swung the body into his arms and carried her outside. This time, she did go in the trunk, but he wouldn't be driving on traveled roads. Instead he went along the dirt track until it just . . . ended. From there, he took her on foot. No need for a grave. He had been studying the art of death for years, and it seemed to him that the Green River Killer had been very good at disposing of bodies without being caught. That had always surprised him, given that Ridgway had an IQ of eighty-two. How then was he able to elude capture for twenty years? He'd learned a great deal from the man; sometimes raw animal cunning beat pure intellect.

Fortunately he had his share of both.

Next time, he would try something different. To be worthy, to put his father to rest and get his voice out of his head forever, her death had to be perfect. And it would be. There was no shortage of brunette, brown-eyed women in the world.

He'd get it right next time.

And then Daddy would say, at last, *Good work, Son. I'm so proud. You finally made them pay for what they done.* Then he could move on. The old man would be exorcised, and he could finally live his life on his own terms.

He found the place beneath a stately pine. Elm and hickory didn't offer the same carpet, which made him feel he was laying her to rest in a worthy place. With great care, he unrolled her from the plastic and used a gloved hand to brush her hair from her face. It still wasn't right, somehow, and then he remembered the red satin ribbons. Dreamily, he twined them about her arms, lacing them like a dancer's shoes. She would be elegant eternally, hiding the ugly wounds he had inflicted.

Inexplicably a fragment of a poem he'd read in school came to him.

> *That moment she was mine, mine, fair,*
> *Perfectly pure and good . . .*

He wished he could remember the rest or at least the author's name so he could look it up. But clearly it was true. In this moment she belonged to him, and she was innocent in death. So he scooped up two handfuls of dry leaves and covered her genitals.

There. That was better.

As he went back toward the car, he realized he wasn't afraid anymore. Instead a sense of peace and completion suffused him. His father's voice was, mercifully, silent. He had the sense the old man approved. Perhaps this hadn't been the right way for Geneva Harper to die, but it was a step in the right direction. The old man approved of persistence and commitment to quality.

For his next girl, he had something special in mind.

It did not take long for him to get back to the house. He gathered the girl's effects, including her purse and her clothing, and dumped them into a rusty barrel. Next went the plastic. He doused it all in lighter fluid and set it alight. Nobody would think twice about somebody burning trash out here. People did it all the time.

For long moments, he stood and watched the acrid smoke curl skyward. Then he pulled the car keys out of his pocket. He needed to check on his mother.

"How long do you think she's been out here?" the deputy asked Hebert.

He shrugged. "Too many factors to say for sure."

Animals had been at her; part of her face had been eaten away by insects and she bore bite marks on her extremities. It was made more grotesque because of the rest-in-peace arrangement of her limbs, offered in vivid contrast to the slashes. He was looking at those, too. They wouldn't have bled enough to kill her. At this point, it was impossible to say what had.

"Somebody has a lot of rage toward women," the deputy said.

"Like that couldn't be said of most men who kill women. He's probably also between twenty-five and forty-five, Caucasian, and hates his mother."

The deputy laughed. "You should be a profiler."

Funny. Except it left them with too many suspects and too much territory to cover.

Hunters had stumbled across the girl, chasing a deer. They'd stopped and called it in, thanks to cell phones, and now here he was, dealing with it on his first day off the desk.

The locals didn't have the resources to deal with a naked unknown murder victim, so they'd called the ABI. It was his job to figure it out.

The tech crew had just arrived. His stomach hurt, but it was hard to know if it was residual damage, phantom pain, or nerves. Without Rina at his back, he'd lost some confidence in himself. Or maybe the stabbing had done that. Whatever the reason, he wasn't the man—or the agent—he had been, but maybe he'd get back there. In time.

He focused on the scene. She was obviously posed, arms crossed on her chest. Then there were the red ribbons, twined around her arms and legs. They'd suffered some from exposure to the elements, but the inclusion tugged at him. What did it mean? There was always a reason for whatever weird fucking thing these people did, and if he could work it out, it would tell him something about the killer.

Hebert studied a little longer. Maybe a dancer had gone missing. That seemed like a too obvious solution, but he couldn't afford to overlook any angles. So why here? What was special about this spot? It had an access road nearby. He'd already walked it; there would be no traffic here. Nobody to see what someone carried in his arms. So privacy, for sure. Had the killer known who owned the land and wanted to make trouble for him?

He went over to the hunters, who were all middle-aged and clad in flannel. Two wore glowing orange vests. One of them, Gerald Franklin, owned the land. Hebert needed to talk to him in particular.

"Emil Hebert." He offered a hand to be polite, and they shook all around. "I'd like to ask you a few questions."

Unfortunately, they didn't seem to know more than they'd told the county boys. None of his questions revealed additional information, but their stories had enough variance that he didn't suspect them of covering something up. One guy remembered seeing a rabbit just before they found the girl, and another argued it had been a squirrel. He suppressed the urge to tell them it mattered fuck-all if they'd seen the ghost

of Bambi's mother out there. Only the dead girl signified anything. Since they didn't know who she was, he cut them loose,
except for Franklin.

"Do you live on this property?" he asked.

"Nah. I'm from Birmingham. There's a cabin out here, but
I don't stay in it often. Mostly when I've pissed off the wife."

"But you make regular hunting trips."

Franklin nodded. "But only in season. We have all the
licenses."

"You didn't recognize the victim?"

"Not at all. Poor girl." His face was pale, and his hands
still weren't steady.

Hebert understood. Even if you hunted, it wasn't the same
dealing with a human body. "Do you rent your property to
other hunters?"

"No, it's just for my friends and me."

So limited traffic and an absentee landowner. He wondered
if the killer had known that. If he did, it suggested someone
local with knowledge of the area. "Do you have any enemies,
anyone who would want to make trouble for you?"

"Like *this*?" Franklin asked, wide-eyed. "Hell no. Look,
I sell used cars. I've pissed a few people off in my day, and I
don't give refunds, but I can't imagine . . . no. No way."

The guy seemed sincere, but one never knew just how far
some people would go to get even. Normal ones didn't kill
women just because they'd bought a lemon. The more direct
route would be beating the shit out of Franklin.

"Do you have any game cameras out here?"

"Actually, I do. Want me to show you?"

"Please."

As it turned out, he had three of them. They checked the
first two and found nothing but animals, but the third was
more or less in the path between the access road and the
tree where she'd been found. Hebert checked this one, while
Franklin stood by. A shiver went through him. The killer had
brushed right past it. Unfortunately, it hadn't caught his face.
But it gave him some idea of the man's build. He was tall

and lanky; he'd carried the woman, wrapped in plastic, like a bride. The plastic hadn't been found with her, which meant he'd taken it with him.

"Damn," Franklin said, peering over his shoulder. "I guess you need the chip, right? Do you have to take the whole camera as evidence?"

"No, the chip's fine. Thank you for your time, Mr. Franklin."

"I can go then?" The man looked eager to get out of these woods. Daylight was fading, and he couldn't have any fond memories of today's business.

"Of course." Hebert strode back to the scene, where the tech crew was finishing up. "Did they turn up anything?"

The deputy on scene shook his head. "Sorry, no."

He fought his instinctive impatience. Overall, despite their inexperience, they'd handled things as well as could be expected. It wasn't their fault that they didn't have the resources, and half the time, Hebert didn't, either. *Fucking budget cuts.* They always made it look so easy on TV.

"Good idea."

This wasn't the primary scene. No blood. No trace evidence. Someone had just quietly brought her out and dumped her. But no, that wasn't right, either. The killer had taken care with her. That much had been evident by the way he'd held her in the footage. He'd had some pride in his work, judging by where he'd placed her. In the winter, the pine resin didn't drop, so he'd wanted her protected by the evergreen. Did that imply a relationship with the victim?

Maybe.

But they wouldn't be able to rake her past with a fine-tooth comb until they knew who she was. Running her prints and dental records would take weeks, but he was grateful the killer hadn't pulled her teeth or cut off her fingertips. Of course, that would signal the job as pro-work, someone experienced in preventing anyone from identifying the deceased, not just a gifted amateur.

Since he'd arrived last, everyone else was just waiting for him to give the word, so they could pack it in. No weapon, no vic ID, nothing helpful at all. This wasn't the way he wanted to get back in the game. But there was no arguing the circumstances. He cued them to wrap things up and move out.

Hebert signed off with the locals and then got in his car. Ordinarily he'd have quite a few notes to go over by this point, but this hadn't offered the usual informational buffet. That made him uneasy.

His phone rang then. There was always another mess to clean up.

CHAPTER 9

Thanksgiving came and went. Zeke spent it with Neva, much to his aunt Sid's chagrin. They made a turkey, along with all the trimmings, took care of the kittens, talked, and listened to music. Sometimes at night, she read. He liked her complete focus while she turned the pages of her suspense novel. At least, he guessed at the genre, based on the man on the cover with a gun.

It did things to Zeke now, watching her chew her lip as she studied the lemon yellow paint on the kitchen walls. No doubt it brightened the room up, but so did she. They had finished in here tonight, after the clinic closed. Paint splattered her T-shirt and smeared her jeans; there was even a streak on her cheek, and he'd give twenty years of his life to cup her face in his hands and bend to touch his lips to hers. He hurt with the need of it.

"You like it?" she asked, turning to him.

He nodded because his throat was too thick for words.

They'd done the parlor first because they hoped it would

be dry by evening that first weekend. He'd opened a window
to allow the breeze, though as the can promised, the stink
wasn't too bad—at least not for anybody with a normal sense
of smell. He'd felt like the inside of his nose had been burned
with an open flame.

They'd switched off caring for the kittens because Neva
didn't want to stop working. Like him, she didn't seem to
enjoy sitting around. Which made him feel better about his
own restless energy.

There are better ways to burn it off. But Zeke couldn't
listen to those instincts. The animal inside him wanted her
so bad that it snarled constantly. It didn't understand why he
couldn't have her. *She's here,* the beast whispered, *in our territory. The house smells like her. That means she belongs to
us.* Well, he wanted that to be true more than anything, but
it wasn't, and he had enough man left in him to know that.
He feared the day when that stopped being true—and what
he might do, then. Sometimes he felt like he was climbing a
muddy slope in the rain, clinging to slippery roots that would
tear free when he least expected it.

"I can't believe we're just about done."

She'd been thrilled they had enough paint to do the hall,
too. They hadn't planned for it, but once they started on the
parlor, it looked so bad she insisted they had to keep going.
Scraping the bottom of the can, they'd managed to finish it.
And tonight they'd wrapped up the kitchen.

"Good work," he said, because she clearly expected something.

"I've been thinking. If you want, we could try a daubing
technique I've been reading about. We have enough yellow
left from the kitchen and it'll be a subtle effect on top of the
Bavarian Cream."

"Uh-huh."

He had no idea what she was talking about, but it made her
so happy, in that moment, he'd have let her paint the whole
house pink if she wanted. Because the darkness had gone
from her eyes; she was alive, glowing with pleasure, and he

understood joy in fixing what was broken. They were alike in that way. He liked shoring things up, too. Sometimes you just couldn't because they were beyond repair.

She paused. "Why are you looking at me like that?"

Like I want to push you to the floor and lick every inch of your pretty skin? Can't imagine.

"Above my pay grade." Zeke jabbed a thumb into his own chest. "Handyman, right? Not a decorator."

"You don't mind?" Worry flashed in her eyes, acorn brown, rimmed in gold. He knew that from working close to her. "I don't want to overstep."

Zeke wanted to say the farm was hers as *he* was hers. But they were here together because somebody had been cruel to a mama cat and her apartment ceiling had a leak, not by her choice. She was only helping with the house because she liked doing such things and she didn't enjoy being idle. *Nothing like cashing a reality check.*

"Nah. Place needs some love." Afterward, he wished he hadn't put it like that because her gaze sharpened, as if wondering if that statement extended to him as well.

"I'll make us some sandwiches."

He watched her work in his kitchen with painful pleasure. Living with her might kill him. It had been two weeks, and she was a good roommate. Zeke had no complaints there. She pitched in, doing chores and fixing up the farmhouse, and never acted like she thought she deserved something better. Even though *he* did.

He'd seen Harper Court, but only ever set foot in the kitchen. They'd let him eat his lunch in there, as part of his pay. So he knew what she was used to and wondered why she chose to live as she did. Most people would be happy having stuff handed to them on a silver platter.

But she was different . . . and he liked having her around. Everything was better. His panic dialed back over the things he sensed; it got easier to accept and not fear what it meant, or if he was walking his mother's road. To him, she felt like a good-luck charm—if she was here, nothing bad could happen.

She looked less exhausted, too. Tonight, after work, they sat in the front room, listening to the radio. Neva always sat with her legs curled to one side, leaning on the arm of the couch. He wished she'd drape herself on him that way, so he could hold her and breathe her in. He'd learned she used honey-almond lotion after her bath, which explained the sweetness, but not his reaction. Mixed with her natural scent, it hit him on a gut-deep level, and he found it all but impossible to keep from reaching out to see if her skin was as soft as it looked.

They carried their food into the parlor and sat at opposite ends of the couch. With the fresh paint on the walls, he became conscious of how bare the room was otherwise. Zeke had taken down all the pictures of his family, anything that could serve as a reminder. He'd also put away his mother's knickknacks years before.

"Why don't you have a TV?" she asked at length. "I couldn't help but notice you don't have a computer anywhere, either."

He didn't want to admit the truth, but he couldn't lie, either. So he shrugged as if reality didn't sting. "No money."

Times had always been tough, even before things got really bad. Before his mom fell down the dark hole and never came up again. Before his dad started drinking to forget. He could still see her swinging in the barn; she hadn't been dead long. He had been nine at the time. He remembered feeling puzzled and running for help, someone to get her down and wake her up.

The truth hadn't sunk in until later.

His dad spelled it out, a few years on, in a drunken rant. *Everything was fine before you came along. Fucking kid. She never wanted you and neither did I.*

"There's that look again."

Zeke wished he *did* have a TV so she'd stop paying such attention to him. But then, he liked her interest in him . . . and he didn't. It made him want things he couldn't have. It made him want her to have a reason for caring how he felt, and then he felt doubly like an ass for hoping.

"What look?"

"The one that says you have sad secrets."

You have no idea.

"Everyone does," he muttered.

"I'm sorry. I didn't mean to pry. I just thought we'd . . ." She hesitated, as if she wasn't sure of the right word. "Become friends in the past weeks."

Is that what we are? He didn't think there was a word for what he felt for her, some awful mix of adoration and helpless longing. And it knotted up inside him, leaving him mute and sick with the impossibility of it.

Given his past and hers, he'd known that going in. He'd still wanted to help her because her problems offered a welcome distraction from his own. But he hadn't figured on just *how* hard it would be, seeing her first thing in the morning, right after she got out of the shower, at the breakfast table, and in the middle of the night, hands brushing while they cared for the kittens. Familiarity didn't change his ache, and the more time they spent together, the more he needed to remember why he could never have her.

She's better than you, Noble. Not your kind.

If he didn't do something, he was going to make a mistake, a big one. He was starting to forget why she was here. Plain and simple, he was just getting used to having her around. It would hurt when she left, but he was used to pain.

Belatedly, he noticed her downcast reaction to his silence. She'd taken it as a rejection. Well, Christ Almighty, he couldn't let that stand.

"We are," he said, though it nearly killed him.

Friends.

Need clawed at his gut, each time she spoke, each time she touched him gently. There was nothing sexual in her fingers on his forearm when she sought his full attention, but God, how he wanted it to be. He needed her hands on him in the worst way; he spent half the days hard and aching.

She didn't make it any better when she put her hand on his biceps and gave him a gentle rub like he was a skittish critter she thought to tame. His tension sent the wrong message, giving her the impression he was in pain. Well, he was—just not the way she believed.

"Did you hurt yourself at work today? Let me see." Neva slid off the couch and circled around behind him. When she set her hands on his shoulders and tugged the neck of his shirt aside to look, a groan escaped him. She sighed, taking that the wrong way, too. "You did, didn't you? Was it when you lifted the rottweiler? It's probably a pulled muscle."

He couldn't have spoken to save his soul. Instead he sat and let her massage him, her fingers gentle but firm. Pleasure began in tiny pinpricks and expanded into the glowing heat of fierce arousal. His cock swelled against his jeans, aching for her touch. Her fingers brushed the nape of his neck and it was all he could do not to shift and tug her over the back of the couch. At last he could take no more.

"Much better," he rasped.

He pushed to his feet and muttered some excuse about checking something in the barn. The truth was, he needed the distance. Sadly, the cold didn't dampen his desire any, but he could get out of the house at least.

By the time he went to bed, he was wound so tight he might break. Time to take matters into his own hands. He made sure the door was shut and the house was quiet and then he lay down on his bed. Instead of the old fantasy, he built a new one.

Neva, as she'd looked today. Only she wouldn't talk about being friends or wonder whether he'd hurt himself doing manual labor. When she came to him, her eyes would show the same heat he felt. He imagined pulling the shirt over her head to reveal her pretty breasts. She had a small waist and a sweet flare of hips. He didn't want to rush this. If this was all he'd ever get of her, he'd make it last. *Jeans off, now.* She wore nothing but a tiny pair of panties and she spun teasingly to show him her delicious ass. He'd drag her down on him so he could watch her face.

I want you, she'd whisper. *I've wanted you for years. I can't wait.*

He knew that wasn't true. Right now that didn't matter at all.

His breathing quickened. With his own hands, he touched himself as he wanted her to. Delicate, teasing fingertips on belly and chest. Not him. Her. Phantom fingertips brushed his balls and his inner thighs. He felt her mouth on him, hotly kissing a path down from his neck.

In his encounters with women, they'd expected him to do all the work. And he knew how. A man put in the time to earn the prize. But in this fantasy, *she* made love to him while he lay beneath her. The real Neva probably wouldn't be like this in bed, but in his head, she wanted to please him.

Nobody ever had, and it was such a powerful picture that he lost it. He forgot he wasn't alone in the house. Zeke wrapped his hand around his cock at last. A low moan escaped him. It had been so fucking long.

A whisper of movement outside the door stilled him. Nobody else would've noticed it, not right now. *Especially* not now. But he felt her as much as heard her, lingering there. Smelled her honey-almond lotion. Did she know? She made no sounds, and she didn't move away. If she wanted something, she'd call out, surely.

It would kill him to go see what the problem was . . . and he couldn't do it right away, but if something was wrong—and then came the slow turn of the knob. The door inched open a fraction, and stayed there, just a slice of darkness. Still no movement. No hint anyone was there.

For all her talk of friendship, she wanted to watch, and that knowledge lit a fire in him. It meant she was curious about him as a man. As Zeke closed his eyes, his hand started moving almost on its own. It wasn't a conscious decision. He felt her gaze on his body, traveling over him like a touch.

Yeah. See how crazy you make me.

Her breath hitched, and it sparked him hotter to know she liked what she saw. He wished she'd push the door open, but if she did, then he'd have to stop. This way, he could pretend he didn't know she was there. He could finish the secret show.

Working faster, he knew it wouldn't take much longer. If she hadn't shown, he could've controlled himself. But she drove him wild with her unexpected curiosity and her quick, shallow gasps. Soft sounds reached him.

Oh, God, was *she* . . . too?

Even if she wasn't, the mere idea offered more push than

he could stand. A low grown tore from him as he came. Her footsteps whispered away then.

Zeke lay there, shaking. Pleasure streaked through him. For the first time in longer than he could recall, he felt like a man—and it was because of her reaction. He couldn't be as worthless as he'd thought, if she had any interest in him. Maybe she just liked watching, maybe it was a secret thing of hers, but he couldn't help the cocky feeling that came over him. He found himself smiling for no reason at all.

He waited until she was in her room before he got up and hit the shower. Though it might be weird, he didn't plan to let it be. From this point on, he'd pay attention to the details. His view of her had been colored by his memory of her as an unattainable dream. If there was any chance she wanted to do more than watch, he'd do damn near anything to make that happen. But he had to tread softly. He didn't want to scare her off.

Two days later, Neva still couldn't believe what she'd done. Not in an I-wish-I-hadn't kind of way, but in an I-wish-I-was-naked-with-him-right-*now* way. It made it damn difficult to focus at the clinic—to the point Julie had noticed, and now she wouldn't leave it alone.

"Something happened," she said. "Spill."

She put on her boss hat. "Get to work. You have a spay to prep for me."

Surgeries took up such a long block of time that she cleared several appointment slots in order to get them done. Which meant she wouldn't be seeing sick animals or doing any vaccinations this morning. The owner had dropped the dog off early, and with any luck, she would be going home that evening. Some vets kept animals overnight to charge a boarding fee, but in most cases, Neva found that wasn't necessary. Only a complication or unexpected reaction to the anesthetic would prompt her to suggest that.

But by the time Zeke showed up, the dog was in recovery. No sign of the truck, which meant he'd run, *again*. Julie thought she was being sly when she sang out, "I'm taking my lunch break now."

Like she needed to be alone with him.

Her friend suspected they'd hooked up. She'd done worse, in fact. Violated his privacy. That night, she'd gone to his room to apologize for pushing when he hadn't wanted to talk. The massage had clearly been over the line. But she hadn't been able to resist her urge to touch him; in a way, she could pretend it wasn't sexual and that she didn't flush with heat anytime he brushed past her.

That was how she ended up outside his room, listening, first to see if he was asleep, and then because she was sure he wasn't.

Remembered excitement flashed through her. Arousal had been immediate and overwhelming. She'd squirmed and clenched her thighs together listening to the noises he made, little growls and impatient huffs of breath. Pretty soon imagination wasn't enough and she had to peek. She'd never done anything like it before in her life, but the impulse had been irresistible.

Moonlight had silvered his skin and he was beautiful. Lean. Hard. Uninhibited. Everything she'd ever wanted in a lover, if someone would just look at her with the wildness she'd glimpsed in his face. His need had struck her as visceral, one he had to sate. *She* wanted to make him look that way.

And now she had to keep working with him while pretending nothing had changed. So when he popped into her office, a hot blush washed her cheeks. He'd die if he knew she'd spied on him.

Zeke seemed happier today somehow, a mischievous smile tugging at the corner of his mouth. "Need anything special done?"

"I—no, that is. Everything's fine. Just the usual stuff." God, she couldn't sound any stupider if she tried.

Stop looking, she ordered. But it didn't help. Now she'd seen him in action as a raw, sexual animal and there was no going back from it. He had gorgeous hands, lean and long-fingered, but callused, too. She told herself he had the hands of an artist, even if he didn't have a creative bone in his body.

"Sure?" There was no explanation for the look he gave her. None. But she'd almost call it flirtatious.

"Yeah, I'm good. Thanks."

Once he went about his business, she dropped her head on the stack of patient files on her desk and groaned. She tried to make notes after each appointment but sometimes the day got away from her. Neva never went home without updating, however. If she didn't, memory might fail her and a pet would suffer down the line. So she often worked through lunch, writing up the visits while they were all still fresh in her mind. Julie helped out by logging test results. Credit for any success Paws & Claws achieved had to be shared.

Julie teased her some more once she got back from lunch, but Neva held firm. No details. She stayed busy with her afternoon appointments and then counseled the pet owner who showed up at six to pick up her newly spayed darling. They always sent home a care checklist, along with signs of trouble in recovery.

As usual, her friend left first. Unfortunately, her day wasn't done. As the only vet in the county, she also worked for farmers in the area, and Howard Bailey had a pregnant heifer he wanted her to check out. She was near calving, but he'd been in the business long enough to recognize budding complications.

"Set?" Zeke appeared in her office doorway, wearing that same inscrutable half smile.

It was like he'd woken up that morning and decided to drive her crazy. He was also holding her jacket. Such a small thing but it made her feel . . . protected, like it was a silent message: *I'll take care of you when it's cold outside.* Stupid. Even Freud would say a coat was sometimes just a coat, and she was his ride home.

"I have a call to make out at the Bailey place. You want to come with me?"

"Anywhere," he said quietly.

Oh. Hard not *to react to that.* Even if he didn't mean it how it sounded. She could get used to these one-word answers fraught with a metric ton of nuance. Her hands shook a little as she let him help her into her coat.

"I'll get the kittens wrapped up. It's colder than usual tonight. Will you stay with them in the car?"

"Sure."

After locking up and setting the alarm, she led the way to her Honda. She'd been out to the Bailey's place more than once, so she knew the way. Zeke probably did, too. It wasn't like the town was so big you could get lost in it. Not if you'd grown up here, and they both had.

Apart from those mysterious months when nobody had seen him, he had always lived in Harper's Creek. After they'd eaten at the diner, people made a point of mentioning him to her, along with all the old gossip. Said he'd end up like his mother or his daddy, one way or another, and good riddance to bad blood. She knew the bare bones of his story, but the bones were no longer enough.

"What's it like?" he asked, breaking the silence as she drove.

"What?"

"Being a Harper."

Nobody had ever asked her that. Not even Julie, who knew her better than anyone. Everyone else assumed it was sunshine and roses, and she was just a stubborn pain in the ass for bucking parental expectations. They saw her work as a phase she was going through, not something she loved. So she gave the question serious consideration—and she offered him the honesty she'd never given anyone else.

"It's not what people think," she said. "All dress parties and satin and money in the bank. It's pressure and . . . suffocating weight. If you're not a Harper in the right way, then you might as well not be one at all."

"That why your brother left?"

Her hands tightened on the wheel. People didn't ask about Luke, much in the way they did not ask about Camilla Beauregard's son, Jackson, who wasn't dead, but might as well be,

since he lived happily in San Francisco with his life partner
and ran an antiques store. Everyone pretended he had died
heroically in some war and spoke of him in past tense in
Camilla's hearing.

"He didn't. He just . . . disappeared."

But he hadn't abandoned them. Of that much, Neva was
sure. The private detectives had found no trace of him and
no use of his credit cards since that last day. Her dad still
demanded a report from Sheriff Raleigh once a week, not that
the man had anything new to add. It was a sad ritual, one that
left them all heavier each time.

Luke had gone on a business trip, looking for cheaper supply alternatives. Everyone had been hit by the recession, as
her parents made clear to her at every function. And if she
had any sense of duty at all, she would marry well. If not
Ben Reed, then someone like him. Ben didn't have money,
but he had connections. In their world, those could be just as
important. They'd really like to transition away from a failing
industry and she could facilitate that, if she'd only consider
her heritage and do the right thing.

Like hell.

The Bailey farm was halfway to Zeke's place, but she turned
off on county road 1 N first, and followed the bend around until
she saw the big red barn. Howard Bailey stood waiting for her
in a fleece-lined jean jacket. He was a weathered man in his
early sixties with a shock of white hair and a weary smile.

"Evening, Doc. Thanks for coming out."

Despite being tired, she said, "I'm happy to help. She in
there?"

He nodded. "She's in distress."

Neva shouldered her pack, which contained basic supplies.
Inside the barn, she saw at once that Bailey was right; the cow
showed all the signs of dystocia. He had two buckets of soapy
water waiting; he knew the drill. She scrubbed up and then
lubed up with mineral oil, so she could perform a pelvic exam
while Bailey soothed his heifer. *Breech birth.*

"We have to pull," she told him. "It's malpresentation, hind
legs first."

Bailey knew what that meant, so he went to get the chains. With the second bucket, Neva cleaned the area around the birth canal, rinsed with clean water, and then slid her arm inside, leaning in to find a hoof. Movement reassured her that they hadn't lost it yet. Speed and timing mattered now; the umbilical was pinched between the fetus and the cow's pelvis, so blood flow was diminished. She straightened the calf and then attached the chains, one to each leg. The cow bleated in protest, but she seemed to know they wanted to help her.

"Ready?" Bailey asked.

He'd helped her before, so he knew when and how to pull. They did it incrementally, walking it out, which allowed the calf a chance to catch its breath as they went. Eventually they got it clear, but her shoulders ached by then. Neva cleared mucus from its throat and mouth, then tickled its nostrils. The heifer took over.

"Make sure it nurses within the first hour," she said.

"How much do I owe you?"

She smiled tiredly. "I'll send you a bill."

Zeke had been in the car for quite a while, and she was eager to get home. With a parting wave for the farmer, she headed out of the barn. It was cold enough that she could see her breath, and overcast, with a whisper of a crescent moon nipping at the night. The darkness filled her with foreboding, though she couldn't have said why. Her skin crawled with the suggestion of someone's eyes on her. A passing car reflected on something in the trees, just a momentary flicker, light on glass.

Binoculars?

In the distance, toward the tree line, she saw a shadow, or the silhouette of a man moving away from the farm. No cars. No other signs of life. She was shaking when she let herself back into the Civic. Since the motor had been running, it was delightfully warm. Neva rubbed her hands over her face.

"What's wrong?"

God, he read her so well. It wasn't the first time she'd thought as much, but his insight was uncanny. Before Zeke, she'd never thought she broadcast her moods this way. "I don't know. I'm probably just tired."

"Tell me." He didn't give up easily, either.

"It's going to sound dumb, but . . . I saw somcone. Out there." She gestured toward the far edge of the field. "And I think he was . . . watching me."

"Your ex?"

She shivered, buckled up, and put the car in drive. "Surely not. That wouldn't make sense. Ben is many things, but he's not crazy."

He eased out of the car and stood peering into the darkness for long moments, as if he thought he could see something out there. As Neva watched, he cocked his head, listening. She heard only the wind. When he got back in, he seemed tense and jumpy, as he had early on. And she didn't feel safe until they reached the farm and Zeke locked the door behind them.

CHAPTER 10

When Zeke woke, he wasn't where he should've been.

The dark forest surrounded him. He wore nothing but a pair of jeans. This wasn't the first time it had happened; only the most recent. A bitter curse escaped him because he'd dared to hope he had these dreams under control. No time for weakness, though. He needed to figure out where he was. Pushing down the fear, he spun in a slow circle, looking for a landmark.

Something slicked his hands. He didn't need to raise them to the moonlight to know it was blood. The sweet coppery stench nearly overwhelmed him as bile filled his throat. He wiped his palms on the bark of a tree and sought the source. *Please let it be an animal.* A few yards away, he found a dead deer. Its throat had been torn out. Judging by the evidence, he guessed he'd done it with his bare hands, and the sour taste in his mouth made him think he might've eaten some of its raw flesh. Normally he might wonder if that would make him sick, but he was so far past normal he couldn't even imagine what it might look like from here.

He listened to the night noises. Other wild creatures shared the woods with him. By scent and by sound, he recognized them: raccoon, squirrel, owl, and coyote. Mice left the smallest signs of all but he heard them, too. Zeke fought his first instinct—to run. The darkness protected him. Another animal would eat the deer carcass. He just needed to clean up and get home before Neva missed him.

This was why he hadn't wanted to spend the night with Aunt Sid. If this happened in town, and it was somebody's dog he went wild on, he'd be lucky to wind up in a mental hospital. More likely, they'd shoot him as rabid and ask questions later.

Tremors shook him. Out here he had no way to shut down the unwelcome thoughts about that . . . place. Mostly he tried to pretend it had never happened, that nothing had changed. Impossible. He remembered the recurring nightmare: the screams and the needles and the weird, flickering light in his cell. Probably nothing worse than a faulty fluorescent bulb, but in his memories it became a torment of its own. He'd had no control over *anything*, and there would be no justice. It comforted him to know the bastards had died in the fire, but that offered no answers. Little wonder he was crazy. But he didn't want to chase the rabbit of his past down a dark hole. He just wanted to move on. Build something brighter and better than he'd had before.

At length Zeke gave up on trying to use his mind to puzzle out where he was. Trees. Dead leaves and branches. His brain was all but worthless anyway, so he closed his eyes and focused on home. Like a horse galloping for the stable, he knew the way, but only if he didn't think about it. When he was sure he could run without losing himself to the wildness in his blood, he did, long strides that carried him through the darkness.

He had no sense of time. Once, he stopped at a tiny trickle of a stream to wash his face and hands. On the off chance Neva might be up with the kittens, he didn't want to scare her more than necessary. God, if she saw him like this, there was no question that she'd go. Maybe he should let her. He shouldn't get involved with her and yet he couldn't stop himself. Need for her sawed at his belly like a rusty blade.

When he reached the farm, he came up on it from behind, rounding the barn to find he'd left the back door open. *Shit.* This couldn't go on. *What if someone came in? What if someone hurt her?* A growl began in his throat. If they did, he'd hunt them by scent and tear them apart with his bare hands. But that wouldn't bring her back or heal her hurts. *Oh, God, I can't do this to her.* He closed the door behind him softly. The kittens mewed as he came from the kitchen into the parlor and headed for the stairs.

Zeke showered quickly, washing away all traces of blood. He scrubbed at his skin until it felt raw, and then once wrapped in a towel, he brushed his teeth four times, like that would change anything. With an angry hand, he swiped the steam from the mirror. The same face stared back at him, eyes a little tired, jaw rough with stubble. *Funny.* He didn't look like a monster.

After dressing in sweats and a T-shirt, he went to care for the kittens. This, at least, he could do without causing harm. He seldom slept eight hours straight anymore anyway. He'd found he napped more like an animal, a few hours here or there, but always lightly, and with a wary sense that roused him the instant anything shifted in his territory.

So when Neva's phone rang upstairs, she didn't hear it, but Zeke did. He sat on the sofa, listening to it chime, and then he pushed to his feet with a growl. It had to be important. Why else would anyone call at this hour? But if it was Reed, he'd feed the guy his fist. Maybe a beating would get him to answer whether he was the crazy fucker stalking her wherever she went.

By the time he got to her bedroom, the call had quieted. He stood for a moment, watching her sleep. The moonlight kissed her skin, so she almost seemed to glow. Deep down he still couldn't believe she was here. More than anything he wanted the right to curl up behind her and set his head on her shoulder. That was the last thing he should ever do; he needed to drive her away before she got hurt. Or before she broke his heart. Of the two choices, one would be inevitable.

"Neva," he said, sinking down on the edge of the bed.

She half stirred, rolled over, and put her hand on his thigh. He felt the touch keenly through the soft cotton. Maybe he should've put on jeans before coming to wake her. The pleasure made him rigid, so for a long moment he couldn't think.

Her eyes opened, but by her dreamy smile, she wasn't fully awake. Her hand went farther up his leg and she mumbled, "It's about time you got here."

Did she even know who he was? For a moment, he considered letting her do it. But if she roused fully, she'd be shocked and embarrassed by it—and she'd wonder why he didn't stop her. It just about killed him to lift her hand before she got where she was going. He'd save the feeling for a private moment; that was how it had to be, and pretty much all he could have of her.

"Phone was ringing."

Finally, she pushed herself upright. "What?"

He handed her the cell. "Here. Check your messages?"

"I—Okay."

Being an animal doctor, she was probably used to calls in the middle of the night. She dialed into her voice mail and listened, a frown forming. Neva closed her phone and rolled off the bed, scrambling for her clothes. He discovered she slept in a tank top and she favored high-cut briefs; they revealed enough of her to make his mouth go dry. But she wasn't thinking of that as she bent over, rummaging in her bag.

"That was the alarm company. There's been a break-in. The police are probably there by now."

Zeke pushed off the bed. "Getting dressed."

She paused in the midst of hopping into her jeans. "You don't have to come with me. I'll be fine."

"I know. Still going."

Relief surged through him when she didn't argue. It didn't take long for him to throw on some real clothes and bundle up the kittens. This would take a while, certainly longer than a quick trip to the hardware store. Though he'd been awake when her phone rang, chances were, it would've woken him anyway. Sometimes birds in distant trees kept him up if he didn't block them, and he couldn't control that as well as he wanted. But her voice always gave him peace.

Zeke met her at the car, box in his arms. She drove fast, obviously worried about the clinic, and he didn't have the words to make it better. Fifteen minutes later, they pulled into the parking lot, where a deputy was already waiting for them. Neva got out and hurried toward the squad car. He could hear them, even with the radio on, even with the windows closed, and debated if he should join her. Though he hadn't wanted her driving alone at night, maybe she'd find it hard to explain his presence and might prefer him to stay low.

"How bad is it?"

"The inside's pretty tore up." Zeke recognized the other man's voice—he'd gone to school with Bobby Pickett. "You'll have to take a walk-through and tell me what's missing."

The guy had been a year ahead of him and pretty popular from what he remembered. Bobby had done some kind of sport and went around with Janette Hanes, one of the cheerleaders. Funny he could recall that, but not the color of his mother's eyes, or if he had liked chocolate ice cream before his incarceration.

"How did they get in?" she asked, walking with Bobby toward the front doors.

She didn't look back at the car or give Zeke any sign of what she wanted, but he made sure the kittens were wrapped up and then climbed out of the car. Maybe she'd need him to help clean. That was his job.

"Jimmied the back door. Come on, I'll show you."

Zeke swept the lot with a glance, seeing a car that shouldn't be there. All the businesses were closed. Strange. Instead of trailing Neva and Bobby around back, he went toward the far end of the parking lot. It wasn't the car her ex had been driving. This was an older one, even junkier than Neva's. It had splotches of paint and primer along the sides, poorly covering the rust.

But worse than the way it looked? The smell. Halfway, he stopped, overcome by the stink the wind carried to him. Something dead.

Clutching the box to his chest, he sprinted back the way he'd come and rounded the building. It was black as sin back here; someone had smashed the lights above the door, which stood open at a drunken angle. Glass crunched under his feet as he stepped into the clinic. The emergency lights were on, giving the place a queer orange glow.

"Power not working?" He spoke into the dark.

Neva answered, "Seems like they cut it, trying to get the alarm off."

"That'd be my guess," the deputy agreed, taking his cue from her. "But who's that?"

Easily he found the other man in the half light. He didn't give Neva a chance to explain him away. Though he knew it was too soon for him to be anything else to her, he didn't want to hear himself described as help. "Zeke Noble."

They shook, and then continued the walk-through, Pickett shining his light around. "Can you tell what's missing?"

"I'll have to take inventory, but it looks like they went for the painkillers."

"Junkies," Pickett said in disgust. "They'll shoot up with anything."

Neva's voice rang heavy with fear. "Deputy, this stuff is strong enough to kill somebody. They stole what I use on farm animals."

Pickett grumbled a word and then apologized for saying it in front of Neva. "I need to fill out the report, but if you'd rather, we can do it in the morning."

Obviously he didn't know her very well. Zeke wasn't surprised when she answered, "No, let's get this over with."

He stashed the kittens in a safe corner and left them talking. It seemed unlikely junkies would know how to cut the power in any permanent way, so he went to check it out. Five minutes later, after tinkering with the fuse box, he had the lights back on.

The place looked worse that way. Everything that could be broken had been, not just the medicine cabinet. Someone had taken the computer from her office desk and thrown it on the floor. The rampage puzzled him. To him, it looked like the people who'd done this hated Neva, and wanted to hurt her. By her crushed expression, they'd sure succeeded. It tore his heart.

Pickett was asking her a series of questions. Zeke wanted to get the broom and start cleaning, but he knew better. The sheriff's office might not have much in the way of resources, but they'd get someone out here to print the place at least, so he made sure not to touch anything else. He kicked a spot on the floor free from glass and sat down to wait.

The kittens mewed, not from hunger, but because they sensed something bad in the air, maybe the same thing Zeke had smelled outside. He slipped a hand inside the blanket and his spirit settled a little when all three of them wriggled over to his hand and lay down on his fingers like live little mittens. He sat quietly until a break came in the questions.

"Check that car in the parking lot," he suggested softly.

Pickett glanced his way with an arch of a brow. "What car?"

"Nothing's open. Why's it still here?"

"I didn't even notice it," Neva said. "I wonder whose it is."

The deputy got to his feet. "Maybe somebody had car trouble, or went home with a coworker." But even as he offered the possibilities, he was heading out to have a look.

That raised his stock in Zeke's eyes; he felt less like growling at Pickett, as he had ever since Neva sat down with him. *Damn. Really gotta get a handle on this.*

He lifted his eyes from the kittens to find her watching him. "You know something."

His heart sank. Surely she didn't think he had anything to do with this break-in. It'd kill him to walk away from this job—and her—under a cloud of suspicion. He could only ask, "What?" in a voice he hoped didn't give away his fear.

"There's a reason you sent the deputy to look at the car." She sounded sure, dark eyes steady on his and demanding the truth.

Zeke nodded, without meaning to, because it invited other questions.

"Why?"

* * *

Neva held her breath, wondering if he'd answer. Wondering if he'd be truthful with her. She'd put so much trust in him, relatively quickly, and what did she know about him, after all? Lillian would be appalled.

His answer surprised the shit out of her. "Smelled bad."

"The car?"

Zeke wasn't looking at her anymore; his next nod came slower as he stroked the kittens. She could see his fingertips moving slowly, delicately beneath the blanket. Getting answers out of him was like pulling teeth.

"Bad how?"

"Like there's something dead in it."

His words hit like a ball-peen hammer in her chest. For a minute she couldn't even breathe. This couldn't be happening. Not here. The worst crime anybody had committed here in years involved Sam Pitney shooting his wife's lover in the ass—and Ollie Wendell didn't even die. Zeke had to be crazy. Had to be.

But he knew other stuff, didn't he? At times, he almost seemed to know things he shouldn't. Or couldn't. There was a terrible weight and wisdom in his eyes, as if those came as partners to the sorrow. Zeke slipped out then, probably to escape more of her questions, though he said he wanted to check the damage.

When Bobby came back in, he looked sick. "I called the sheriff."

Oh no.

"What did you find?" Neva asked through numb lips.

The deputy sat down, looking sad and shaken. "A dead girl in the trunk. I ain't never seen nothin' like it." She knew she shouldn't ask—so she didn't—but Bobby seemed to have forgotten their existence, murmuring, "Poor gal didn't have a stitch on, except those red ribbons."

For Neva, that conjured an awful, vivid image of pale skin and satin that gleamed like blood. She wanted to cling to her disbelief: things like that didn't happen in Harper Creek. But the deputy's shaken face said otherwise.

"Do you think this has anything to do with the break-in here?"

Bobby shrugged. "It's not for me to say. I'll need you to stick around. There may be questions."

Sheriff Raleigh arrived quickly. In his early fifties, the sheriff was still fit, but showing his age in the speed of his movements and the silver in his hair; his face was all craggy lines in the half morning light. He greeted her first, which she thought was a waste of time, but he'd never forget who her father was. Once he'd done that, he went to look in the trunk. Neva slipped outside to watch the action; Zeke stood off to the side, doing the same.

"You were right to call me," Raleigh told Pickett. "I'll let the staties know we got work for them."

Just before dawn, the parking lot filled with vehicles from the county crime lab and the coroner's office. Photographers snapped pictures and all Neva could do was repeat that she'd come in response to a message from the alarm company.

Raleigh gave Neva an absent smile; he golfed and hunted with her father. No surprise there. Conrad Harper made a point of cultivating the acquaintance of anyone who mattered or who might one day be in a position to do him a service. She'd never imagined a scene like this outside the movies. The other deputies all looked about like Bobby Pickett, tense and unhappy. They were trying to sound professional, but they didn't handle business like this. Not here. She made sure not to get in anyone's way, but she listened, too.

"No visible wounds. No bruising. She hasn't been dead long."

Zeke had known. Whether he'd actually smelled death from across a parking lot . . . well, that claim strained credulity. They weren't saying she was in bad shape, so the stench wouldn't carry on the wind. And offered more disturbing possibilities. *How* else *could he have known?*

I'd have heard his truck, if he'd left, she told herself. And then a little voice whispered, *But he runs. Would you hear him running? You didn't even hear your phone.* She'd woken up with him perched on the side of her bed. *What do you know about him, really?* Neva slid him a glance out of the corner of her eyes. Was he too interested in the proceedings? But no, he had been with her; he couldn't have made it back to the house before the alarm went off. Unless he'd left the car and some-one else broke into the clinic. Were the two crimes related? Her head began to ache.

No, she didn't believe he had the capacity to hurt anyone. She trusted him.

"Not natural causes," one of the deputies said. "You don't put a girl in the trunk of a car if she died in her sleep."

Pickett agreed with a nod. "Damn shame. She looks so young."

"Do we know who she is?" Raleigh asked.

"No ID on her. No purse in the car, either."

"Did you run the plates before popping that trunk?" the sheriff demanded.

"Yes, sir," Bobby said nervously. "It was reported stolen in Birmingham five days ago."

Birmingham. Without realizing she'd been holding her whole body so tense, Neva relaxed. That poor girl had noth-ing to do with the clinic, nothing to do with Harper Creek. She just had the misfortune to wind up dumped here by some maniac traveling through. Not that she was pleased to imag-ine he might get away with it, but it was worse to think it might've been done by somebody she knew.

"Cold out," Zeke said at her left shoulder. "Come inside."

Sheriff Raleigh broke away from the car and strode toward the clinic. "I got a better idea. Go on home. I'll supervise the team myself when they get to the inside of the clinic and then lock up for you. Bobby doesn't need anything else. If he does later, he knows how to use the phone."

Because she was a Harper, they weren't going to ask her any questions. She should be pleased she could leave but the unfairness ate at her a bit. Anybody else would be interviewed and asked if she'd seen anything useful. But she was too tired to argue.

"Thanks, Cliff."

"Anything for you, Geneva." His insistence on calling her by her full name, because her mama and daddy did, set her teeth on edge.

She didn't let it show as she walked away. Zeke got the kittens and then caught up with her. It was almost time for their next feeding, and they spoke of their hunger in plaintive tones. She drove them back to the farm in weary silence; he didn't press her, no words at all as he went to fetch the supplies.

They cared for them without speaking. The sun had come up fully by the time they finished. She watched him settling the kittens and she dismissed her momentary doubt. Still, she couldn't help but wonder:

"How close did you get to the car? You didn't touch it, did you?" If they found his prints on the vehicle, it would cause Zeke no end of trouble.

"No."

There was something strange about him, but she didn't think there was any harm. He'd gone out of his way to help her, more than once, without any expectation she'd reward him with introductions to her father or give him money he hadn't earned. Few people did, and she felt guilty over her momentary doubt. Maybe he just had a keen sense of smell. Hadn't she gotten mad at Ben for refusing to put any faith in her gut feelings? They'd started fighting about Luke—and his worry that she was setting herself up for worse pain by believing her brother wasn't dead.

Like I need to think about him now, like I don't have enough trouble.

"It'll be a while before we can clean up and reopen for business." Her voice broke. "Longer before I can replace everything they smashed."

Likely she should be more upset about the dead girl, but they hadn't let her get a look, so it didn't seem as real as the destruction. Or maybe she was just tired. She didn't know how much more resolve she had left. One of these days, the fight might become too hard. Maybe at that point, she'd be ready to live as her parents wanted and just coast on their expectations and accomplishments.

"I'm so sorry."

At first she didn't know why the sentiment sounded so strange, coming from him, and then she realized. He'd used all the words, pronoun and verb, with intensifier. Three little words, but they meant so much more. She raised her face and found him standing very close. Not towering, but near. His proximity felt like a question: *I'm here if you want me. Do you?*

Neva answered by taking two steps closer and then his hands curled around her upper arms. He drew her in as if he were afraid she might shatter. When her cheek met his chest, a sigh slid out of her. He smoothed his hands up and down her back, and she wound her arms about his waist. She noted the way his muscles tensed and leapt at her touch.

"Every time I get close to being settled, something like this happens." An emotion akin to despair coiled through her.

"What else?"

"At first it was little things. Vandalism outside. Windows broken. And then there was a small fire. To make matters worse, I can't keep anyone but Julie on staff. I don't know why. I don't think it's a bad place to work. I swear, it feels like I'm cursed sometimes." She exhaled shakily. "I'm sorry. That sounds melodramatic."

"Sounds like somebody trying to make you fail."

She'd thought so once, too, but she'd installed a few cameras, and never caught anyone sabotaging the place. Which made her feel even stupider. *It couldn't just be bad luck, could it?* Well, maybe.

"Maybe it's just not meant to be."

There would come a time when she couldn't afford to start over anymore. But she wouldn't just conform. If that time came, she'd leave Harper Creek and go to work for another veterinary practice. She'd hate leaving her patients, but she'd be damned if she'd choose a life she hated instead.

"Fuck *meant*," he growled.

His tone startled her, so she tipped her head back to gaze into his face. He wore a look so intense she almost took a step back. But there was no anger in it, only fierce determination.

"Zeke?"

"Do what makes you happy."

"The clinic does," she said softly. "And . . . *you* do."

That shocked him; she saw the flash in his eyes. But the corners turned up on the edges of his mouth. The heat of his hands shifted as they glided down her back to the curve of her hips. "Yeah?"

Gathering her courage, she nodded. Despite the long, awful night, a spark of brightness gathered at her core, as if she hid a star inside her. The glow brightened into delight when she saw how he stared at her mouth. Nobody had *ever* looked at her that way, like she embodied all his sweetest dreams. She no longer cared what people would say or if it was suitable for her to feel this way about someone who worked for her. That one moment of doubt aside, she trusted him. Now she only cared if he wanted her back.

"You're not like anybody I ever met."

"That a good thing?" He sounded none too sure.

"A *very* good thing," she said fervently.

"Okay to kiss you?"

"You don't need to ask."

CHAPTER 11

Toku dipped his head, half expecting her to stop him. His mouth brushed hers, and her lips parted. She raised on tiptoe and twined her arms around his neck. He lost every word he knew at the feel of Neva in his arms; better than he'd ever imagined. And he'd wondered about it a lot.

Her honey-almond scent went straight to his head. He kissed her as he'd always wanted to—first with a boy's tentative desire and then a man's need. He wanted to remember each brush, each gasp, in case she never let him do it again. A shiver rolled through him as she cupped his head in her hands and deepened the kiss.

Lips clung, teasing touches of tongue. He tasted her, and with each whisper of contact, the ache intensified.

"I want you," she whispered. "But will it be weird, afterward? I don't want you to feel pressured—"

He couldn't help it. He laughed. Couldn't she tell how much he needed her? He shook with it, just from that one little kiss. Two hours of nakedness with other women hadn't gotten him this stirred up.

She pulled back, eyes wide. *"What?"*

"Can't make a man do this if he don't want to. Least, not without blue pills and a coil of rope."

Neva grinned up at him, appreciating the joke. That warmed him as nothing had in the past months. It made him feel like maybe he wasn't so broken after all. Maybe he could still live in the world with other people and have some small part in her life. Even if there was nothing more than this night, it'd be enough. It would be something real to take the place of all those empty dreams of her.

"Then . . ." She shifted and he sucked in a breath at the painful pleasure of it. "I guess that means you're . . . interested."

"Ain't the right word."

The smile still lingered, but he couldn't leash his intensity, even if it scared her. In fact it was all he could do to finish the conversation, so there could be no doubt she wanted this, too. If she touched his bare skin, he might carry her off like a caveman. He hoped she said yes and stopped talking soon because he was losing the thread of her words in the sweetness of her body against his. She said some other stuff and he nodded like he was listening, then this got through:

"Let's go to your room."

That was what he'd been waiting for. With a hungry little growl, he swept her into his arms. She squealed and wrapped her arms around his neck, making him grin even more as he jogged up the stairs. Though he knew she had some weight to her, she felt like a bag of feathers.

"Damn," she breathed. "It must be all that running."

Must be. He didn't want to think about all the ways he was different than other men right now. He wanted to lose himself in her and not think about the forest noises and the other intuitions whispering at the edges of his mind. Right now, there was only Neva, not the girl from his dreams, but better, because she was real and she wanted him, too.

In his bedroom, he set her on her feet and looked at the scuffed floor and dingy paint. The morning sunlight showed all the faults, down to the worn places on the sheets and the faded quilt his grandmother had made. It suddenly didn't seem good enough for her, and he wasn't, either. The edge of desire didn't go away, but it gained a layer of desperation and sadness.

"Wish I had someplace better for you." He wished *he* was better, too, but that he didn't say out loud.

"Please don't let this be about me being a Harper," she said softly. "I thought it didn't matter to you. Please don't let me be wrong about that."

Her words eased his burden. In her way she, too, had carried the weight of a name she didn't want and couldn't put down. Sure, her people brought with them a different kind of expectation, but it couldn't be any easier than the path he'd walked. And it didn't matter, except that it had brought them to this point. He had to say, he'd do it all again, even the terrible and tormenting parts, for the right to step closer as he was about to do.

"Not wrong," he answered.

Still feeling tentative, Zeke pulled her shirt over her head. She had beautiful skin, soft and smooth, delicate shoulders and pretty breasts. Hands shaking, he skimmed away her jeans. He'd seen these panties earlier; it was her hips and thighs that claimed his attention.

Before he could decide what to do first, she responded in kind and yanked his shirt off. He wished he had the muscles he'd once had to wow her, instead of showing so much rib, but she didn't seem to mind. Her eyes went wide and avid. His breath gusted into a moan when she set her fingers against his belly, exploring the ridges, and his cock throbbed in his pants, practically begging for her touch.

Her hands were on his belt buckle when she paused, as if something had occurred to her. "I'm not on the pill. Do you have protection?"

A low curse escaped him. "Hell, no. Why would I?"

He'd never brought a woman out to the farm. Before he was taken, he'd hooked up a few times, but never here, and it was always some barfly who didn't want to see him the next morning and probably wouldn't remember his name. It had never meant anything before. The one time he'd liked a girl well enough to ask to see her again, she'd laughed at him, and said, *Oh, honey, I don't think so.*

It spoke volumes that not even a good-time girl thought he had anything to offer. And that was before. Now even he didn't think so, and it made him question the wisdom of what they were about to do. But her next words drove all doubt from his mind.

"Because you're beautiful."

The pleasure he felt in hearing her say that almost sent him to his knees. Women didn't say such things to Zeke Noble. They saw only his family history and the fact that he drove an old truck and couldn't buy them expensive gifts. His heart almost broke at the awful joy.

He looked oddly vulnerable, Neva thought. She felt self-conscious standing in nothing but her panties, but when he skinned out of his jeans, it didn't matter. He seemed to shake off the mood then. Zeke lifted her in his arms and tumbled them both into bed. His unexpectedly playful nature brought a smile to her face.

"Know we can't . . ." He made a gesture with his fingers that should've been offensive, but instead Neva laughed because he'd obviously done it to avoid using a coarser word. "Still want to—"

"Fool around?"

"Yeah." His relief was obvious.

How adorable. He found it difficult to use certain words around her, like she was too ladylike to hear them, let alone do such things. Unlike the men who pretended such care, he meant it. Tenderness spilled through her in the wake of arousal. It felt like it had been years since she'd wanted anyone like this—or had someone want her back in the same way.

"We should probably have a conversation first." How she hated this part of modern life. "I've had four partners. Always used protection. You?"

"Three. And me, too."

Huh, she had never been the experienced one in a relationship before. It was kind of nice. "Then I'd love to get naked and roll around with you."

"Need these off." He pulled on her panties and she lifted her hips.

With deft hands he drew them down, each delicate touch a caress that lit her up. She'd never felt anything as good. For a few seconds, he gazed at the panties in his hands and then tossed them over his shoulder with a wicked, delightful smile.

No going back now.

Zeke wore his boxers this time, and she started to take them off, but he stilled her by flattening a palm on her belly. The clinic didn't leave her much time to work out, so she was soft, not tight. But he seemed enthralled. With his fingertips, he drew patterns on her skin and shivers went through her. Then he propped himself on an elbow and just lay beside her, studying her body. He now looked solemn in a way that couldn't be good, considering they were in bed together.

"Everything all right?"

God, please don't let him change his mind because he's seen me naked in daylight. Nerves started to overwhelm her. *Maybe this wasn't such a good idea . . . I do have to work with him afterward.*

"Just . . . scared is all."

She forgot her fears in the face of his. "Why?"

"Never had it matter so much before. Doing it right."

That was it. She fell. Her heart had been dancing on the edge of it from the first moment he heard her troubles and offered to solve them, from the first day he partnered with her in caring for those kittens. She had been fighting it tooth and nail because it seemed wrong for so many reasons. But now she was just *his*, and that was all.

"Would it help if I went first?" That seemed right, somehow. "But . . . there will be rules. You can't touch me until I say so."

A little tremor rolled through him. From his rapt expression, he liked the idea a lot. Neva wanted to please him more than she wanted her next breath. She didn't wait for a verbal answer; she eased onto her side and kissed his throat. His head fell back. Zeke folded his arms and tucked them beneath his head.

She'd never done anything like this before; her sexual encounters had always been pretty basic. Some had been pleasurable, but she'd never needed to blow someone's head off before. It mattered, partly because she wanted to erase any memory he might have of anyone else's touch. Such possessiveness was also new.

Instinct kicked in. She planted kisses between his neck and shoulder, then used her teeth to nip him gently. He sucked in a breath and his knees came up. She thought he'd reach for her then, but he managed to keep his hands beneath his head. Impressive self-control, though longing radiated from every tense muscle.

Knowing she could make him feel that way . . . heady and empowering. And she hadn't even done much of anything, yet. Neva nibbled a path down to his shoulders. She paused to admire his lovely lean build; his concave stomach sloped into his pelvis. She stroked his lower belly with her fingertips, tracing the muscles. His cock jumped in his boxers and he lifted his hips, breath coming faster.

"Please," he whispered.

But she wasn't going to let him rush her. Open-mouthed, she nuzzled his chest, rolling half atop him so that both her thighs framed his. His skin felt hot against hers, lightly roughened with hair. She rubbed against him, letting him feel her wetness. A low moan escaped him as she touched her tongue to his nipple. He was shaking now, incessant shivers and panting breaths that said he was hers to do with as she willed, and that certainty sent desire spiraling through her.

Neva rubbed her lips over his skin, licking and biting gently, until she found his other nipple. She alternated tongue and teeth, slowly working her hips against his thigh. He lifted it, and the new angle abraded her clit with the sweetest friction. Much more of this and she'd come all over his leg.

"You like this?" She knew the answer. She just wanted to hear his voice again, raw with passion.

"Love," he growled. *"Love."*

He imbued that one word with impossible layers of meaning—somehow, spoken so, it became endearment, demand, and declaration. The front of his boxers showed damp with his excitement, clung to his cock. She couldn't wait any longer to see and touch it. When she eased off him, he groaned in protest and reached for her, but he checked himself at her teasingly reproachful glance. Zeke bit off a gravelly curse and tucked his hands behind his head again.

"It's still my show. You'll get your turn."

"If I live," he muttered.

Still, he arched so she could skim away the last barrier between them. *Beautiful.* His iron-hard cock jutted from dark pubic hair—the tip glistened with his precome, and the whole length had flushed a ruddy hue with his desire. It twitched as she admired it and he moaned, but not in pain. Sheer need drew the sound from him.

He seemed to take pleasure in her gaze, but that didn't content her long.

Neva spread his thighs with her hands and settled between them. But she didn't go immediately for the prize. Instead she licked and nuzzled, teased his sac with little scrapes of her nails. His groans became incessant rather than intermittent; she loved the lovely torment in his arching body. Zeke writhed against her mouth, and when she licked the curve of his hair-rough skin, he went wild.

He bucked, offering himself to the air, and she couldn't deny him a second longer. She licked the ejaculate from his crown, and then took his shaft fully into her mouth. He thrust with a relieved groan, quick and shallow movements that told her he was close. But to her surprise, he stopped almost at once.

"Turn around." It wasn't a request.

He still hadn't touched her but she found herself doing as he'd asked. She knew what he wanted and how to arrange herself. She lay down on him, knees on either side of his head. He didn't use his hands, but *oh, his mouth* . . .

Neva undulated, almost forgetting what she ought to be doing. Her hands shook as she guided his cock back between her lips. No finesse or teasing this time. She wanted to finish him almost as much as she wanted her own orgasm.

Pleasure built from the sweet, relentless sweeps of his tongue. His mouth felt like hot, damp satin and the gentle abrasion of his cheeks added to the sensation. She rocked faster, and his hips gained speed in tandem. Each shift brought them closer.

They came together. Her body stiffened and shook as she drank him down. For endless seconds, she savored his taste and the sweet little shocks that wracked him. Boneless, Neva let him turn her and draw her into his arms. They fit, soft and hard nestled together. She put her head on his chest and luxuriated in the feel of his heart against her ear, so strong and steady. *This* was a man she could count on. He wasn't like other men—and that was the best part about him.

"How was that?" The ultimate exercise in vanity because she knew.

"Perfect." Zeke buried his face in her hair, and each breath he took sent a shiver through her.

"We'll get condoms for next time."

He levered up on one elbow to gaze into her face. "Next time?"

"You don't want to do it again?" God, if he'd only wanted a one-time hookup and a chance to blow off some steam, she might die of shame. In that case, she'd misunderstood everything. She'd thought—

"'Course. Wasn't sure *you* would."

She laughed shakily. "Don't scare me like that, Zeke. I mean, I thought this was . . . something. Or that it could be, at least."

"Not something," he said gravely. "Everything."

CHAPTER 12

Emil was tired. Oh, he could've taken the promotion that Birch had offered, but he still didn't want it. He'd spent eight years in the army avoiding officer bars, and he didn't intend to start climbing rank now. Plus being overworked meant he had less time to mourn. He'd once loved being out in the field and making a difference. Even now, he occasionally managed to find some satisfaction in his work, despite everything he'd lost.

Today wasn't one of them.

The dive crew finished up while he supervised. A girl had gone missing near the river, and so they started a search. First they confined their efforts to the shore but as the hours wore on, it became clear they needed to look in the water. To his dismay, they'd found her half an hour ago. As senior officer, he got the pleasure of telling the parents, who were waiting at home for word. He'd sent them away from the scene because the mother's constant crying wasn't helping anybody.

With a faint sigh, he climbed in the car. The victim's parents lived fifteen minutes away; he let GPS plot the route and worked out what he'd say to them. Rina had been better at the people skills. But she was gone. *Gone, gone, gone.* He'd put roses on her grave, and they would be dead by now, too, petals curled in, blackened and dry with the evening frost. That was how he felt inside. And ancient, too, as if he'd lived past his expiration date.

He listened to country music on the way. That would surprise people, he thought. They probably pegged him as a classical man, based on his taste in clothing. But everyone had secrets. Long ago, he'd compensated for his very Cajun name and eliminated all trace of Louisiana from his accent, unless he was stressed.

Hebert felt like he was wearing prison ankle weights as he went up the walk. *Hate this part of the job.* They knew as soon as he rang the bell. Mrs. Winston dissolved into sobs and her oldest daughter had to lead her away. Michelle had been the baby of the family.

Mr. Winston invited him in. It was a nice house, well kept, and decorated in typical Southern style. He refused coffee and perched uneasily at the edge of the sofa.

"The dive team found her a little while ago," he said. "We don't give this kind of news over the phone."

"I appreciate that. What . . ." The older man trailed off, not wanting to say it.

"It appears she drowned. We won't know for sure what more happened—if anything—until the report comes back from the medical examiner's office."

"Kim had a fight with Michelle earlier today. About some boy she wanted to date. We thought he was too old—she was only seventeen!—and she ran out of the house. That was the last time we saw her. Do you think . . . you don't think—"

"I can't speculate, sir. It's best we wait for the facts. But I'm very sorry for your loss."

Did that sound sincere? It *was*; he just wasn't good at showing sympathy. That had been Rina's job. She would lean forward and offer a consoling hand on the shoulder. He'd often wondered if motherhood had any impact on her public manner, whether she'd been different before. But he hadn't known her then. They'd worked together for ten years, and her kids were three and four when they met. Thirteen and fourteen, now. She'd had them in her late twenties, married Preston fresh out of college. And sometimes he wanted to demand of the universe, *Why didn't she wait for me? That was supposed to be* my *life.*

Don't think of her.

At least work offered more relief than sitting at home, but it was . . . harder than it had been, too. He had to do things differently to compensate for her loss. They had been partners for a long time; such feelings were expected, according to the shrink. He just didn't know what to do with them. God knew what Marlow would say if he knew the true depth of Hebert's loss. He probably wouldn't have released him.

After fielding a few procedural questions from Winston, he left. Hebert sat in the car feeling sick to his stomach. Maybe he should've taken the promotion after all. He liked the investigative aspects . . . the personal interactions, not so much. If one was in a position of authority, it mattered less if his subordinates found him distant or abrasive.

As he started the engine, his phone rang. His nerves jumped. Touching that phone was the last thing he should ever do, because it only ever meant bad news, but he did it anyway.

"Hebert."

As he'd feared, Hal Birch spoke. "Got another job for you."

"That's great news." His dry tone drew a laugh from his lieutenant.

"Not for the girl. There's a Jane Doe down in Harper Creek. The locals don't know what to make of her."

He was already bringing the town up on GPS. It wasn't more than an hour from where they'd found Michelle Winston. It had already been a long night, but they'd give him the day off to compensate. He did occasionally need to sleep.

"Sec. I'm putting on the headset so you can brief me while I drive."

Hebert plugged in his phone and made the connections, then curled the earphone mic around his ear. He pulled out of the driveway then. He wanted to get away from the grieving family inside more than he felt they couldn't afford a five-minute delay.

"Ready?" Birch asked.

"I'm plugged in."

"A weird one. Locals responded to a B and E report from the alarm company and investigated a suspicious vehicle in the lot. Since the plates came back as reported stolen, they popped the trunk and found our girl inside."

"Tell me about her."

"From what they said, no ID or unusual marks. Mid-twenties, brunette. But get this . . ." The anticipation in his boss's voice put his nerves on edge. "She was all tied up in red satin ribbons."

He froze, hoping this wasn't going where he thought it was. "Like a Christmas present?"

"Not exactly. More like the laces of ballet shoes."

Just like the girl we found in the woods, a few weeks back. Birch was describing the same general physical type, too. That made two.

If the MO is the same . . .

"Any marks on her?"

"Nope. But you'll see for yourself soon enough."

That was unusual. But there was no overlooking the laced red ribbons. The two cases had to be connected. A sour feeling swelled in his stomach. Birch was right; this was a weird one, and he had a feeling it would get worse before it got better.

"Did you call the tech team?"

"Yeah, they're on their way and will meet you at the scene."

He hoped the locals had enough sense to cordon the area off. He'd seen more than one scene compromised by well-intentioned incompetence. This was a different county from the vic the hunters had found, so he could expect different personnel. Hebert drove through the sunrise, and it was full morning by the time he got there.

They had, indeed, secured the area. The car sat isolated while the sheriff and his deputy milled around, barking at passersby. The lot had more than its share of lookie-lous. Unfortunately, there was a sandwich shop in the mall that served breakfast so everyone who stopped there on the way to work had seen the flashing lights and the tape and then spread the word. *You gotta love the digital age.* A surprising number of people had turned up to see the show. He guessed this town didn't have much in the way of entertainment.

Since they wouldn't let anyone in the lot, people had parked along the streets and stood with coffee or some other steaming drink, watching the show. First Hebert skimmed the crowd for anyone showing undue intensity or excitement. But they all expressed standard-issue morbid curiosity and interest. Then he went over to introduce himself to the Halpern County Sheriff.

He extended a hand. "I'm with the ABI. Emil Hebert."

"Nice to meet you, Agent Hebert. Cliff Raleigh." The other man shook hard, proving a point, he guessed. "Your men got here before you did. Seem to be efficient, too. Taking pictures with their Rebel digital cameras and all."

His good-old-boy façade might fool some people, but Hebert wasn't falling for it. When he first started out, he'd been taken by that *I'm just a rube* ruse and been burned by it. He kept his expression neutral. There was no call for this to turn into a pissing match. The sheriff had obviously known he needed outside help.

"They're good at what they do. Walk me through what happened?"

He listened to what Raleigh had to say and his report matched what his boss had told him. "You have some names and addresses for me?"

He needed to talk to the two people who had been present when they found the body. Maybe some other workers would have some idea when the car had arrived in the lot; it wasn't a huge parking area by any means. And the vehicle itself was pretty distinctive in its ugliness.

"Yes, of course. But please be extra polite when you visit the lady who runs the clinic. Geneva Harper's people—"

He set his jaw and blanked the rest. *Not this again.* Hebert cared fuck-all for local politics. He didn't care if she was born of Jesus and Mary Magdalene; she still needed to answer his questions. If they wanted him to investigate, they couldn't set up roadblocks. Rina would've smoothed over his icy look, but she wasn't here, and he had to deal. It also pissed him off Raleigh would try to tell him how to best do his job.

"I'll need to talk to them. And I want to see the report from the alarm company. Are there any cameras in this lot?"

Raleigh laughed. "Don't I wish. Geneva—that is, Ms. Harper—had some in her shop, but the thieves busted them in the break-in and there are none outside."

This case was going to be a bundle of laughs—he just knew it. "Then why don't you start by showing me our girl?"

After they both donned protective gear, Raleigh led the way. Hebert lifted the tape and stepped under. He'd seen a lot of strange things in his day, but this gave him pause. With the lid raised, the trunk looked like a coffin, a resemblance further amplified by the white satin she lay on.

But no damage had been done to her. Eyes closed, lashes in dark contrast to her pale skin, she looked serene and almost peaceful. Few murder victims did. He didn't know what to make of the red ribbons, but it clearly had a ritual significance. It meant something to the killer.

Yeah, he had a feeling he'd be seeing this guy's work again.

He'd enjoyed watching them discover her.

While the sheriff waited for outside help and rubberneckers stopped to gawk, he'd stood in the shadows and admired the response to his handiwork. This one had been closer to right, but still not perfect. He'd used some of the drugs he'd stolen from the clinic, and she died quickly, but not accidentally. This time, it happened in accordance with his will, not due to incompetence, and the old man was pleased.

How amusing to slip in and take the drugs silently, no alarms, no notice, and then return to her to do his work. Once he finished, he'd come back and trashed the place, setting the alarm off. These stupid cops probably thought it was a coincidence. He had been a little surprised they'd focused on the car so quickly. He'd thought it might take a little while, although he hoped not. He did want her found while everyone could appreciate the expertise.

But that wasn't the death he wanted for Geneva Harper. She required more drama. More passion. In time, he would learn how to do it.

Practice, practice. He was starting to like it.

He'd taken pleasure in this one, arranging her limbs and winding the ribbons about them in a pretty counterpoint to her pale, pale skin. This time, there had been no ugly wounds to hide, but it looked right; he didn't question why. Closing her eyes had been inspired.

Had they noticed the way he'd spread a pristine white sheet in the trunk before placing her inside? Doubtless, yes, which meant they would be checking the tags and the fabric and trying to deduce who he was from such small details. It wouldn't work. He'd taken care to buy a common brand in a different town. Nobody would remember him, and countless thousands of these would've been sold in a week's time.

No leads. You will wonder about me. You may even pass me on the street and have no idea who I am.

Now, he sat in silence, waiting. This was his special room, no windows, just cement walls, and a door. Six by six. It had been used as storage by the old farmwives who lived here, once upon a time. Ancient jars still sat on the shelves behind him, homemade pickles swimming in brine, canned beets, and a pair of eyeballs. He hated the waiting, but the old man would come. He always did. It was better if he dealt with him here in private, where nobody else could see or hear.

From out of the darkness, the old man stumbled toward him. His face was lined with drink and he limped because he'd lost a foot fighting for his country. *So you're finally doing what you were born to do, boy. What took you so fucking long?*

He knew his father was dead, of course. But he couldn't make him rest until the work was done. *Break them for me,* the old bastard would rage. *Leave them with nothing.* And he was an obedient son. He had found he heard the old man less, after taking a girl. They calmed him; he liked to watch.

"I don't know."

The old man made him feel weak. Impotent. Too well he remembered the nights in the dark in his own filth and the days he hadn't eaten, until he would've promised anything to make it stop. He had promised, in fact.

It's because you're pathetic. Your mother coddled you. I tried to make a man of you. God knows I tried.

He put his hands over his ears and shut his eyes. It had been too long since he laid that pretty, pretty girl to her rest. The old man was getting impatient. He'd done so much killing in the war that he hungered for more. He clawed at his own neck, feeling the old man's teeth there. *Vampire. He will suck the life out of me.* A low moan escaped him, and he crouched down, arms over his head, and began to rock.

It was a long time later before he came to himself again. It was nearly dark, and there was a chill in the air. Carefully, he put his things away. He couldn't take his work home, after all.

He climbed in the car and drove away from the desolate house. It was no more than a ruin to anyone else's eyes, rotten clapboard and broken windows. His dreams had died there, long ago.

His mother had breakfast waiting when he got home. As ever, she seemed pleased to see him. She was a fragile little thing, who'd once dreamed of becoming a dancer; in happier times, she would get out her red ballet shoes and tell him how she'd planned to go to New York to join a famous dance troupe, but those days were long gone. It seemed impossible to him that she could've survived his father's fists, but as he got older, he had stepped in whenever possible to take her place. She had wept over it, but she'd never once tried to put herself between them. Once, she'd tried to take him away, but the old man dragged them both back. They sat for twelve hours under the threat of his shotgun while he screamed and drank. He had been sure he would die then, but in the end, he only pissed himself and then the old man made him crawl through it like a dog.

"I made waffles," she said, laying the table.

Her movements were jerky and fearful, after all these years. She couldn't meet his eyes, and he had never hurt her. But he was starting to see why the old man had slapped her around; the constant cringing woke a monster in him, too. Sometimes he wanted to scream at her, just like the devil had. So far, he'd contained the urge.

"Thank you."

"Thanks for fixing the heater. I don't know what I'd do without you." She touched his cheek with gentle affection, and he fought not to recoil.

Weak, pathetic mama's boy. Why don't you just fuck her now that I'm gone?

Revulsion swelled in his stomach. He made himself ignore the evil, insidious voice and sat down at the breakfast table. He desperately wanted them both to shut up, but they never, ever did.

"Can I do anything else?"

The old man's laughter rang caustic in his ears. *Hike up those skirts, pussy boy. She hasn't had a good seeing-to in years, and since she can't have a real man, you'll have to do.*

She was smiling, like she didn't *know.* "No, just enjoy your breakfast. I'm going to the market for a few things."

He couldn't eat a bite. Once she'd gone, he scraped the pastry with its sticky syrup into the trash. Feeling trapped, he went down the hall to his old bedroom. He was exhausted, but sleep didn't come easily. Eventually, he drifted off, and his dreams were dark as night.

When he woke, he found her there, as she always was. She had curled up at his back like a ghost, one hand on his head. There existed here no sense of what was right or fitting. If he protested, she would sob, and say how lonely she was. *You're all I have left,* she would weep. And he hated her tears almost as much as the old man's vitriol. But then she would cry anyway, so he had no choice but to hold her. As if she knew he was awake, she started sniffling on cue.

He rolled to face her. Close up, he saw the lines on her skin and the deep bruises beneath her eyes. Not from a man's fists anymore, but from lack of sleep. Years after the old man's death, she still feared his reach, or maybe she feared something else more, now.

"You're going to *leave* me. You spend so much time away from home."

This was an old argument. He didn't even live here anymore. This was her place, and he only came when he had to. This woman was truly wretched, and he wanted nothing to do with her, for all she had carried him in her womb. He wished she would find some purpose that did not revolve around him. She was as likely to sprout wings. In that the old man had been right; she was worthless except when it came to cooking and cleaning. She herself could not imagine doing anything else, not so long after her dancer's dreams went to dust by way of a man's brutality.

"Mother . . ." But he could not find words to refute her claims. They clogged in his throat, and his fists clenched at the failure. He wanted to hurt her and could not.

Feeble, the old man said scornfully.

"Oh," she cried. "You're still mine. Still my beautiful boy."

She hugged him to her and covered his face with kisses. Her arms strangled his neck, squeezing, squeezing, and he loathed her closeness and loved it at the same time. His prick hardened because she was close and warm, and she had *always* done this to him. She'd once done more in the guise of educating him. But he knew it wasn't right, even if his body remembered otherwise.

"What a good boy," she whispered. "Such a sweet boy. Nothing like him."

No, I would've had the bitch on her back by now.

He rolled away, onto the floor and went toward the door at a crawl. How he hated them both.

"Where are you going?" Her voice went shrill.

He needed quiet. No matter what, he wouldn't come back here until he'd finished. He had a devil's bargain to execute, and then . . . a life to live.

Lives to *take.* The thought let him climb to his feet, bolstering his strength. He steadied himself on the doorframe, and then left her apartment at a run, pretending he couldn't hear her crying. It was hard to tell how much of her grief was real, and how much she feigned to bludgeon him with guilt. He'd played the game before.

This time, he would win.

CHAPTER 13

Zeke slept for a few hours, and when he woke, there was no panic or disorientation. This time he knew instantly where he was and who he held in his arms. He'd expected her to be gone, like she was a dream too dear to keep. Since his escape, he'd suffered nightmares, unrelated to the recurring one, about them finding him . . . not that he knew why they'd taken him in the first place or what they'd done to him while he was there. He tried not to think about it. *They.* There was no surer way to make someone think you were crazy than by talking about *them*.

He hadn't walked in his sleep, at least, or woken up in the woods again. She soothed the beast. Zeke shifted slightly and gazed into Neva's face. The sixteen-year-old boy in him couldn't believe it. She'd slept with him. And she was still here.

He heard her tentative voice saying, *I thought this was something.*

Lord knew he didn't understand her reasons—she could obviously do better—but it almost made him believe in divine intervention, like somebody was watching out for him and

saying, *Here, man, you're due a break*. He laced his hands
through her hair, gentle so he wouldn't wake her just yet. The
late afternoon light caught threads of red and gold, turning
the plain color into a shining autumn crown. Zeke wasn't
ready to end these private, peaceful moments where she'd
given herself wholly to him. That meant serious trust.

He also wanted her again, but the ache was manageable.
Easing his lower body away helped. But she shifted at the
movement and followed him, throwing her leg over his. Her
arm fell across his waist. And maybe he'd have acted on his
desire, if he hadn't heard the kittens mewing.

Still tired, he rolled out of bed without waking her and
went to tend to them. They were simple. As long as they were
cozy and warm and fed, they didn't complain. In addition to
the hours of human contact, the plush cat fulfilled their need
to snuggle; they didn't seem to notice the difference. But they
were always happy to see him; their little minds felt like tiny
pinpricks of joy. At first he'd tried to keep them out, but that
was more trouble than it was worth. They didn't hurt him;
Zeke just understood he shouldn't be able to sense them this
way. It wasn't normal. But maybe that was okay.

Their eyes were open and they tried to explore with unsteady
little steps. It was harder now to keep them in the box.

By the time he finished, Neva had gotten up. Still not wide
awake, she stumbled into the kitchen doorway, wearing his
discarded T-shirt. The loose fabric made her shoulders look
small and feminine while it clung sweetly to her round butt.
Desire spiked to insane levels; it wasn't her *just fucked* look,
though her tousled hair struck him as sexy No, it was the sight
of his shirt on her.

The need to claim her permanently rose in him. Not that
he was sure how to make such a claim. He only knew an urge
to mark her and make her smell like him from the inside out.
Easy. Give her some time.

"I feel like I'm taking advantage of you," she said on a
jaw-cracking yawn.

He let his gaze wander down her bare legs. "Hear me
screaming?"

Neva grinned. He shared her humor because he was sure it wasn't directed at him. She didn't own that brand of unkindness.

"Funny." But her eyes revealed contentment and she smelled . . . happy. He didn't know how to put more words to the feeling, but she told him more with her scent than he could learn from her words. Right now, she gave off faint hints of nutmeg and allspice, warmed from her skin.

"Sometimes." In truth he never had been. He kept to himself, had few friends, and enjoyed simple pleasures. Zeke knew he'd never been extraordinary—and now he was freakish—so it made no sense that she wanted him, but maybe he could light some candles in hope she never figured out the wrongness of it.

"I'm not going to the clinic today." She paused as if she expected him to argue with her. "They may well be done by now, but I can't face it. You know the minute we show up, people will be all over us with questions."

He nodded. "Probably looking for you right now."

"Shit. I bet my parents are going crazy."

His heart sank like a lead weight. "Didn't tell 'em where you are?"

She ran for her cell phone without answering. There could be all kinds of reasons for that. It didn't necessarily mean she was ashamed of him. *Doesn't mean she's proud to be with you, either.* Though she went back upstairs, he heard her clearly. This time he didn't try to block it out.

The click of the buttons in the quiet house told him she was dialing. Otherwise, there were just kitten noises, the settling wood of the old house, and her breathing. She must be listening to her messages. Then she dialed again.

"Don't panic," she said to whoever picked up. "I'm fine."

A long pause.

"I'm sorry. I should've realized you'd worry."

This time, the silence was even longer.

"I don't have to tell you that." Zeke guessed they'd asked where she'd been spending her nights. "It's none of your business." A brief break and then, "I don't give a shit what Ben says. I'm *not* cheating on him. We're not together!"

More waiting.

"And I'm sorry for that, too. But Luke's gone and I can't—" Her voice broke. "Just know I'm all right. Yes, I'll come to Sunday dinner." She didn't say she loved them before hanging up.

Then he listened to her crying softly. Zeke didn't reckon it was the time to dump his doubts on her. Sometimes you just had to choke it down and do the right thing for someone else. So by the time she reappeared, a good half hour later, she'd washed and dressed, no sign of his shirt or the woman he'd made love to.

He greeted her with a warm cup of coffee. Neva drank it with milk, no sugar. She also liked chai tea, meatball sandwiches, and rainy days. When it rained, her hair tried to curl, but it was too long and heavy, so it became a mass of unruly waves, and she used a honey and keratin shampoo to tame it. The first time he'd seen her stuff in his bathroom, it gave him the strangest feeling, like she might stay, and if she did, then the shadows could be banished from this place for good. The farm might be a home again.

Zeke didn't ask about her phone call. He figured if she wanted to talk, she would. Prying never helped.

She sat down, cup in hand, at the old kitchen table. For long moments, she stared at the scarred surface while seeing something else, and when she looked up at him at last, her face was haunted. "Do you ever feel like you let people down constantly, just by being who you are?"

He thought about making a sympathetic noise, but he couldn't. "No."

"Must be nice." A faint sigh escaped her.

Again, he gave her the raw truth. "Not really. Means nobody cares what I do."

That surprised her enough that her coffee cup paused mid-air. "I know your folks are gone, but what about your aunt?"

He struggled to find the words. They balled up inside in a knot of feelings. "Loves me, but . . ."

"What?"

"Doesn't expect anything."

If he didn't become a drunk like his dad or kill himself like his mom, that'd be enough for Sid. But he couldn't say it like that. She loved him, but she thought he was too broken to amount to much, given his family history. He hadn't known that until he came back—and he could smell it on her. Pity had a distinctive scent.

"I'd think that would be nice."

"Could be, I guess."

It was just too hard to explain. With everything she had going on, it was no wonder she hadn't commented on his strangeness. When she did, it would be all over because he couldn't put it in terms that would ever make sense. And even if he did manage it, she'd never believe him.

Thankfully, her own issues weighed too heavily on her to dig into his. "This isn't. My parents are pushing me to get back together with Ben. They're saying he's just what the family needs—and what I need, too."

Christ, it hurt to hear that. He'd guessed as much from her call—and the man's visit the other night—but it raised every hackle for her to speak his name. He had been polished and sure of himself. He drove an expensive car and didn't have calluses on his hands. Just like that, Zeke wanted to kill him.

"That true?"

Neva noticed his tension belatedly. He wasn't sure of himself . . . or them. And here she was, rambling about Ben. It was a cardinal rule of any new relationship: *thou shalt not talk about the ex.*

"It might be the right thing for my family. I know a political connection would make my dad happy, and Ben has been helping out at the mill since Luke went missing. But I'm *positive* he's wrong for me."

"Sure?" he asked quietly.

"I had him, Zeke. I threw him back because he wasn't big enough."

His twilight eyes twinkled. "That so?"

She grinned. "You on the other hand . . ."

When she stepped close, he reached for her and drew her down on his lap. He was already hard, but he didn't seem to want that, at least not right now. Since she was raw inside, both from the problems at the clinic and ongoing family drama, she curled into him and put her head on his shoulder. His arms wrapped around her and it felt like the most natural thing in the world.

"Want you to know," he said softly. "I'm not going anywhere."

Oh, God. That sounds like a promise. She wanted to beg him not to say it if he didn't mean it. Down the road, things would get complicated . . . and when they found out, her family—and Ben—would surely make trouble for him. Neva wouldn't blame him if he did bail down the line, but it'd just hurt more if he'd sworn to stay.

Before she could answer, Zeke tensed and cocked his head, listening to something she couldn't hear. Once more that struck a familiar note. She'd seen animals do it more than once. A minute later the sound of a car crunching down the gravel drive reached her.

"You heard that *way* before I did." It wasn't a question.

He didn't deny it, but neither did he explain. Zeke eased her off his lap and went toward the front door. Neva followed him. By the time he opened it, the vehicle—a plain Ford— had stopped, and a man in his late thirties climbed out. He had dark hair, cropped close to his skull, and caramel skin that bespoke some mixed ethnic heritage. His features were fine and even; some might even call him handsome, except for the ice of his pale green eyes and the stern expression. His tailored clothing showed signs of a hard night and his shoes had lost their pristine polish.

"Zeke Noble and Geneva Harper?" he asked.

"That's right." She guessed he already knew that, or he wouldn't be here. "And you are?"

"Emil Hebert. I'm with the Alabama Bureau of Investigation. I have a few questions for you." He came up on the porch and offered a hand to each of them.

Zeke didn't seem thrilled about touching the guy. In fact, now that she was thinking of it, he avoided direct contact with everyone but her. She filed that away for future reference as they went into the front room.

"I'll get some coffee."

She didn't offer either of them a chance to demur, just went to the kitchen. In times like this she liked having something to do with her hands. The men didn't speak, probably engaged in taking each other's measure. When she returned, she had three cups on a glass platter. It was probably meant for holiday cookies, but it doubled as coffee service with a jug of milk and a bowl of sugar. She knew how Zeke took it, of course, but she served Hebert's black, and permitted him to doctor it as he preferred. The men had chosen seats opposite each other, agent in the chair, Zeke at the end of the couch. She sat in the middle beside him, and it felt like he relaxed a bit.

Hebert took a sip. "It's good. Thank you."

"Is this about the break-in or the girl?" she asked.

"The girl. They don't call me out for anything the locals can handle."

That made sense. "Well, we don't know anything but what we already told Bobby Pickett and Sheriff Raleigh. But ask away."

"Did you notice anything unusual last night?"

"Besides the car?" Neva shook her head.

Hebert nodded and focused on Zeke. "I'm told they investigated the abandoned vehicle at your suggestion. Can you tell me about that?"

"Seemed strange it'd be there at four in the morning."

Neva managed not to react. But that was a lie. He'd told her it was because of the smell. Even in her head, however, that still sounded implausible, so that was probably why he didn't want to repeat it to the investigator. Unease prickled. Maybe she *had* been too quick to trust him, and God, she'd slept with him . . .

The agent took a few notes, his expression closed and neutral. "Did you have any reason to believe they would find something?"

"Thought it might belong to the burglars," Zeke muttered. "Maybe they had car trouble after the break-in and had to flee on foot."

It wasn't the worst story ever, but from Hebert's expression, he thought it was just that—a story. "I see."

Neva fought the urge to begin some nervous babbling. That would only make things worse. She caught a hint of thinly veiled dislike in the man's eyes when he shifted his attention. A pang went through her. *What'd I ever do to* him?

"You own the clinic, Ms. Harper?"

"I don't own the building. I lease it. But yes, I run the place. I'm a veterinarian." Being able to say that still gave her a quiet rush of pride; she had achieved it on her own, not only without support, but occasionally despite real resistance as well.

"Is business good?"

Her brows pulled together in a frown. "I'm not rolling in money, but we're in the black, yes."

Where was he going with this? Did he think she'd staged the break-in for insurance reasons and that girl caught her at it, so she'd killed her and stashed her in the trunk of a car? Surely not. There were far too many holes in that theory.

Hebert scrawled in his notebook some more. "I understand Mr. Noble works for you?"

Beside her, Zeke tensed.

"That's right," she said.

"And are you living together?" From his tone, he already knew the answer.

She almost said, *I don't see what that has to do with anything.* But Zeke was quivering; leashed anger rolled off him in waves. Whatever her private doubts, however she'd felt last night—wondering how he could know there was a girl's body in the trunk when she hadn't been dead long—she wasn't going to let Hebert make her feel ashamed, and she wouldn't answer in a way to make him fear for his place in her life. Deliberately, she covered Zeke's hand where it rested on his thigh, flipped it over, and laced her fingers through his. He seemed to take comfort in the contact and some of his intensity dialed back. She didn't know if the agent had noticed

Zeke's near explosion, but he didn't miss the intimacy of the gesture.

A low growl escaped Zeke. "Watch it."

"I still have an apartment in town, but I can't bring my work home. We're caring for three orphaned kittens. Zeke offered to let me stay here for a while, so I wouldn't have to spend the night at the clinic."

"Given the break-in," Hebert said, "it's a good thing you weren't there."

She hadn't even thought of that. Cold rolled through her. "Anyway, I've been staying here for about a month, I guess."

Hebert nodded. "The rest of these questions are just routine, if you'll bear with me a little longer."

It took another half an hour to content the man with what they'd already told local law enforcement. *Never seen the car before. No, we don't think it has anything to do with the break-in, but who knows for sure?*

At the end, he said, "Thanks for your time and the coffee. I'll be in touch if there's anything further."

Once he'd gone, a tense and peculiar mood fell between them. Zeke pulled his hand away and shoved to his feet. He didn't look her in the eyes.

"Are you all right?"

"No," he snarled.

And he went out the door at a run.

CHAPTER 14

Zeke ran.

As Hebert asked his questions, the air grew sour with Neva's secret fear. She'd noticed the difference in what he'd told her and what he said to the agent. And he felt sick at the idea she thought he might be capable of . . . that.

True, they hadn't been together long, and trust took time. But it raised a deeper issue. It meant she'd noticed his strangeness and that was the spin she'd put on it. She knew he was hiding something, and he would have to confide in her . . . or lose her. Which meant he'd lose her either way.

And so he ran from that certainty. He pounded over rough ground, ducking dry branches and feeling the wind on his face. There was no doubt in him anymore. Even in peak physical condition, he couldn't have set this pace. Certainly couldn't have sustained it. Zeke would bet if he timed himself, he'd break some records. Not that he intended to tell anyone.

Well . . . anyone but her.

If he didn't at least try, though he had no idea how to convince her he wasn't crazy, then he'd never forgive himself. It'd be the same as quitting on the best thing that had ever happened to him. But they couldn't go on as they were. Her doubt would poison everything and then she'd make excuses not to see him.

Because he didn't know what else to do and he needed to burn the anger out of his blood, he pushed on, long past sunset. He'd run miles by the time he stopped, breathing in ragged gulps. The stars rained light down through the naked tangle of branches overhead. Zeke turned his face upward and squeezed his eyes shut.

What am I going to do?

As if in answer, a howl sounded in the distance. Loneliness. He got a feeling from the sound. Not like the kittens. This was fierce and feral and hunted. The creature's kin had been shot, probably for killing pets or chickens, and it was alone. No answering call came, and loss weighted the silence.

A normal person, realizing he was alone in the woods with a hungry beast, would run the other way. Instead Zeke focused on the otherness of it and jogged toward it. When he neared the creature, it didn't flee. It stilled so that even its mind quieted, trying to determine if he was threat or prey.

Neither.

He knelt in the dry leaves and dropped his hands between his knees. For the first time, he tried to use the odd link. Zeke sent an invitation, for one could not compel such creatures. Curiosity touched in response, layered with uncertainty.

And then a tawny coyote stepped out of the undergrowth. He had lighter fur beneath his chin and on his belly. Golden eyes gleamed in the dark. The animal paused some distance away, studying him. But he did not seem fearful or timid. Confused, maybe.

I get it, Zeke thought. *What you smell is not what you see. Under the skin, you know I'm more like you.*

Hesitantly the animal trotted closer, sniffing. When it got within touching distance, he held out a hand. Images washed through him. He saw the death of its loved ones and mourned as blood stained their fur. More confusion. Hunger. They were feelings more than thoughts, impressions wrapped around pictures.

Without considering what he did, he sent the invitation again, along with feelings of safety and belonging. The coyote let out a little yelp and fell in behind him. This time, when he ran, he wasn't alone, and the joy in sharing the night replaced everything else.

It was very late by the time he remembered he wasn't a coyote and that he had a woman waiting for him at home. He also didn't know how to get rid of the animal now that he had him. He knew coyotes weren't suitable pets. They *ate* people's pets.

But he couldn't bring himself to send the impulse that would drive it away, so he let it trot at his heels. There were no animals on the farm, he reasoned. Except the kittens, and he wouldn't let the thing come into the house. But how to explain it—

It hit him then. This was a good thing, a way to show her, without starting at the *forget it, I'm not listening, you're crazy* mile marker. Normal guys didn't go out for a run and come home with a coyote.

He stopped as they reached the yard. The lights were on, at least, and her car was still in the drive. That reassured him until he realized she couldn't leave. Not when it meant abandoning the kittens, her home was a mess, and the clinic was still wrecked. Basically she *had* to stay, which sapped his pleasure in finding her there.

The coyote whined, sensing his mood, and he sent a wave of reassurance, natural as breathing. A question flowed back to him—not words so much as a sense of *what're we doing here?*

"Taking a leap," he said aloud. And then he called, "Neva!"

The cry echoed louder than he expected and the animal beside him cringed. Standing here beside him went against all its instincts. It had seen its family killed for venturing too close to someone else's farm. Zeke aimed another wave of warmth at it. *Don't run off just yet. I need you.* The coyote stood before the porch for long minutes, tense as a yard dog straining at its chain.

Finally she peeked out the front door. The hall light showed she was wearing one of his shirts and a pair of fuzzy pink slippers. She couldn't be too mad at him if she'd gone rummaging through his clothes. He didn't know why women did that, only how much he liked it.

"Are you drunk?"

"No."

"Did you bring home a dog?" She stepped out onto the porch. Then she took a closer look and seemed to realize what was standing in their yard. "Zeke, what did you do?"

He wouldn't get a better lead. "Not what did I do. What *can* I do?"

"I don't understand."

He turned to the coyote, knelt down, and stared into its eyes, making it understand the importance of this. Then he sent the idea of pack, of safety and belonging, wrapped up in this female. The creature seemed none too convinced at first, cocking its head doubtfully. When he set his hand on its head, it yielded with a whine.

The animal slunk toward Neva, reluctantly overcoming its own nature because he begged it to. It lay down at her feet, trembling all the way. She bent, probably to check it for injuries, but she'd find it whole. Just terrified. Waves of it came off the creature and he felt bad for subjecting it to this.

"It acts like you're influencing its behavior," she said unsteadily.

"Exactly. Gonna let it go."

Go on now. Thanks, little brother. The coyote leapt to its feet and sprinted for the woods. The lure of freedom was far stronger than the whispers of pack he'd offered before, especially when coupled with a known threat. Neva wasn't like him. Her kind hunted theirs.

Her bewilderment was obvious. He took her arm and drew her back into the house. She was cold. Once he'd shut the door, he headed for the kitchen to make some hot chocolate. He'd noticed that she ordered it pretty often at Armando's. The chore also gave her time to process. He put the pan on the stove and added cocoa and sugar. By the time he'd finished making the drink, she looked less shocked. He poured the hot chocolate into two mugs and set hers on the table. She seemed thoughtful more than anything.

"Was that a longtime pet of yours?"

"No."

A shuddering sigh escaped her. "Then you must have a story to tell."

"Yep." He paused, trying to think how to put it. It was impossible to look her in the face and see her loss of faith, so he busied himself at the sink. "Got . . . taken. Dunno by who or why. Spent six months locked up while they . . . did things to me."

Her breath caught. "What things?"

"Bad." He didn't want to talk about it. But he had to. "Got out, along with some other folks. Six of us. But we were all . . . different when we left."

There was no way she'd believe this, despite the coyote. How *could* she? He curled his hands into fists and leaned against the sink.

"Different, as in you have an affinity for animals," she said softly.

God, he didn't dare hope. He didn't turn. It would kill him to see everything change between him, but how the hell could he expect her to accept this? He rubbed a hand over his chest, trying to soothe the pain building inside.

"Yeah."

"That's why you know what's wrong with half my patients before I examine them." She didn't sound surprised.

"Yeah."

"Zeke, look at me."

Taking a deep breath, he did.

"I believe you." She felt slightly insane for saying those words, but hadn't she already known he was different? His strength, his hearing, his instincts around animals, his sense of smell all bore out the story.

And everyone knew he'd disappeared for months and nobody knew why. The part about him being locked up and people experimenting on him—that was the toughest to swallow. But how else to explain the unusual things he could do?

The way he knew things he couldn't possibly know. Like the
dead girl in the trunk. If he had senses keen as a coyote, he
might honestly have smelled the whispers of decomposition
carried on the wind. Just as he'd claimed.

"Really?" He took a step back, bracing a hand on the counter behind him, as if he hadn't expected that, and relief left
him weak.

Or maybe she was reading too much into his reaction
because she *wanted* him to care.

"Do you know their names? Maybe we could figure out
what y'all had in common? Why they took you there?"

Anger flashed in his face, supplanting relief. "*No.* Soon as
we got out of there, we ran. For our lives. Didn't care why. Just
wanted to be free." He paced, his strides tight like the kitchen
caged him.

"Are you worried they'll find you again?"

The question hit him like a lash, and she was sorry she'd
asked when she saw him flinch. His throat worked for a few
seconds before he choked out a single word: "Yes."

This was so far beyond anything she'd ever dealt with—
Neva tried to ask logical questions, but maybe that wasn't
what he needed. "Have you thought about leaving Harper
Creek, so they can't?"

His blue eyes showed bleak, like a storm-tossed sea lashing an empty coastline. More secrets lurked there, toothed
and threatening, like the broken mast of an ancient, sunken
ship. "And go where? Do what?"

God, she didn't like seeing him so hopeless. "I don't know.
Sometimes I've considered taking off myself."

He mustered a hint of swagger, a smile curling the edges of
his well-shaped mouth. Her gaze lingered on the pretty divot.
So kissable. Lord help her, he was, even in pain, like this.
Maybe especially in pain, because she was, by nature, a fixer,
and wanted to kiss him better.

"Asking me to run away with you, Dr. Harper?"

She smiled back. "Maybe. Let's keep the option open for
the moment. But I'm here for you and I'm trying to understand
what you went through. I'm . . . having a hard time with it."

Zeke gave a jerky nod, as if it were nothing more than he'd expected. "Think I'm a freak?"

"I already knew you were special," she said slowly. "I just didn't know why."

"Look." To her surprise, he skinned out of his jeans, leaving him clad in a pair of boxers and his T-shirt. But she didn't think this was sexual, despite her attention to his mouth. "Closer."

Obediently, she knelt as he worked the leg up and lifted his testicles away from his inner thigh, soft skin, tender and sensitive. Or it should've been. Zeke was covered in tiny pin-prick scars, a whole network of them. Needles. Repeatedly, and over time. She knew he risked everything by showing her this. Someone else might take this for a junkie's secret shooting site, well concealed from anyone looking for signs of his habit. But this wasn't a good place for self-administered drugs. Most junkies used the arms or the femoral in the thigh. A few who had blown their veins used the feet, or even the penis, but never here. Zeke fit his underwear back into place, once he saw she'd gotten a good look. Now he wore a defiant expression, daring her to judge him.

"It wasn't your fault," she said softly. "Someone did this to you. Medical research, maybe? But it wasn't your fault. I'm surprised you let me . . . you know."

"Not scared of you." Wild and wary he might be, but she believed him. He let her touch him when he flinched away from everyone else. For whatever reason, he'd dubbed her worthy of skin privileges.

"What were they like? The others."

He shrugged, halfway into pulling up his jeans. "Didn't know 'em. Was in my cell, watching the light flicker, or in the big room, getting shocked and jabbed."

"I'm so sorry." It killed her to hear it, made her hands furl into impotent fists. She wanted to hurt someone on his behalf, but there were no faces or names. Just anonymous evil.

Neva had heard rumors that companies snatched the homeless off the streets for product testing and then dumped them back once they'd served their purpose. Many of them sickened and died and nobody cared. It broke her heart to think something similar might've been done to Zeke. Instead of his inexplicable Doctor Doolittling, he might've come back with a fatal illness. The very idea rocked her.

He took a couple of steps and folded her into his arms. She could smell the night wind on him and an echo of the forest: pine and hickory and a whisper of cool wildness, nothing that could ever be bottled. It lingered, and she breathed him in, turning her cheek against his chest.

"One girl had red hair," he said, low. "She could heal people. Of anything. Tall guy had electricity in his hands. He busted us all out. Black-haired lady . . . don't know about her. And a blond woman . . . I remember them saying she could walk in people's dreams. Touch 'em. Change 'em."

"Counting you, that's only five."

"Giant. Bald. Silas," Zeke added, as if the name was a revelation to him, too. "Called him a failure but kept him locked up down there, too. Made him work."

There was no doubt in her. Something terrible had been done to him. Neva didn't know why he trusted her with it, but she'd deal.

"You did smell that girl, didn't you?"

His hands moved on her back: long, measured strokes, as if she were the one who needed comforting. "Yeah. Can hear stuff I'm not supposed to, too."

Her cheeks heated, remembering the nights she'd masturbated, thinking about him. Maybe she'd even whimpered his name, softly, behind the closed door. His sober expression melted into a heart-stopping grin. Nobody else ever saw this look, she realized. He saved it for her, and only when they were alone. The rest of the time, he offered the world a wounded wariness, like he was waiting for the next blow to land.

"Oh God, you *knew.*"

He nodded. "Changed everything."

"But you're okay with it? I mean, you do want this? Us?"

She hated the thought she might've pushed before he was ready. Maybe impulse had overcome him. If he was more in touch with his animal nature, he might not be able to resist temptation, no matter his emotional state. Might be that any warm body would do.

"Want you more than I want to live," he said quietly.

He couldn't mean that. Only she recognized the fervent sincerity in his stormy blue eyes. But it also hinted at darkness and desperation she hadn't known he hid. Given what he'd gone through, then he might be damaged irrevocably. Beyond repair. A voice of self-preservation wondered if she wasn't in over her head. How could he possibly be ready for a relationship? She needed to back away and suggest counseling, before she got in too deep.

"Right." He took a step back, pushing her away from him. "Knew it was too good to be true. Figured we'd end up here. S'fine for you to go. I get it."

"What—" And then she knew. "You can read my moods. How?"

"Dunno."

He thought she was leaving him, so there was no point in talking more or explaining anything. That was so not fair. She hadn't spoken her worries out loud; that meant he had no right to them. Anger sparked to life, edging out the uncertainty.

"This is a lot to absorb," she snapped. "Don't you see that? I'm trying to parse everything."

His voice came bitter and low. "Why? What's the point?"

"Fine. I can't make you talk to me. But I guess you don't care as much as I thought you did." Her heart ached. She didn't want to argue, but she didn't know how to shake him out of this terrible resignation, either.

"Challenging me?" he demanded.

Some dark emotion sparked to life, animating his face, a blend of possession and desire she'd never seen. His hands curled into fists at his sides, his breath coming in ragged rasps. Need rolled off him in white-hot waves. Even without any special abilities, she read his leashed longing; he wanted to settle the dispute in the most primitive of ways.

"Zeke . . ." Neva didn't even know what she was going to say.

She wet her lips with her tongue. He seemed more imposing now, shoulders straight. Despite herself, her gaze went to
his groin. His cock strained against the zipper of his jeans,
telling her what he intended if she didn't start running. Or
maybe that would just make it worse. Maybe he'd like it better
if she ran.

A pulse of uncomfortable arousal surged through her. A
modern woman shouldn't admit that it turned her on, thinking about being chased by her man, and pinned down beneath
him. But she liked that idea as much as she'd enjoyed having
him helpless and yearning beneath her.

"If you're going, you should go," he growled. "I can keep it
together for another minute or two."

Complete sentences. But the snappish way he bit them off
revealed the depth of his strain. Part of her wanted to flee. But
the rest of her wanted to see what would happen if she stayed.

"Take me," she whispered.

A shudder rolled through him. He pounced on her. That
was the only word for it. In one graceful leap he had her in
his arms. He ripped his own shirt off her back, tore the fabric
with his hands. A low growl escaped him as he buried his face
in the curve of her neck. This time he used his teeth on her,
not hard enough to break the skin, but fierce animal nips that
made her want to fall back and give him her throat.

Zeke ran his hands down her back and cupped her bottom in his hands, drawing her up against his burning erection.
He was so hard it almost hurt when he ground against her.
She whimpered as her core went molten for him. He tore his
own clothes off and they fell onto the kitchen floor as if the
ruined clothes made up their nest, reinforcing her sense that
he wasn't in control.

He pushed her down onto the fabric, demanding her sub-
mission. His silence, coupled with his intensity, ratcheted her
own arousal up to flash-fire levels. Neva didn't think he had
any words left; he'd forgotten them for the moment. With
brute strength, he rolled her onto her stomach and pulled her
hips up.

Oh God, like this?

He entered her in one fierce thrust. Hard. Fast. His hands hurt a little, but it was a pain that made her lift up higher to push back against him. Her field of vision went white with the pleasure sparking through her. His low grunts of pleasure woke an answering atavistic need in her. Nothing mattered, nothing but this.

Zeke ran his hands over her as he moved, possessive hands cupping her breasts and playing with her nipples. They skimmed down her belly and stroked between her legs, not expert but inexorable. The demand drove her higher, and she writhed, glorying in the feel of him filling her up.

Hot. Hard. Hers.

Their bodies made a sweet liquid sound as they strained together. And then, just as suddenly as he'd claimed her, he stopped, though it drew a powerful, anguished groan from him. Her whole body protested. He slid out of her and rolled away onto his back. His cock shone with her juices, still jerking with deferred pleasure. He was a raw, beautiful sight and her whole body protested his loss.

"What's wrong?"

"Can't," he snarled. "Remembered, just before . . ."

Shit. Still no protection. That had been stupid and reckless of them. She should be grateful he hadn't gone off inside her, but the lizard brain just wanted to climb on top of him and finish the job before she died of frustration.

"This, then. We can do this."

She did crawl on top of him and framed his thighs with her own. Once before she'd done this, and she had secretly wanted to come all over his leg right then, marking him with her scent. Zeke should appreciate that urge, more than she'd first realized. He set his hands on her waist as if to pull her away, and then he seemed to realize what she intended. So instead he wrapped his arms around her.

Neva lay down on him at an angle, her belly warm against his cock. He was slick from her body, and slipped against her as she circled her hips against his hard thigh. At this rate it wouldn't take much; she just needed to get enough pressure on her clit. Tremors ran through her as the pleasure built. His

muscles tensed beneath her, and he raised his leg to give her
better purchase. She raised her head in arching her back to
find him staring at her with a dazed hunger.

"Come," he demanded.

She bore down, rubbing her belly against his iron-hard
erection. "You, too."

He drew her up a little higher so that her pussy hit his hip,
as close to his cock as she could be without taking him inside.
He wanted it so bad he shook beneath her, rubbing against
the side of her thigh in sweet, helpless friction. He hunched
upward faster and faster, the quick motions telling her he was
close.

Neva came in a cascade of heat. Moaning, she swept a hand
beneath and wet her fingers, riding them as she flicked her clit
to another orgasm. Then she eased it outward and encircled
his throbbing shaft. Squeezed.

"Mine," she whispered. "I marked you. You smell like me."

He gave a possessive growl and went with a raw groan,
spurting hot from her hand all over her thigh. As if he couldn't
help himself, his hands slid down and stroked it into her skin.
Making her smell like him. It would linger too. Maybe not for
anyone else, but his heightened senses would always detect it.

"Christ." His head fell back onto the floor.

A devil took hold of her then. Instead of letting him pull
her into his arms, as he clearly intended, she nuzzled a path
down his body and studied his softening sex. His penis gave
a halfhearted jerk when she put her face near, but it didn't
have the resolve again so soon. That wasn't what she wanted
anyway.

"I want to taste us," she breathed.

He groaned as she licked, dainty, delicate licks that sam-
pled their flavor. His and hers, and oh, it was good. Arousal
whispered through her as if she could come again but she
damped it down. This was something else, tenderness and care
she sensed he'd never known. His hands threaded through her
hair, still unsteady as aftershocks rippled through him.

By the time she finished, he was half hard again, but the
initial insanity had passed. She let him pull her up and into

his embrace. Neva nestled her head on his chest and listened to his heart. The kitchen floor had to be hurting his back, but he didn't complain.

"What was that?" he asked.

A smile started at the bottom of her and worked its way up. She felt fearless and joyous and perfectly desirable. There would never be another man who fit her better, even with his strangeness. She went for it.

"Love."

His breath rushed out like she'd hit him. "That mean what I think it does?"

"Yeah. I love you." It felt good to say it, like she could stop being afraid.

"Glad you're not just using me for my body."

"Oh."

Not the reaction she'd hoped for. But maybe it was too soon. Maybe she'd let endorphins from spectacular sex push her toward a precipitous declaration. She started to roll away, but he held her fast and tilted her face to his.

"Never had a woman say that to me before," he said, eyes intent on hers. "Never said it to anybody myself, either. So not sure I even know what it is. But you make me feel like I did when I was small and Ma would have one of her spells and there'd be no supper that night: cold, hungry, and empty. Only with you there's this hope I won't always be, like you could be the light to warm me."

It was, without a doubt, the longest speech she'd ever heard from him. And those words told her so much about him, maybe more than he'd meant for her to know. She melted.

"It's okay. You don't have to say it until you're sure."

He shook his head, blue eyes brimming with desperate sweetness. "Still don't get it. Been loving a dream of you since I was sixteen. Can't believe this is real. You're here, saying these things to me, and I'm scared if I say it, too, I'll find I never did get away from that place. 'Cos you're just too good to be true."

Nobody had ever, *ever* felt that way about her. They might want something from her or want to use her, but not this.

Never this. Neva wanted to laugh and cry at the same time and ask him what he meant about loving her so long. Only the words wouldn't come past the tears streaming down her face.

"Oh, *hey*," he protested. "Don't, sweet girl. Please don't."

"I'm fine. Don't worry."

"Can tell that just by looking." His dry tone summoned a watery smile. "Shower?"

She became aware they were still on the kitchen floor on the pile of destroyed clothes. The kittens would need to eat soon, and she felt like she could, too. Once he'd stormed out, she hadn't wanted much dinner. With his uncanny strength, he brought them both to their feet in one motion.

"Sounds good."

CHAPTER 15

Monday was a bitch. No wonder people hated them, Zeke thought. He wasn't ready to return to the real world. He feared he couldn't be part of *her* real world, only a shadow on its fringes. They had gone to bed together, but after the wildness in the kitchen, he had just been content to hold her.

Zeke didn't wholly understand why she hadn't left. He'd come to realize he didn't always understand her motives, even though he could scent her moods. Now they were at the clinic, much to his regret.

Cleanup took all day.

At midday he ran out to Tom's Diner because Neva wanted pie, and Armando's only had cookies for dessert. While she took his carryout order, Emmylou didn't flirt with him, which meant the whole town knew who he was sleeping with. The thought actually put a smile on his face.

After Emmylou handed him the plastic sack full of food, he turned and nearly smacked into his cousin Wil. He didn't see Jeff, or his uncle Lew; Zeke felt grateful for small favors.

Talking to them offered as much fun as a brick upside the head.

The other man looked like his dad, the same bitterness, only with Wil it came from frustration, not loss. "Guess you're too good for us, now that you're tapping that Harper ass. How is she, cuz? Does she like it hard and dirty?"

His hand lashed out, and his cousin hit the floor, before he had any idea he meant to attack. The beast in his head wanted Wil dead. Zeke planted a foot on his chest and wrestled with the urge to do worse. Everyone in the diner was staring; he could feel the eyes on him. Not even a whisper broke the stillness.

"Don't talk about her," he growled. "Mean it."

With that he stepped over Wil and headed for the door. Rage washed over him in red waves. He wanted to go back and finish the job, beat Wil Noble into paste. But if he didn't leave, someone would call the sheriff. He didn't want to end the day in a holding cell. As he opened the door, conversation resumed.

"You think he's crazy like his ma?" a man asked.

Mrs. Gillespie answered tartly, "You heard what Wil said about Ms. Harper. I wish more men demanded respect for their women like that."

Huh. He'd never have guessed the old biddy would defend him. She had seemed so shocked when she saw him and Neva in here eating dinner together. Of course, that had been before there was anything to it, at least on her part. He couldn't remember a time when he hadn't wanted her, though he'd learned to ignore the feeling and pretend it didn't exist.

"That's what you get when you run around with white trash," someone else said. "People fighting over you in public."

Vaguely shamed, Zeke let the door close behind him and strode toward the car. He swung into it and drove back to the clinic, still wrestling with his discomfort; he would probably never feel at ease behind the wheel. He hoped Neva wouldn't get word about this. She had enough on her plate.

He hated seeing her sad, and she was, the entire time they were at the clinic. Getting rid of the broken glass wasn't enough; they couldn't reopen until she received all new supplies, including a new computer. He could tell she was worried. They ate lunch without talking much.

To make matters worse, Reed showed up, looking bewildered and sympathetic. "What the hell happened here? Is there anything I can do?"

Neva stopped what she was doing to talk to him. She stepped over the broken computer and met him at the front door. "Not really. It's kind of you to ask." Polite words, blank face.

But looking at them together, he couldn't help but wonder if the other man had ever touched her. He imagined them together, Reed's hands on her soft skin. A growl began low inside him.

"You've had a lot of trouble lately." Reed frowned. "You might want to consider the possibility you have an enemy."

She laughed. "Sure. Wait, I bet I know who's behind all this. Connie Lacrosse hated me in fourth grade because Derek Jansen gave me his extra Twinkie. She does know how to hold a grudge."

"What has to happen before you take this seriously?" Reed demanded.

That sobered her up fast. "I do. I just don't need you in my business. Go help my father, why don't you?"

"That's actually why I came by."

Zeke read her surprise. "What's up?"

"He doesn't want you to know, but he's heading to Birmingham tomorrow to have some tests run. I thought maybe you might want to go see him."

"What kind of tests?"

Reed shook his head. "I've said too much already. I really think you just need to go see him. If there's nothing I can do, I guess I'll get back to the mill."

This guy had her family's seal of approval; that bothered him more than he'd admit. Zeke watched until Reed left his territory, climbed into his overpriced car, and drove away. Then he turned to her.

"Need to go?"

She shook her head. "We're going to dinner on Sunday. Even if it's bad news, it'll surely keep until then."

He froze. Surely she couldn't mean that like it sounded. "We?"

Now *she* seemed unsure. "Well . . . yeah. I want you to go. I'll feel better if you're there."

Put that way, he couldn't refuse, even though the idea made him ill. Zeke Noble, as a guest at the Harper dinner table? Her parents would eat him alive. But it didn't matter what he felt; only what she did. If she needed him, he'd be there. It seemed so unlikely she could need him for anything.

"Sure," he promised.

"I think we've done all we can today. Now we just have to wait for supplies."

For the next few days, Neva saw emergency patients at the farm; people drove out there without complaint, and she also made a few farm calls. Julie proved herself a good friend, offering hugs and support instead of asking about her paycheck. She was taking a week's unpaid vacation, so Neva didn't have to fret about her, at least. Zeke was glad about that.

"Seriously, don't worry about it," Julie said, just before she left. "Travis makes good money."

He knew it wasn't that Julie didn't want to help, only that Neva would feel compelled to pay her if she did. And it was going to be hard enough for her to rebound from this—he only wished he could do more.

That night, he tried not to obsess over the looming dinner with her parents. Sunday. Three days away. They were in the kitchen, cooking together, when he heard a car slowing as it approached his drive. She hadn't noticed it yet, wouldn't until it turned down and got about halfway to the house.

"You expecting a patient?" he asked.

She shook her head. "Why?"

"Company's on the way."

Neva went to the window and two minutes later, headlights appeared, as he'd predicted. She no longer showed any surprise. Instead dismay flashed on her face.

"That's my mother's car."

Zeke swallowed a cuss word. "Guess she wants to see what you're up to."

"You think?" She offered a wry smile.

He let her get the door while he pulled the roast out of the oven. The house smelled delicious. Peeling back the foil revealed perfection. If her mother wasn't here, he would be setting the table and calling her to join him, maybe kissing the nape of her neck as she sat down.

"Hello, Geneva." The frosty tone reached him easily. Might have anyway, even if his hearing didn't permit him to listen to the mice running around the barn.

"Mother."

"I can't believe you made me track you down like this."

"Excuse me?"

"Ben told me he came to see you and you still haven't visited your father. He left today."

Tension laced her voice. "If this is another guilt trip to get me to come home, then can we please just skip it? I've had a long day.

That did it. This was his house, and he wasn't having anybody hassle her in his territory. He came into the doorway, and he leaned against the wall as if he didn't know what was going on.

"Zeke Noble." He didn't extend a hand because Lillian Harper wasn't like to exchange such courtesies with him anyway. "You staying for dinner?"

To his surprise, Neva's mom swept him up and down with a thorough look. It was almost uncomfortable. "Aha. I see what's keeping you busy these days. I heard the rumors, of course, but I didn't know if they were accurate."

Could that be a smile tugging at the corners of her mouth? Since her face had been worked on so much to preserve her beauty, she didn't show much expression. So he couldn't be sure. Neva seemed equally stunned.

"How long have the two of you been . . . involved?" Mrs. Harper asked. "Is he why you keep turning Ben down?"

Pain twisted Neva's expression, mixed with embarrassment. "Not at first. Ben and me, it's never going to happen. But yes, now Zeke would be why."

God, how he loved hearing that—and she'd claimed him before her mother, of all people. He felt like he could do anything, as long as she believed in him.

"Can we talk on Sunday?" Neva asked tiredly.

"Of course. And I'm sure Ben understands that you need to sow some oats, darling. We all had our . . ." Lillian's gaze raked him up and down once more. "Wild days. Before settling down. But my dear, one does not marry the help."

Her words hit him like a fist in his stomach. Good enough to fuck. Not good enough for anything else. Maybe it was because he secretly shared her opinion, but nothing had hurt so much in a long time. Not since he'd come home, anyway. Pain had been a regular part of the experiments.

Mrs. Harper let herself out. She hadn't ever spoken directly to him, as if he were too dumb to understand her words. And hell, maybe she was right. Fuck, he couldn't even read, little better than a trained monkey. He felt sick at the idea Neva might be using him for sex too dirty to get anywhere else. She'd said she loved him once, but she never said it again. He was afraid to believe she meant it, because if she didn't, if it had been a sex-fueled impulse, then he would die. Better not to ask about her feelings when he could barely manage his own.

"Zeke, no." Neva ran to him and took his hands in hers. "She doesn't know anything about me. Please, please don't look like that."

He sighed. "And you want me to go to dinner with you. Gonna be fun."

"If Luke was here, everything would be better. You'd like him, I know it." She laid her head on his chest and he put his arms around her, mostly because he didn't know how *not* to. It was impossible for him to have her within arm's length and not to touch her. But he didn't let himself swell with the need that always wracked him when she was near. Not this time. "He always distracted Mom and Dad, kept them off my back. He didn't mind being perfect so I didn't have to be."

"As far as you know." As soon as the words were out, he regretted them.

Her stricken look cut him to the core, but it was too late; she'd worked it out. "I never once thought of that. He might've hated it just as much as I did, but he did it anyway. For *me*. Do you think that's why he left?"

Desperate hope shone in her eyes. She wanted to believe her brother had simply had enough, run away and changed his name. That would be better than thinking he lay dead in an unmarked grave or had gone unclaimed in a city morgue somewhere.

Zeke shrugged. He couldn't lie to her. Maybe somebody else could—and if she wanted that, she should go find him. He wasn't that guy.

"Supper?" he asked, changing the subject instead.

Her shoulders slumped. She felt his distance and it hurt her, but he couldn't help it. He needed to pull back some before he gave her everything. The past few nights, she'd slept alone in her bed, and he wasn't sure enough to ask her to come to him. He'd decided she needed space. Fair enough, so did he. He didn't know what to call what they were doing together. Zeke knew he wasn't a catch; he wasn't datable. Still, he couldn't help hoping for happiness.

In town, on Monday, he'd bought condoms, expecting to need them. But she had been quiet and withdrawn after they got back from the clinic, and it seemed wrong to expect sex just because they'd fooled around a couple of times. So he'd put them in his dresser and tried to pretend they weren't there.

Now he just felt raw from being hit by the truck Neva called her mother. He wanted to have supper, hold the kittens, and listen to music. And not feel anything at all.

"Yeah," she said sadly, stepping away from him. "Let's eat."

She'd done something wrong. Problem was, Neva didn't know what, and she feared if she brought it up, they'd get into an if-you-don't-know-then-I'm-not-telling-you type of discussion. Not that she thought Zeke would come out and say that. She suspected he'd just leave instead; he wasn't much for talking. Sometimes she didn't mind; other times, she found it frustrating.

Fortunately, she had work to keep her busy. Replacement supplies arrived, though she had to completely tap her meager savings to get everything she needed. Other stuff she ordered on credit with her suppliers. It would be a tight couple of months, but by Friday, she had the clinic open for business again.

People had put off their nonemergency pet-care needs while she sorted things out, but today, after realizing she was back in business, they buried her. A clinic forty-five minutes away offered the only alternative, and people didn't want to spend half the day trying to get their dog vaccinated.

Julie showed up for work, unexpectedly, half an hour after she opened. "How come you didn't call me?"

"How'd you know to come in?" she countered.

"You have to ask? Emmylou got her morning coffee at Armando's." She tilted her head toward the café. "And texted me."

She laughed. "No secrets in this town. She doesn't like the brew down at the diner?"

Julie grinned. "She likes the guy who works the counter here in the morning. Which is also how I know you've been keeping company with our new hire. I thought you said you were only staying with him because of the kittens."

A hot flush stained her cheeks. "Well—"

"Oh, my God, tell me!"

Thankfully, her first patient arrived, so she snatched the file and retreated to the exam room. Julie gave her pointed, mock-threatening looks throughout the day. By early afternoon, she was tired of dodging, but the nonstop appointments kept her from thinking, at least.

When Zeke arrived, she quelled the longing to kiss him hello and claim him. She didn't like the way Connie Lacrosse eyed him. But Neva had to admit, he looked fine, the way his lean muscles rippled beneath his shirt. Even when he worked outside, he didn't bother with a jacket, another sign he wasn't like other men. Between patients, she managed to take care of the kittens; they each walked around with one of them tucked into their shirts.

Around three, the squeal of brakes signaled a delivery, but Zeke would handle it. As she finished up with Tiff, she gave the cat a soothing stroke and said to her owner, "Here's your invoice. Take it to Julie, check out, and you'll be all set."

She had a ten-minute break, since that appointment hadn't taken as long as anticipated, so she went into her office to record her observations of Tiff's annual checkup. Instead of going straight to Julie, Connie paused where Zeke was stocking the food storage closet. They sold expensive brands of specially formulated pet food; enough people bought it to be worth the space.

"Are you new?" Connie asked, a smile in her voice.

"Been working here awhile."

That's right. His two-week trial had passed long ago, and neither of them had even noticed. She felt a bit bad about that, but it wasn't like she'd promised him a raise or anything. Neva eavesdropped, no longer even pretending to work on the cat's chart.

"Do you like it?"

"Well enough." She heard the shrug and could picture his expression. Funny how well she already knew him. Connie would be frustrated by the lack of give and take.

Apparently the woman liked what she saw enough to go for it. "That's good. Anyway, I was wondering if you'd like to go out sometime."

"A date?"

Neva froze. She'd expected a flat no from him. She curled her hands into fists and laid them on her desk, not wanting to hear the rest of this conversation, but she didn't have a choice, now.

"Yeah. There's a steakhouse—"

"Sorry." He cut her off. "Seeing someone. But thanks for asking."

Her whole body relaxed, and she let out a breath she hadn't realized she was holding. *So polite.* Maybe he'd just wanted to be sure it wasn't a platonic invitation before turning Connie down. She ducked her head and she went back to scribbling on the cat's file.

"Oh." Disappointment colored the word, but Connie rallied. "Well, let me know if it doesn't work out."

A minute later, Zeke tapped on her open door. Neva glanced up as if she'd just become aware of him, but by his expression, he wasn't buying it. A smile played at the corners of his mouth, and he stepped into her office without awaiting permission.

"Worried I was gonna say yes, huh?"

What the hell? She tried to deny it. "I don't know what you mean."

"Can hear every move you make." With a half smile he quoted The Police.

Crap. She'd forgotten about that. He knew all kinds of things she wished he didn't. Neva frowned at him and lowered her head. She'd worn her hair down today, so her hair fell into her face, providing a welcome screen from his too sharp gaze.

"You haven't made any promises," she said.

Or even told me you share my feelings. Uncertainty flooded her. The click of the door brought her gaze up, and she found him perched on the edge of her desk. His ability to move so quietly sent a chill through her. She could think of any number of frightening uses for that skill. *Trust. You* trust *him, remember?*

"True. Want some?" If his tone had been anything less than serious, if his expression had not been grave and sincere, she might've brushed the question aside and called it a joke—not a nice one.

"Maybe it's too soon to be speaking of them. But I *would* like to know if you plan on seeing other people."

"No." He set his palm against her cheek, long fingers curving beneath her ear.

Pleasure purled through her and she resisted the impulse to rub herself against his hand like a cat. "Things have been . . . different between us since my mother came. Can we talk about it tonight?"

Zeke nodded. "Probably should."

He swooped down and planted a possessive kiss on her mouth, just enough to leave her tingling and wanting more. But they both had work to do.

The day went quickly after that, and she was dead tired by the time they locked the front doors. Julie had gone home an hour before; Neva finished before Zeke for once, but it didn't take long for him to wrap up. He met her at the back door, kitten box in hand.

She drove without asking if he wanted to. Maybe nobody else would notice, but she paid attention to his reactions; he hated being behind the wheel of a car. Now she suspected that was the reason he preferred to run everywhere. Not only did it offer a nice workout, it also saved him from driving.

They passed the ride in silence. He'd left the parlor lights on at the farm, so the windows showed golden, comforting against the dark. She liked feeling like she had a real home again, though she knew, of course, she couldn't just move in an a temporary arrangement and then just   stay. People didn't make life-altering decisions like that.

Zeke bounded out of the car, box in hand, and jogged around to her side to open the car door. Funny. He hadn't always done that, just since that first morning they'd hooked up. The difference in how he treated his boss versus his lover delighted her. Not that they'd done much loving lately. He unlocked the front door and she preceded him into the house.

"Thanks."

He inclined his head. "Gonna heat the chicken casserole."

The kittens were hungry, so Neva fed them before doing anything else. Julie had pitched in during the afternoon, freeing her to see patients, but she was glad to get back to them. These little guys had beaten the odds, and with each passing day, they got a bit stronger. In a few more weeks, she could wean and transition them to soft food mixed with formula. She would be grateful when they could use the cat box; they could go to the bathroom on their own now, but orphaned kittens tended to run a little behind on litter training. *Only another week or so,* she told herself. Once they'd eaten and gone to the bathroom and she cleaned up, she tucked two kittens into her shirt. They were soft and furry with tiny claws raking at her skin. Zeke took the other little guy.

They carried plates of leftovers on the stove and ate in the parlor. Amazing how little they spoke, but she felt comfortable; it wasn't an awkward I-wish-I-could-think-of-something-to-say silence, but a we'll-talk-when-it's-important feeling.

And now it was time to get down to it.

Zeke sat down at the far end of the couch. He couldn't touch her and say what he needed to. Nothing had ever scared him so much.

"Did this all backward," he said without looking at her. "Working together, living together, then—" He made the gesture that she seemed to understand meant *fooling around*. "Never did it . . . right. No dates. No normal stuff. And I don't want to feel like I'm somebody you need to hide."

"How could you imagine I'm ashamed of you? I asked you to come with me to dinner this weekend."

"Maybe just to piss off your mother."

"You think *that's* why? No wonder you've been distant," she said coldly. "I wouldn't want anything to do with someone I thought was using me, either."

Shit. He was fucking this all up as he'd known he would. Which was why he'd been avoiding the conversation, only things were getting worse between them, and not better. Another inch and she'd be out the door. That wasn't what he wanted.

"*No.*" He fought for the right words. If she were an animal, he could share what he felt without needing the words. Helplessly, he tried, and the kittens cried plaintively. "Just want to feel like I'm good enough for you. That's all."

He chanced a look at her, and she'd thawed a little. "I think you are. Maybe the problem is that *you* don't. And that's not something I can help."

Those words hit him like a punch in the chest. He hadn't been fair. She'd never once hinted he wasn't enough. He just thought she deserved better because he knew what he had to offer: this farm, manual labor, and precious little else.

"I'm happy with you," she went on, more gently. "At home for the first time in years. But I feel like I'm more invested in this than you are. And that scares me."

God, she was fearless with her brown eyes and firm chin lifted at an angle that dared him to clip her on it. It wasn't true, of course. He was hers. Zeke just hadn't wanted to admit it, for fear she'd realize he was nothing special and leave, just as soon as she figured it out. But if he didn't tell her, that made him a coward.

He put the words together slowly, like a complicated jigsaw puzzle. "Would do anything for you. Too soon to say it and maybe too soon to feel it." Zeke shaped the last sentence with care, so she understood its importance. "It's not that you matter less to me . . . it's that I . . . care so much I don't have the words."

Love didn't encompass it. She was every bright and beautiful thing in his world, but she'd once seemed as untouchable as the moon. In some ways, it was a tough adjustment. Not bad, just different, allowing himself to picture a future that put her beside him. He didn't know how to lose the fear that admitting his feelings would draw down some terrible curse. It wasn't logical, but he'd already lost the ability to read. He also feared as time went on, he'd lose even more of his mind. Would she still want him when he could only lift heavy things for her, grunt, and hump?

That was why the idea of jumping with both feet and accepting they could be together terrified him. If he could barely tell her how he felt about her, how could he tell her *that*? Neva studied him, as if trying to read him like he could the kittens and the coyote. God, how he wished it could be so easy.

"So you're good enough," she said in summation. "And I'm not using you. That established, what do you want, Zeke?"

"Want everyone to know you're mine." The answer slipped out before he'd even formed it in his mind: her parents, their friends, his family, and especially that fucking Ben Reed. If the guy came sniffing around again—well, he'd been polite the first couple of times; he didn't have any more patience to spare.

She surprised him by nodding. "Me, too. I didn't like it when Connie was prowling around you. Most relationships start light, but I don't think I can do that with you. It's too hard."

He couldn't have said it better himself. Zeke nodded, relieved he didn't have to say it. Pleasure coursed through him at knowing she felt possessive. He wanted to belong to her. In fact, he already did, but it soothed his hackles knowing she wanted him like that. Soothed him and stirred him at the same time. The raw lust he'd leashed came roaring back.

"Enough talk," he growled.

If she was his, then she was, and he wanted her right now. No more waiting. The kittens, he settled in their box before pouncing on her. Neva wore a look of comical surprise as he snatched her up. Normal men probably didn't do this; he was beyond caring. Beyond her gasp, she didn't protest.

He took the stairs at a run with her dangling over one shoulder. Instead of fighting him, her hands wandered down his back, teasing at the skin above the waistband of his jeans. Oh, she'd pay for that.

Once he got to the bedroom, a ravenous kiss spoke of her eagerness. Her tongue stroked his, teasing, but he didn't let her take control. *She had her chance. Now it's my turn.* And this time he wasn't stopping until she came all over his cock.

Zeke brought her up against him hard, grinding their hips together. With a soft little moan, she softened and let him do it while his lips ravished hers. *Mine. All mine.* She nipped his lower lip and the tender pain drove him higher. His cock throbbed as she moved with him. The layers of clothing only heightened his arousal because he remembered the heat and softness of her skin.

"Can't go slow this first time," he warned her, biting down on her shoulder. "Been missing you in my bed."

The hitch in her voice did things to him. "Then go fast. Please."

And that little *please* broke him. With a snarl he dug into the dresser and got a condom. Neva took it from him and unbuttoned his pants. His cock sprang out, so hard it hurt for her to touch him. A woman had never rolled the latex on him before, and with her head bent to the task, he almost came from the pleasure of it.

With rough hands, he peeled off her scrubs and panties, then backed her against the wall. Even the bed seemed too far; he had to be inside her right now. Still, he had enough mind left to make sure she was ready. He knelt and pressed his face between her legs, breathing her in. Her body was wet but he licked her up and down to be sure. He offered no finesse or gentleness; he just tasted and took.

She loved it.

"Fuck." She shuddered when his mouth brushed her clit, but she wasn't coming. Not yet. Not like that.

Take her. She's all yours.

At last he heeded the beast voice inside him. Zeke straightened and lifted her up, flattening her back against the wall. He tilted her hips and drove forward. Hot. Tight. Perfect. A shudder rocked him.

By her reaction she'd never done this before; her weak, polished men probably couldn't manage it. He held her easily, for once glorying in his strength. Zeke thrust hard and fast while she figured out how to roll her hips against him. Her wetness kissed his pelvis with each inward push. Neva clutched his shoulders, her head falling back as pleasure overwhelmed her.

Her contractions drove him over. His whole body tightened and he urged himself into her over and over, trying to imprint himself on her. *Nobody else for you, ever. Only me. Just mine. Love you. Mine.* The words melted into a kaleidoscope of cascading colors and feelings. He wrapped his arms around her while they both trembled. Tingles spilled through him, lighting him up from base of spine to base of skull. He'd never known anything like it.

At last he stumbled from the wall to the bed with her still in his arms. She rolled off him and disposed of the condom. Not romantic, per se, but sticky and somehow more real. She wasn't afraid to touch him. Not any part of him, and it gave him some hope that maybe she wouldn't be disgusted when she learned his last secret.

"Wow," she breathed, snuggling into his side.

He put his arms around her and buried his face in her hair. If he was like other men, he'd tell her nobody else could ever take her place. He'd tell her she made him feel like a million bucks. Maybe he'd find a way to say everything that mattered. Instead he could only lay with her and listen to her breathe.

Sunday came all too soon. Neva knew Zeke wasn't looking forward to it. Truth be told, neither was she. Her first sign of *how* tense he was about it came when she caught him ironing four hours before they were due at Harper Court. He had a pair of black slacks and he was putting a crease in them with such ferocity she expected the pants to cry uncle.

"You all right?" she asked.

"No." He pulled a face as he hung the slacks on a rack and moved on to his white dress shirt.

Plain clothes, almost painfully simple. Was he worried he'd look like he was wearing a waiter's uniform? She'd never seen him in anything but jeans, sweats, or his bare skin. Neva preferred the latter.

"You're nervous." It wasn't a question.

"Duh." His smile softened the syllable.

She sighed. "I don't blame you. My mother gave you reason to worry. But it won't just be us, if that helps any. My folks don't know the meaning of *intimate family meal*. There will be people my father wants to cultivate and those trying to get something out of him in turn."

"Sounds like fun." His dry tone put a smile on her face.

"I'll stay close, I promise. I won't let her at you again. We'll circulate, minimize your contact with them."

"Make 'em sound like poison oak."

Grinning, she answered, "That's not a bad analogy."

Some of the tension eased out of him. "Don't have many ties. Maybe help me pick the best of the lot?"

"My pleasure."

Yesterday she'd run to her apartment to pick up some more clothes and wound up bringing over a box of other stuff, too, towels and linens mostly. She had a weakness for Egyptian cotton, and there was no point in her expensive sheets going to waste in her hall closet. *It's just a few things,* she'd told herself. *No problem to move back in a few weeks when the kittens are old enough.* Neva didn't let herself think about how much she didn't want to go back; the repairs weren't finished, and by the look of the equipment sitting around, it would be at least another week. *Thank God.* Since they'd painted the place together, the farmhouse had begun to feel like home. She had to stop herself from planning all the little things she'd do to improve the place or how perfectly some of her pictures would brighten up the walls. There was even a place for her TV armoire in the parlor.

Zeke led the way to the bedroom they now shared. Her stuff was still in the other room but she hadn't slept there in two days. In the closet he had a meager assortment of ties. She studied them and then chose a black and purple one. Since he was wearing black and white, he could afford a splashier pattern.

"This is the best."

"Really?" He gave it a dubious glance.

"Trust me."

"I do," he said gravely.

"You can't know how much I need you there."

By his expression, he understood what she meant. Zeke nodded. "Only reason I said yes."

She left him to finish getting ready; he mumbled about needing to shave, and she went to put on her good black dress, the same one she always wore. It wasn't like one looked so different from another, after all. For once, she left her hair down and put on makeup. As she frosted her lids with shadow, outlined her eyes, and painted her mouth, she knew she wasn't doing it for her mother's guests.

Neva wanted Zeke to see her, for once, looking her absolute

best, not in baggy scrubs or with her hair caught up in a tail. She wanted him to see the graceful slope of her shoulders and the way the dress nipped in at her waist and hugged her hips. She wasn't the most beautiful woman in the world, but he made her feel so.

His reaction when she came down the stairs was everything she could've asked. His breath caught, and his stormy eyes went dark with a need she recognized. In answer, it coiled deep in her stomach. Zeke took a step toward her, and then checked himself. The sweetest tension rose between them, an ache that had never been assuaged. She stood in the parlor, breathless at the ferocity.

"Beautiful," he breathed.

And that one word meant more than a barrage of orchestrated flattery. Other men might say it more eloquently, but when Zeke said it, she believed him. Neva spun so he could take in the whole picture.

"Are you ready?"

"To strip that dress off you."

God, he was good for her self-esteem. This guy would *never* choose TV and beer over her. Neva smiled up at him. His dress clothes were a little loose, but fortunately with a belt and judicious tucking, it didn't matter much. His build showed to advantage anyway, giving him a razor-lean look.

"Later, I promise. You look wonderful. Shall we?"

"No."

Neva paused, glancing at him over her shoulder, and found him breathlessly close. His hands settled on her hips and he kissed the side of her neck as he worked her skirt up. Each movement constituted a caress, and despite the fact that she was ready to step out the door, a whisper of arousal flickered through her. Other men wouldn't even think of this; they had plans, someplace to be. But he wanted her too much to consider anything else. *And what a turn on . . .*

A shiver ran through her. "Quickly then."

"Mmm." He made a noise of assent as he lifted her skirt all the way up.

She was glad, now, that she'd put on stockings instead of

hose. He dipped his fingers down the satin front of her panties and stroked her. His hands promised, *I* will *fuck you before we go.* Her pussy slicked in preparation, aching for him. She fell back against his chest, lost in the sweetness of his touch.

Zeke tore off her panties then. He was hell on her wardrobe—and his own—but she found his wildness irresistible. He pushed her forward a few steps, so that she fell across the arm of the couch. Just high enough. And she knew what he intended.

His breath rasped. Then he unzipped his pants. The crinkle of a foil packet reassured her. Quiet sounds, inextricably linked to sex.

"Spread for me."

She almost came at his white-hot instruction and rose on her tiptoes, quivering from head to toe in anticipation. Zeke sank himself home in one long thrust; a satisfied growl tore free as he pumped into her, rough and hard. Neva tried to support herself on her arms, but they trembled. She couldn't think, only feel. Her whole body shook at his mastery. The position put extra pressure on her clit, and he struck the sweetest spot. Repeatedly. Pleasure nearly blinded her as he held her still with a hand on her back. She could only squeeze her muscles against him and let her breath come in panting moans. Nothing had *ever* felt like this.

"Can't do this unless you're mine," he growled. "Can't be in the middle of all those people unless I feel it. Unless I'm sure." He thrust harder, dragging her hips back against him in primitive demand.

"Oh."

"Say it."

"Yours. I'm yours." In speaking the words, she came, long, glorious waves that nearly broke her.

He arched into her and snarled, rocking with quick, almost pained movements. Neva felt his shudders for long moments, and then he pulled out. She moaned in protest. She knew only that he'd left her, but when he returned, he had a damp cloth to clean them up, a spot-bath. Zeke helped her step into a fresh pair of panties, and she would've fallen if he hadn't caught her.

Hands on her waist, he wore a hard, focused look. "Remember this, while we're there. Remember it."

Neva let him guide her out to the car, but it was a minute or two before she stopped trembling enough to start the engine. He seemed incredibly pleased with himself. "Took care of the kittens just before I changed."

"Excellent. Now we have an excuse for not staying longer than a few hours."

She briefed him about the sort of guests he could expect to encounter, but his inattention made her stop talking when he lost the thread for the third time. *Damn. He's really nervous.* Neva took one hand off the wheel and put it on his thigh in reassurance. His muscles tensed.

He closed his eyes and growled, "Don't distract me, woman."

How utterly heady. We just . . . But she heeded him and went back to driving with her hands at ten and two. The countryside sped by, brown trees and damp farmland, until Harper Court appeared around a bend like a fairy-tale manor. Her mother said it aroused envy in the hearts of all who passed by, nestled like a jewel in the gentle rise. The white stone caught the wan afternoon sunlight, gilding the place.

"And here we are."

They had valet service, so she turned her keys over to the boy in the yellow vest. He raised a brow at her old Honda, but Neva ignored him. It wouldn't hurt any of the Mercedes or BMWs with its proximity.

Zeke took a deep breath and offered his arm. "Sure this is a good idea?"

"Trust me," she said. "It'll be fun."

And things went well at first. He cleaned up well enough that even her mother didn't seem to recognize him, so she didn't come over to spread her special brand of tolerance. She introduced him to a senator and a congressman, not local boys; he owned the knack of nodding and looking interested, so that worked in lieu of actual conversation. Most of her mother's guests had an agenda and a message to espouse.

"So that's why you want to vote for me, Son," the politician was saying.

Zeke kept a drink in his right hand and his left hand on her waist, so he didn't have to touch anyone. He was careful enough about it that she didn't think anyone else caught it, but she needed to ask him about that. She didn't think it could be mysophobia—a fear of germs—given the work he did at the clinic, but perhaps haphephobia? Strange that the fear of being touched didn't apply to her as well, though. So maybe that wasn't it.

Once everyone arrived, they had a sit-down meal, thirty guests for dinner, which one of the Yanks called lunch, and earned a round of ribbing. Zeke radiated tension beside her. He tried not to show it but he didn't like having a strange man on his left, and liked even less that she had one on her right. He kept sliding the guy—a businessman from Mississippi—wary looks. She hadn't realized it would be so hard for him; he chewed his food doggedly and kept his eyes on his plate.

She absorbed some of his tension until her shoulders ached. It was a relief when maids collected the dessert plates, and they were free to move around again. It was time to go talk to her father anyway and see what Ben was talking about with those tests.

"I need a moment with my dad," she said to Zeke. "Will you be all right?"

Momentary panic flashed in his blue eyes, but he offered a terse nod. "Gonna step outside for some air."

As she'd known she would, she found her father smoking in his study, drinking with a couple of his cronies. Neva nodded in greeting. "Gentlemen, could I borrow him briefly?"

An assenting chorus came in response—not that anyone ever said no to her, and it was a wonder it hadn't ruined her character—then the men filed out with their cigars, leaving her alone with Conrad Harper. He looked tired and old, hair thinner, and far grayer. But he still had a powerful presence. He rose and gave her a hug.

"Good to see you, my dear. What can I do for you?"

Had it come to that, then? The only reason she'd possibly seek him out was if she wanted something? In fact, he could make her life easier, if he released her trust fund. But she wouldn't ask. She had chosen her course.

"Ben told me you went to the hospital." A question laced the statement, inviting him to explain.

To her surprise, he rubbed a hand tiredly over his face. She couldn't remember ever seeing him so vulnerable. He was Conrad Harper, larger than life. "The results came back yesterday."

"And?"

"I have lung cancer."

Impossible. He couldn't have said what she thought he had. That would imply he could die and he couldn't possibly. He'd be around to order their lives for decades yet. Lillian couldn't function without him.

"No. You . . . you're still smoking!"

"Why quit?" he asked. "That would be like closing the barn door after the horse got out, wouldn't it? It's a death sentence, sweetheart. I'm not putting myself through chemo for a few extra months. When I go, I want it to be quick. I won't put you and your mother through a long illness. Not . . . not on top of everything else."

Luke, he meant Luke.

Her father went on, "But it would mean a lot to me if you could see your way clear to making up with her. She needs you. Misses you. And she'll need you a lot more after I'm gone. Both of you are just so dang stubborn."

She gazed at him, unable to believe it hadn't been just another of Ben's ruses. He was really sick. Dying. No, it couldn't be true.

"How long?" She forced the words past numb lips.

"A year at the outside. The doc made a guess but it's up to God."

"Oh, Daddy." Tears filled her eyes, and she regretted how callous she'd been, dismissing Ben's concern.

"Don't smear your makeup over me. I'm not worth it." To

her surprise he didn't try to capitalize on the moment, didn't push her toward a life change to make an old man happy. He just hugged her, and he smelled of expensive tobacco and Ralph Lauren cologne, as he always had.

"I'm so sorry. I'm a terrible daughter."

"I won't win any prizes, either," he said gruffly. "Go back to the party or your mother will come looking for us. We don't want that, do we?"

A shaky laugh escaped her. Neva shook her head and turned for the door. She managed to get a few yards down the hall before she had to stop. The tears she'd been fighting trickled down her cheeks. She leaned against the wall, taking deep breaths to try to control herself. *Talk about a sucker punch.*

"He told you, I take it?" Ben's voice didn't surprise her.

When she opened her eyes, he was coming down the hall toward her. The guy always knew where she was and what she was doing. Great situational awareness, if it hadn't been so annoying.

"He did."

"Hell of a thing. I'm sorry."

Tentative as he never was, Ben put his arms around her and she let him hug her. If only he wasn't so insistent about marrying her, they might be friends. They stood like that for a few seconds. She closed her eyes and struggled with conflicting emotions. Neva didn't want to go back to the party, but she had to find Zeke so they could leave. After she had some time to deal with the news, then she'd tackle her dad's request and see about making peace with her mother.

She didn't hear Zeke approach. Just one minute he wasn't there, and the next, he was, spinning Ben off her with brute strength and slamming him into the wall. His hand curled around the other man's throat, squeezing until his face went ruddy and his breath came in choking gasps.

"Touch her again," he snarled, "and I kill you."

"Zeke, no! Let him go."

For an agonizing instant, she feared he'd murder Ben. There was nothing human in his face, just a fierce and bestial anger. At last, with a trembling groan, he dropped his hand and stumbled back, rubbing his hands on his thighs. He shook his head as if to clear it.

Horror dawned and he backed away from them both. "Shouldn't have come."

Ben glared after him. "Your new boyfriend is *crazy*. He shouldn't be allowed to associate with normal people."

And until this moment, she would've argued that wasn't true.

CHAPTER 16

At last Hebert had names for his two dead girls: Gwen Davies and Sheila Palmer. Both came from Birmingham. So it was still his problem. Not that he minded. The heavy workload kept him busy, at least.

The other agents treated him differently these days. They were gentler, none of the no-holds-barred ribbing from before, like they thought he couldn't handle it. That pissed him off, but he didn't say so. He didn't want anyone thinking he was unstable or needed more counseling.

Davies had been a single mother who worked as a beautician. Fortunately, they could pinpoint her disappearance to the day she'd first failed to pick up her daughter, Minnie, from the babysitter. The woman had called the girl's grandparents. Now, they waited for him to ask the questions that would lead to answers.

He sighed and killed the car engine. The Davies lived in a small brick house near Five Points. The streets were narrow near downtown, full of houses restored or in the process of it. This one was well kept, with a tiny lawn gone brown with coming winter. He let himself in through the wrought iron gate and went up the walk. Inside a tiny dog yapped, signaling his arrival.

Mrs. Davies met him at the front door. She was short, no more than five feet, and she'd gone round with age, sort of comfortably pigeon-shaped. A little girl held her hand, eyes wide and sad in her small face. From her other hand, a stuffed bear dangled by an arm. The house smelled of gingerbread, rousing sweet memories.

"We were just baking a bit," Mrs. Davies said. "Would you like coffee and cookies?"

To make this seem like a social call instead of an interview. He understood the impulse. Plus, who could turn down fresh gingerbread? Not him.

"Yes, ma'am. That would be very kind."

Minnie went with her grandmother with a final look over her shoulder. He took stock of his surroundings, mostly finding the access points and exits. It was something he did as second nature, but the warmth of the house also registered. They had decorated for Christmas. Lights twinkled around the windows, and boughs of holly had been fastened to the wall at regular intervals. Combined with the gingerbread, the place smelled wonderful.

Hebert settled on the edge of a gold sofa. Mr. Davies wasn't in evidence. Unfortunate. He might have to come back.

When they returned, Mrs. Davies carried a tray set with cookies and her good china. She poured his coffee and gave it to him with an intense look. He recognized it: *you're the man who will fix this.* In the beginning they all wanted the impossible from him—for him to make the truth untrue. Once they realized he couldn't, then they would shift to a need for answers. If all went well, he could provide them. But sometimes . . . sometimes he couldn't. The reality was, some murders went unsolved, or they went cold for years, until some fluke event brought new evidence to light. He didn't have any investigative magic. He could only promise persistence until someone demanded he close the file and move on.

"When was the last time you saw Gwen?"

"Let me think . . . It was about six weeks ago, I suppose."

It had been a month since they found the body. He made a note. "Did she mention anything strange to you at that time?"

"Like someone stalking her?" The older woman surprised him with her directness.

"Yes. Or an old boyfriend who wouldn't leave her alone? What about Minnie's father?"

"He's down in Childersburg in the work-release program."

She didn't say what crime had landed him there, and he didn't ask. Being incarcerated provided a pretty sound alibi. He'd do some checking, of course, just to be sure. Part of the job. Hebert tapped his pen against the pad. If this killer was targeting random strangers, à la Ted Bundy, then it might be nearly impossible to catch him.

"I saw a man watching us."

Minnie was all of five, which meant he could take her statement with a grain of salt. Kids her age also saw fairies, the Easter Bunny, and Santa Claus. They hadn't yet gotten good at separating fantasy from reality. But he didn't shut her down.

"Oh? What did he look like?"

"Tall. He had a red hat."

Hebert stifled a sigh. All men looked tall to a kid. And a red hat? He couldn't even take Santa off the suspect list.

"When did you see him?"

"The day Mommy didn't come get me." So much sadness in her big dark eyes.

Just maybe this wasn't a coincidence. If only he could get a better description out of her. "Can you remember anything else about him?"

"He wasn't brown like you."

"Minnie!" Mrs. Davies chided.

"No, it's fine." He didn't mind a child stating the obvious.

Hebert made another note. White male, red hat. "Where did you see him?"

"At Tina's house."

Tina was the babysitter, who had kept Minnie two full hours before notifying the grandparents. He needed to talk to her next. If the man had followed Gwen from the sitter's to her place of employment, then it indicated a stalking pathology. Watching a subject from afar and building fantasies around them was the first step. Eventually the killer would be moved to try and make those dreams come true. When the victim didn't respond as scripted, then it escalated into what the hunters found in the woods. He tried to keep his face neutral.

"Was your daughter dating anyone?" If there was a boyfriend, he needed to look there first.

Mrs. Davies shook her head. "She was waiting for Minnie's dad."

Commendable loyalty, if somewhat misplaced. But maybe the guy was sincere in his desire to complete work release and turn over a new leaf. People could change if given sufficient motivation. A woman like Gwen and a daughter like Minnie would be enough for any man with an iota of sense.

"Has he been notified?"

She gave a jerky nod. If the couple hadn't been married, the job would've fallen to her. He didn't envy her the task, and it would suck even more to learn someone had murdered the woman you loved while you were locked in a state program and couldn't protect her. He wished he didn't have this empathy; before Rina died, he'd had none. Now he knew too much about loss.

"What's his name?"

"Theodore Mosely."

He wrote that down. Hebert ran down his list of questions, but as he expected he didn't get much more out of them. He drank his coffee and ate his cookies, then rose to his feet. "Thanks for your time. I'll be in touch when I know more."

First, there was Tina, and then he should talk to the boyfriend. He wasn't a suspect but he might know something. Maybe his associates had targeted Gwen as an object lesson for him. The way this case was shaping up, it didn't seem likely, but he'd never get anywhere building on assumptions.

An hour later, he sat on Tina Hedwig's couch, having refused an offer of refreshments. The sitter was around thirty with artificially blond hair and olive skin. She lived in a tidy red-brick duplex. Since she only watched Minnie, along with her own two kids, there were no state licensing requirements, but he could see she had taken care to childproof the house.

"I still can't believe it," she was saying, hands clasped so tight they showed her knuckles. "Poor Minnie."

"How well did you know Gwen Davies?" Hebert didn't enjoy cutting her off, but he had been around enough grieving people to know they would repeat themselves and talk in circles if he didn't ride herd.

But she pulled herself together. "We were friends in high school. We aren't as close now as we were then. But when I heard she needed a new sitter, I called and offered. It's tough to be a single mom."

"So you've known her a long time." That meant she probably knew the baby daddy, too. "What's your take on Theodore Mosely?"

"No good," she said without hesitation. "Opposed to an honest day's work."

"How did you feel about their relationship?"

She offered a wry, weary smile. "In high school or now?"

"Both." Hebert watched her face.

"It was bad enough in school. He was wild then. You know girls and their bad boys. They have—" She corrected herself with a flicker of pain. "*Had* this messy on-again, off-again thing, and it went on for more than ten years."

"Do you think he had anything to do with this?"

Now Tina did hesitate. "Honestly? I don't know. I would've said no, once. But . . . he hit her the last time she tried to leave. He said he couldn't live without her."

He made a note. "He's in Childersburg now. Wouldn't that have been the time to make a break and file restraining orders?"

"Sure . . . if she didn't love him deep down. Nobody else could push her buttons in quite the same way."

The whole thing sounded pretty toxic. He needed to find out whether Mosely had checked in on time, the day Gwen died. He worked a day shift in a machine shop, and then had to be back in lockup. He had a rough time of death from the medical examiner's report.

"Minnie said she saw a man lurking outside your house the day her mother disappeared. Caucasian male, red hat. Does that ring any bells?"

Tina frowned. "I'm sorry, no. But I'm running all day long with three kids."

"Can you think of anything else that might prove helpful?"

"Do you have a card? If I do, I'll call you."

He nodded and offered it to her. She read it and then rose to tuck it into a folder on the bookshelf above the television.

"Thanks for your time, Ms. Hedwig."

With that, he left. He took Highway 280 south out of Birmingham, heading toward Childersburg. Traffic was awful, worse than usual, and it took an hour and a half to make it past Inverness and Chelsea. Fifteen minutes more, and he arrived at Randall's Tool and Die, where Theodore Mosely worked during the day.

Hebert flashed his badge, and the manager escorted him to a break room to wait. It was a grim place, with plastic furniture, grimy floors, and a couple of dilapidated vending machines. Not even a fridge or microwave. Newspapers lay discarded on the tables along with candy wrappers and soda cans. The fluorescent bar overhead badly needed changing.

"I can't have you on the floor," the man said, sweating. "You understand. Insurance reasons."

Hebert suspected he was more worried about the immigration status of some of his workers, but he wasn't here for that. Legal employment was somebody else's wheelhouse and they were welcome to it. Five minutes later, a lanky blond-haired man ambled into the lounge. He had some cuts on his jaw from shaving with cheap safety razors, and a chip on his shoulder fit to weigh a body down in a dark river. Minnie looked nothing like him; no wonder Gwen had named her that. She was, in all ways, a replica of her mother.

"What's the po-po want with me now? Ain't I already locked up?"

Great, another white man who thinks he's black. Hebert had often received the reverse complaint—that he was a man of color who was white on the inside. He didn't let it bother him anymore; he was who he was, and that was mostly the sum total of his work, including all his successes and failures.

"I'd like to talk to you about Gwen Davies."

The man's whole demeanor changed. He lost the swagger and he just about fell into his chair across the table from Hebert. Raw pain lit him up as if someone had jammed a Roman candle in through his ear.

"I don't know nothin' bout that, man. But y'all find out who did it, and I will kill the motherfucker." No bravado—it was a promise.

Hebert had heard enough threats to know when one had teeth. He filed that away for future reference. It was just as well Mosely would be locked up for a while yet or he might get himself the death penalty, playing the Punisher. Honestly, he thought that would be a bad call. Sometimes people had it coming, but it wasn't an opinion he'd ever share with another law enforcement professional. It would get him sidelined faster than he could blink. In his line of work, he was supposed to catch vigilantes, not sympathize with them.

"When did you see her last?" There was no question who he meant.

"Two months ago, I guess. She brings Minnie to see me sometimes." Desperate devotion and pride shone in his tired face.

"I'd caution you against doing anything irrevocable." Hebert surprised himself. This was the kind of thing Rina would do. "You have a little girl out there who needs you. She needs you to straighten up and do the right thing. Her grandmother won't be around forever. Do you want to let her down again?"

"Fuck no." Mosely ran a hand over his shorn head.

"Can you think of anyone who would hurt you by going through Gwen?"

The other man froze. "Like for revenge or some shit?"

"Precisely."

While Hebert watched, Mosely ran a mental tally. He could see him going through old scores and people he'd pissed off over the years. Finally he shook his head. "I ain't never done nothing to earn that payback, swear to Jesus. They'd steal my shit or trash the car I got parked at my brother's place. Not this. Not Gwen."

Fuck. Hebert believed him. That meant he just needed to verify the man's alibi. He asked a few more questions and left. In the car, he called Childersburg, gave his badge number, and asked about the time of death. Theodore Mosely had been locked up when Gwen Davies died.

Back to square one. He hated this goddamn case. On the plus side, they'd caught the guy who'd killed Michelle Winston. It was, unsurprisingly, the guy her family hadn't wanted her to date. Sometimes the job literally made him sick.

But it was better than where he'd come from, better than a life of endless poverty. At least he'd gotten out. Many of his friends couldn't say the same, not that they'd recognize him. When he'd left Louisiana, he left all of that behind. And as always, he had work to do.

He studied the paper, a faint smile playing about his lips. So they'd identified the two girls. He had been watching the Birmingham paper and reading the obituaries. They had both appeared, now. So the ABI knew their names. It wouldn't do them any good. He had been too careful, studied the work of too many others before he started. Though his father had claimed he was a coward, his precision was paying off now.

Reading the obit made him feel strange, almost like a child with a secret. He'd known that Gwen was a stylist and that Sheila worked as a dental hygienist, and he'd known, of course, that Gwen had a daughter. But the other facts about their hobbies and interests and those they'd left behind? He almost felt like a voyeur.

Still, there had been no articles about the cases being connected or a killer on the loose. The press wouldn't have gotten wind of it yet. And that was a good thing. He wasn't doing this for notoriety. In fact, he would prefer nobody ever knew. But unless the agent assigned was a complete idiot, he couldn't help but see the connection. As the body count rose, they'd form a task force and his job would get harder. Hopefully he would discover the perfect death soon.

Folding the newspaper to avoid showing any undue interest in the obit section, he went to see what his woman was doing. He found her in the kitchen, banging on a steak with the meat mallet. Lately he had been distracted around her, not as present in the relationship as he should be. He apologized by nuzzling the back of her neck.

It won't be long until I'm all yours. I just have to finish a few things first.

"In a better mood?" she asked.

She'd picked up on his tension earlier and he'd snapped at her. He regretted it. If he drove her away, it would destroy him. This woman was all that stood between him and utter darkness.

"I'm sorry. Work's been a real bitch lately."

She nodded. "That new project has you buried, huh?"

Her choice of words made him smile. "You could say that. I appreciate how patient you've been. I hate traveling for the job, but it's necessary right now. Anything I can do to help?"

"Peel the potatoes? I've got the water boiling already."

"We could just bake them." Since the first girl, he hadn't wanted to touch a knife. Odd, that. But it reminded him too sharply of his loss of control. He dropped a kiss on her upturned mouth.

"Then could you prep them?"

"Of course." He liked doing such simple things with her.

She didn't know what his early life had been like. Because her childhood had been pretty and perfect, she assumed every one had grown up the same way. Using the fork, he stabbed several neat holes in the potatoes, then oiled them and dipped them in salt. That was the proper way to make a baked potato. People who wrapped them in foil were simply doing it wrong and ruined the skin. There were, definitely, right and wrong ways to do things.

He still needed to find the perfect method.

Without being asked, he dumped the hot water down the

drain for her and turned on the oven. He stashed the potatoes directly on the rack with a cookie sheet beneath to catch the drippings. No mess. When he turned he found her watching him with a faint smile.

"What?"

"You're so careful."

That gave him satisfaction on several levels. "If it's worth doing, it's worth doing well."

"Don't I get on your nerves then?"

Well, she was a bit of a whirlwind, somewhat slapdash in her habits. But her sweetness made up for all of that. "You know I'm crazy about you."

He took her in his arms and breathed her in. Her hair smelled natural and clean; she used an organic shampoo bar that she ordered specially from a company in California. It had sandalwood powder and other ingredients to brighten and bring out the highlights in her hair. She didn't mess about at salons, and in his opinion, she didn't need to; she was already so beautiful she took his breath away.

"Mmm." She gazed up at him, love in her eyes. "Me, too."

"Want me to fire up the grill?"

"It's freezing outside!"

That was an overstatement. It was forty-five. "With a jacket, I'll be fine once the coals heat up."

She'd eat it from the broiler but not with the same pleasure. So her eyes lit up even though she kept arguing, just for appearances. He ignored her protests.

"Marinate it while I get ready?"

"Sure."

He grabbed a coat from the hook beside the back door and went outside. After pulling the cover from the barbeque, he arranged the briquettes to his satisfaction. The steel grill gleamed in the moonlight. Since the potatoes were baking— and that would take an hour or so—he didn't use lighter fluid. In his opinion, using it tainted the taste of the meat. A primitive palate might not notice the difference.

By the time she delivered the steaks, he was ready. The flesh hissed when it met hot metal. A delicious smell wafted up, making him forget the cold. They bled as he pierced them to flip them over. *Ah, perfect.* Since they both enjoyed their steaks rare, he pulled them and carried the plate back into the kitchen.

"The potatoes just finished. They look wonderful." As she set the table, she added, "I made a salad, too."

He smiled. "You are too good for me."

How true. More than she knew. But it didn't matter. He had ample proof that people didn't get what they deserved. Sometimes he felt almost as if he were two men: the one who did his dark work alone and the one who loved her. Oh, he knew it wasn't true. He didn't have dissociative identity disorder in the clinical sense. He didn't black out and wake up wondering what he'd done. He always knew.

The best part about her? Daddy couldn't talk when she was around. Her strength and her goodness worked on him like Kryptonite. When he was with her, he was only himself, but without the vulnerability and the weakness. It was a blissful feeling and he would do *anything* to keep it.

Once they'd finished eating, she asked, "What do you want to do tonight?"

What he wanted to do, and what he had to do were two different things. "I'm afraid I have to put in some extra hours tonight."

"Again?" Disappointment colored her voice.

"I'm sorry. But it won't be for too much longer. I'll be done soon."

"You promise?"

"I swear."

That much, he could guarantee. If he had to, he would take more girls and finish them quicker, exploring the possibilities. There were . . . so many. Sometimes, if a woman felt sufficient pain, her screams became a song, like the mourning cry of grieving women in Afghanistan. A most ghastly music. The old man approved. He wanted Geneva Harper to know that special brand of agony.

"Guess what I heard today?"

How cute. She loved to gossip. It was her one feature that

could be remotely considered a fault, but he liked hearing her silly stories. He leaned forward, chin on hand. "What?"

"It's Harper related. You know how this town is."

He did indeed. They ran everything, owned everything, and thought themselves the next things to God. "So tell me. I can see you're dying to."

"Apparently there was an altercation up at Harper Court. One of the guests threatened to kill another."

"Really? Why?"

"I think it had to do with Geneva, but I'm not sure."

"Interesting." It remained to be seen if he could make use of the information. "Let me know if you hear anything more?"

She paused in clearing the table, surprised. "I didn't know you cared about stuff like this."

"I have my seamy side, too."

"*Sure* you do. I know you're just humoring me but I love you for it."

So easily she spoke those words, and yet they meant everything to him. He had to finish this soon, so they could move on together. She'd never know. This wasn't something he did because he wanted to; he had an obligation to the old man. This would let the bastard rest—and *finally*, he could just be normal. The voices would stop; the panic would stop.

It was all the Harpers' fault. They had to pay. His lips shaped the words without him meaning to, a breath of sound.

"Did you say something?"

God, no. None of this could touch her, ever. He thought of the girl waiting for him in the dark, wondering why he'd taken her.

"Just mumbling about the project. I should get back to it, and that requires a research trip. Don't wait up."

CHAPTER 17

Since Neva had the car keys, it wasn't like Zeke was inconveniencing her. The nightmare of the party fell behind him as he ran. He resisted the urge to pull off his shoes and leave the road behind. He must look quite the fool, running in slacks and a dress shirt. The woods, where this kind of shit didn't matter, beckoned.

Inside him, the beast roared with shame and humiliation. It knew no middle ground, and most times, neither did he. If another male had his hands on his woman, he was the enemy. But those rules didn't belong to her world . . . and neither did he.

Zeke covered the miles back to the farm in record time. The cold didn't bother him, or the distance. He wasn't even breathing hard when he came up the drive. Mewing kittens greeted him; their heating pad was still warm, but they didn't much like being alone. They were also getting hungry.

He changed his clothes first, tearing off the dress pants and tie. There was no end to the mistakes he'd make, apparently. It did no good, trying to be something you weren't. Jeans and

T-shirts covered him; that was all that mattered. Zeke turned on the radio in the kitchen as he gathered the supplies.

Caring for them helped him calm down some, but it didn't change his surety they needed to end this. It would hurt like a bitch, but he couldn't be the man she needed, no matter how he felt about her. Sometimes longing wasn't enough; sometimes *love* wasn't enough. It sure hadn't made his mother want to live.

Zeke tucked the kittens into his shirt, knowing they needed the warmth and the reassurance of his heartbeat. Their little claws scrabbled at his skin and left tiny scratches; he didn't mind. He needed them, too—and without them, he wouldn't even have had these few weeks with her. God, it hurt, as if someone had smashed a fist through his chest and were even now crushing his heart to pulp.

He heard her car on the road long before she turned down the driveway. By now he could identify her engine from the unique way it rumbled, its tiny knocks and pings, much as he could tell different birds apart in the woods. They each made a unique sound. If you had good ears, the sounds told a story.

God, he didn't look forward to this conversation.

She came in through the kitchen instead of the parlor. Zeke listened to her moving about, distinct from the music, and then she came to the doorway. Her mouth was pale and tight, all the lipstick chewed off. He could smell disappointment on her, and it stung like lye.

"We need to talk about what happened," she said.

He scented her fear, too, a sour-milk stink beneath the lye. It had taken a lot of guts for her to face him alone—and maybe lack of self preservation, too. Even now, she wasn't sure it was safe, and that made the beast roar. *She's ours.* With effort, he fought down its anguished outrage. His animal self felt like she'd kicked it. But he'd given her reason to doubt him. More than one.

"Gonna sleep in the barn while you're here." It was just too much temptation otherwise. If he saw her moving around his home, he wouldn't be able to keep his hands off her. The beast wouldn't let her be; in his head, it roared in protest. Even now he wanted to stroke her and tell her everything would be fine, that he'd never let her go and they could fix anything bad between them. Most of all, he wanted to keep that promise: *I'm not going anywhere.* But promises were made to be broken, and someone like him had no business making them to a woman like her.

Her breath hitched. "What are you saying?"

"Know what I'm saying." He couldn't meet her gaze, and it hurt way worse than he'd thought it would, like an echo of needles beneath his skin. Added to the heartache from before, it became damn near unbearable.

"You don't want to be with me anymore? Because of this? It was a little . . . over the top, I admit, but I understand why you thought I didn't want him touching me. But that was a special circumstance."

Wonderful. She didn't get it. Her emotional state mattered not at all, didn't count even slightly when it came to his animal impulses. Her preferences hadn't even dawned on him.

"Can't say that was a one-time thing, Neva. If you're around him—or *anyone*—and you're mine, then I'll do it again. Next time, might kill him."

"But why?"

Zeke focused on the critters inside his shirt, their contentment instead of his own pain. "Can't stand to see somebody else's hands on you."

"It doesn't mean anything." Her forehead creased. "He was comforting me. I found out—"

"Don't matter." He cut her off, not wanting to hear why.

Her scent shifted from fear to hurt. In doing so, it darkened, a touch less sour in his nose, more like meat soaked in brine. But that was no better, just a different kind of wrong.

"Maybe you could learn to control it. I mean, obviously it's not . . . all right. What you did."

Zeke shoved to his feet, startling the kittens. He caught them and deposited them back in their freshly cleaned box. He turned and headed for the door. Words couldn't fix this. Nothing could change what he was and he didn't believe in endless talking that only turned the knife in the wound. He had been beyond stupid to think it could work, even for a little while.

"So that's it?" Her voice rose. "We're done?"

He went out the front door without looking back. Zeke almost expected her to follow him; he hoped, though it would only make the parting more painful. If she pleaded or cried, he might not be able to stand firm. God help them both.

But she didn't. From outside he heard her moving around the house. It took him a minute to realize she was packing. *Did you think she'd stay?* She'd rather be anywhere but here, now.

So in a way, I did keep my promise. I didn't go anywhere. I just made it so she had no choice but to do the leaving.

A flock of snow geese lit in the distant field, resting and looking for food. Their white feathers contrasted with the dark earth. It should have been beautiful, like the cascading call of the winter wren. There was much to admire here, and yet he turned his back on all of it and strode toward the out-building: the perfect place to hide.

When the front door opened, it took everything he had to stay in the barn. Cold wind blew through the cracks in the rotting walls. Empty stalls and rusted tools gave the building a haunted air. This was the worst place on the farm, where he'd found his mother's body. Sometimes he thought she lingered here, trapped and hopeless as she'd been in life. Fitting he stood in these shadows now, listening to love leave him.

Zeke didn't budge until he heard her engine start and the car drove away. She was five miles down the road before he stepped outside. Funny, he felt the cold as he hadn't since his escape, but it didn't settle on his skin. Instead he felt it in his bones.

The house was too quiet when he went back inside. She'd turned off the music, probably to save electricity since she didn't know when he'd come back. But the silence felt to him like the grave, heavy and final.

He sat down to grieve, one night only. Zeke didn't believe in brooding for long on things that couldn't be changed. As things stood, he would have to give notice at the clinic and start looking for other work. There was no way he could see her every day and not die of the pain. Better to make the break clean and permanent. Hell, maybe he should even sell the farm, if he could find a buyer. Start over somewhere else. That might be best.

Hours later, a car slowed near his drive. That meant the person intended to turn. He wasn't in the mood for company, but he stood, ambling to the window to see who it was. Sid parked and climbed out of her old Ford, then went to the trunk and started unloading. The wicker basket in her hand would be loaded with dishes, if he knew the woman at all. Time to turn on some lights and pretend he was fine.

Zeke sighed and went to open the door. "Evening, auntie."

"Oh my," she said, marveling at the bright walls. "You've done wonders for the place, you surely have."

"Glad you like it."

"I brought leftovers." She leveled a chastening stare on him, "Last week you promised you'd come to Sunday supper, after church let out. When you didn't show, I figured you plumb forgot."

Shit. The last time they'd talked, he *had* promised. Neva had a way of edging everything out of his brain, not that his mind was a steel trap on the best of days. Another reason she'd do better without him. Zeke never could've imagined he'd miss the average IQ he'd had before.

"Sorry."

Sid brushed past him, heading for the kitchen. He followed her. She clucked over its humble state. "Good thing everything's still warm. Have you eaten today?"

Had he? Yeah, at the luncheon, but he'd been too tense to enjoy it much. He took a seat at the kitchen table. It brought back memories to see her here. While he was a kid and his dad was still alive, she'd often come over with that same basket full of food. If she hadn't, no telling what would've happened to them.

"Not supper," he admitted.

"Then I'll fix you a plate and you can tell me what went wrong."

He froze. "Huh?"

"I heard your girl moved out."

Did the whole town know everything about everyone? Christ, it had only been a few hours. The wound hadn't even scabbed over, and they were already gossiping. It must be worse for Neva; she'd risked her good name by taking up with him.

"How?" No point in denying it. Sid knew her information was good.

"The housekeeper at Harper Court called her cousin to say she'd be staying late because they needed her to prepare Geneva's bedroom. She was supposed to have Sunday supper with Gladys."

"Gladys."

"The housekeeper's cousin. And she goes to church with my friend Judy."

"Who called you?" He wasn't sure he understood why, but he didn't ask.

Gladys probably called somebody in her prayer chain; telephone lists worked equally well for spreading juicy news. His aunt Sid had been guilty of doing the same a time or two. He just wished it didn't involve him directly.

"Lands, yes. You and Geneva have been the talk of the town, and she hasn't spent a night at Harper Court in a while now. For her to go home . . . well." His aunt smiled. "Things must be rough on both of you, and I figured you'd need cheering up. Don't worry, baby. You'll meet a girl who appreciates you."

He almost laughed. She figured Neva had done the dumping; it made no sense the other way. Why would a man like him break it off with a woman like her? No point setting the record straight; even Aunt Sid wouldn't believe him.

The forest sounded better and better.

What could he say, except: "Thanks."

With grim resolve, he ate the food she'd brought: fried chicken, peas and carrots, and apple cobbler. Zeke let her comforting words pour over him in a vague rush of noise. He made the right sounds and nodded now and then, wanting nothing more than to be alone. Eventually she left and the silence came back. Tonight, he didn't stick around to listen.

Instead he went to the woods, where he belonged.

Could things get worse? Neva was with her mother of all people, unpacking in her childhood bedroom. Suite was more like it. Everything was pink and gold—a dream come true, if she were eleven and still dreaming of ballet. In fact, her last pair of slippers still sat in the closet, waiting for a little girl who didn't exist anymore. She didn't know whether to be touched or horrified. Nobody had cleaned the place when she moved out permanently, as if leaving these things here would ensure she came home.

And look, here I am, a perfect example of functional sympathetic magic.

"You want to talk about it?" Her mother was making a real effort to be kind, though she had to be thrilled, after what she'd said about not marrying the help. She paused delicately. "I . . . heard about what happened."

Neva tensed. When she'd turned, horrified at Zeke's behavior, there had been a few guests milling around; no doubt they'd wasted no time in spreading the story. People would be talking about this for weeks. Since she was a Harper, it made the furor worse, too. It had taken all her courage not to bolt like Zeke had. Instead she'd taken Ben's arm and spent an excruciating hour pretending the stares and whispers didn't bother her. She'd learned early on that running only made it worse.

"Not really." She hung up the last shirt in the enormous closet; her bathroom at the apartment was smaller.

And it's still not livable. Thank you, Mrs. Popović and grandson.

Lillian sighed. "You should. If not to me, then to Julie. You won't be ready to move on until you accept it's over."

Oh, subtle.

"We're not talking about Zeke anymore, are we?"

"Did you want to talk about Luke instead?" Her mother

shifted, crossing her legs elegantly even while she perched on the edge of the bed.

"I don't want to talk period. I just need to stay until the kittens are big enough not to need overnight care."

And she didn't want to impose on Travis and Julie, though she expected they'd be happy to have her. They'd find some way to work around his allergies, if they knew she really needed help. She was just conscious of not asking for favors from friends; it tended to strain the relationship. Whereas her relationship with her parents could hardly get worse, so it didn't matter. It might be a little awkward, but the house echoed with space. She could stay out of their way, if she could just get rid of her mother first.

"Fine." The other woman capitulated unexpectedly. "I understand you spoke to your father . . . and he told you."

Since it was at least off topic, she nodded, shutting the closet doors and turning to face Lillian. "I can't believe it."

"I suppose he gave you the same speech?"

"That we need to cut each other some slack, because soon we'll only have each other?"

"That's the one." Lillian studied her hands, and Neva did, too.

Though she was well kept and lovely, cosmetics couldn't hide the signs of age on her fingers. Her fingers had thickened slightly, the knuckles a touch knotty. As her mild arthritis worsened, it would show even more. Her mother hated that, and had even stopped wearing her beloved rings, hoping people wouldn't notice. Neva remembered when she'd worn diamonds on just about every finger. She remembered pulling them off to try them on her thumbs—and her mother hadn't scolded her or complained she might lose them. It hadn't always been . . . like this, between them. Maybe she could make the first move.

"I'm sorry I can't be who you want me to be."

She sat down on the bed, seeing how old her mother looked—without her makeup and in her at-home clothes, Lillian Harper showed her years in the small lines about her eyes and the ones bracketing her mouth. Luke's disappearance had hit her hard. They'd all depended on him, maybe too much, and his absence left a hole.

Her mother took her hand. "I'm the one who's sorry. With your brother gone and now your dad sick . . . I feel like I'm lucky I still have you at all." Tears brimmed in her eyes. "It hurts me to see you sad. Did I have anything to do with this?"

So it takes a dying man and broken heart to dig any real emotion out of you, huh? She squished the uncharitable thought and tried not to remember what an ice queen her mother had been out at the farm. It wasn't like that mattered anymore. Zeke had walked out on her, and she wouldn't be crawling back. She didn't want a man who was always running instead of fighting.

"With my breakup?" Though she didn't know if those words even accurately represented the situation. They'd never had an official date; she didn't think she could count that meal at Tom's Diner. In all the ways that mattered, they'd never been together like normal people, and the one time they tried, it blew up in a huge way.

"I was a bitch to him," Lillian said flatly. "And I did it on purpose because I still had it fixed in my head you should be with Ben."

That surprised her. "You don't think so now? Why the sudden change of heart?"

For her mother to admit she'd been wrong, it might mean the end of days. Perhaps she should be looking for a rain of toads, blood in the rivers, locusts in the fields, and fire in the sky. Neva glanced out the window, just in case, and saw only darkness. She wondered if Zeke was still out in the barn, or if he'd gone back inside as soon she left. The idea didn't sit right. God, she wished she'd had a chance to tell him off before walking out.

"I saw you two together at the party today . . . and your father had a . . . talk with me after you left," she added. "I admit it. There's no spark. I know why Ben wants the marriage . . . and I understand why you don't. We've been using him as a stand-in for Luke, and asking you to marry under those circumstances is just . . ." Lillian grimaced. "A hundred kinds of wrong."

She didn't even know what to say. Part of her feared the woman was just setting her up for something worse, but she appeared sincere. So she made an effort, too. Her dad would be happy, at least.

"It wasn't your fault. Zeke has some stuff to work out." To put it mildly. "He's a hard man to understand."

"They all are. Do you love him?"

"It's a little early to be throwing that word around. We hadn't been together very long." A shrug.

"Did I ever tell you how I met your daddy?"

Hell, no. Since she got old enough to talk about such things, Lillian had been the last person she'd want to share them with. As a little girl, she'd loved her mother's tales, though. But since she was really trying, Neva could do no less.

"Uh-uh."

"Would you like to hear the story?"

"Of course."

"This isn't the story we tell people, but I was at a honky-tonk in Birmingham." Her expression said she sympathized with Neva's current plight. "I met a handsome man, wearing a blue-check shirt and worn-out Wranglers."

"Dad?" she guessed.

Lillian laughed. "No, he comes later. I did some dancing with that fella I probably shouldn't have and it gave him . . . ideas about my intentions."

She couldn't help but chuckle, too. "Really? What happened next?"

"I'd had too much to drink by that point, so I wasn't thinking right. I let him edge me out to his truck. We were kissing up a storm, and if he'd finished the job, your last name might not be Harper." Her mother grinned a little, less formal than she'd been in years, and Neva wondered if she had been drinking *today.* "As he rounded second base, some of the liquor wore off and I thought better of what I was doing. I'd only wanted to dance and be a little wild. Not *that* wild.

"So I started to fight and scrambled out of the truck. He chased after me, but before he could do more than call me a tease and give me a shove, another man came out of the bar.

He had an open Jack Daniels in one hand, and he was drunk as a skunk, singing some Johnny Cash song, 'Oh Lonesome Me,' I think it was. He saw I was in trouble and came charging in. He whacked that cowboy upside the head with his bottle and he went down."

Neva could picture the scene so clearly, dark parking lot, an old truck. It made her parents seem more human, somehow, but it was hard to picture her mother wearing jeans. She hadn't seen her in anything but pastel suits for so long. Her doubt must've shown because Lillian smiled and shook her head.

"I wasn't born wearing Dior, you know. Your daddy was so drunk, I had to drive him home that night. If I'd known we were going all the way to Harper Creek, I might not have offered."

"You had no idea who he was."

"Lord, no. I'd never heard of the place. I just knew he'd done the right thing and saved me, even though he could hardly walk straight. When I pulled up in front of Harper Court, I like to died. I had to help him up the walk and the housekeeper thought I was some cheap floozy with my lipstick all smeared and my hair gone wild. My mother-in-law never let me live that down."

"Grandmother Harper?" Funny, she'd never wondered what it had been like for her mom. The Devereaux family had some money—enough for her maternal grandparents to send her to college—but nothing like the Harpers. They certainly didn't have any towns named after them.

The older woman nodded, her mouth pulling tight. "I won't say I was sorry when she passed on."

Realization dawned, and it explained a lot. Everything, in fact. "And that's why you were so hard on me. You probably heard about how your daughter was showing your common roots."

Which was funny. Her mother's people weren't trailer trash by any means. But Grandmother Harper had made her assessment based on one night's events, and hadn't let anything in subsequent years change her mind. Neva just wished Lillian hadn't allowed the old woman to leach all the life from her. But habits formed over time, and a brittle shell grew where affection used to be. Only her husband had been spared the ice.

"Yes. But it was worth it." Remembered warmth kindled in Lillian's eyes. "I fell in love with him that first night. Oh, we courted and didn't marry for two years, but I knew, right then. And I'll tell you: I never regretted a minute I spent with him, even with Mother Harper carping on every little thing I did. How I spoke, walked, dressed, ate, and raised my children. I'm only sorry—" Her voice broke.

That it's coming to an end.

"Oh, Mama . . ." Tears stung Neva's eyes, and she reached out.

She couldn't remember the last time they'd hugged. Maybe when the deputies came to tell them they had found Luke's car abandoned on the highway. She had no clear memories of that day, just residual shock. Today Lillian didn't smell like Chanel; she wore a floral scent, something light and sweet. Her mother's hands stroked her back as they had when she was a little girl and had a nightmare.

"The heart wants what it wants," Lillian said softly. "And if your daddy had turned out not to be such a catch, if he had been a miner or a mechanic, I would've married him anyway, no matter what my parents said or thought. I guess I got so wrapped up in being worthy of this name of ours that I forgot it doesn't matter a damn unless you're happy."

That did it. Neva started bawling. It had been years since she'd broken down this way; she could handle anything in the world except her mother being sweet. In between quiet sobs, she got out, "I want to come home."

"Anytime, baby. Anytime. We'll pay off your lease on the apartment."

Maybe it was weak, but Neva didn't demur. She had been brave and stoic and dealt with Luke's loss on her own. She had forged her own path, and chosen a career she loved, but she just couldn't deal with a breakup, business trouble, and a dying father all alone. There was no reason she should, either. They held each other for a long time, sniffing into each other's shoulders. She'd missed this.

"It warms my heart to see my girls together . . . and not fighting." Her father spoke from the doorway, wearing a melancholy smile.

Neva became aware there might not be many opportunities like this left. She got off the bed and hugged him, too. "I guess you heard I'm moving back in."

"With the problems you've had at the clinic, I'm glad. That girl they found—"

"That's nothing to do with me," she reassured him.

In his condition, he didn't need to be worrying about her. But she knew better than to say so. He hated fussing, even when he had a minor illness. With this, Neva suspected he'd prefer to pretend nothing was wrong, until the very end.

"I hear you brought kittens. Maybe your mother will let me keep one."

She expected Lillian to protest the trouble or the mess, but her mother nodded. Apparently her dad could ask for anything, now, and get the wifely seal of approval. "Can we see them?"

Neva nodded, feeling like she would wake up soon. Neither of her parents had ever shared her interest in animals. But she went to get the box and brought it to the bed. The kittens were adorable balls of fluff now, eyes open, and full of curiosity. The biggest one had medium fur, patterned in black and white. His brother was mostly gray with white feet, and their sister was an orange marmalade tabby.

"They're all adorable."

A devil made her say, "You should keep all three. You have the space and the resources to feed them and pay for their medical care."

To her surprise, her mother shrugged. "How is three worse than one? At least they'll have each other to play with . . . and they're used to each other."

That was true. Cats from the same litter tended to cohabitate better once they were grown with less territorial conflict than if they were integrated later. And it was how she knew her mom had really changed—or maybe it was more accurate to say she'd thawed. Because she hadn't always been so frozen.

And she understood. Sometimes you had to suffer loss in order to remember what mattered.

CHAPTER 18

Zeke found a body in the woods.

And he couldn't be the one to bring it to the attention of the authorities. Not after his tip led to the girl in the trunk. They just wouldn't believe he had nothing to do with it. But he didn't feel right about leaving her here, either.

She hadn't been in the wild long. No animals had touched her. Tear tracks had been wiped from her cheeks, but in the moonlight, with his extra-sharp vision, he made out the signs of where she'd cried. Her lips were cracked, as if she had been denied water. Water made a woman piss and reminded a murderer she was only human, not a symbol or a vessel, or whatever he wanted from her.

The killer had surely painted her face after death because no woman would make herself up like this: eyeliner too thick, shadow too dark, lipstick too bold. Stage actresses wore it like this from what he remembered, and maybe so did whores. Zeke didn't know enough about the latter to be sure.

Ribbons twined around her arms and legs like creeper vines, and someone had placed a bouquet of daisies on her crotch. From two flowers, the white petals had been plucked, and the yellow eye covered each of her nipples. They must be glued or stapled; or the wind would've carried them off. He took care not to get too close and certainly not to touch her.

The only marks came from where someone had strangled her. Deep, livid bruises glowed against the pallor of her throat. He didn't know enough about corpses to tell if it had been done with bare hands. Maybe the sheriff could, or the uptight agent from the ABI.

Zeke only knew he couldn't put it off anymore. He had to call someone. First he made a note of where he was, exactly, and then he ran back to the house for the truck. Sweeney's Service Station had the nearest payphone, but he drove fifteen miles farther to a convenience store, where nobody knew him, and the phone was outside and around the corner from the cashier. He felt a little sick at what would surely be called cowardice, but he couldn't be open about this.

He slipped from the truck and deposited his coins. The call connected. On the other end, the county dispatcher asked what he needed. Zeke deepened his voice as much as he could. "There's a body in the woods."

"Quit," the woman said. "This isn't funny."

Maybe they'd gotten prank calls? He hadn't figured on that. Now he needed to find the best way to persuade her—and fast. An edge, born of nerves and impatience, came into his voice. "Write it down, woman. I'll only tell you where, once."

Her breath caught. "Oh, crap. You mean it. Wait, I'm getting a pencil. Don't hang up." Rustling noises came across the line. "Go ahead."

Zeke gave the directions as best he could and waited while she scratched them down. The sounds told him she did take him seriously now. If their county had any resources, he might worry about a trace but it would take a while to set something like that up, and he'd have to call a second time. He didn't intend to do that.

"And there's where you'll find her," he finished.

"Why are you killing these women?" she asked. "What do you *want*?"

Shit. She thought she was talking to the murderer. It was a reasonable guess under the circumstances, but he did not want to be caught in that net. Zeke cut the connection and sprinted for the truck. He was nearly back to Sweeney's when blue and red lights whizzed past him, heading in the opposite direction. The car used its sirens, too. Maybe they couldn't trace a call, but they could use caller ID and then get an address for the number. He hoped nobody had seen him, but if they had, he was royally fucked, because they would remember the truck. Maybe the deputies wouldn't ask the right questions early on, and the clerk would forget.

By the time he pulled up at the farm, he was shaking. His first thought was for the kittens, but . . . they weren't here anymore. Not his responsibility. Like everything else sweet and good, they belonged with Neva. Not him.

Zeke didn't sleep much. He kept waiting for engines in the night and a knock at his door. And anytime he closed his eyes, he saw the dead girl in the moonlight; she haunted him with her painted face and her staring eyes. In the morning, he worked around the farm at jobs that didn't call for his brain to kick in.

He managed to show up for work on time, but he didn't speak to Neva. She didn't look him in the eye when he went past her. Sadness covered her from head to toe, smelling of lemons and vinegar, and he couldn't get away from it. Since he lacked the courage to do it to her face, he stopped at Julie's desk while Neva saw a cocker spaniel with a piddling problem.

"Giving my two weeks," he muttered.

The redhead slammed her pen down on her desk, and her brows pulled tight with anger. "They got to you, too, huh? How much did they offer?"

He raised a brow. That was the last thing he'd expected her to say. "What?"

"You mean you're not quitting because they bribed you?"

"What the hell—"

Neva stuck her head out of the exam room and called to Julie to bring her something, ending the conversation. It left Zeke with more questions. Somebody had been paying the help to quit on her? That made it seem like she had an enemy, and he'd be a real piece of work to leave her drowning in trouble. But did it have anything to do with these gift-wrapped dead girls? *Shit*. The one he'd found in the woods had been a bit younger and slimmer, but she'd had brown hair and brown eyes. Could be it didn't mean anything. But his animal self growled in warning. *Nobody better try and hurt her. She's still ours.* Maybe he could stick it out for another month or two. Do his job and not think about how sweet she smelled, or how good she felt. If it hurt him, then he had it coming for making her so sad.

When Julie came back, he was still standing by her desk. "Why are you quitting if they haven't approached you?"

"Never mind that," he said. "Tell me what's up."

Julie checked the exam room door to make sure it was closed, and then came back, lowering her voice to a whisper. "Just what I said. The last guy who had your job told me he was offered a thousand bucks to quit. So I went and asked the one before him. Same thing."

"Who? Why?"

She shook her head. "I have no idea. They received the offer by e-mail, the first part as a money order in the mail, and the second payment once they left Paws and Claws. It's crazy, right?"

"Does she know?"

"No! And I'll kick your ass if you tell her. She has enough problems right now."

"Don't think it might help?" Julie knew Neva. But Zeke had to wonder if it would make her feel better, knowing they hadn't left because her clinic was terrible, cursed, or she was just a bad boss.

"I'm afraid she'd start digging," Julie said quietly. "And discover her parents were behind it. See, they're patching up their differences now. Her dad is dying." She misread his expression, seeing confusion instead of the stunning pain he felt. "Cancer. Since nobody has tried to bribe you—and they just made up—the pieces seem to fit. So I don't want her hurt more. They love her. They just don't understand her. I'm sure they don't realize how much damage they did with their good intentions. They thought if she couldn't keep help, she'd give up and come home. Instead it just made her work harder."

He got it now. At that fucking party, she'd just learned her dad had a fatal illness. Ben, the bastard, had been on hand to comfort her. He hadn't. Never mind that he should've been; it was a wonder she'd wanted to talk to him at all, afterward. Zeke felt like slime on the bottom of a river rock.

"Won't tell her then."

Julie's face softened. "Good. I know you care about her, too."

There was no point in denying it. But he shrugged. "Think they were behind the break-in, the vandalism, and the fire?"

"Hope not. That's a lot worse than bribing staff, isn't it?"

He nodded. "Criminal, even."

Neva's friend was persistent and didn't let his change of subject stick. "Look, I don't know what went wrong between you guys, but I hope you make up. With you, she was happier than she'd been for a while." She glanced at the time. "Crap, Travis is expecting me to be home by now. I'm sorry you won't be coming for the next movie night."

While he looked on, she grabbed her things and hurried out, glowing with eagerness. Had Neva ever looked like that about him? Maybe they hadn't been together long enough for it to ripen into what it could be. Still, he thought he'd done the right thing, even if he felt like he was dying by degrees. Food didn't even taste the same, and his house ached with emptiness.

Because his job was done, he left the clinic. But he didn't go home. Instead he went over to the sandwich shop and ordered a soda. The girl behind the counter made eyes at him as she filled the paper cup; he couldn't help but notice she had clumps of black goo caked on her lashes. It made his own eyes water in reaction. Ignoring her, he took a seat facing the window so he could make sure she got off okay. Knowing her, she would stay stupid late and walk out alone in the dark, long after everyone else disappeared. Only Armando's was open as late, and the clerk paid no attention to the parking lot. Right now, she had on a tiny music player and was dancing to some thumping music. He had some idea he ought to find her swiveling hips and gunky eyes sexy. God help him.

At ten minutes to eight, Neva came out of the clinic. He heard her lock up, several shops away, but didn't see her until she started walking toward her car. The animal part of him wanted to run to meet her and to apologize. Beg on his knees if need be. He wanted her safe and close, and the rest didn't matter.

Only it did.

His truck was parked at the farm; he had run to work today, so he couldn't follow her to make sure she got home okay. And he wouldn't, even if he could. Some lines you didn't cross, or it would drive you crazy, yearning after the impossible.

All he could do was watch her drive away.

On the way home from the clinic, Neva drove by a stalled vehicle. As she passed, a man climbed out of the driver's side. He was tall and lanky, and he signaled her, miming a request to use her phone. She slowed, but warning bells went off in her head, and she remembered Luke's abandoned vehicle. Caution kicked in; instead of stopping, she called Tim Sweeney. Since the Honda was somewhat unreliable, she had him on speed dial.

"There's a guy who needs a tow." She gave the location and mile marker.

"Thanks, hon," Tim said cheerfully. "It's coming up on the holiday season, so I can use the money. I'll go help him out."

When she got home, she was understandably nervous. Her mother had talked her into letting her care for the kittens while she was at work. Lillian had said, "Trust me with them.

I promise you I can help. And I need something to keep me busy."

She'd replied, "You understand they're messy and——"

"I know. Just like all babies. I can do this for you, darling. Let me." It was the ultimate olive branch, and she had been unable to refuse.

So she had taught her what needed doing and how often to care for them. She'd told Lillian they needed to be held as much as possible. It would be the last straw if her mother hadn't done a good job, had forgotten them or fobbed them off on the staff. *She promised——*

But when Neva came into the lavish sitting room, decorated in blue and silver striped wallpaper, she found her mother cuddling all three kittens. She had fur and formula on her sweater . . . and she looked remarkably happy about it. A knot dissolved inside her. She remembered a time when Lillian hadn't been so rigid, and it appeared her mother did, too. The chasm between them wasn't unbridgeable.

"They're fine. See?" Lillian held the orange one up. "She's so lively!"

"Yes, they'll be ready to start exploring a bit soon. But you'll need to keep an eye on them. They could easily get lost in a house this size."

Her mother seemed thoughtful. "What about a playpen? One of the new ones with the netting? I looked at your old one up in the attic but it has wooden bars. They'd slip right out."

Astonishment dawned. "That would be perfect. You could put a few soft toys in there for them. More space for them to play, but not enough for them to get lost or feel frightened."

"They need to be in their box at night, of course. I'm sure they're used to it." Lillian stood, all three babies cradled in one arm. "I'll send the housekeeper out. Would you make a list of what toys would be suitable for them?"

Tears prickled at her eyes. Ridiculous—she hadn't cried in years—and now that she'd started, she couldn't seem to stop. It meant so much, maybe more than it should, to see her mother taking an interest in what she loved, even if it was just three orphaned kittens. Before she could embarrass herself, her phone rang. Neva glanced at the screen and was surprised to identify the caller as Tim Sweeney.

"What's up?" she asked.

"Are you sure of the directions you gave me?"

She frowned. "Absolutely. There's only one route to Harper Court from the clinic. I was on Harper Road." Embarrassing, but the street had been named for her great-grandfather because he brought money in when the town needed it most, during the Great Depression.

"Well, when I got there, I didn't see any stalled vehicle. Just an oil stain."

"Maybe he got the car moving again?"

"I guess. Next time I'll just wait for the customer to call me."

"I'm sorry I wasted your time."

When she hit end, she looked up to find her mother watching her. "What was that about?"

Neva summarized, feeling uneasy for no reason she could name. She remembered the shadow out at the farm and the glint of light on what might have been binoculars. Rubbing her hands up and down her arms didn't banish the chill.

And then Lillian put a finger on it. "If his car wasn't really broken down, and you'd stopped . . . oh honey. I'm so glad you were careful."

It was a predatory trick. Unease flared, leaving her shaken. "I just had a feeling. You know, those instincts Ben always makes fun of?"

"And thank God for it. Do you think we ought to call Cliff?"

Ordinarily she would dismiss it. But they had found a dead girl in a trunk. Maybe that woman had stopped to help and wound up killed for her kindness. Maybe the same thing had happened to Luke. There were so many places to dump a body around here. Acknowledging the possibility hurt, almost more than she could bear.

"Yes," she said through numb lips. "I think maybe we should tell him. If it's nothing, then he can decide it is."

Lillian nodded and took Neva's phone. She had the sheriff's personal number memorized, probably because she arranged his golf meetings with Conrad. "Cliff, it's Lilly. Could you come out to the house? I'm sorry for the short notice. You can stay for dinner if you like." A rumbled affirmative came in answer. She hung up and said, "Good. He'll be here in about half an hour. Do you want to go change? I'm fine with them."

For once, Neva didn't take offense to the suggestion. She did smell like she had been working with animals all day. Since her mother wasn't precisely pristine, either, the question lacked teeth. It was a considerate offer, nothing more.

"Yes, I think it'll bolster me before talking to Cliff."

"Go on then, darling."

On impulse she dropped a kiss on her mother's cheek as she went by. The sudden mist in Lillian's eyes ratified the decision as a good one. Neva took the stairs at a slow jog, nodding at a maid or two as she went by. In their black-and-white uniforms, they were neater and better dressed than she. But it didn't matter.

She washed up quickly and changed into a pair of jeans and a red sweater. By the time she got back downstairs, the sheriff had arrived. As she approached, she heard him making small talk with her mother.

"I'd name that one Garfield, I surely would."

Lillian smiled at him and shook her head. "It's a girl, Cliff."

"Oh. Then maybe not."

"Ah, here's Geneva." Her mother didn't get up, understandably, as she still had kittens all over her lap.

If I could just get her to call me Neva, things would be perfect. But she was happy with the middle ground they'd found. It wasn't like she hadn't heard the argument before: *I called you Geneva because it's a beautiful name. If I had wanted to shorten it, I'd have done so on your birth certificate.* No bitterness attached to the memory this time, though.

Cliff strode over and shook her hand firmly. Some men got old and dumpy, but Sheriff Raleigh really did look good for his age. "Your mother says you have something to tell me?"

"It may be nothing, but . . ." She filled him in on what had happened with the not-stalled car.

He wore a frown by the time she finished. "People do use it as a ruse. Sometimes they rob or rape the person who stops, but I've also read about killers who use it as a method to lure victims."

She stilled, hardly daring to breathe. "Do you think we have someone working the highways and county roads around here?"

"I'd love to tell you no because the very idea it might be happening on my watch offends me. But the truth is, there's a lot of pavement out there and a lot of psychos. It's . . . possible." The sheriff studied her for a moment. "The girl we found at the clinic, she looked a little like you."

Lillian drew in a sharp breath. "Are you suggesting—"

"I'm not saying anything. But maybe I should get the word out that brown-haired, brown-eyed girls should be careful. That's all." He turned to Neva. "Can you tell me anything about the car?"

Crap. At the time, she hadn't known it mattered—and it had been dark. *If Zeke was with me, he could say. He has better night vision.* But if Zeke had been with her, they wouldn't have driven that route at all. They'd have gone to the farm instead.

"Chevy. Light colored, late model. That probably doesn't help a whole lot."

Raleigh just nodded his thanks. "Anything about the man?"

"He was tall, at least six feet, I'd say. Rangy build. Red hat." Of that, she felt sure. When he'd stepped in front of the headlights, signaling her, she'd noted the ball cap in the rear-view mirror.

The sheriff pushed to his feet. "I don't feel able to say whether this means anything or not. I'll get on the phone and give this information to the ABI agent. He's the one handling the murder investigation. If you'll excuse me a minute?"

Raleigh went out into the hall for privacy, but Neva could still hear him in the silence of the house. The quiet used to weigh on her like a smothering hand. Now she was just happy to be home.

"Agent Hebert," she heard Cliff say. "This is Sheriff Raleigh. We met when you were in Harper Creek?" A pause. "I'm not sure if this signifies, but I figured you should know." He told Neva's story, almost word for word. When he came back, he seemed unsettled. "He said we should keep an eye out for the car, just in case."

"Anything else?" Lillian asked.

"He's coming to talk to Neva tomorrow." Raleigh faced her then, instead of her mother. "Will you be at the clinic?"

She gave a tense nod. "Usual business hours. If he comes later, I'll be here."

He nodded. "That's what I told him. Just . . . take care. I don't like the way this feels, and your dad would have my . . ." Raleigh swallowed the coarser word, no doubt in deference to their ladylike sensibilities. Neva stifled a snort. "Er, backside if anything happened to you."

"I'd do what now?" Conrad Harper stood in the doorway of the sitting room, surveying them with equal parts puzzlement and alarm.

He had to be remembering the last time he'd come home to such a scene. The sheriff had been delivering the unpleasant news that they had found Luke's car . . . but no sign of him at all. Her father seemed to take comfort in the fact that Neva was sitting there, safe and sound. Not gone.

But I might be. If I'd stopped. The thought chilled her.

Lillian passed her the kittens and hurried to kiss him. Not a social peck, but a smooch that made Neva turn away with a grin. Her mother whispered to him for a few seconds, likely filling him in. She wished they had better news.

"It's okay," she said quickly. "I'm fine."

Her dad hugged her anyway, as if he feared losing her. She had spent so long focused on how she wasn't Luke, she had forgotten that they loved her, too.

"I'm glad you're out of that apartment," her father said. "I'll beef up security. You're staying to eat, right, Cliff?"

The sheriff agreed, "Wouldn't miss it. I smell Caro's luscious roast beef."

Caroline James had been cooking for them for twenty
years. For the last ten, Sheriff Raleigh had been saying
he'd marry her and take her home with him. Which might
even work if she wasn't seventy years old and disinclined to
younger men. For the first time, Neva realized how lucky she
was, because she had memories like this.

Some people, like Zeke, were totally alone. Maybe he had
an aunt or cousins, but he was apart from them in ways that
couldn't be mended. For a little while she'd thought she could
reach him, but no. He was too far from her, too, and the ache
settled into her chest again, but she resolved not to let it own
her.

They ate a delicious dinner, and there was laughter in the
house for the first time since Luke went missing. Afterward
they played with the kittens and set up the playpen in the sitting room. Raleigh stayed late, and Neva watched her parents
together, feeling like it might be the last time. The doctors had
said her father had a year but he might go downhill quickly.
But from the research she'd done later, life *with* treatment
could be worse. She respected his choice; she just wished it
wasn't breaking her heart, too. But she put that aside. Tonight
was not the time for such dark thoughts; it was an oasis, and
a respite.

Tomorrow she would meet with Agent Hebert, answer
his questions, consider the dangers, and take up her burdens
again.

CHAPTER 19

Coming out of the supply closet, Neva smacked into Zeke. He had an armful of dog food, so she stepped back to let him through. Before, he would've stolen a kiss and nuzzled his face into the curve of her neck. Remembered pleasure curled through her, chased by an ache that it was lost. She didn't intend to speak, but that seemed churlish. Though the effort might kill her, she would be better than that.

So she fixed a fake smile in place while he stacked the supplies, and said, "Everything all right?"

"That a joke?"

"No." She was surprised to find that true. "We're still friends. It didn't work out between us, but that doesn't mean I stopped caring what happens to you."

"Too sweet for your own good," he said softly. "Ought to hate me. Wish—"

"Don't. Don't say it." Hurt and longing swamped her in equal measure, and she wasn't strong enough to go down that road with him again. "Please don't make me think about it."

It hadn't been nearly long enough for her to forget. He let

out a slow breath, and she had the unmistakable impression he hurt as badly as she did. If she stood here much longer, she would beg him to tell her why. Because that was the worst part of this: she couldn't make sense of it.

But he'd always been good at reading her moods. "Can't control it. Those feelings. Wanted to kill him, and it's unlikely to get better, so . . . better this way. Better without me. Can't live in your world and play the part you need me to. Wanted to, so damn bad." His voice dropped, leaden with sorrow and finality. "Can't."

In front, Julie was playing a Christmas CD, Faith Hill singing "O Holy Night." Neva heard her friend moving around, hanging the usual decorations: lights, garland, ornaments, and pictures of their pets the children from the elementary school sent over, so full of cheer when she felt bleak as a salted, fallow field.

"You say that," she said, "and I have no way of proving you wrong. But I'll always be sorry that you didn't even try."

He flinched at that, back against the steel shelving. "Not true."

"*One* party isn't a real effort. And yes, you fucked it up. You could have apologized and pushed past it. But all you know how to do is run. So fine, that's your call. But don't look at me with those sad, sad eyes and act like you had no choice. You just made the wrong one."

Neva pushed past him and went straight to her office. She had five minutes before her next patient arrived. She wrapped her arms around herself, shaking from head to toe. It felt good to tell him off; she'd been saving up those words for days, but it hurt as well because she'd wounded him, and she was still close enough to him to feel when he suffered. Instead she waited until she could face her client with equanimity, listening to Julie do the intake and settle them in the exam room.

Mrs. Jones wanted Kady's teeth cleaned for the holidays. Scraping gunk off poodle teeth wasn't exactly the glorious animal-saving mission she'd signed on for, but it paid the bills. Unfortunately, the dog didn't enjoy the process, so she had to sedate her. Thus Neva kept busy until lunch, when she had an appointment.

"I'm going out. Can you hold the fort for me?" Julie had already done so much—Neva felt bad about asking more—but this was nothing she wanted, not a fun outing.

Her friend smiled. "Not a problem. I actually brought my lunch today."

On impulse, she gave Julie a quick hug around the shoulders. "Don't know what I'd do without you."

"Live the most boring life imaginable and pine away to nothing?"

"For sure."

"Are you coming to our holiday party this weekend?"

Travis and Julie hosted a big bash in December each year. They did it before the rush, so they were guaranteed good attendance; people weren't yet sick of Christmas carols, cheese log, and wassail.

"I wouldn't miss it."

Julie grinned. "Then you won't mind helping me decorate on Friday night."

"Not at all."

With a wave, she collected her coat and stepped out into the wind. The tan jacket flapped in the wind as she strode along the walk. The nail salon was doing a brisk business; Neva lifted a hand in greeting to a girl she recognized from high school currently buffing the dead skin off Mrs. Jones's feet. Kady watched from her oversized handbag, still groggy from the sedative. Pink neon framed the windows, where they advertised that walk-ins were welcome.

Down at Armando's, she found Hebert waiting for her. He hadn't yet taken a seat and drew interested glances from women eating their lunches nearby. The agent seemed unaware of his eligible status; Neva decided not to enlighten him. It would be entertaining to watch.

"Thank you for meeting me," he said.

"I needed to eat lunch anyway and they do great sandwiches here."

"What do you recommend?"

"I usually order the special. It saves money, and everything is good."

From his expression, he thought money shouldn't be a concern for her, which meant Raleigh had filled his ears about her being the first daughter of Harper Creek and needing to be afforded all deference; it also explained his mild dislike on their first meeting. She might be back on good terms with her parents now, and her financial problems would disappear soon enough, but that hadn't always been the case.

Today, they had a turkey and Swiss combo on sale, so she ordered that. For seven dollars and ninety-nine cents, she got a drink and a side as well; Neva figured that was a decent deal, and why Armando's did a good business. They waited in line together, making small talk, so they could pretend this wasn't a business lunch. From the shadows in his eyes, Neva didn't reckon that fiction worked any better for him than it did for her.

Wax vegetables and plastic leaves lined the top of the glass counter; she had seen them countless times. From the pictures of food on the walls to the faux wood tables, everything here was familiar, but it felt strange with Agent Hebert standing at her left. After receiving their trays, they settled at a table near the back and ate for a while in silence. Just as well. Once they got started, the food probably wouldn't go down at all.

It didn't take long for the curiosity to start. A woman she'd gone to high school with stopped by, wearing an inviting smile. Though she greeted Neva, her attention lingered on Hebert. The woman asked, "Are you here for the holidays then?"

"Pardon me?" Clearly he didn't come from a small town.

"I'm on the welcoming committee. It's my job to keep tabs on all the new faces." Her name was Melissa McDonald, Neva remembered. Twice divorced, unless she was thinking of her sister.

He managed to glare her away with his ice green eyes, but two more hopefuls stopped by, digging for information, though the third one tried asking Neva if she had a new boyfriend. "We were all so glad to hear you cut that awful Zeke Noble loose."

That did it. She gave the bitch her best Harper stare, until she slid away. For good measure, she leveled the look on the whole place in case anyone else had ideas about approaching their table. She couldn't afford to be away from work the whole afternoon; they needed to get this done.

"Helpful," he observed. "Your mama teach you that?"

"Among other things."

"Why were they so persistent?"

She raised a brow. "You really don't know?"

Hebert half shrugged with the lifting of one lean shoulder. "Should I?"

"You're young, handsome, and they presume gainfully employed. Your clothes bear no tobacco stains. That qualifies you as a catch, Mr. Hebert."

For the first time, he seemed flustered and eager to change the subject. "Are you set?"

"Yes. I've already told Sheriff Raleigh everything I can remember. But it's no problem to go over it again with you."

It wasn't as if she disliked the guy. In fact, the agent struck her as handsome enough when he wasn't staring at her like he despised the air she breathed. Today he'd lost some of his edge. He merely looked weary, his green eyes like imperfect emeralds in contrast to his brown face.

"You said the man was driving a late-model Chevy, is that right?"

She nodded. "It wasn't a Corvette or a Camaro. That's about all I can say."

Hebert drew a laptop out of his bag and set it on the table between them. A sticker on the window said "Free Wi-Fi." She waited while he made the connection and clicked some keys. Then he spun the screen toward her. He'd brought up the Chevrolet home page.

"Just take a look at each model. You might remember more than you think."

She clicked past the Malibu and the Impala, and then paused. "It might've been an Aveo or maybe the Cobalt Coupe."

"Can you recall how many doors it had?"

"Two. I'm pretty sure."

"Was it a hatchback?"

Neva shook her head. "It definitely wasn't."

"Then it must be the Cobalt Coupe. Could you look at the colors for me? I know it was night time, but if you could narrow it down more than *light*, that would help a lot."

There were only two possibilities, in fact: silver ice metallic and summit white. The rest were just too dark. She studied the two shades and said, "Summit white. I don't think there was any shimmer to it."

Hebert made a note. "I'll see if any cars matching those parameters have been reported stolen recently. You've been very helpful, Ms. Harper. Do you still have my card in case anything else comes to mind?"

She dug into her purse and checked the slot in her wallet where she collected them, then she said, "I do. Will you be in town long?"

"It depends on what I find while I'm here."

That was as cagey a response as she'd ever heard. Neva furrowed her brow, scrutinizing the minute differences in his appearance. As a vet, she often made diagnoses based on small symptoms, but sometimes it boiled down to a feeling.

"She wasn't the only one," she said slowly. "That's why you look so tired. How many, Agent Hebert?"

"I can't disclose details of an ongoing investigation."

"Did they all look like me?"

Hebert didn't answer that question, either. At least, not aloud. But she saw the flicker of his lashes as he glanced away. Cold coalesced in her stomach like a chunk of dry ice.

"I won't take up any more of your time," he murmured. Something in his voice shifted, though. A whisper of a drawl? She'd never noticed it before. It didn't sound like Alabama, but she'd need to hear more in order to tell where he might be from. With economical grace, he wiped his mouth and stood. She gathered up his trash for him, then stacked it on her tray, and he drew up short, startled.

"What?"

Hebert just shook his head. "It doesn't matter. Good day, Ms. Harper."

Not surprisingly, after that conversation, she didn't feel like going back to work, but she still had a full afternoon of patients to see. With the holidays thundering toward them, pets needed vaccinations before they could be boarded or go on a trip. They needed checkups and teeth cleanings and medicine for motion sickness. With a faint sigh, she cleared the table and went back to work.

Geneva Harper wasn't like he'd expected, based on Sheriff Raleigh's comments. Hebert decided he liked her. And a maniac was killing women who bore more than a passing resemblance to her. He knelt where she'd seen the car—faint tire tracks, but nothing that struck him as distinctive. He took a few pictures, more to be thorough than because he thought it would prove vital to the case. But one never knew.

Time to pack it in and head for the sheriff's office to use the NCIC database. As he got back in his car, his phone rang and Raleigh's voice came across the line. "I think you need to get over here, if you're still in town."

"What's up?"

"Last night I told my boys to keep an eye out for any reports related to light, late-model Chevrolets."

"An unofficial BOLO?"

"More or less."

"I take it they found something?"

"Strangest thing . . . but, yes. The Willigs called and reported their car missing. They'd gone on vacation in Europe, but the missus started feeling poorly, and wanted to come home early. When they arrived, they found the back door of the garage standing open and the car gone."

"Let me guess," Hebert said. "It was a Cobalt Coupe, summit white."

"How did you know that?" Raleigh sounded impressed.

"Never mind that. What's the status on the vehicle?"

"I've got it in impound right now."

"Already?" Now Hebert was impressed.

"They had OnStar. That's why we tracked it down so fast.

The thief must have fled on foot, as soon as he realized it had a tracking system. The truly strange thing? It was only a few miles down the road from the Willig place when we found it."

Strange, indeed. He had the sense they were missing a vital piece of the puzzle, and if he could just work it out, then everything else would fall into place. But if the guy had been forced to abandon the vehicle earlier than planned, he would've left evidence behind. *Got you this time. Foiled because an old woman didn't like French cooking. That has to sting.*

"Don't let anyone touch anything. I'm calling my crew."

Hebert did that first thing and received a promise the full team would arrive as soon as they could. Hair, fiber, prints—anything they found on the car could prove useful, assuming a connection between the man who had tried to lure Geneva Harper into stopping and the one Minnie Davies had seen outside Tina Hedwig's house. If not, then they'd have a ridiculously strong case against anyone they arrested for joyriding in the Willig coupe.

Then he drove downtown, such as it was. He could tell it had been restored recently because most of the buildings carried the same brick façade. In winter it was quaint, the light poles strung with white lights. Somebody—the town beautification committee most likely—had planted trees along the sidewalk at regular intervals, and they too had been wrapped in lights . . . and red ribbon. Most likely, it meant nothing. Red ribbons were a common holiday touch. Yet he stared hard at those trees as he went past.

The Halpern County courthouse was an old colonial building with smooth white columns, surrounded by lawyers' offices and bail bondsmen. They were doing a brisk business, too. These days, crystal meth had become a problem even in rural areas. Hebert grabbed his bag and exited the vehicle; he clicked the button, locking the doors, as he hurried up the steps. A chill wind bit through his jacket. It was hard not to feel for the girls he had found out in the woods.

They'd discovered another one. Anonymous tip. He didn't like those. Didn't trust them. And the girl . . . this death had been the most personal—and the most artful—yet. He could still see her in his mind's eye, pale and pretty and covered in flowers. Someone had choked the life out of her. The count had increased. He'd escalated, gone from experimentation to perfecting his method. This kill displayed none of the tentative exploration from before. Now they were dealing with someone who had discovered what gave him the greatest satisfaction. Less time would elapse between victims, though he might become cleverer about disposing of them. Or he might become more flagrant, seeking the attention inherent in quick discovery. Some dreamed of starting their own cult of personality and did not mind they could end their days in prison or in the execution chamber.

His people had swept the area and this time, they hadn't come up empty-handed. Unfortunately, the results took time. The labs were all backlogged, and the approaching holidays didn't make response times better. If only he could sit down at a computer and get instant results as they did on detective shows.

He pushed through the heavy doors and found himself in a hallway, where everything was made of burnished wood. Hebert paused at the directory and then followed the arrows to Sheriff Raleigh's office. Once inside, he found himself in an large open room full of desks used by his deputies. There was a jail cell to the left, and straight on, an ornate door inset with frosted glass stenciled with Raleigh's name and title. He made straight for it.

A few officers nodded or raised a hand in greeting. Nobody tried to stop him. He did knock before stepping into the other man's domain. It was only polite.

"Come in!" Raleigh called.

Hebert did. They had a lot of ground to cover, and he had a new theory. One that just might catch a killer, if the evidence bore his idea out.

CHAPTER 20

You're a fucking failure. *Shoulda drowned you at birth.*

This time, nothing he did made the old man's voice go away. It drilled into his skull like an ice pick. *You're gonna get caught before you do her. Because you don't have the balls. Way to go with that car, genius. That was a real brilliant plan.*

A shudder went through him. The worst part was that he'd been thinking the same thing. Having the couple return just before he brought the vehicle back had been catastrophic, derailing his master plan. Nobody would've ever known it was missing, and he would've had the opportunity to wipe down the car just in case, and then park it in the garage. But then Geneva Harper was rumored to be kind; she should've stopped for him.

As her brother had.

A roar escaped him. It didn't matter out here. The only one who could hear him had been without recourse for months. Maybe that would make him feel better. Maybe the old man would like to see Lucius Harper bleed.

He had kept him alive this long because it was perfect
and diabolical; after everything else he'd suffered, Luke also
had to watch his sister die. And he knew precisely how to do
it, now. He was ready for her. Feeling the soft flesh give in
his hands, silencing the gargling cries and incoherent wails?
Godlike. Just thinking about it gave him a silent rush. Unlike
the others, he had kept something of hers to remember her
by. She had been the perfect victim, offering him the perfect
death. He wished he could do it again and again.

But now everything had been ruined. He'd left evidence
behind. If they ever figured out that everything centered
around the Harpers, they would start digging. And it wouldn't
take long to find his family's history of threats and griev-
ances. The old man had left a trail a mile wide.

*Never left them a stolen car with my fingerprints all over
it,* the old bastard said.

It might be a little tougher to track him. He'd changed his
name for that very reason. But it wouldn't stop a determined
investigator. Soon enough they'd realize that Donnell Carson
had a son. They'd figure out how he had been fired from the
mill and spent his years thereafter drinking, beating his wife
and child, and spouting threats against the Harper family.

I was so close, he thought, heart heavy.

Now it was all falling apart. Funny how one mistake could
change everything. Now he raced the clock to see if he could
finish what he'd started before they put the pieces together.
With the evidence he'd left behind in the car, if they started
looking at his family, then he was done. His name change was
a matter of public record, and the truth would lead right to him.

He strode through the ruined house and out the back door.
Chain and padlock secured the root cellar, which offered perfect privacy for all his dire work. When they found this place,
they would know. But he wasn't in custody yet. He had a little
time.

Pulling the key from his pocket, he unlocked the base-
ment and climbed down the ladder, pulling the doors closed
after him. He heard the other man breathing in terrified gulps.
Each time he came down, Harper feared it meant the end,

and he had gotten to the point, after his long captivity, that he didn't know what he wanted more: freedom or death.

In the dark, with perfect ease, he found the chain and yanked, summoning weak illumination. This underground room smelled of human filth and fear. Lucius looked weak and sick from his incarceration. He had scabs on his wrists from where he'd tried to escape time and again, before accepting the cuffs weren't coming off unless he chewed his own thumbs off. He was too civilized for that. For a while, he hoped for rescue and maintained a brittle defiance. Now Harper was more of a beaten dog. He knew that feeling well.

The water bottle beside him was nearly empty, and the bucket in the corner was nearly full. He hadn't come down here in a while.

"Come to finish me?" Harper asked, toneless.

"Not just yet." But he did lash out with a booted foot to sate his anger.

He moved close enough to snag the water bottle and fill it from the tap, then he set it on the floor just inside Harper's reach. Next he found an old loaf of bread on the pantry shelf. By now it would be stale and moldy as well. If Harper was hungry enough and if he wanted to survive, he'd choose to eat it. And then, for the little time remaining him, Harper would burn with that awful desperation. He placed the bread beside the water bottle.

Down here it was dark and cold, nothing but dirt and cement block. The old man liked seeing the great Harper heir so reduced. It quieted his rage to manageable levels, freeing him to think. Maybe all was not yet lost. Maybe he could still triumph; surely he was not destined for a quotidian end in a gloomy cell.

"Why are you doing this?" The question came in the tone of one who had long since given up hoping for an answer.

He smiled. "You'll find out soon enough."

His tone must've penetrated because Harper focused on him, really focused, and fresh fear kindled in his face. "What does that mean?"

"It means you'll be seeing your sister before too long."

"No!" Despite weakness born of captivity and deprivation, the man lunged for him, straining at his chains. "Leave her alone!"

"Your parents are going to be devastated, you know. Both their children in one year . . . who could bear that? Your mother already looks so fragile—"

"You're not human. Haven't you done enough to my family already?"

"No," he said gently. "I'm only just getting started."

When he left, he carried away with him the beautiful sound of Harper weeping. He felt near tenderness for the man; he'd spent days down here himself. As a child, he'd tried to resist the old man's attempts to shape him into something else. He'd just wanted to eat and sleep and play like other children. But the darkness and the rats soon cured him of it. The old man had been proud when he came back and found him surrounded by corpses.

Now they won't bite me anymore, he'd said, angry and defiant.

And the old man had unlocked his chains, for once approving. He'd ruffled his hair and said, *Good work, Son. You faced your fear. You killed your enemy. Now you're worthy to eat at my table.*

For the first time in his life, he had been proud. His mother, weak and cringing cow that she was, ran his bath and fussed over his wounds. She didn't understand he'd come out of the ground in triumph, changed from that pathetic, crying, wetting thing. He had harnessed the darkness, as the old man intended. He could mold it to his will and make others dance as he desired. There was such power in that. If he could just succeed in silencing the old man's voice forever, then he would be free.

It was a risk, driving his personal vehicle out here. But he could not risk a theft each time he needed to visit. So instead, he sat with his lights off, some distance from the ruined house. For long moments he watched the road, making sure it was clear in all directions, before he pushed out of the overgrown drive. Two cars passed, their lights blazing in twin halos. If someone stopped and asked why he was parked here, what would he say? He'd have to kill them. His pulse thundered as if he'd been running. *Thud. Thud. Thud.* The rhythm reminded him of a shovel striking the dirt—funny, even his own heart sounded like the grave.

But nobody noticed him. The old man had taught him well. Once the way was clear, he pulled onto the road and drove sedately home, where his woman waited for him. She was cooking when he arrived, which meant he was late.

"Did you get the cherries and the cognac?"

He stared at her, nonplussed. She'd asked him if he would run out to the store for her. A pound cake sat cooling on the counter, filling the house with a delicious, buttery aroma, lightly touched with sweet vanilla. The black cherry cognac sauce would provide the perfect touch to the dessert—and he'd forgotten the reason he'd left the house in the first place. Stress built at the back of his head. He couldn't think of a single excuse.

She paused, frowning. "Are you all right? Did something happen?"

"I almost hit a deer." The lie came out smoothly, supplied by the old man. "I never made it to the store."

He felt the old man staring out of his eyes. Avid. Lustful. This was the first time he'd ever taken control, and he was so relieved, he let him.

You owe me. Remember that. And he knew what the old man wanted. To ride her the way he had his mother in life: cruel, vicious, and domineering. When the time came, he'd fight that. She couldn't be damaged as he had been.

"But you didn't? You're not hurt." She took a tactile survey, her hands gentle.

"Just a little shaken. It was a close call." He couldn't afford to slip up like this again. The disaster with the car had shaken everything loose—distracted him and made him careless.

"Well, dinner's almost ready now. Don't worry about the sauce. Whipped cream and powdered sugar will do fine."

She laid the table, talking about her day at work. They

ate. So normal. So unlikely. He tuned her out, listening to the
old man's whispers. But when she mentioned his mother, she
gained his full attention.

"I still haven't met her," she said, frowning. "I know you
said she hates the idea of us being together, but it's been so
long. Does she really dislike me that much, without ever
meeting me?"

Anger lashed its dragon tail inside him. "We've been over
this before. You can't meet her. She's never going to give her
blessing. I . . . I don't have a normal family like you. If you
want to be with me, you have to accept that."

"But . . . we talked about getting married. You want to do
that without giving me a chance to win your mother over?
She'll like me, I promise. Everyone does."

"I said *no*," he snarled, and the old man's voice came out.

*No. No, no, no, no. Not here. Not with her. Don't touch
her. Don't.*

Her fear rose up like a ghost in her face, shadowing the
way his mother had always looked. Always. Always. He
closed his eyes so he wouldn't have to see it, but the old man
was still looking. Smiling. Women only understood one way:
the belt or the boot. He'd teach her respect.

No. But he'd swung around the other side of the one-way
door with a mirror in it. He could watch, but he couldn't do
more than pound his fists and scream while his body moved.
Her eyes went wide when his fist balled up. Blood stained her
pretty mouth. She tried to flee, scrambling away on hands and
knees.

Oh, no, don't run. Don't run. That only makes it worse.

As he had always done, when things were darkest, he
closed his eyes and began to sing. *Don't you laugh when the
hearse goes by . . . cause you might be the next to die. They'll
wrap you up in a clean white sheet . . . and put you down
about six feet deep. They put you into a wooden box . . . and
cover you over with earth and rocks.*

The worms crawl in . . . the worms crawl out . . .

He did not hear what happened next.

* * *

They must know.

It had taken longer than Zeke had expected. It was almost Christmas now, but when he heard the vehicle coming down the road a few miles distant, Zeke froze. He remembered the sound of it, and for an instant, he considered running. They'd never find him in the wild, but if he did that, then he said good-bye to his humanity. Out there, he would lose himself faster.

It might happen anyway. He'd noticed without Neva around, he cared less how he appeared to others, and instinct fought with logic constantly. Little by little, he was forgetting what it meant to be human. So maybe this was for the best. Maybe he'd been wrong to think he could live a normal life, after what had been done to him, and he belonged in a cell, now. Even if he hadn't done this, he might do something worse down the line. He remembered the deer and his bloody mouth and a shudder rolled through him.

Going out on the porch, he watched for those who would lock him up. When the car rounded the final curve to his house, he saw Hebert behind the wheel. Zeke felt remarkably unmoved. He did wake up in places he shouldn't be. Even he couldn't swear on a Bible he hadn't done this, so he couldn't feign surprise as the agent eased out of his car and climbed the steps to join him on the porch.

"Do you have a minute to talk?" Though the guy kept his tone friendly enough, Zeke knew if he said no, they'd go downtown and make it official.

So he turned and opened the front door. "Sure. Come on in."

He didn't bother making a tray of coffee like Neva, what seemed so long ago now. There was no altering the purpose of this visit. He dropped down into the armchair and propped his ankle on his knee, waiting for the accusations to start.

Hebert showed more interest in the house this time around, too. The agent moved around, examining the picture books on his coffee table. That would be fun to explain. He'd bought them trying to see if he could puzzle out simple words, if they were set apart from others and written in big letters. But he could tell the agent found children's books in the home of a single man more than mildly creepy.

Eventually he sat down on the edge of the sofa and clasped his hands between his knees. Sitting so, he could reach his weapon fairly easily, so Zeke read readiness in case he tried to make a move. At that, he almost smiled. If he wanted to kill the guy, he'd never see it coming. Good thing for Hebert he didn't.

"We know you made the anonymous call," he said quietly. "When I asked the clerk about it, she remembered your truck because it was loud and old. She puts you there at the time the call was made from the payphone outside."

Even he knew if they had a case, he wouldn't be chatting with Hebert in his living room. He didn't like the breach of his territory, but he would like being confined even less. Remembered horror rolled through him. "And?"

"That means you're the one who found the girl."

He nodded. "So?"

"Why didn't you come forward in a more forthright fashion?"

"Didn't want to get involved."

"Or maybe you wanted to make sure people found and admired your work. She was the prettiest one yet, wasn't she?"

"Didn't do that to her," he said, though by the flicker of Hebert's expression he found the denial unlikely. "Knew after the first girl, you'd see me finding the second as more than bad luck."

"Explain it to me then. How did you come to find them both?"

That would take a case of beer and eight solid hours of talking. It wasn't like he could just go get a coyote for Agent Hebert, either, and even if he did, the man wouldn't take it as proof of anything. Unlike Neva, he had no reason to trust Zeke and every reason to want to lock him up and throw away the key.

"Can't."

"I see. Mind if I take a look around?"

He shrugged. "Suit yourself."

There wasn't a secret killing room on the premises. The agent could dig around to his heart's content, and the only thing he'd find would be the bottle of shampoo Neva had left behind. Zeke didn't have the heart to throw it away; sometimes he popped the top and breathed it in, missing her until his hands shook.

Hebert took him at his word and poked around for a good fifteen minutes. Zeke heard him rifling through drawers, though he'd tried to be quiet about it. If movies could be believed, he expected to find souvenirs like pictures, shoes, locks of hair, or chunks of polished bone. If the guy thought him guilty, it was a wonder he was brave enough to stay out here alone, having spoken of his suspicions. Maybe he had a death wish.

The agent smelled angry by the time he came back to the parlor, angry and frustrated. Those scents were sharp and spicy, like jalapeño peppers and thyme. "Thanks for your cooperation."

Maybe it wasn't smart but he couldn't resist asking, "Find anything good?"

Hebert responded with a soft, cruel laugh. "By the way, I think I've discovered the connection between victims. We already knew they all had brown eyes and brown hair. But it seems they all wore a uniform, too. We have a beautician, a dental hygienist, a registered nurse, and a cafeteria worker. Who else do you know that fits that profile?" He paused, visibly enjoying Zeke's distress. "But you probably already knew, didn't you? I mean you tried to snatch her already. After she left you."

And the chill of that fear sank straight into his bones. Zeke scrambled for his keys. It didn't matter that she hated him and she wanted nothing to do with him. He had to keep her safe. Maybe Hebert had planted that seed just to see what he would do. Maybe the guy had been lying, or this was a trap. But he couldn't take chances with her safety.

This meant he'd have to brave Harper Court again—and

her parents, as well as that smug son of a bitch who'd put his hands all over her. The anger rose up, and the beast part of him roared in outrage. He flattened it, and the creature responded to his dominance as it never had before. It quieted, acknowledging him as master. Though it was a part of him, he ruled it, and not the other way around.

The truck took three tries before it started. Probably wouldn't run much longer. But as long as it got him where he needed to go this time—and faster than he could run—he'd be grateful to the thing forever. No matter how much he hated driving. The old fear kicked in as soon as the engine caught.

Sweat beaded his brow but he ignored that, as he ignored the beast whimpering in his head. Zeke stomped on the gas, spitting gravel behind his rear wheels. *She's probably safe,* he told himself. *Hebert was fucking with you. Pushing your buttons. He was just mad he didn't find anything. He's hoping you'll lead him somewhere. Your killing field.*

But he couldn't quiet the animal terror swamping him in waves. It didn't come from the unnatural speed at which he hurtled down the rough, country road. Twilight now. The trees were spindly skeletons reaching for the car. Too fast. He shouldn't be moving this fast. It made him sick especially with his own hands on the wheel.

No choice. Got to make sure she's okay.

He'd find her safe and sound at Harper Court, eating her dinner and angry to see him turn up unexpectedly. Maybe she'd yell at him some more for being a coward, and that would be fine, too. *Just, please, let her be there. Keep her safe.*

So pale it glowed against the night sky, the house was so beautiful it shook him, with its manicured lawn and graceful columns. *This* was where she came from. He'd known that all along, and yet he'd dared put his hands on her. How crazy.

It took all his courage to climb out of the truck with its awful rusted side panels and the engine that kept knocking until he pounded with both fists on the front door. Long moments passed—and he died repeatedly in his head—until the housekeeper tugged the door open. She regarded him with frosty disapproval.

"All maintenance work is done through the back door," she scolded, "and we have no repairs scheduled today. It's nearly supper time!"

"Neva home? She all right?" The beast whined, cowering from the images in his head. Their woman dead in the woods, eternally cold and pale . . . strangled by some monster's hands.

No.

"Young man, I demand you leave at once! You are hardly the sort of person Ms. Harper would—"

"What's all the fuss?" a familiar voice asked.

Zeke recognized the sound of Lillian Harper's voice and the smell of her perfume long before she came into sight. He pushed past the startled housekeeper and strode into the foyer, his breath coming in ragged gulps. How he wanted to see Neva following behind her mother, but she wasn't there. Confusion and ire scented the room, black pepper mixed with lime.

"Neva?" He spun in a slow circle as if they could produce her from thin air.

"She said she wasn't coming straight home from work tonight," Lillian said slowly. "I believe she meant to help decorate Julie's place for the Christmas party."

He was finding it hard to form words. The beast wanted to run and to fight, preferably both. It wanted an enemy to maul for making it feel this way. So did he.

"Call. Please."

"Trudy, you may go. I'll attend to Mr. Noble."

The housekeeper stomped off, muttering about men with the manners of wild pigs. He ignored her as Mrs. Harper led the way to a formal study and picked up a cordless phone. She dialed, her scent wafting in layers of muted alarm mixed with expensive perfume. The phone rang for a very long time; he listened to each one, and then Neva's voice mail kicked in. He heard each word as if she whispered in his ear.

I can't come to the phone right now. Please leave me a message.

Can't. Why did that word sound so terrifying?

"I'll try Julie's place."

But he already knew it was pointless. Her mother got the answering machine and now her alarm ripened into fright. Her hands clenched around the handset.

"What should we do?" Mrs. Harper asked him. "I trust you have reason to fear for her. What do we *do*?"

He shrugged. The beast surged again and this time he let it lead.

"I have to call my husband. He . . . he'll know what to do. No, not again. Not like this. Not Geneva." Mrs. Harper trembled on the edge of a complete breakdown.

They were such small signs of something out of place, and it was too soon for such a reaction. The police might say they had to wait twenty-four hours before she officially became missing. And most times, those twenty-fours would make the difference between life and death. Then again, Sheriff Raleigh answered to the Harpers for his election money, so he might mount a search right this minute. That was their business.

If he didn't act now, he would lose her for good. No second chances. No, maybe-someday-when-I-get-my-shit-together. *Forever*. He couldn't face that—life without her would be unbearable. If he had to face an endless death march of days, knowing she was dead and rotten in the ground, then he'd take his mother's road.

Zeke ignored Mrs. Harper, racing through the house to the veranda doors he'd used to flee the night of the party. He slammed them open and went into the dark. Now that he let himself think about her again, now that he wasn't blocking all signs of her existence, he could smell her on the night wind.

Sour. Acrid. Terror. Somewhere, Neva was fighting for her life.

CHAPTER 21

Neva woke in darkness.

She remembered coming out of the clinic and pausing to admire the Christmas lights, then a stinging in her neck. Everything went sideways after that, no more than bits and pieces. The backseat of a car floated up, swimming as if through disco lights, and next, a rumbling engine. Broken whispers. *Wasn't supposed to be like this. Not like this.* Someone had moaned those words with such pain, that she had felt almost sorry for the speaker. And then the lights went out.

Damn. I was drugged. Knowing about the potential danger hadn't saved her in the end. It had seemed so harmless, that pause, admiring the white lights twined around the poles, and taking pleasure in how they twinkled in the dark. She'd been sad since breaking up with Zeke, and it was nice to enjoy a simple thing after a long day. *God, I'm so stupid.*

Panic tried to swamp her and she fought it off. *No. Not your fault. You didn't do this. Your job is to stay calm and find a way out. You're not a victim. You won't become a statistic.*

An evil little voice whispered, *Wonder if the other women thought that at first, too.* The world swam again, and the next time she knew anything, she was somewhere else. Hard floor—and it reeked.

Her wrists had been tied behind her back, and she ached all over. Getting out of her bonds had to be the first item on a long, impossible list. A tiny sob escaped her.

"I'm not going to let him hurt you."

"Luke? Oh my God, *Luke.*" If she hadn't gone mad, that was definitely her brother's voice. If only she could see—

"Shh. Try to stay calm. As soon as he realizes you've come around, he'll be back to finish us."

"Why's he doing this?"

"He never said. The only thing I know is that he wants me to watch you die before he kills me." His flat tone worried her, as if he had gone far beyond the emotions wracking her.

She trembled with fear and cold. Behind her, she felt the individual blocks of a cement wall. Between her fingers trailed loose dirt. It stank of human excrement and urine, mildew and must. A faint breeze blew in from somewhere, indicating they weren't too far from freedom. But in which direction?

"Do you know who he is?"

"The voice is a little familiar, maybe, but he stands behind the light so I can't get a good look at him."

So it was someone they knew. So hard to fathom—someone in Harper Creek hated them that much. Their parents must be going crazy, losing not one child, but two. *And Luke doesn't even know about Dad . . .* but this wasn't the time to tell him. She had to fight past the fuzz in her head and come up with a plan.

"What can you tell me about him?"

"He wasn't himself when he brought you in. Out of control and raving. I think he'd been drinking. I never smelled it on him before tonight . . . and he'd sometimes come in several times a week to stare at me. Taunt me."

"Christ, you've been here for months. You need a doctor."

Luke made a soft sound. "Forget that. You only have one

chance." He paused, and she heard him breathing. "I'm too weak . . . I've been here too long. But I can help you get away. I'll distract him."

Sickness roiled in her stomach. "No. I'm not leaving you."

"I'm lost," Luke said softly. "And if you stay, so will you be. When it's time, run and don't look back."

"Run *where*?"

She couldn't see the way out, nor did she know where they were. The dark assumed nightmare shapes. Neva had no idea how Luke had survived with his sanity intact; she'd only been awake for a few moments, and she was already sick with terror. Her brother was far stronger than she'd known.

"He comes in from the right. In daytime, you can see enough to get a sense of the place. It's a root cellar, though I couldn't tell you exactly where."

"What happened, Luke?"

"I stopped to help somebody I thought had car trouble."

That tracked. So when he'd tried it with her, he had the assurance of having used the lure successfully before. Something must have happened, leading him to grab her boldly outside the clinic and say *to hell with finesse*. There might even have been witnesses to her abduction; Armando's had still been open when she left work.

"I appreciate you wanting to save me, but we're both getting out of here." Trying to be quiet, she wriggled around and then scooted until she could feel him behind her. "Can you cut me loose?"

"The chain's rough and rusted. I might be able to saw through. I can't unpick the knots. I told you . . ." His voice fell, nearly soundless. "I'm . . . not well."

All the more reason for them to get the hell out of here. Maybe Luke couldn't run, but if they could slip away before the maniac returned, he could hide somewhere. The most important thing had to be getting out of here. Her shoulders were already burning from being pulled back for a few hours. She couldn't imagine how Luke felt.

They didn't speak while he worked on her bonds. The sawing occasionally hurt, but she made no noise. Each heartbeat sounded insanely loud in the dark. Neva grew conscious of Luke's labored breathing, like there was fluid in his lungs. Shit, he hadn't been exaggerating. All this time in the cold, improper nutrition—not to mention the darkness and maybe festering wounds, too—God, she had to save him. Fate wouldn't be so cruel as to prove her intuition right—that Luke was alive against all odds—only to make her watch him die. Or worse, force her to save her own skin while he sacrificed himself.

No, that wasn't happening.

"How's it coming?" she whispered.

His fingers brushed over the bonds in a rattle of chain. "About halfway. It's starting to fray."

"Enough for me to break it if I strain?"

"I don't think so."

She tried. While the rope gave a little, it wasn't enough, and she only succeeded in hurting her shoulders. "Keep at it. Once you untie me, I'll find a way to get you out of those cuffs."

"So stubborn," he breathed. "You always were."

"That's why I'm a vet now and not a politician's wife."

Fear wanted to bubble up through the cracks in her defenses, but she refused to let it. This situation would've been much worse if she'd woken alone. Luke helped her keep it together, whether he knew it or not. If he could survive as long as he had, then she could manage this, too, however impossible the task seemed.

At last the final knot snapped and she pulled free. Pins and needles prickled through her forearms, and she was cold, but things could be a lot worse. Neva felt her way around the room, finding with her fingertips what felt like animal bones. *Oh, Christ.* A soft whimper escaped her.

"What's wrong?"

"Nothing. Just looking for something to cut you free."

This time, he didn't try to convince her to leave him. Most likely he knew it wouldn't work. Waste of breath. "Let me think. I know what's down here . . ." He trailed off on a sigh. "There's nothing. No tools. Just a few jars on the far shelves."

She had already worked that out for herself. "Then you may not like plan B."

"I like being here even less."

Luke had always been able to make her smile. "Point. I need you to be quiet then, no matter how much it hurts."

"What?"

"I'm going to pop your thumbs and pull your hand out before it swells. I'll have to do it to both hands. I'm sorry."

"Quit talking about it. I'm ready."

Maybe he was. She wasn't. The plan sounded good in the abstract, but in practice, she hated the idea of hurting him. Nevertheless, she steeled herself, found his hand in the dark, and brailled the location of the shackle versus his thumb. He'd lost weight since they had been attached, so that would make it easier. Neva took a deep breath and snapped, then in a quick motion, she dragged the shackle over his hand.

Luke swallowed a sound, but she didn't think it would be audible in the house, though they seemed to be on the other side of the foundation wall. His breath came in pained rasps, and she put a hand on his filthy hair. She wanted so bad to hug him but they didn't have time for that. They needed to run. Right now, in her shoes, somebody else might be making plans on how to kill the bastard; she just wanted to save her brother.

"Ready?" she whispered.

With her palm on his head, she felt him nod. Time for round two. This time she went even faster because she knew what to do, and he swallowed his scream. He wrenched forward, his thin chest colliding with hers. Neva held him for a few seconds, and then she got her hands beneath his elbows. Using the wall for purchase, she levered him to his feet.

"This way," he said. "Try not to step on anything."

Each step they took felt like a mile. Neither of them was particularly steady on their feet, Luke from the long captivity and the fresh injuries she'd inflicted, and Neva from the residual effects of being drugged. Still, they managed to get to the stairs: old rickety things of creaking wood. If the wind hadn't kicked up outside it certainly would've given them away. Any moment she expected to see a murderer's form looming above them, a boot lashing out to kick them back down into the dark. Terror sent tremors through her. She went up behind Luke, sometimes shoving him up another step when he faltered. He fumbled with the latch. Oh no. If they'd gotten this far, only to be turned back—

"Is the door locked?"

"I can usually hear him putting the chains on. Don't think he remembered this time. Something was wrong—and got it." With a grunt of effort, her brother pushed the doors wide. They banged against the ground with a soft thud, rattling the chains the killer had left open in distraction or despair, whatever drove him.

Shit, he's going to hear us. Even if he's drunk, even if he's not at the top of his game, this is still his territory. We have to hurry.

Luke scrambled up, falling forward onto his knees. She came up beside him. Nothing had ever been more welcome than the brisk, fresh breeze pouring over her. *Damp ground, and the scent of pine . . .* Neva spun, trying to figure out where they were. She'd never seen this house before, set deep in the forest. Boards had rotted away in places like jagged, graying teeth. Someone had covered all the windows in black tar paper. It looked . . . desolate, ruined, like a place that campers found in the woods, just before the axe-wielding maniac beheaded one of them.

This is not time for my imagination to kick in. If she let it, she'd conjure demons in each dry branch and gust of wind. Already the cracking limbs reminded her of breaking bone. They needed to find a road or a house with normal people inside. Something slammed nearby, like a door, or possibly breaking furniture. Had the bastard heard them? They needed as much of a head start as they could manage, and they couldn't count on him leaving them alone forever. It had been a lucky break that she shook off the drugs quicker than expected.

"I know you're tired," she said desperately. "But get up, Luke. Please."

Moonlight emphasized the new lines of pain and exhaustion etched into his face as he pulled himself up. God, he was a shadow of his former self; down in the dark she hadn't realized. Neva pushed aside the pity also. It wouldn't save them.

As a lone coyote howl split the night, they broke into a run.

Zeke nearly blew up his truck getting from Harper Court to Julie's house on Ringer Road. He didn't think she'd be there. But maybe Julie knew something. She generally left the clinic before Neva, who had gone missing at some point between work and Julie's place. Mrs. Harper had called the sheriff after she rang up her husband. Raleigh found out for them right away that Neva's car wasn't in the lot.

And then her mom just kept moaning, *It's happening again, just like Luke,* over and over, her dread scaling up until the whole house stank of it. He'd stayed until Harper himself got in and then he took off at a dead run. Let them do their own thing and go through channels. He'd use his godforsaken curse to find her.

As he got out of the car at Julie's, he still had a sense of Neva, but it was vague and impossible to follow. Not like he could just put his nose to the ground and run. He wasn't a dog, though that would be fucking handy right now.

Another smell blazed in the dark. If it had a color, it would be red: coppery and darkly sweet. Surely not. Surely this was just like the owl and the mouse. He couldn't trust himself. Zeke ran up the front walk, raised his hand to knock, and then froze. The front door stood open, light streaming onto the porch to reveal smears on the tile. Carols played merrily on the stereo; somebody was singing about a white Christmas while he stared at the blood.

He backed away as lights blazed up from behind. Another car was pulling into the drive behind. *Fucking Hebert. He didn't waste any time.*

"Got a mess in there," he said as the agent opened his car door. "Didn't go in. Didn't touch anything. Know Neva is missing, I guess?"

If the guy listened to police chatter on his radio, he knew.

That was doubtless how he'd gotten here so fast. Raleigh had been lighting a fire under every deputy, on or off duty, for the last hour and a half. They all knew if they didn't find her before dawn, chances went way down they'd find her at all, at least, not living and breathing. She'd become a murderer's toy, all painted and posed. A roar built behind his eyes; he could actually hear his own heartbeat inside his skull.

"I thought you'd lead me to her," the agent admitted.

"Sure gonna try."

"No," Hebert said. "Not like that."

Zeke had neither the time nor the patience to sort through what was in Hebert's head. They could have a beer later, if the guy really felt bad about pegging him for it wrongly. "Know you thought I was the guy. But I'm not and he's got her. Maybe grabbed her here?"

"Could be. If he did, then he's got Julie, too. I'll call it in."

"You do that," Zeke muttered.

Thinking hadn't gotten him a damn thing. Now it was time for something else. It made no sense on the surface, but he left his truck parked and took off for the woods at a run. Huge stretches of them grew around here, from a small copse of trees to a darker tangle of forest that ambled toward the national park.

Behind him he heard Hebert call out, but he didn't hear the words. He knew the other man didn't understand where the hell he was going—or why. But he was beyond caring what anyone thought of him. The only thing that mattered was finding Neva before it was too late. And so he was done cursing this gift that made him different. If it could help him save her, then he'd be grateful for the rest of his days, even if she never spoke to him again.

As he covered the ground in long strides, he heard rustling around him: animals curious about the commotion. He touched their minds in glancing contact, gaining all they knew. Sadly it didn't amount to much. They told him of good places to hide and acorn stashes, nothing he wanted to know. Even farther back, he heard signs of the agent trying to keep pace with him. *Good luck.*

Her scent floated before him, but he couldn't track it.

Eventually he stopped, clothes torn and his skin ripped from his flight through brambles. He still had no better sense for where she was, and he was only wearing himself down. Despair sank its claws deep into his guts.

As if the emotion called to sound, a howl rang out—and he knew it. Not just any coyote. *His* coyote. The pitch, the notes, the feeling; they were all familiar. Zeke cast outward, eyes closed, drifting on the wind. His old friend was miles away, but still within range. They'd run together; that made them pack. Zeke had introduced him to his woman.

Surprise and then welcome blazed through him. The coyote remembered him. It was still alone, still cold, missing the heat of its kin. But it got by, hunting and running and staying away from human farms. Except his. In a rapid wash of images, it told him it had pissed all around his property so nothing else would come near. He couldn't help but laugh at that, despite the serious situation.

Next Zeke sent a sense of Neva. *Remember her? Find her.* Promises of piles of juicy steak accompanied the request, along with the promise of a cozy straw den in his barn. *Home. Pack. Our territory.*

Another howl rang out across the miles, this one affirmative instead of lonely. The coyote had a job to do. It loped off, happy to be helping. Animals craved a purpose, almost as much as people did. This one was used to being needed to hunt meat for the young and protect the old. They both ran in tandem, bonded but separate, and he didn't fear or hate what he had become anymore.

Smell her. Close. Not words but the surety this was the female its brother wanted. Zeke reacted. Now, a new thing: one he'd never tried before, at least not on purpose. When it happened with the owl, it had been accidental. God, it had never mattered so much. He opened the link slowly, widening it like a throttle until his vision receded some and he saw what the coyote did. It was fucking nauseating, like trying to watch two TV shows at once, and he didn't even *like* TV.

He saw a flickering image of two people, running. So she was in the woods, and she had someone with her. That couldn't be good. Except for crazy Zeke Noble, nobody came out here to run around for fun. If they came out, they brought weapons and hunting permits.

As best he could, he concentrated on closing the distance between himself and his four-footed partner. But miles lay in between them and he'd already run a long way from Ringer Road. Though he was stronger and faster than most men, he had limits, and he hadn't been sleeping or eating well since Neva had left him.

The coyote paced her as she raced through the dark trees. She kept glancing over her shoulder as if she heard it, and Zeke wished he could tell her not to be afraid. He might not be there but he was *with* her. But no.

That wasn't what she feared. Not one small coyote.

He heard what the animal did: something big crashing through the undergrowth after her. And it was gaining, because she kept stopping to support the man with her. He wheezed in the night air like each breath might be his last. Neva pushed him onward. Damn, he wished the coyote spoke English, but through its ears, the words were only noise. But it knew the thing chasing these humans sounded angry.

It also recognized the sound of a hunting rifle. One of them cried out in pain.

They pushed onward, zigzagging. Lower to the ground, he could see the way the terrain shifted. But trees disguised the drop off, and they spilled down the gully, rolling head over heels, and then landing hard. More blood scented the night air. The coyote shared the idea they were done, and Zeke shook his head fiercely, putting on more speed. If he pushed any harder, his heart would explode.

But he wasn't going to make it. He knew he wasn't. He was just too far away. He wouldn't be there when the bastard caught up to her. He'd failed to keep her safe.

Rage powered him through the unthinkable. He let his own body fall—it was just meat; he didn't need it—and went sailing along the link he'd formed with the coyote. It tried to fight him at first and he soothed it with soft whispers.

It's all right, brother. Let me in. I won't stay long.

The animal yielded to gentleness when it would've fought force even to its own death. It took him a few tries to get used to driving and then he bunched his muscles to spring. Neva was down at the bottom, trying to pull the man to a standing position, but he could tell by the way the ankle bent, he wasn't going any farther. He was also bleeding, a distinctive smell.

"We'll find a place to hide," she whispered. "Come on. You can't quit on me now, Luke."

Her brother. Oh Christ.

"Grab me that stick. I'll try to slow him down. I think the fall bought us a little time, so you can find help. I don't hear him right now anyway."

With his sensitive ears, Zeke did. But he was moving off in the opposite direction, at least for now. He wanted desperately for her to agree. He'd guide her out of the woods.

But as he'd known she would, she shook her head. He knew how much she loved her brother. Hell would freeze before she left him. "If you're fighting, so am I."

Brave, brave woman. My woman. Without thinking about it, he slipped out of the brush to stand beside her. She jumped back a foot, and then froze, peering down at him. He raised his ears and wagged his tail. Sharing headspace with him, the coyote complained about being out in the open. Was this smart? They should forget this troublesome female and go catch a rabbit.

Mmm, rabbit . . .

"Is that a goddamn coyote?" her brother asked. "Could things get worse?"

She smiled, and the sight like to broke his heart. Even the coyote forgot that he wanted some fresh meat for a minute. "Don't say that. It'll start raining." Then she knelt, her movements slow and deliberate. "Dear God. I recognize your markings." Neva glanced at Luke, as if self-conscious about what she was about to say. "Did . . . Zeke send you?"

He still didn't have fine motor control of his canine body, but he managed to raise and lower his snout in a fair approximation of a nod.

"He knows I'm in trouble then?"

Another nod.

"Holy fuck. You really do have a way with animals."

"It's not me," she said. "And it's a long story."

She fetched a couple of stout branches, as Luke had asked. If the crazy chasing them had a gun or a knife, it wouldn't help a whole lot, but maybe they could take him down in sheer numbers. Zeke wished he had a wolf body or even a bear, but this little coyote would have to do.

He planted himself in front of Neva, bared his teeth, and braced for battle.

CHAPTER 22

This was not one of Hebert's shining moments. He'd followed Zeke Noble into the woods, knowing that waiting for backup might mean hauling a whole bunch of dead bodies out of the woods, come morning. That decision might make Marlow accuse him of having a death wish, but he hadn't expected the man to take off like a fucking deer. He'd never seen anybody run like that, and these days he just couldn't keep up. Truthfully, he *never* could have, even if he hadn't spent the last few months in the hospital. By the time he stopped trying, he had a stabbing pain in his side. Just a pulled muscle, he hoped, and nothing worse.

Now he had no idea what—or who—might be out here with him, but his gut said he was looking for the guy who had been killing women and dumping them in these woods. Hebert didn't even know if he could trust Noble. This might've been his last mistake, but at this point, he could only keep moving forward, because he couldn't find the way out to save his life. He stopped and listened.

In the distance, he heard the sound of people crashing

through the trees. He wasn't a woodsman by any means, but he angled in that direction. A flicker of movement in his periphery some distance off had him spinning but it was too late. Fire slammed into his gut, just like before, and he staggered back against a tree. Instinctively he covered the wound with his left hand and in the same motion whipped his gun from the holster. He emptied his magazine in the general direction of the fleeing figure, and he nailed him at least once. A muffled cry of pain floated back on the wind, but the footsteps receded, stumbling into the distance.

With shaking, blood-slick hands, he replaced the cartridge in case the son of a bitch came back. Then he got out his cell phone and prayed for a signal. *One bar. Good enough.* He dialed Sheriff Raleigh and slid down against the tree trunk, palm back on the wound. *Slow the bleeding. Hang on until help arrives.*

"Where the hell are you?" the older man demanded.

"Woods, east of Julie Fish's house."

"You don't sound good. What's up?"

"Call the cell carrier and have them activate the tracking. Need help. Been shot. Think it was our guy. Nailed him at least once. He's got the Harper girl."

"I'll get rescue to you ASAP and flood those woods with my people. Just hold on. He won't slip the net." Hebert heard Raleigh barking orders; the man hadn't cut the connection in order to start the trace, so he must be using another phone. "Pickett, we've got an officer down out there. If he dies while you're eating that sandwich, Son, you won't be able to get a job collecting tolls in this state. I said *move.*"

But Raleigh's voice was getting fainter, as if through a tunnel. Soon the words didn't sound right anymore, some other language, and it came in distorted. The phone slipped from his fingers, but he could still see the light. *Slow blinks.* The tree branches overhead wavered in and out of sight as if they were waving good-bye.

And then he saw Rina, coming toward him in a white dress. Which was all wrong because she hated skirts. She claimed she'd gotten married in slacks over at the courthouse. Her feet were bare despite the cold, and they didn't seem to touch the ground. In death, she'd come to see him home. He gave the mental finger to her husband since he couldn't seem to move his hands.

Fuck you, Preston. We'll see who spends eternity with her after all.

"Everything happens for a reason," she said.

"You're not here."

She smiled. "No. It's probably just the blood loss. You don't believe in an afterlife, remember?"

"No." But their religious differences hardly mattered now. "I always loved you, you know."

"I know. But it wasn't the kind of love that you build a life on. If it had been, you would've told me. You wouldn't have been able to keep it in."

"I didn't want to ruin our working relationship. Your friendship meant too much to me, and I knew it would be awkward—"

"Keep telling yourself that, Hebert. But one of these days you'll meet her . . . and you'll know. You won't be able to stop yourself, not for a husband or children. Not for anything. Because she's meant to be yours."

Romantic crap. He felt vaguely ashamed to have it roiling around in his unconscious, a remnant of the young idiot he had once been, who studied the meaning of flowers to pick the perfect bouquet as a secret message of love. Rina faded then. Or everything did. He fell into the dark hole he remembered from before, and it was full of tooth and bone, a mass grave full of murdered souls whose names he did not know.

He spent eternity there. Then, overhead, a white and terrible light shone down.

Zeke smelled the murderer before he heard him. The wind carried the scent of human blood. And so he listened, pinpointing the approach. Since he couldn't tell her what he intended, he loped away to scout.

"Guess it's bored," her brother said.

"No. I think he'll be back." But she didn't sound sure. She sounded scared, and it killed him he couldn't take her in his arms.

Zeke located him quickly, following his nose. That coppery trail might as well glow in the dark. The man was limping, more determined than strong. But he was also armed. Bad, bad news. Her brother had a broken ankle, and he'd taken a bullet somewhere. Luke Harper might be beyond stoic but he couldn't walk out of here on his own. They had to kill this bastard. The coyote cringed away from that idea; it hadn't experienced good luck tangling with mankind. He soothed it before fear could take a deep hold and it started fighting for control. Not yet. He couldn't leave with the job half done.

Zeke paced him as he drew closer to the gully where the other two prepared to make their stand. When he broke from the trees and started sliding down, Zeke launched himself, knowing he'd only have one shot. He sank his teeth into the arm holding the rifle and tasted his meat and bone. Horror surged through him, but the coyote part of him didn't mind at all. He dodged the kick and clamped his jaws around the rifle and towed it away as fast as he could. If the man hadn't been injured, it wouldn't have worked. As it was, the weapon went banging away down the ridge, lost in the dark. Zeke growled and lunged, but this time the kick landed, solid in the ribs. His body went flying, and he landed hard, dazed.

The coyote whined and fought him. It wasn't ready to die here. Its instincts surged harder than spiritual kinship. He wrestled, but he didn't want to hurt the brother who had already helped so much. His control slipped, and the animal floundered, trying to get to its feet. Wanting to run. But the pain overwhelmed it; that kick had certainly broken bones.

The killer closed. If he died in this coyote body, what did that mean? Would that be it? Somehow he didn't mind, regardless. She was worth everything. Worth dying for. It might even be the best thing he'd ever done. He bared his teeth and snarled.

But Neva surged into view in the dark, scrambling up over

loose dirt and rocks. She had a stick in one hand she was using
as support. The bastard wheeled away and went after her.

His voice sent a chill through Zeke, raising his hackles.
"You're gonna pay. I'm gonna make you hurt for such a long
time. Oh, I've got a different playroom for you, and you won't
get out this time."

"Travis," she choked out. "Oh my God, you? *Why?*"

"That piece of shit's dead. I should've known if I wanted
something done right I'd have to do it myself."

Neva seemed frozen on the side of the gully. "Where's
Julie? What did you do to her?"

"Don't," he roared. "This is your fault. All of it. If you'd
just stopped to help. If you'd just *died*—"

"Nobody's dying tonight but you." She lifted the stick and
its broken end looked like a spear.

Travis lunged at her and she slammed her weapon home,
using her deceptive strength and his momentum to pierce
his wound. The smell of blood grew stronger as she twisted,
her expression fierce. She was a lioness defending her cub,
a mother bear roaring in claim of her territory—all things
feral and terrible and heartbreakingly beautiful, all the wild
places he loved. The coyote stopped thrashing as it saw his
mate protecting them.

The man who had killed so many gazed down at the wood
jutting from his belly, and his hands curled around it as if he
would pull it out and keep fighting. Instead, he fell forward;
he bounced down the loose dirt slope.

Luke Harper stared down at the corpse beside him and
then up at his sister. "I wish I could've done it. I wanted to.
But thank you."

Zeke wished he could tell Neva how proud he was, but he
felt odd. Disconnected. The coyote wasn't fighting him anymore, but he had the sense his own body was very cold. And
so far away. A whine slid free of the animal's throat, but it
couldn't keep him. He floated up, but there was no connection
to bring him back, and he went sailing on the wind, like a
dandelion ghost of summers lost.

* * *

The pain was excruciating. But it was satisfying, too. Travis Delaney, who had been Delroy Carson, smiled. Because he'd won the game after all. Not the old man. He'd denied the bastard his final revenge. Drinking that bottle of Jack Daniels had been the best idea he had ever had. It had slowed him down. Dulled his wits. He'd lost his way, or maybe it was more accurate to say he found it again, near the end.

He had never been strong enough to stop it or turn aside. Never. He had been fooling himself with thoughts of a normal life. Too long ago, he had been broken, no matter how hard he tried to pretend. What he'd wanted could never have been. The voices never would've stopped. Ever. They were only getting stronger—and he had enough of himself left to realize there was no good ending. Since the first time the old man had locked him in the dark room, he'd never had a chance. But in the final hours, he had sabotaged himself, just enough.

And so he had been right. He would not finish his days in a gloomy cell. It was a cleaner, wilder death, and one more worthy than he deserved. The pain faded.

Darkness gathered. Cold crept in. Though his eyes were open, he could see nothing anymore. There was only silence. And it was good.

Neva shook in reaction. The baying and barking of hounds said help wasn't too far off, but she'd done it. Saved them. She stumbled down and bent to wrap her arms around her brother. He might be older by ten minutes, but she felt incredibly protective toward him.

"He shot you while we were running. How bad is it?"

"Flesh wound." Like Luke would admit anything else. "I need to get warm, eat a decent meal, bathe, and sleep in a real bed. Oh, and have someone set this ankle." Still no complaints—that had never been his way.

She was always the one who fought with their parents if

she didn't get what she wanted. Not him. They were going to be so happy to see him.

Up the hill, the coyote struggled to its feet. It was obviously hurt, but it limped off into the dark. Neva felt like she should call out a thank-you, but—the animal paused. Whimpered at her. It staggered down a few feet and then back up.

"I'm not leaving him," she told it.

It responded with a soft, urgent yelp. This time, it stumbled all the way to her and lay down, crawling on its belly. If she wasn't mistaken, she'd call this begging. She cut a look at Luke.

"The rescuers will be here soon," he said. "Listen. They're getting closer. I'll send them after you. Maybe you should go see what it wants. It did help us."

Zeke. It had to be. Without knowing she'd made a decision— taking a leap that Ben Reed would call ridiculous—she pushed to her feet and nodded at the coyote. "Show me. And this better not be a dead squirrel."

She snagged another stick to help her push her way up. The coyote had almost as much trouble as she did with its wounds; it had taken a couple of brutal kicks. Poor thing. Up top, it set a gentle pace, leading her through the maze of trees. After all they'd been through, she couldn't believe she'd left her brother alone in the dark. If anything happened to him, she'd never forgive herself. And yet she *knew.* It was beyond explanation.

It seemed as if they walked for miles, but eventually she saw what it was desperate to show her: a prone form lying, pale as death in the moonlight. She broke into a run, hoping it wasn't him. *Not Zeke. Please, no.*

But it was.

Neva gathered him into her arms. His skin was cold, lips already turning blue. If he had a pulse, it was too sluggish for her to tell. *CPR.* She'd taken the class, and she was certified. Pushing down her anguish, she laid him flat and went to work, breath and compression.

Nothing. The mirror test would tell her if he had no breath at all, but she didn't have any supplies out here. The coyote prowled in worried, limping circles, whimpering.

"I know," she whispered. "I know. You were him. Somehow. And he was you. But he's not anymore. He's lost and he can't find his way home."

Tears filled her eyes and spilled down her cheeks. Once more she gathered him in her arms, and instead of CPR, she pressed her lips to his. Heat. Not enough. Neva touched her brow to his.

Come back to me. Come back. We're not finished yet. We're not. Please don't give everything for me. Not when the last time we spoke, I yelled at you and called you a coward. Don't let those be the last words you ever hear from me.

She said it aloud, hoping it would help. Repeated it over and over again.

"Come back to me. I love you."

Just when her heart broke, just when her tears froze, and she stopped believing in miracles . . . he did. His lashes flickered, and then rose, revealing dreamy twilight eyes, drenched in moonlight. He was still too pale and too cold, but it meant everything that he was alive.

"Oh, Zeke," she whispered, as she had done at the farm, what seemed so long ago now. "What did you do?"

He remembered. "Not what did I do. What *can* I do?"

"I don't understand." She spoke the line mostly to give him the opening she sensed he wanted.

"Drive a coyote better than my old truck."

Zeke raised up on one elbow and reached out a hand. The animal nuzzled his fingers, and then limped away into the dark. Probably it heard the sounds of the rescue party. Luke would've sent them along.

"You ready to go? I think the cavalry's here."

"'Bout fucking time," he said.

She rode in the ambulance with him and found her parents waiting at the hospital. Neva had never been hugged so tightly in her life. But she understood when they followed the doctors— and Luke. He'd been through so much; he needed the attention more, and she wanted to be with Zeke.

Later, she used her position as a Harper shamelessly to get into Zeke's room after visiting hours. They'd put him in with

Agent Hebert, who had come out of surgery just before they
arrived. The rescue party had found him just in time. Now
there were crews in the woods, picking up the pieces, but
nobody died out there except for Travis Delaney. Under the
circumstances, it was a Christmas miracle.

Not surprisingly, Zeke wanted to check himself out.

"Am fine," he kept muttering. "Nothing wrong with me."

She folded her arms and gave him her mother's best frosty
glare. "You were unconscious in the woods for God knows
how long."

"Not for medical reasons."

"Regardless, that mandates an overnight hospital stay."

"You two gonna fuss all night?" Surely that drawl hadn't
come from Agent Hebert. Groggy from the anesthesia, sure,
but damn. He sounded like a different man.

She blushed over bothering him. "No. I'm sorry. We'll
keep it down."

Neva settled herself on the bed beside Zeke and curled into
his side. The nurses could suck it if they didn't approve. She
was a Harper, and that meant in this town, she could do whatever the hell she wanted.

But he clutched her hand, worry written in his face. "The
kittens?"

"They're fine. My mom left them with the housekeeper.
You wouldn't believe how much she loves them. She named
them Larry, Curly, and Mo."

His lips quirked in a tired smile. "Which one's Mo?"

"The little girl. It's short for Maureen."

"Cute." Zeke relaxed then and drew her fully into his arms.

Neva knew they had some talking to do yet, but there was
time. Right now, she needed sleep. Everything else would keep.

In the morning, hospital staff woke her at an ungodly hour
to check the two patients. Just as well. She'd visit Luke while
they did undignified things to Zeke. His blue eyes promised
retribution as she made her escape.

Neva ran into her mother in the hallway. Lillian swept
her into a tight hug, choking off tears. "I can't believe it. You
found him, I sat with him all night."

"That's not quite how it happened."

Lillian went on, obviously not listening, "When you went missing, I prayed like I never have in my life. God, darling, I was so frightened. I think I promised to build this hospital a new wing if you came home to me. And you're both *here*."

Her father came down the hall toward her, looking tired but happy. The fluorescent lighting brought out the new lines in his face. He wrapped his arms around both of them, seemingly unable to speak for long moments. It took him three tries.

"I thought I'd lost both of you. God knows I put the mill before you kids more than once. I was always worried about profit and loss. But I promise in whatever time I've got left, that's going to change."

"I'm glad," she whispered, tears clotting her throat.

Her parents didn't even look like the esteemed Harpers right now. They were wrinkled and disheveled from a night spent in the hospital. Neva imagined she didn't look much better. She didn't care at all.

"The doctors say Luke will be fine . . . in time." Lillian's voice broke, and she turned her face away.

But Neva knew how her mother felt; she'd given her son up for dead, along with everyone else. Inadequacy and guilt stung her, too. If she'd tried harder, fought harder, they might have found him much sooner. But Sheriff Raleigh had been doing everything he could.

"Let's get some breakfast," her father suggested. "The nurses are attending to your brother right now."

Which would explain why they weren't in the room. It was just that time of the day, she supposed. She should have expected the nurses would be attending to Luke, too, now. Neva nodded and followed them down to the cafeteria. But her heart was heavy; she still didn't know what had become of Julie.

CHAPTER 23

After the nurse had her way with the two patients, Sheriff Raleigh came into the room, hat in hand. The morning sunlight revealed evidence of a long, tough night. But he wasn't there to see Zeke. Instead he sat down beside Agent Hebert's bed.

"How you feeling?"

"Like I've been shot," came Hebert's slow response. "The doctors tell me the scar tissue saved my life."

Raleigh laughed, even if it wasn't a joke. "Your people have been invaluable. Your boss Birch came down and he's directing things. Never seen such a mess in my life. But look . . . if it was me and I missed the wrap-up, I'd be chafing for some news."

"I'm listening."

"Seems Travis Delaney wasn't a newcomer to Harper Creek. He grew up here. When he left, he changed his name. He used to be Delroy Carson. Father Donnell, mother Celia. Appears the elder Carson worked at the mill at one time, but they fired him after he caused an accident due to on-the-job drinking. I can only guess that started the grudge, though why the son was acting on a grievance so many years later, I have no idea."

The agent lifted one shoulder. "It's hard to reckon crazy. Anything else?"

"On Birch's request, we did a property search and located the place Carson grew up. It's a ruin now, but we're sure that's where he held Luke Harper . . . and all of the girls, most likely."

Zeke watched the slow smile build on Hebert's face. "Good work."

"But that's not all."

"There's more?"

"Unfortunately. We're already swarming with reporters. It's impossible to keep something like this under wraps. Somebody's leaking information and they're already on the TV talking about the Red Ribbon killer. I guess we're just lucky they didn't latch on while we were trying to catch him."

"Out with it already," Hebert said, clearly losing patience.

"We found his mother in her bed. Just bones after all these years. And right beside her, the nearly unrecognizable body of Julie Fish."

Shit. Neva was going to be heartbroken. A soft sound, almost like an animal in pain, drew his gaze toward the door. She stood there, hand to mouth, absorbing what she'd overheard. Zeke slid out of bed and went toward her. He was still a little weak, but nothing time wouldn't cure. When he put his arms around her, she leaned into him like he'd feared she never would again.

"Aw, shi—oot," Raleigh said. "I didn't want you to find out this way, Geneva. I'm so sorry, honey."

Misery weighted her pretty face. Zeke stroked her hair, wishing he could do more. She must feel like shit. Survivor's guilt, he thought it was called. Maybe he'd once felt the same way about his mother—that if he hadn't been such a pain in the ass, she might've wanted to live. God knew his dad had offered that suggestion more than once, but it hadn't driven him crazy. And now, he'd be okay because Neva needed him. There were no other options.

"Do her people know?"

The sheriff nodded. "We notified her mama early this morning."

She gave a jerky nod, verging on a breakdown, and she hated for people to see her cry. That did it. He needed to get her out of here. Zeke stepped back, went to the closet for his clothes, and then slid into the bathroom to get dressed. The other three stared when he returned. Good, he'd distracted her from her hurt.

"What do you think you're doing?" she demanded.

"Taking you home."

Neva planted her feet. "You haven't been discharged."

"Don't care." He sat down on the edge of the bed and put his shoes on. "Got somebody waiting on me."

Her face went blank for a moment, and then she remembered. The idea of a wounded animal in need of attention trumped her argument, as he'd known it would. She was just too tender for this world, and he worshipped the ground she walked on. He always would.

"Come on then," she said. "I'll drive you."

"What am I supposed to tell the doctor when he comes in?" Raleigh asked.

Zeke shrugged and followed her. His street clothes were dirty, but it was early enough they didn't attract too many looks. It helped that he didn't seem sick. By the time they walked out the automatic front doors, he'd decided nobody would give chase. Half the staff was probably camped outside her brother's room anyway. It wasn't every day the Harper heir rose from the dead.

A passel of reporters stood waiting. Regional news vans had set up in the parking lot, and they seemed to recognize Neva. A tall blond woman strode over in the lead, microphone extended.

"What can you tell us about your brother's miraculous rescue?"

"Is it true you were taken but survived the Red Ribbon killer?"

Neva glared at them with her best Harper look and snarled, "No comment."

He backed her with an expression that said he wouldn't mind a fight, and the press melted back far enough for them to move around to the car. The vehicle she unlocked by clicking a button wasn't her old Honda. At his look, she explained, "The cops have it. He drove it when he took me, so . . ."

It was part of the mess, for the moment at least. This was a slick new Volvo, midnight blue, interior done in gray leather. He slid into the passenger seat, admiring the car's lines.

"Nice."

"This is my dad's spare."

That drove home what different worlds they came from— and it didn't matter at all. He no longer cared about their differences; only the ways they were the same. Tears trailed down her cheek now and then, over Julie, he guessed, and Zeke put his hand on her knee, a comforting gesture. Sometimes touch said what words couldn't.

"I'm going to miss her so much," she said softly. "It *hurts*."

"So sorry, sweet girl. Wish I coulda saved her."

It was a bright day, the sky bluing up overhead, because it didn't know or care that down below, people were grieving. He watched the wires attached to the electrical poles whip by, and it reminded him of a game he'd played as a kid, flicking his fingers each time he passed, making believe he had super speed and he was running alongside the car, swinging around each pole like a hero in a comic book. Funny he'd remember now. But then, no dream ever truly died. It just grew small and quiet until you needed it again.

She pulled off the main road into his drive, and the Volvo took the gravel smoother than he would've guessed. Without waiting for her, he slid out of the car and let his mind go walkabout, looking for his coyote brother. He found him cowering in the barn, because Zeke had asked him to come and wait, and they were bound now. They'd walked together in the same skin.

"Here," he said, and she followed him.

"He needs some blankets and food and water. Will he let me check him out?"

Zeke sent the question. Would he? The coyote shivered,

but didn't move. He took that as a yes. She raced for the house, and if he knew her at all, she was glad of the chance to think about something besides her loss.

After she examined him, she said, "Looks like broken ribs, but I don't think he's got any internal bleeding. I'd need an X-ray or CT to be sure, but I can't imagine he wants to go to the clinic."

"Did what we can."

They left the coyote with food and water and a nest of old blankets. He could wiggle out of the barn the same way he came in, but Zeke hoped he would rest first. In his condition, he couldn't hunt for himself too easily.

He led the way back to the house and took her coat. As usual he didn't have one. Didn't need one, either. The house felt warm and welcoming with its bright new paint, but it was only half done. He needed her to help him brighten up that bedroom where his father had died in his sleep, and then the upstairs, too. If he let her, Neva could change everything. Without waiting for her to speak, he swung her up in his arms and carried her to the couch. He wanted her in his lap and right now he didn't much care how she felt about it.

Zeke rested his cheek against her hair and whispered, "Didn't think I was gonna make it in time. Thought I'd lost you."

"I felt the same way when I found you in the woods." A shiver went through her.

He tightened his arms. "Got some things to say. Want you to listen and not talk 'til I'm done. Okay?"

"Go on," she said, resting her head against his chest.

Because it mattered so much, he called up all his words. He'd never be as eloquent as he could've been before, casually, but he had to try. Feelings fought with the right way to get them out into the world, and he tensed. *Make it right.*

"Know you said you loved me, 'fore I fucked it all up. Dunno if that's still true, but . . . I do love you. Ain't even the right word 'cos it's like breathing, not something you stop unless you die."

When it seemed she would speak, he held up a hand. "What

they done changed me." He closed his eyes and the shame didn't seem so heavy as long as he could feel her heart thudding against his. "Can't read. Not even a little. Or figure out complicated stuff. Sometimes when you're talking, I lose the meaning. Not 'cos I don't wanna listen but 'cos there's just too many words. May get worse. Can't promise I won't be worthless to you someday, just a strong back and no more. And . . . sometimes I roam in the night and I'm like an animal when I do. Partly s'why I ran. 'Cos I don't wanna hurt you. Not *you*. But it don't happen so much when you're close. Think maybe I did it 'cos I was lookin' for what I'd lost."

"Are you done?" she asked quietly.

He let out an anguished breath. If she laughed at him, or walked away, he didn't think he could survive it. "Yeah."

"Then it's my turn." She framed his face with her hands, brown eyes intent. "I don't *care*. Loving you means I embrace everything you are. I understand you're not like other men, and that's fine. I love what you can do. If you hadn't noticed, I like animals more than people most days anyhow. And if that affinity means you had to give up some things, then I'll just have to love you more, so you won't miss them. Do you understand now, Zeke? I'm not afraid of who you are—and I wouldn't have you any other way. I'm in this, if you're done running."

"Can help you at the clinic," he said slowly, testing her.

"Of course. You're great with the animals. I'd be sorry to lose you."

"And can probably get some work doing repair work. Good with my hands."

She grinned. "You are. But do you really think money's an issue for us?"

"Used to be."

"One benefit of leaving you . . . I made up with my family. My dad will be unfreezing my trust fund, and I don't feel like I have anything to prove anymore. I intend to pour money into this place and make it beautiful again."

Male pride gave him a flicker of discomfort. He wanted to take care of her, not the other way around. But maybe he could do that in other ways. If she didn't mind, he wouldn't let it sour the joy of knowing she loved him, however unlikely it seemed. He was still Zeke Noble with that terrible old truck and a rundown farm; he still came from a family laden with sorrow. And it all seemed pretty unimportant now. He stepped out of those memories like an ox slipping its yoke.

"Parents won't mind you settling?"

She smiled. "I'm not. But they know you played a part in saving Luke and me. You have nothing to worry about, trust me."

"Guess there's only one thing left, then."

"What's that?"

"Makeup sex."

Neva's heart ached; there was no escaping from reality, but if he could make it go away for even a little while, then she was on board. Afterward, all the details would still be waiting: respects to pay and services to plan. Julie's mother would need her. But for now, she wanted the sweetness of his mouth and the solace of his body. She could have so easily lost him last night, too.

In answer she wrapped her arms around his neck and he pushed off the couch in a graceful motion. She'd never get over how strong he was, despite his lean frame. It sent a fresh thrill through her. Running her hand down his chest, she felt even more of his ribs. He hadn't been eating much since she'd gone. Well, her, either—she'd lost eight pounds in a short time.

The sun warmed the wood floors, gilding them in light as he carried her across the front room and up the stairs. In that moment, Neva felt oddly like a bride being borne to her marriage bed for the first time. He had that tenderness about him, and it melded so beautifully with the wildness that sang beneath his skin.

She ate him with her eyes, drinking in his masculine allure, from the golden bristles on his jaw to the smooth bunch and pull of his muscles. But he lacked the ferocity of their first few encounters, as if he managed the beast inside him instead of the other way around. Something had changed for him out there in the woods; he had come out of that gauntlet in a manner refined, still himself, but at peace with it instead of forever fighting.

Outside the bathroom door, Zeke set her on her feet and then pulled her shirt over her head. It was like he read her mind. She'd cleaned up a bit at the hospital, but after her ordeal, she wanted a shower before anything else. His storm blue eyes darkened as he peeled away her clothing. Now the intensity kindled, longing limned in adoration. How he'd ever thought she could want anyone else, after this, after *him* . . . well, thinking clearly wasn't his strong suit.

"Like a fresh start," he said softly.

Neva nodded. "Symbolic."

When he stepped back, she saw what he'd done. Though she had left before the renovations were complete, he had put her ideas into practice. The walls had been painted pristine white and he'd hung the ivy border around the top of the room. But he hadn't stopped there. One night, she had been chattering about what else she'd do in there—and suspected he hadn't been listening. Apparently she had been wrong, because he'd hung tiny Victorian portraits, the frames ornately and artfully tarnished, along with wicker baskets of ivy. He had even found a white lace shower curtain with a liner.

Every item she'd mentioned, he had acquired, making her dream come true, and maybe it would seem trivial to someone else. Her throat thickened. It was just a bathroom. Just paint, time, and a few knickknacks . . . and it wasn't. This room offered a promise from him to her, and by God, she would hold him to it.

Zeke tilted his head, indicating the fuzzy green rug and the green marbled soap dish. "For you. Just like you wanted."

"I love it," she breathed. "But . . . you knew I'd be back?"

"Hoped. Someday. If I ever proved myself worthy."

"You always were." Neva became aware she was standing in her bra and panties, gawking at the bathroom. "Did you want to wait outside while I—"

"No." He'd never be a talker, but as he stripped his shirt off with measured intent, she didn't mind. Zeke started the water running and shucked his jeans.

My God, he's so gorgeous. She ought to be used to the sight of him by now, but it had been awhile. Neva knew he'd never believe her if she said it out loud, but her eyes didn't lie; he had a runner's body, taut and lean and well defined. Her gaze wandered down his chest to his ridged abdomen over the concavity of his pelvis. He was already hard, and she hadn't even touched him. No kissing. But the promise appeared to be enough.

He stood, serious and still, as she studied him. "Water's warm."

In reply she swept the fancy curtain back and stepped into the tub. Zeke followed close behind, and when he touched her, she felt the tremors in his hands. He wasn't remotely in control, but he'd been trying to pretend. For her. So their makeup sex would be sweeter than the way they'd fucked on the kitchen floor.

"It's all right," she whispered. "I just want you."

The words seemed to break something in him, and he gathered her close on a little growl as the water cascaded over them in a silver spray. It patterned his skin and she drew damp fingers down his side, reveling in his heat and power. He found her throat with his mouth, and then his teeth, nuzzling in the way that she remembered.

Zeke drew her hard up against him, and she went boneless at the rasp of his chest against her breasts. His cock jabbed against her belly, and he circled his hips, a creature of instinct now.

"Meant to go slow," he growled. "Take my time."

"Too late for that."

"Mmm. Always is, with you."

But she had in mind to tease, so she slipped away. With wet skin it was easy. She put a bar of soap between them and lathered her hands. "Let's finish the shower first. You can wait, right?"

He hissed as her foamy hands slid over his chest. Lower. "Gonna kill me."

Neva watched his face avidly as she washed him, fingers playing over each muscle group. He stood like a beautiful statue, so hard she feared he might break, and she almost hoped he did. Except that would be frustrating.

At last she finished rinsing him and he turned the tables on her. She'd expected him to push her against the wall, but instead he plucked the soap and went to work on her breasts, by now achingly sensitive; each touch sent pleasure careening through her. Neva arched, wanting his mouth, but instead he merely went on. He caressed everywhere: breasts, belly, hips, thighs. When he parted them to tenderly soap between, she almost came. But he didn't give her enough stimulation, not quite enough, and then he splashed water, rinsing her. And he still wasn't finished. The bastard washed her hair in soft, seductive swirls.

Her whole body felt flushed and hungry. "Now? Please, now."

His reply came when he hitched her up and sank into her. Neva locked her ankles behind his back, gloriously full. He made her feel soft and small and so cherished. She rolled her hips, tightening her muscles on his cock. Zeke moaned. He gripped her hips and thrust in long, deep strokes.

"Oh. *More*."

"Mine," he whispered.

"Always."

He bent his head and ran his mouth against her throat, biting a path to her shoulders. She wrapped her arms around him and held on, reveling in being taken. The water rained down, and she felt dimly amazed it didn't evaporate on her skin. He held her with one arm and slid the other between them, fiercely focused.

She clenched and came, quaking in his arms. An answering growl rumbled from his chest, and then he pinned her to the shower wall, each push a little harder than the last. His shocks mingled with hers, leaving her sweet and fluid with satiation.

Thankfully he still had some coordination, or she would've collapsed in the tub. Zeke maneuvered them out and guided her, still dripping, down the hall to his bedroom. It was a little chilly, so they scrambled wet into the sheets and drew up his grandmother's quilt. As she snuggled up to him, she realized—*oops*.

But he shook his head, apparently reading her look. "Didn't forget. Never wearing one again. Want you to mother my children."

The feminist in her considered bristling at his peremptory statement. But at base, she wanted children, too . . . and she was fine with the pregnancy happening when it would. Maybe if her father lived long enough, he'd even get to see his first grandchild. That possibility roused a warm glow.

"No telling how long it will take. Sometimes people have trouble."

"Willing to keep at it."

"That's selfless of you."

She felt him smiling against the top of her head. His fingers sifted through her hair, finger-combing the tangles. "Isn't it, though?"

"But there's a price."

"Shit. No free lunch?"

"Afraid not."

Zeke sighed. "Tell me."

"Dinner with my parents this weekend."

"Reckon that's not too steep, given I aim to marry their daughter."

"Really?" She threw an arm across his waist. "I don't remember being asked."

A wickedly delightful smile curled his mouth. "Think this is the right time? Figure you're too weak to get away."

"Try me." Scooting up in bed, she tucked the sheet beneath her arms and then folded her hands primly in her lap.

To her astonishment, he bounded off the bed, allowing her to admire the tight curve of his backside, and padded over to the dresser. Surely he hadn't—but yes. When he came back, he held a blue velvet box. Eyes on hers, he offered it to her.

With trembling fingers, she flipped the lid, and nestled in ivory satin, she found two matching rings: white gold, art deco style. The wedding band had diamonds inset, and the engagement ring had several smaller stones instead of one big one.

"Belonged to my grandmother," he said softly. "Found those when I was cleaning the place. Had 'em polished for you."

"When?"

Zeke ducked his head, adorably bashful. "'Fore you came to stay. I been wanting you so long, I can't remember nobody else." He came to his knees on the bed beside her and put out his hand. "Will you, then? Be with me always?"

Other women might get more lavish proposals or more eloquent ones. But they didn't come with Zeke Noble, and his wild, beautiful soul. Her heart sang like the meadowlark and whippoorwill outside in the trees, who didn't have the sense to know it was winter, and they should be elsewhere. Or maybe, just maybe, knowing Zeke, they had come just for this reason, for this moment. She could expect such marvels in a life with him.

"I will," she whispered.

CHAPTER 24

It was not a glamorous party. For one thing, kittens frolicked underfoot. Each wiggle of the shoe brought out pouncing instincts. They were all litter trained now and eating dry kitten food, content in their new home.

Neva's mother had invited none of the crème de la crème, nobody who could boost their social status. Instead it was a relatively small gathering. The guest list consisted of herself, Zeke, Sheriff Raleigh, Luke, her parents, Ben Reed, and unexpectedly, Agent Hebert.

She'd thought he would've been glad to see the last of this town, but he'd agreed to come to please Lillian Harper. Maybe his supervisor, Hal Birch, had something to say about it. For whatever reason, he was here sipping his wine and making small talk with the sheriff.

It had been six weeks since Julie's funeral. They'd hired a new tech to replace her, but she'd never be Neva's best friend. That ache would never go away. She had helped the Fish family make arrangements; she'd bought flowers and made sure they had food in the house, and she still felt it wasn't enough.

Like she should've known somehow and saved her. But outwardly there hadn't been any warning signs or clues about Travis's secret life. Not until the end.

Agent Hebert made his way to her side, moving gingerly; he was on leave from the ABI. From what she'd heard, it was his second medical absence that year. If she were him, she'd take it as a sign maybe he should consider a change of career.

"It's not your fault," he said quietly.

He wasn't one for small talk, no more than Zeke, and she liked him for it, more than she'd expected the first time he turned up out at the farm, quietly annoyed at the sheriff's warnings to handle her with kid gloves. Sometimes you found friends in unlikely places.

"No?"

"You'll drive yourself crazy unless you accept that you can't save everyone. Maybe that means I'm a bad cop, I don't know. But I've realized loss is inevitable."

"It doesn't. It means you've taken some knocks. We all have."

Despite the brightness of the chandelier overhead and the luxury of maids circulating with trays of hors d'oeuvres, none of this felt like home to her. She nursed no bitterness any longer, but she belonged at the farm now. Neva watched Zeke, but in this smaller crowd he seemed to be more at ease. It probably helped that everyone here accepted him without question.

"As you probably guessed, I didn't come over to talk philosophy."

"No?"

"Zeke invited me to stay with y'all for a few weeks. He said he wants to take me fishing and make up for the fact he almost got me killed."

That surprised her. But she didn't object. Her man didn't take to people readily, so if he liked Hebert, she wouldn't argue. The farmhouse had three bedrooms, and they only needed one. Hebert could stay downstairs in the newly renovated room. Zeke still didn't like to go in there, despite the fresh paint, and last night, he'd confided in her as to why. But death didn't linger; you could sweep away memories with fresh air and laughter. Everything went in its own time.

"You're welcome. I appreciate what you did for us. If you hadn't shot him, if he'd been stronger . . ." Well, things might have turned out differently for everyone.

The events of that night gave her the sense the universe might be connected in grand and mysterious ways. If not for Zeke's abilities, if not for that coyote, if not for a cautious man choosing to take a risk instead—and the list went on. Because it all aligned, she'd saved her brother and come out stronger on the other side. Because she'd offered Zeke a job, she had her family back. This year she had much for which to be grateful.

There was loss, too, of course, and an ache that would never go away. But all told, things were better than they could've been, given the circumstances.

It was a little awkward at first, but Ben wasn't ever going to stop being a friend of the family. Zeke apologized to him and they shook hands. Ben was cool, but he'd lost to the man, and then nearly been throttled by him. Neva figured that was to be expected. Though she doubted they'd ever be friends, it was a start. After the uncomfortable exchange, Ben spent his time with her father, talking campaign ideas. If he couldn't marry Harper's daughter, he could still benefit from Conrad Harper's undoubted political acumen.

They ate family style, passing bowls around the table, and she couldn't remember ever enjoying a meal at her mother's house more, at least not since she'd been grown. In her childhood there had been secret midnight suppers in front of the TV, sticky peanut butter and jelly fingers and a whispered order not to tell Grandmother Harper. Neva felt glad the old martinet no longer ruled this place from her grave.

Afterward, Sheriff Raleigh got to his feet. "I reckon y'all know I have an announcement to make."

She glanced at the bulge in Zeke's pocket. They did, too. There was a reason she hadn't worn her ring. He wanted to make it official in front of her folks and ask permission formally. He hadn't wanted to do it so soon after they'd broken up, lest her family thought they were rushing things.

But she leaned forward, chin propped on her hand, as

Raleigh went on, "That business over the holidays made me realize something. I don't want another term. I've had this job for twenty years, and it's time for me to retire."

Nobody protested, which meant they'd known it was coming. Her father said, "I understand, Cliff. Do you have anyone in mind as your successor? Is there somebody in the department who could step up?"

Raleigh snorted. "Like who? Bobby Pickett?"

Even Neva smiled at that. Pickett was a good guy, but not upwardly mobile.

The sheriff continued, "I was awful impressed with Agent Hebert. He'd need to move into the county, and run for office when the time comes, but you could help with that, couldn't you, Con?"

Her father smiled. "I reckon I know a thing or two about winning elections."

Watching his face, she decided this offer didn't take Agent Hebert by surprise. Zeke's hospitality would permit him to take the town's measure when he wasn't trying to catch a killer and decide if it was a place he wanted to settle.

"I'm flattered," Hebert said. "And . . . interested, I believe. No promises as yet, but I could use a change."

That called for a toast. Once she would've resented being part of the secret meetings that dictated the town's future, like she was better than everyone else. But it made up part of who she was, the family she came from, and no point in being angry when there were so many good things in the world. No, the Harpers weren't perfect, but she loved them.

When the talk died down, Zeke pushed to his feet beside her. "My turn."

"You have something to say about the sheriff position?" her dad asked.

"No, sir."

He flipped open the box and showed the rings around the table. Smiles built because everyone knew what was coming. Only her father remained stone-faced, eyeing Zeke with apparent disfavor. She knew that look; it was meant to test her man's mettle.

Zeke froze, and her heart sank. He'd spent so long and memorized each word so he could do right by her, and she knew how hard it was for him. How it all got scrambled when he was nervous. She touched his thigh.

It'll be all right. You can do this.

It all came out in a rush and without much inflection. "I want to marry your daughter. I'll sign any form you'd like, saying I don't have a right to anything she owns. I just love her and I want your blessing."

"You have it," Lillian said. "No prenuptial needed."

"Lilly—" Her father began, but his wife shushed him.

"I know people. Just *look* at him. He doesn't care about the money."

Neva dared to raise her eyes then, and she saw it, too: that luminous look of perfect devotion. He glowed with it. There was no subterfuge in him; what he gave, he gave completely and without reservation.

I am so lucky.

"I never could argue with my wife," Conrad Harper said.

After the toast, she made her way around the table to Luke's side. In good lighting, he looked older. Captivity had aged him and given him a new gravity. He didn't laugh as readily. No surprise there.

"How are you holding up? If Mom and Dad start driving you crazy, we have room out at the farm for one more."

"No, it's fine. I'm good here." His dark eyes, so like her own, roamed the bright, luxurious room. "I feel . . . safe. Dad's doubled the guards on the grounds, at least until I'm less of a pussy."

"Don't say that. I'll never forget how brave you were."

"And I'll never forget that you fought for me. Congrats, by the way. He seems like a hell of a guy."

"He is." She knelt beside him and kissed his cheek. "I never gave up hope you know. I knew you were out there, somewhere."

"Such as I am." Luke was broken in ways no simple hug could fix, and he tensed when she touched him.

So she pretended she hadn't noticed and straightened. Her

gaze found Zeke; he stood listening to her father and Sheriff Raleigh. He could market that attentive look. People would probably pay a fortune for it. She was the only one who knew he was flying somewhere in his head, listening to the wind.

Once the party ended, Zeke got Neva out of there as soon as he could. Maybe he'd learn to fake it, but he'd never enjoy such things, although he'd admit her family wasn't as bad as he'd first feared.

"Can't wait to get you home," he said, and the word thrilled him because it was right and true.

Emil would be joining them in a couple of days. Before he left, he'd said he needed to pack some things and settle some details at work. It would be weird to have a friend again, but he thought maybe he'd like it. If he was going that route, there would come a time when he'd have to tell the guy some things, and he was okay with that, too. You didn't build a life on secrets, and other people could choose what to believe, whether to walk or stay.

While they waited for the valet to pull the car around, her father came out, bundled against the late-winter air. "I'd like a private word with your young man, if you don't mind." The words were polite enough, but his face was pure steel.

Neva evidently recognized that, too, because she said, "Maybe I'll just go see if Caro has any leftovers."

Beneath the weight of the older man's gaze, he straightened his shoulders. "Yes, sir?"

"I don't know if she's told you about me, but—"

"Yes." It seemed best to save time. Zeke knew about the cancer.

A relieved sigh escaped Harper. "So let me cut to the chase. The doctors gave me a year, and I'm putting a good face on it because God knows this family's had enough sadness lately. I want them to enjoy Luke being home. They shouldn't be fretting about me."

"Would feel the same," he said.

"But I'm not going to make it that long." Even as he spoke,

he broke into coughing that sounded rough and painful. Harper pressed a handkerchief to his mouth and it came away damp with blood. He smelled of sickness, a deep-core rot. It came up from his chest and tainted his breath.

"Guess you need something from me, then." Zeke couldn't imagine what.

When he tucked the cloth away, he seemed frailer and more tired, his breath a wisp of smoke in the night air. "I won't be around to watch how you treat her. I won't be here to see if you remember her birthday or bring home flowers on your anniversary. I won't be able to kick your ass for making my girl cry. You seem like a man of your word, so I want your promise, here and now, to a dying man, that you will do right by her."

That hit him like a fist in the gut. He'd lost his father twice, once to the bottle, and once to the grave, but maybe he had a second chance. Zeke put out his hand and flattened the other across his heart. "Swear on my life, sir, I will be good to her."

Harper shook it, and then yanked him into a back-slapping hug. It was awkward and awful and wonderful at the same time. And Zeke found he didn't mind because of the man's connection to Neva—he could bear it.

As he drew back, he asked, "Did you bribe her staff to quit?"

A flicker of shame offered his answer, and Harper didn't try to deny it. "I regret that. I regret so many things. I thought I knew best for her when I should've just wanted her to be happy."

"Been there," Zeke said, remembering how he'd thought he couldn't live in her world and had hurt her enough to make her leave him.

The woman he loved cleared her throat as she came out the door to make sure she wasn't interrupting anything. The night glimmered in her hair, painting her face in silver and starlight. Her loveliness made him ache all the way down to his bones, but it was a sweet feeling because she belonged to him and he had just made a promise to her father. This was forever, one foot on a road that he wanted to walk all the way to the end, as long as she stayed by his side. As long as she did, he could do anything and he feared nothing. It didn't even shame him anymore that he couldn't read a story to their children when the time came; she could read to all of them, and she would, because she loved him back.

"Are you finished?" she asked her dad with a faint half smile.

"I am, baby. You have yourself a good man, here."

"I know," she said, taking Zeke's hand. "Let's go home."

EPILOGUE

JUNE, FOUR MONTHS LATER

The grounds at Harper Court glowed emerald against a backdrop of roses. Staff hurried around with trays of food on silver platters, and a guy staggered by with a giant swan carved out of ice. A woman was setting up folding chairs and tying some sparkly fabric over the top while she yelled at her assistant to work faster. The gazebo had already been covered in flowers and more sparkly fabric. Zeke had to admit it was pretty. And scary.

If he had to live here, he might go out the veranda doors. But no. He'd deal, if Neva wanted to make this their home. Thank God she didn't. The servants would surely ask about the coyote running around and the squirrels who came up to the bedroom window to chatter before dawn.

As he stared out over the lawn, Zeke could only be glad he hadn't been the one pushing the mower. Impossible to imagine he'd ever be here like this. Turning, he tugged at his tie.

The tuxedo felt strange, and he'd only agreed to this to please
Neva's mother. Lillian had asked him the other day to call
her mom. Before, he had been so alone, despite his aunt Sid
and his numerous cousins. Now he was about to become a
husband, and with that step came Neva's family. Because she
loved him, they acted like he was doing them a favor to consider joining their ranks.

"You yanked it crooked." Emil's tone held impatience, but
he didn't smell the same way. He was pleased to be here. Like
Zeke, he didn't make friends easily. "Here." The other man
stepped back, evidently satisfied with the adjustment.

"Got the rings?"

"Yes." He patted his pocket. "Stop worrying."

"Just want everything to be perfect for her."

"She loves you," Hebert said. "So it will be."

Zeke had to smile at that. "Thanks. Y'know . . . the role of
best man's played by a guy's best friend." He felt stupid, but
sometimes shared danger created a deep, unbreakable bond.
In this case, it had.

There were other bridesmaids and groomsmen, but they
didn't mean much to Neva or himself. Lillian had chosen
them for the way they'd fill out their suits and dresses and
whether they'd photograph well. Though she wasn't the frosty
bitch he'd first met at the farm, some things didn't change.
She cared about the way things were done, and she'd needed
the distraction of a big wedding. Neither he nor Neva had the
heart to deny her this spectacle.

The other man grinned. "I know. I just wanted to make
you say it. But please don't kiss me. Neva might get jealous."

"Got it." Zeke laughed, his nerves easing as Hebert had
intended.

This was the right thing to do. In half an hour, he would
go to meet the woman he loved, and then she would stand
before all the world—Lillian had invited the whole town, at
least—and tell them she was his. The beast in his head rumbled its approval. Ever since he'd put his ring on her finger, it
had quieted. No more outbursts, though it made its presence

known from time to time. It told him things about people. As long as he took regular runs and stayed out of big crowds, it was bearable.

Regardless, he'd never be normal. Ever.

But he had made peace with it. She'd made it clear she belonged to him, no matter what—even if things changed in him for the worst. But there were no guarantees even for regular folks. You just had to take it one day at a time and live your life. He could do that. In fact, he looked forward to it.

"You're a lucky man, you know."

"Yeah. Thinking about Rina?"

Once, his friend would've flinched at hearing that name. Hebert had confided in him that spring while they'd been fishing, so he knew the story. It had been peaceful that day. Sometimes friendship just meant showing up.

"Not in the way you mean. I think . . . it was easier than trying to meet someone I could have loved. That way, I had this perfect, untouchable dream instead of disappointment."

Zeke nodded, knowing Emil must be going somewhere with this line of talk, and he just needed to listen. He was best at that anyway.

"Being around you and Neva has made me realize I cheated myself. And that maybe I have to forget about Rina, at least . . . like that. She was my partner, and my friend, and that's all. It's enough."

"Moving on then?"

"I think I'm ready."

"Wedding's a good place to get lucky," he observed.

Emil punched him. Before Zeke could respond, the other man's cell phone rang. "Hebert." He listened briefly, a frown forming. "Huh. It's for you."

That was weird. But maybe it was somebody who knew he didn't have a cell and that Hebert would be with him this morning, doing best man duty. If it was a last-minute cancellation or addition, Lillian's head might explode. "Yeah?"

The voice that came over the line sounded tinny. Not real. "I understand you're getting married. The bride looks especially lovely today."

Fear coiled through him. "Who's this?"

"You can call me Mockingbird."

"What—"

"I just have a message for you, that's all. Consider it a wedding present."

This had to do with the people who had taken him. He just knew it. "Talk."

"They're not looking for you. They're not coming for you. You were a failure, so to speak. No money in your genetic evolution."

"Who *are* you?"

"As I said, call me Mockingbird. We've been watching you, Zeke. Trying to decide whether you would be a good fit. But unfortunately, we want different things. You don't care about revenge. But you sensed us, did you not?"

So he hadn't imagined the eyes on him. He wasn't crazy. Not even a little bit. "Yeah. Why tell me now?"

A distorted laugh rang out. "I just thought you might crave peace of mind, today of all days. You don't want to look over your shoulder for the rest of your life, do you?"

"So they chose me. Not at random."

"Yes," Mockingbird said. "But if you want to be happy, if you want *her* to be safe and happy, then let it be. Others will fight the good fight for you."

"S'all I have to do? Walk away?"

"Yes."

Zeke cut the call by hitting end and handed Emil back his phone. The other man studied him. "You all right? Want me to find out who that was?"

"Doesn't matter," he said, and went out to meet his bride-to-be.

It's almost a cliché, Neva thought, gazing down at the ivory satin dress. She had the shoulders for strapless and her mother had insisted. Not that she'd required much persuading. It was a gorgeous gown.

She studied herself in the mirror, hardly daring to believe

it as Lillian settled the wreath of white baby roses on her dark
hair. The elegant updo suited her, though she wouldn't want it
every day. But for one day? *This* day? Absolutely. And as long
as Zeke found her beautiful, everything else would be worth it.

"You take my breath away," her mother whispered. "I
wish—"

Neva covered her mom's hand with her own. "Yes. Me, too."

Her dad hadn't lasted nearly as long as the doctors esti-
mated. It had been a matter of months, not the year they'd
given him. And the end came quickly. She wished he could've
given her away, too. Every woman wanted her daddy on hand
to walk her down the aisle.

"The music's starting." Even now, so many months after
he'd returned to them, Luke's voice still had the power to send
joy streaming through her veins.

These days he couldn't stand dark rooms or closed spaces.
Loud noises made him cringe. He'd gone back to work at the
mill at least, and he was keeping things afloat, as he'd always
done, without regard to his own well-being. Neva wanted so
much for him to be happy. He had a lot of healing left to do,
and he'd never be the man he had been before. Too many old
scars and bad memories.

But he looked handsome in his tuxedo, and he stood
ready, offering his arm. With a tremulous smile, she took it.
Her brother walked her down the aisle in time to the music.
She didn't have a ridiculous train, so the attendants followed
behind. They stopped at the gazebo and Luke offered her
hand to Zeke.

Neva barely heard the words the minister spoke, too lost
in eyes bluer than the sky and twice as beautiful. Finally, he
would be hers in the judgment of the whole world, and she
could prove how proud she was of him. Not that there had
been any doubt for months. But she wanted this. Hell, they
needed this.

In a couple of months, the wedding dress probably wouldn't
fit anymore.

The ceremony itself passed in a blur. She spoke her vows
and he repeated his with excessive care. Neva alone knew how

terrified he was of signing his name on the marriage certificate. It was the one place he might trip up, so with her help, he'd practiced a scrawl beforehand. Doctors did it all the time.

At last the minister said, "I now pronounce you man and wife. You may kiss the bride."

And what a kiss; Neva heard tell afterward that a lady in the front row fainted after the first forty seconds and had to be revived with smelling salts. She wouldn't know, of course, too busy enjoying the heat and magic of Zeke's mouth. He kissed her without pretense of civilization: his mouth said to hers—and the world—*this woman is mine*.

Eventually, people pulled them apart because Lillian's photographer was too important and artistic to be kept waiting by the mundane happiness of the bride and groom. But she wouldn't allow that to ruin her wedding day. Instead she laughed and ran along the grass, hand in hand with Zeke. *My husband.* It thrilled her just thinking the words, and his grandmother's ring caught the light. Once, as a young woman, Martha Noble had worn this ring and experienced the same joy. Such connections mattered.

Zeke's family stopped them. Aunt Sid gave her a hug and then stood back, admiring her dress with tears shining in her eyes. "I'm just that proud. Couldn't love this boy more if he was my own. Welcome to the family, honey."

"Thank you, ma'am."

"Auntie Sid to you. Next week, I'll stop by the farm and show you how to make the ambrosia salad Zeke loves so well."

Behind her, Zeke shook his head frantically; apparently he didn't like the dish, but he was too kind to say so. That sort of thing was common in families—when people cared—and Neva had never felt more connected than this moment with the sun shining down and the sweet smell of flowers on the wind.

Uncle Lew pumped Zeke's hand. He'd done away with chew for the day, and his sons wore their best suits. To Neva's surprise, one of them—she could never remember who was Wil and who was Jeff—mumbled an apology while staring at his Sunday shoes.

"I spoke out of turn," the man said. "And I got what was coming to me. No hard feelings?"

She raised her brows at Zeke, who merely offered an inscrutable half smile. Her husband accepted the proffered hand and shook, though she could tell he didn't like it. Even his family made him uncomfortable. Only she could stroke him all over, and watch as he arched and purred like a powerful cat beneath her hands. There was a delicious power in that knowledge.

She posed and smiled for the next hour, along with everyone else, and then it was time for the toasts and wedding cake. Emil gave an unexpectedly romantic one; during his days in Harper Creek, he'd lost some of his cold, forbidding edge.

"When I see these two together, I am reminded that all things are possible, that we can find beauty in the most unexpected of places, and that if we cling fast to it, that lovely seed flowers into something steadfast and rare. To Zeke and Neva." Emil raised his glass, and she smiled at him, wondering if he knew what he'd done.

When he started his term as sheriff, he was going to be beating the ladies off with a stick. From what Neva could tell, Emmylou Fish already had her eye on him, and that sure would be fun to watch.

Seeing Julie's cousin gave the day a bittersweet flavor. She wished her best friend could've been here. She wanted her; she missed her, and that ache would never go away. But even that sorrow couldn't linger long. Not today. Not in the sunshine, with little girls romping on the lawn in lace dresses, ribbons streaming from their hair. Too much beauty.

When Zeke raised the wineglass to her lips, she shook her head and whispered, "None for me." While pretending to drink.

It took him a moment to work it out. "You—we—"

"Haven't been to the doctor, but I'm pretty sure. I think it was when you pounced on me in the stockroom at the clinic. If it's a girl, I'd like to name her Julia."

Heedless of what anyone might think, he knelt right then and pressed his ear to her stomach. To anyone else, it looked like a knight paying homage to his lady, and a little *awww* rippled through the crowd. But she knew what he was doing. Only with ears like his would that be possible. When his gaze met hers, his eyes shone like dusky sapphires. Tears, though they didn't fall. Zeke wouldn't let them.

"What else could you possibly give me?" he asked, each word pushed through a throat that sounded thick to her ears.

"Everything," she answered.

And then she did.

Turn the page for a special preview of
Ava Gray's next novel

SKIN DIVE

Coming July 2011
from Berkley Sensation!

NINE MONTHS AGO
ABOVE THE EXETER FACILITY, VIRGINIA

Taye prayed his nerves didn't show; he had a whole elevator full of people counting on him to make the right decisions. Insane when you thought about it. He suspected he'd never been in charge of anything before. He bore all the signs of a man who had never amounted to much; he knew in his bones nobody was looking for him.

Not so long ago, Gillie had asked him, *Do you remember who you are? Do you have a family?* He'd answered, *Only bits and pieces. I think I might have a family out there, but I'm not positive. I'm pretty sure they'd given up on me, long before I was taken.* Which made it even crazier that these people were all looking to him to guide them out of this mess.

But hell, I got us this far.

As the lift rose, the sound of distant explosions carried from the facility below, even through all the metal and concrete. Down there, the workers were dying. *Because of me.*

That probably made him a monster by most people's reckoning, but to his view, those who could cash a paycheck without trying to stop what had been done to Gillie—well, they deserved the big boom. The floor heated beneath his feet, and he could well imagine the wall of flames shooting up the shaft toward the car. There were only two stops, top and bottom, and the metal box rocked as it climbed. *Come on, just a little higher. Systems, don't shut down just yet.*

At last, the doors swished open, swamping him in a wave of crushing relief. Promise kept. Gillie glanced his way, seeking direction. She had to be scared shitless, but damned if she would show it. There was a word for a girl like her—indomitable.

Now let's see, where the hell are we? Four walls of textured metal. No visible door. But since the place had been built from panels—

"Start looking for a latch or a hidden exit," the dark-haired woman said.

Took the words right out of my mouth. The woman who had given the instruction seemed different than everyone else, less tentative, less damaged. She couldn't have been there very long, or she would carry fear in her face. Instead, she only appeared determined, as if this sojourn had proven a minor inconvenience. *Rowan didn't have a chance to work on her, thanks to me.* He took visceral satisfaction in that.

Eager for freedom, the others spread out; Silas found the panel after a brief search. The big orderly flipped it open, and Taye called the juice from his own body—precious little left now—to pop the electronic lock. Sizzle and spark, just like underground. When the door swung open, the scent of musty grain wafted in. Tentatively, they moved as a group, peering into the next room.

It wasn't what he'd expected. No barbed wire, no high-tech perimeter. There were no guards he'd have to fry. It was almost . . . anticlimactic. This outer room was lined with straw and held the remnants of an old harvest. That was all.

"Looks like a farm," a man with a faint Southern drawl said.

He was a little taller than Taye, but he wasn't quite as pale, which meant he hadn't been incarcerated long. The blond woman, on the other hand—Rowan must've had her for a while because she was damn near wrecked. And that was everyone: Gillie, himself, Silas, the Southern man, the confident brunette, and the broken blonde.

"We need to get out of here. Right now. Rowan could be arriving any minute." Fear made Gillie's words ring sharp and staccato with urgency.

That triggered a stampede, though nobody pushed or shoved. Silas hit the door first, and it wasn't locked, swinging open to reveal daylight. Taye shaded his eyes, unable to speak for the pleasure of it. Even though it hurt his eyes a little, the fresh wind on his face felt amazing. It was late spring, he guessed, by the color and size of the foliage, so the weather was on their side, at least. Given all their disadvantages, they needed the break. Or it might be early summer, if weather patterns had changed while he was underground.

Taye gazed out over the furrowed fields, breathing in the verdant air. It was sweet and clean, hints of manure and compost, but no chemicals. No pine-scented cleaner. That antiseptic smell haunted him. Flashes still hit him from the time before, when his brain was scrambled, and he remembered screaming as they dumped some solution on him from the ceiling; Rowan aspired to complete dehumanization of his subjects, and in most cases, he had succeeded.

Beside him, Gillie trembled from head to toe. This had to be fucking overwhelming for her. He remembered how she had said, *I want to see the sun again, Taye.* That was when he'd known he'd do anything to make that dream come true, anything at all. And here they were.

He touched her on the shoulder. "It's okay. We made it."

"What now?" the man with the drawl asked.

"We should split up." The black-haired woman spoke decisively. "Looking like this, if we stick together, we'll be caught fast."

Mental hospital pajamas, no shoes, no money, crazy eyes?

No question. They'll round us up and put us on the first short bus they find.

"She's right," Silas agreed.

Gillie managed a grin. "Before we split up, should we all agree to meet at the top of the Empire State Building in five years?"

And that was so Gillie. Lighten the mood, refusing to show fear. She might be quaking inside, worried how the hell they'd manage, but nobody would ever know it. The girl would spit in death's eye, and if he understood her past, she had done it more than once.

While the others gaped in astonishment, Silas gave a slow nod. "I'd like that. Five years—to the day."

The thin, blond woman spoke for the first time. "If I'm alive, I'll come. But for now, it's time to get moving."

A murmur of good-byes followed. Taye didn't take long about it, and he didn't ask Gillie if she wanted his company, either. He laced his fingers through hers and gave a tug.

With a final backward glance at the silo, she followed him across the field. He pushed north, avoiding the highway, because they would certainly attract attention from passing cars. People in their right minds didn't go for a hike barefoot in thin cotton pajamas.

They'd been walking for a while—impossible to say how long—when he glimpsed a white house set well away from the road in the middle of sprawling fields. Farmhouse. He didn't see any cars in the gravel drive, but there was a detached garage, so it was impossible to be sure.

"Let's go check it out."

"Why?" she asked.

He read the anxiety in her expression. Though she tried to hide it, she was more than a little freaked. She hadn't been outdoors in twelve years, and it would be dark soon. Compounding that, they had no money, no food, and no shelter, and she had to rely on him for safety; that would worry anyone with a lick of sense. Shit, it worried him.

"We're not gonna knock on the door and ask for help, if

that's what you're fretting about. But we can't travel like this, either."

She merely nodded. He pretended confidence, striding toward the house. The gravel drive bit into the soles of his feet as he crossed to peer into a garage window. No cars. That ought to mean nobody was around. Setting Gillie on watch, he broke in through the back and stole food, drink, and clothing.

As he came back out carrying a plastic bag, she called, "I hear a car coming."

In tandem, they raced across the property toward the fields: once they put some distance behind them, they paused to change clothes. His were too loose and short; hers looked like they'd previously belonged to an old woman. It didn't matter. At least the shoes worked, more or less, and socks made up the difference.

By then, it was getting on toward nightfall, but they pressed on. He could only think of getting out of Virginia. To the north lay safety and freedom. Or maybe he was conflating old history classes about the Underground Railroad with personal motivation. Strange he could remember those kinds of facts, but nothing about the man he had been. That was more than a trifle unsettling.

Gillie stumbled beside him and he turned to her, shoring her up. "We need to stop soon, huh? You're not used to this."

She didn't deny being tired, but she didn't complain. "I can go on."

"No need." He pointed. "There's a barn. Just a little farther and we'll get some rest."

The red outbuilding was well kept and had been shoveled recently, so the smell wasn't overwhelming. In the stalls, the landowner kept cows, who lowed at the intrusion. Taye ignored them and scrambled up the ramp to the hayloft. There was enough straw to mound for a bed and if someone came to investigate the restless animals, they should be able to hide behind the bales. Good enough.

"It'll get better," he told Gillie. "You'll have your own place. We'll find work."

"But we don't have any identification."

"That just means we'll have to do the jobs nobody else wants for a while. Just until I figure out a better way."

She didn't argue. Instead she helped him arrange a make-shift bed. Though he wasn't crazy about the idea of sleeping together—even like this—he couldn't leave her unprotected. He'd just have to tamp down the unwelcome desire she roused in him; thinking about Gillie that way made him feel dirty and wrong, almost as bad as that bastard Rowan.

They ate some of the bread and peanut butter he'd lifted from the house a ways back and washed it down with tap water. It wasn't gourmet fare, but he could tell she enjoyed it by the way she smiled at him; that look made him feel ten feet tall.

"My first meal as a free woman," she said.

"The first of many."

Then he lay down and tried to sleep, but as the temperature dropped and she lay shivering in her thin polyester pantsuit, he turned with a reluctant growl. "Come here."

Just sharing body heat, that's all. Don't think about that kiss. You can't have her. Not now. Not ever. He gazed up at the slats above his head and tried to resign himself to that. The straw prickled, and they lacked both covers and pillow. *Not an auspicious start, genius.*

"Thank you," she whispered.

"I should've grabbed a blanket, too. I wasn't thinking about sleeping rough."

"I'm glad we didn't take more than we had to from those people. They had nothing to do with what happened to us."

"You're too nice."

Gillie didn't reply right then. Instead, she nestled into his arms. God, why did she have to feel so good, feminine without being fragile. Her small frame possessed a tensile strength; he knew she'd worked out in captivity to stay strong. Some days when he came to visit her, he'd found her running on the treadmill, as if she could outpace Rowan and his cameras, artificial lights, and doors that didn't lock.

Eventually she asked, "Do you want to split up?"

He understood the reason behind the question. After all,

they'd decided as a group that it made sense to go their separate ways. That would be the smart thing. He sensed her tension as she awaited his reply; she wasn't ready to be alone. Which guaranteed his response.

"No. I broke out of there for you, Gillie-girl. I'm not going anywhere without you."

Not now. Not until you're ready.

The world seemed so fucking big. Gillie had all but forgotten the feel of the wind on her face; today it didn't matter if it smelled of exhaust, not as fresh as she remembered. There wasn't much sun today, either, a gray day threatening rain that hadn't materialized yet. But the hint of it hung in the air, a touch of damp that charmed her. She remembered rain and she'd seen it on TV, but the visceral feel of the droplets hitting her skin . . . not so much. Would it hit lightly or sting her skin? She so looked forward to finding out.

Though her feet hurt and her thighs burned from the long walk, the fact that she was free made all the difference. She wanted to dance and spin, but people would stare, and that'd piss Taye off for sure. He had been muttering about staying under the radar all morning.

They had passed through the shabby downtown area and headed off. She hoped he knew where he was going. Apparently he did, because he stopped outside a bank.

Gillie watched as Taye strode up to an ATM machine. He touched his fingers to the screen and sent a gentle jolt of power. To her astonishment, the machine spat out a number of bills. He palmed them smoothly and hurried away, tucking the money into his pocket.

She followed. They'd hiked all the way to Altoona, across the Pennsylvania state line. He'd turned down two offers of rides even on the back roads, and she was wary enough to appreciate his caution; she knew their value to the Foundation well enough. They couldn't risk trusting strangers right now.

He eyed all the storefronts as they passed, until she felt compelled to ask, "What are you looking for?"

"Thrift shop."

"I guess we do need some things."

Eventually they found a secondhand store in a shopping plaza that had clearly seen better days; they bought jackets, jeans, T-shirts, and sneakers, as well as battered backpacks to put the clean things in. Since the place also sold irregular socks and underwear, it set them up to keep moving, blending in on the lower edge of normal. Taye tucked the food he'd stolen at the house in Virginia into his pack; they hadn't eaten since the day before because she'd been worried about buying more. After that ATM trick, maybe she didn't need to fret quite as much.

Still, she didn't feel right about it; the money had to come from somewhere. The bank would pass the loss on its customers, and that wasn't fair. But Gillie would do whatever it took to keep from going back.

God, sometimes it seemed crazy—the idea that she could function in the real world. She'd never stood on her own two feet. Things other people took for granted—milestones like dates, job interviews, and boring birthday parties—she'd never known any of it, and she hungered for the normalcy she had watched on TV with great longing.

"I watched a movie," she said to Taye's back. "About a man who was in prison so long, he forgot how to be free. He couldn't survive without someone telling him what to do. *Shawshank Redemption*, I think it was."

"That's not you," he said roughly.

She didn't argue. He clearly wasn't in the mood to bolster her insecurity, so it was better to ask, "Where are we headed?"

"Right now? The bus station, if I can find it." He stopped at a graffiti-covered pay phone then. This wasn't a nice neighborhood and the directory had been chained to the pedestal to keep people from running off with it. Many of the pages had been torn out, probably people without pens who needed to take an address with them.

Fortunately, Taye found what he was looking for in the yellow pages under transportation. He didn't pull the page, just read it aloud. "1231 Eleventh Avenue."

"I don't think that's far."

He glanced at the addresses on the nearby buildings and nodded. "Just a little longer. You can rest on the bus."

Taye has a maddening tendency to think I'm made of spun glass. But surely if they spent enough time together, he'd get over that. He would see she wasn't an ornament.

"I'm fine," she said.

The rain began halfway into their walk. Delighted, she turned her face up; it was cool and soft, dropping lightly on her skin. Other people hurried all around her, heads down and jackets pulled up. Annoyance radiated from those caught without umbrellas. They couldn't possibly know what a miracle this was.

When Taye glanced at her, his aspect warmed. "First time in a while, huh?"

"Yeah."

"Go on." At her questioning look, he added, "Spin. I know you're dying to."

In response, she twirled, arms out, and belted the chorus to "Singin' in the Rain." He laughed quietly, ignoring the looks they received from passersby. A little dizzy, she stumbled as they walked on, but the distance didn't seem as daunting anymore. When they approached the terminal, she was shivering, and they were both soaking wet. He paused to tug her hood up. That seemed counterintuitive because she was already damp from head to toe. Gillie arched a brow.

"There are cameras inside," he explained. "Since 9/11, they track people more."

From his grave expression, that ought to mean something to her. She hunched her shoulders, feeling ignorant and debating whether she should admit as much. "What's 9/11?"

Rain trickled down his pale face, tangling in his lashes. His stillness told her nothing at all, but she felt sure he thought she was an idiot. But then his mouth softened, and he cupped her cheek in his hand. That was actually worse because she glimpsed sympathy: *poor little thing. She's a little lost lamb in the big bad world.*

Gillie bit him.

He pulled his fingers away, as if *that* was why, like he thought she didn't want him touching her. Men could be such impossible boneheads.

"Don't feel sorry for me," she warned him. "I mean it. Next time, I do worse. I used to fantasize about biting Rowan's pecker off, if he should ever push my head in that direction."

Taye eyed her, his expression mingled incredulity, astonished appreciation, and masculine horror. "Dear God."

"I know, right? I only look harmless. If you hadn't gotten me out of there, I was biding my time. We both know he was escalating."

"Yeah." Then he addressed her initial question. "About 9/11 . . . the situation is tense in the Middle East. There have been wars off and on for years or military engagements, whatever the current buzz word."

"So . . . we're at war?"

"Kind of. It's more complex than that, though. Terrorists who work for enemy factions will target civilian sites. War's not just for armies anymore."

She thought back. "I remember bombings in other countries, something about an American embassy. But I didn't watch the news much as a kid, and that never happened here."

America was safe. That had to be true. At least . . . it *used* to be. Chills washed over her, coupled with a dire sense of loss, as if a way of life had ended before she had a chance to appreciate it.

"It does now," he said.

"And 9/11?"

"The Twin Towers in NYC aren't there anymore. Terrorists hijacked a plane on September 11, 2001 and crashed into them. The death toll was astonishing. Since then, life in this country has changed a lot."

"Like putting cameras in bus stations."

He nodded and pulled his own hood up. "Let's find out where we can both afford to go."

Gillie wondered in frozen silence what other events she'd missed, how else the world had changed while she was confined. Children's TV networks had given her some idea about changing fashion and how people talked, though she never knew how realistic it was, but she'd never gotten news channels. Rowan had locked almost all stations, controlling her entertainment as fully as he did every other aspect of her life. Even the DVDs she'd watched passed through his controlling hands. As she got older, she had to request the things she really wanted to watch and he would decide whether to grant her wish with a DVD.

And he might be out there somewhere, looking for you. He'll never stop. As long as he's alive, he will never *stop.* She refused to let that hateful voice take root in her head. With grim determination, she dug it out and cast those thoughts away.

Once inside the station, they didn't look any different from the other folks waiting to catch a bus somewhere. Most had backpacks, like them. Wore jeans and sneakers. *He's right. This is the perfect way to travel. Provided we can keep out of sight of those cameras.*

They had to stop somewhere, of course. But not so close to the facility; Gillie was with him on that point. She wanted to put miles behind them as fast as they could.

Rowan's face loomed up in her mind's eye—the too minty yet anodyne taste of his mouth on hers—and she caught her breath, trembling with the fear that she'd find him one step behind her. Taye didn't notice, thank God, because he already thought she was breakable. If he knew how frightened she was of this enormous world with its brand-new rules, he'd never look on her as more than a child.

He moved toward the counter. "How much for two tickets to Pittsburgh?"

Big city, random choice. Good call.

The cashier tapped on the computer, which didn't look anything like the ones she remembered. Its monitor was thin and sleek, and the printer was so small. Most likely, they all ran on different systems, not that she had spent much time using her dad's PC as a kid. *Something else I need to learn.* But she could, no question.

"Seventy dollars."

"We'll take them." He counted out the cash.

"All right. Passenger names?"

If she asks for ID, we're stuck.

"Steve Mills and Clare Smith." Taye spoke the lies so smoothly that even she was impressed.

Luckily for them, the attendant didn't care about the rules; her bored face said she was only half here. The woman typed and then printed tickets. "Your bus leaves in an hour and a half. Listen for us to announce the terminal."

Since the building was small, that was probably unnecessary, but Taye thanked her and scooped up the tickets. He swept the room and picked out two seats away from the cameras. With innate wariness, he set his backpack between his knees and looped the strap around his ankle. The gesture fascinated her because it wasn't something she would have thought to do; it was a remnant of a homeless man, who only owned what he could carry and defend.

"Hey," she said softly.

"Yeah?"

"How is it you can remember stuff like 9/11, but—"

"Nothing about myself?" he supplied in a low growl.

She nodded.

His knuckles whitened as he curled his hands into fists, studying them with unnecessary care. "I have echoes. Empty space. Sometimes I think they burned certain things out of me. They ran a lot of voltage through me, and that doesn't factor the experimental drugs."

"So you think it's permanent damage . . . those memories are just gone."

He lifted his shoulders in a shrug. "I don't think I lost anything worth keeping."

Oh, Taye.

In self-defense, Gillie went to the bathroom; they had been making do at gas stations, but she needed to sponge off. Fortunately, she found paper towels and hand soap, which allowed her to do a decent job. After she finished in the stall, she finger-combed her red curls, pulled her hood back up, and then went out to join him, once she was sure she could offer a neutral face. Just as she didn't want his pity, she knew he wouldn't allow that from her, either, even if his truths threatened to tug the heart from her body.

Taye had a soda waiting for her and a couple of peanut butter sandwiches. By the look of him, he'd cleaned up a little, too, wiped away the grubbiness from his face, at least, and that left his eyes more brilliant in contrast with his dark hood. He had a roguish wanderer's charm, like she imagined gypsies used to be. He wasn't a stick-around-forever guy; he was a steal-your-heart-and-run-off-into-the-night man.

"Feel better . . . Clare?"

Gillie laughed softly. Yeah. She did, actually. It would be better once they actually got on the bus, wheels moving. She couldn't remember if she got motion sick.

Hope not.

She ate in silence, feeling the twinge in her arm where the shunt had been removed. *It's a good thing I talked Rowan out of the fistula.* Yet she would always bear a mark there, more visible than those from the constant injections during her early days with the Foundation. Even in her new life, the scars from the old would follow her.

But it was only superficial, not soul-deep damage. Over the years, she'd safeguarded everything about herself that mattered, locked it away from Rowan, wherever he might be.

I win, you bastard. I. Win.

$\mathcal{D}$iscover $\mathcal{R}$omance

berkleyjoveauthors.com

See what's coming up next from your
favorite romance authors and explore all
the latest Berkley, Jove, and Sensation
selections.

See what's new

~

Find author appearances

~

Win fantastic prizes

~

Get reading recommendations

~

Chat with authors and other fans

~

Read interviews with authors you love

berkleyjoveauthors.com

M1G0610